Advance Praise for *Oneiron*

'*Oneiron* is literally a fabulous work. A triumph of the art of the novel.'
Dagbladet (Norway)

'*Oneiron* seems to rise effortlessly to the best of international literature.'
Finlandia Prize Jury

'Laura Lindstedt embodies with breathtaking imagination the idea that we are all equal in the face of death...[weaving] her unlikely story with the finest of writers' hands.' *Svenska Dagbladet* (Sweden)

'*Oneiron* is ambitious and lush...[a] vital, critically-acclaimed novel.'
Stavanger Aftenblad (Norway)

'A prize-worthy, magnificent meditation on the afterlife.'
Dagens Nyheter (Sweden)

'On an international scale this is an exceptionally bright pearl of high literature – a novel that is close to perfect.' *Aamulehti* (Finland)

'Powerful...fresh and inventive.' *Klassekampen* (Norway)

'[Lindstedt's language] is powerful: the sprawling narrative flows masterfully smoothly.' *Savon Sanomat* (Finland)

'*Oneiron* is a shameless, touching and absurd approach to the state we know little about, the space, the transition, the moment when we hover between life and death.'
Torborg Iglan, *Fædrelandsvennen* (Norway)

'Lindstedt uses the tools of literature to form a work of art with its own rules; one can only admire her execution and her ability to depict our world to a startling effect.' *Helsingin Sanomat* (Finland)

oneiron

A Fantasy About the
Seconds After Death

Laura Lindstedt

Translated by Owen F. Witesman

ONEWORLD

A Oneworld Book

First published in North America, Great Britain and Australia by
Oneworld Publications, 2018

Originally published in Finnish as *Oneiron* by Teos Publishers, 2015
Copyright © Laura Lindstedt, 2015
English translation copyright © Owen Witesman, 2018

English edition published by agreement with Laura Lindstedt and
Elina Ahlback Literary Agency, Helsinki, Finland

ISBN 978-1-78607-259-7
ISBN 978-1-78607-260-3 (eBook)

Work published with the support of the Finnish Literature Exchange

F I L I FINNISH
LITERATURE
EXCHANGE

Printed and bound in Great Britain by Clays Ltd, St Ives plc

Oneworld Publications
10 Bloomsbury Street
London WC1B 3SR
England

MIX
Paper from
responsible sources
FSC
www.fsc.org   FSC® C018072

I

When I am not, what will there be? Nothing.
But where shall I be when I am no more?

Leo Tolstoy, *The Death of Ivan Ilyich*

DANSE MACABRE

Imagine you are partially blind. Minus eleven diopters. Imagine a dark exam room at an optometrist's office. You're sitting in a comfortable leather chair, afraid you'll lose your sight entirely. You've carefully placed your old glasses on the table. The plastic rims, electric-blue ten years ago, are scuffed now. You repaired one arm with tape, which you painted blue with permanent marker. For years you've preferred seeing poorly to discovering the true state of your vision. You've pushed away the idea of going to the optometrist the same way other people put off going to the dentist. You know those people. Their breath smells, and they know it. They always speak in a slight mumble, tilting their mouth down and away. They take a step back whenever someone comes too close. But what you've put off is this vision exam. Every year you've acted more strangely, more absent-mindedly— that's your excuse. As soon as something resembling a human appears on the horizon, you lower your gaze to the street, just in case. Your friends play along with the game. "How's that castle in the sky coming?" "Yoo-hoo, anyone home in there?" They wave their hands in front of your eyes as if wiping snow from the windshield of a car. You laugh and tell them what's weighing on your mind this time. Of course you're lying. At least a bit. You fabricate more details than necessary. You don't want to remember that reality isn't a fog. It isn't a shared twilight we all fumble through. Reality has terrible clarity. You don't want to admit that you are seen but you do not see, not now, perhaps not ever again. You're terrified. You fear that the world will run out of lens strengths, Coke-bottle glasses, and minuses. That the next time they'll hand you a white cane, encourage you to get a guide dog, a set of talking bathroom-scales, stickers for your computer keyboard . . . But don't think of these things now. Focus on imagining the dimexam room, the back half of the dim room, the white chart on a white, illuminated wall. It's the old-fashioned kind of chart nowhere has any more. The chart has "E"s pointing in four directions. Letters you can't see now.

The optometrist begins loading lenses into the device resting on the bridge of your nose. Minus eleven diopters, and you see as you do through your glasses. Poorly, murkily at best, but just enough that you can get by. You can only clearly make out the top row of "E"s— the final letter on the following line gives you trouble. Your heart pounds with terror, but let it pound. Focus your thoughts on this brief moment, this blink of an eye, because this is the moment you must be able to imagine. The optometrist adding sharpness to your gaze, one lens at a time.

Move your eyes to the tiny, ant-sized letters on the bottom edge. Things start to happen when you stop being afraid and let time slow down. No lenses are necessary any more, for the desired clarity has been achieved: the tiny creatures have begun to move. They wriggle and tremble and jerk like black pieces of string on an excessively clean floor. Like when you were a child. Don't you remember? You stared at that piece of string hanging from the arm of a chair, head full of blood, eyes heavy with pressure. Then the black snake began to dance. It had its very own rhythm, unfailingly repeating its pattern. That was the magic of your eyes, the magic of your retinas.

Now you're sitting in a comfortable, plush chair where the feeling of heaviness completely disappears. A movie is starting, and the screen is full of light even before the film has begun to roll. But this time more than light fills the screen, because something is stuck to the film gate. Bits of fuzz that vibrate in the air from the fan. You count them to pass the time. There are six in all. Hairs from the projectionist's knuckles? Are they hairs? But don't think of men right now. Stare at the bright white screen and the six pieces of fuzz. They've moved close enough now that you have to believe: *a woman, each and every one.* And they aren't thin bits of fuzz any more, except one of them, the one in the middle, who remains terribly skinny. She walks a little ahead of the others, pulling the rest behind like the leader of a wedge of cranes. An enormous, auburn cloud of curls bounces as she takes nimble, swaying steps through the air on nothing. Behind her walk five women, two to the left, three to the right. They tread the air as if treading water, with some effort, except one who appears to dance.

The women are easy to tell apart. The one to the left has enormous, swinging breasts that barely fit in her magenta polo shirt even though four of the five buttons hang undone. The breasts belong to a sturdy brown-skinned woman, whose face is blank just now, lacking any expression. Next to her traipses a mound of stomach, a blond, pregnant woman dressed in a black shirt and turquoise trousers. She exudes health and wealth. She is wrinkle-free, stain resistant, and Top Quality.

To the right of the emaciated woman with the curls strides an overweight matron, with smeared make-up wearing a knee-length sable fur coat. On one foot she wears a red woolen sock, on the other a heavy boot that extends to her knee. Next to her skips a tall, copper-brown beauty in a yellow dress with an enormous Afro. On the outside right, a little separated from the others, slinks a bald, shriveled woman in a poison-green hospital gown, looking like the most woebegone creature imaginable.

Six women walk toward you out of the white emptiness. You start, as if waking from a dream, turning around, looking to either side, up and down. But you see nothing to anchor your gaze, nothing beyond this peculiar company floating ever closer.

You feel faint. You feel your ears stopping up, your head ringing. Your legs give way. You fall into something. It isn't soft and it isn't hard. Not cold, not hot. You collapse into it as if resting in snow. You close your eyes and wait to wake up somewhere else. At the movies? Just before the end of *Solaris*? In that moment when the camera rises into the sky, revealing that Kris Kelvin's homecoming is a dream, an island on the planet's surface surrounded by a sea with no shore, when the clamorous music accompanying the final scene begins to

surge, to penetrate your body chilled by a fitful sleep. Suddenly the
music stops, and you stare in unbearable silence at the white screen
and the black letters there: КОНЕЦ ФИЛЬМА. You hear nothing
but your own heart, which still pumps in time with the music.

Do you believe you'll wake up that way again this time?

You hear sounds of movement and can't bear not to peek. Instead
of moviegoers rustling as they leave the theater, you see those women
before you, those six beings who appeared from nothingness. They've
fallen to their knees next to you and surround you on all sides.

Suddenly the leader, the one who's all skin and bones, begins to
tug the shoes from your feet. She pulls off your corduroy trousers and
underwear, and bends your knees as she spreads your legs. Two of
the women hold your ankles tight, and two grab your arms. The sad
one with no hair has lifted your neck onto her knees and gently
strokes your hair.

The thin woman shoves her head between your legs, and you do
exactly what is best for you in this situation. You close your eyes
again. You submit. You let it happen, because that's all you can do.
You feel the cool, soft tip of the tongue begin to dig into you. It seeks
and finds your most sensitive spot. No evil is being done to you. The
bony one seems to know how to satisfy a woman. She takes the hood
of the clitoris between her lips and sucks out the tiny protuberance
hiding beneath. The *glans clitoridis*. Or, if you please: the tongue of
Cleite the warrior queen, the pink joy buzzer, the love button, the
little man in the boat, the devil's burning teat . . . This she energeti-
cally begins to lick, at once strongly and lightly, varying the rhythm
with purpose, now pressing more, now brushing only gently.

You submit. You want nothing else.

How is it possible to think of pleasure? You can't. Instead think of
light. Bright, eyelid-penetrating light. You become part of the orange
flame, the solar wind, the plasma flares, the throbbing coronal holes.
Within you is the core of the universe, a mysterious generator, that
divine nodule with its perfect minefield of eight thousand nerve
endings that send fibers all the way to the spinal cord and central nervous system, all the way to the sun and the foundations of the universe.

Your body tenses, preparing for the wave beginning to form deep inside. The surge builds from small, tenuous pulses, radiating ripples to every part. In your toes and fingertips they turn, changing direction, washing back with a greater roar toward the center, shrinking to a single leaden point and diving in. One ring. Two rings. Three rings. Four. Each heavier than the last, each plunging deeper. Five. It almost makes you ache, that gathering—soon nothing more will fit, your body will no longer be able to keep them in. Six. Then comes the seventh ring. It dives so deep that it no longer touches you. It pushes through to a place with no return. Your body knows it. The tension in your muscles begins to release. You know this feeling of irrevocability, the precise feeling that makes pleasure cause dependency. The second before orgasm. The seventh ring, which pulls all the rings with it in a wave, launching them out of their hideaway one by one— opening, expanding, and finally exploding against your pelvic diaphragm.

The women have released their grip on you. They stare intently at your cringing face, your head resting in the bald woman's lap, your mouth releasing a scream, your rising wail. You bathe in cold-hot sweat, your back arching. Your eyes are still closed, and that is good, because when you open them, nothing will be as it was. Believe me.

Agitated words fly all around, the ends of each sentence rising. Questions, in four languages. If only you could catch hold of even one of them, if only you could understand. *Kto vy? Otkuda vy?* Oh, how they wish the joy of understanding would spread across your face, the blissful experience of familiarity as you hear your mother tongue after this shock, this earth-shattering pleasure. *De onde você vem? Quem é você?* They so hope for you to find a citizen of your land, a sister, a friend, a kindred spirit in their group. *Qui êtes-vous? D'où venez-vous?* If only you would open your mouth and tell them what you know. Who you are, where you come from. That's what they want to hear: where you come from and, above all, how you came. And why you're here now too.

You open your eyes. The thin woman crouches between your legs, bony fingers removing hairs from her mouth. She wipes the small black curls on your knee like the tablecloth of a fine restaurant. Black curls? You look at your hands. They are the hands of a young girl. The nails are round, cut short, every other one painted black or white. You look at your bent legs. They're smoother, and much, much more petite, and lighter. Blue veins shine through the skin, you've become so white. You lift your left leg. It rises easily. It's so light and lithe you could easily swing it over your own head. Yes, you have the supple legs of a young girl. You lower your leg again, next to the other, and open your mouth, but nothing comes out.

Good morning, Sleeping Beauty, the thin woman says a little hoarsely, *where do you come from?* Her voice is powerful, and strangely low for such a frail body. She places both hands on your knees, spreading your legs a little and extending her neck toward you. Her voice rises, softening, becoming slightly more friendly, almost inquisitive. *Who are you?*

You say one single word. A name. You say it in the voice of a young girl shrill from crying. The voice that a lost child might use when a nice adult kneels and tries to help, offering to go together to find a lost mother in the crowd.

You say: *Ul-ri-ke*.

You pronounce each syllable in turn, with a tearful insistence that both demands and pleads. You practically beg. Sobbing, you tell them who you are.

You are Ulrike, and you are seventeen.

You don't know where you're coming from, but your home is in Austria. In Salzburg.

SHLOMITH PREPARES TO SHARE HER KNOWLEDGE (FOR THE SIXTH TIME)

Ulrike was the last to arrive. As one might imagine, she was shocked by what had just been done to her, even though it was enormously pleasurable, or perhaps because of that. It was more pleasurable than anything anyone had ever done to her. Hanno couldn't do anything like that. Hanno was Hanno. And now this grotesque woman had done it to her. Completely by surprise, by force, with the help of a large group, and still the experience hadn't been the slightest bit unpleasant. This sort of thing can happen in a dream. In dreams you can end up in orgies, in wanton copulation with complete strangers. But now isn't night, and Ulrike isn't sleeping. She understands that, if only just. She looks at each of the women sitting around her, in a state of shock. She waits. She opens her mouth. She closes it again. And when no one sees fit to do anything, when no one makes the slightest move, when no one sees the need to spit out a single word, the feelings come. Rage first of all.

Ulrike sits up and wipes away the hair matted on her forehead. Her face hardens in Cleopatra-like hauteur: chin up, mouth tightly pursed, nostrils slightly flared, a demonic squint to her eyes.

And because Ulrike's temperament is of the relatively volatile type, she hisses *Scheiße!* And it is meant for everyone. *Scheiße!* And it is meant especially for that skinny monstrosity sitting with legs crossed in front of her. The woman gazes sweetly at her, and Ulrike stares back. She has been violated. This she understands. She feels stupid.

She feels like a complete idiot. The orgy doesn't matter—anything can happen if you're wild enough, and she is. With the right company and enough alcohol, she's up for almost anything. The place and these women don't matter—this is obviously some kind of *Eyes Wide Shut* thing, and maybe they used date-rape drugs. Maybe this is *Candid Camera* NC–17. But they made her cry, and that she does not intend to forgive. They made her tell her name, her age, and nearly her home address, although she never intends to go home again. *Scheiße!* she hisses, barely audibly, and continues her unabashed staring. She will not lower her gaze first. She will not lose this game.

The thin woman has seen this confusion many times before. Five times in fact. First there was she. She alone. Completely alone. Then came Polina the Windbag in her sable coat with one booted foot. Then the imponderable Rosa Imaculada, Crazy Rosa whom she could do without. Then Little Nina appeared from Marseilles with her belly sticking out, then Wlibgis from Holland, from Zwolle, ravaged by cancer, then proud Maimuna from Dakar, and finally beautiful Ulrike from the birthplace of Mozart. Angry, beautiful Ulrike. The youngest of all. Every bit as innocent as the recently arrived tend to be. The skinny woman stares at Ulrike's face. She tries to record the image in her mind: the raised jaw, the forced hardness in her gaze, just now turning away. The girl's bright violet-blue eyes begin to glance cautiously past her, finding the white, which is every-where, which is nowhere. In her eyes, distress.

The thin woman has seen this. Many times she has been forced to speak, but so what? She almost prefers to speak. She is also speaking to herself, repeating over and over how things are, telling everything as best she can. When she speaks, everyone falls silent and listens. Everyone hears, once again, where they are, perhaps, right now. Hearing this is important. Just as taking communion can be impor-tant for some people, or lighting a cigar after a meal. For others it might be a weekly manicure, a pedicure, or a daily trim of the dry skin from their cuticles—each just as compulsive, perhaps a bit pain-ful but undeniably pleasurable. So she will tell. She is happy to tell!

* * *

The thin woman remembers how it feels to wake up here. How it feels to open one's eyes, to sit up, to touch the white beneath in disbelief. Is it land or frozen snow? It isn't cold, and it isn't hot. Plastic? Latex? Painted concrete? It isn't hard, and it isn't soft. She stood up, feeling excellent, empty, and numb in a good sort of way: the pain that had gnawed at her stomach and the staggering dizziness were wiped away. Of course she had managed exceedingly well with her pain and dizziness—she was a pain professional, after all. She was a hunger artist, after all. "No, no, and once again no": that had been the doctors' opinion about her last project. Secretly of course they hoped she would continue to the end. They wanted to see, even though they didn't admit it, how the body and mind would function in controlled extremis. Officially they were obliged to warn her, practically to threaten her. Professionally they could do nothing more than demand that she interrupt the "test" and end her questionable experiment, "full stop". This wasn't the first time she had met scorn even as the same people viewed her with a mixture of admiration and horror.

It all started at the little apartment on Carroll Street. With her mother's gaze. That was where it began. But the fact that her art had begun to arouse scientific interest—that was new and motivated her to push on. Her weight loss methods had been as deliberate as an ascetic yogi's. At times they had driven her into a trance, yet she pressed on with more cycles of the regime. On the final day of the experiment, a few hours before stepping on the stage, she had drunk several tepid cups of an Ayurveda tea named "Internal Peace". Her mind spun in a dervish dance, round and round and round as she reeled in the staff kitchen at the Jewish Museum, in her hand a paper printed with the presentation she would soon read in the auditorium. It was a blissful state and yet frighteningly fragile. Temporary. No person, not even she, could live forever on nothing but adrenaline, pain, and vertigo.

She had learned the dervish dance long ago. She had been hanging around Coney Island, at Astroland, which had just opened, staggering along in a famished stupor even as she rode the Cyclone again and again. That night her bed spun and shook as soon as she closed her eyes. That was her fifth week devoted to losing weight and the first night when she had finally understood: this relationship, and only this relationship, was meant to be for life. Hunger, my love. Under the covers they made a secret pact: I trust in you, and you trust in me. I will never eat you away, and you will never stop fighting by my side.

Of course some minor slips occurred. At a cousin's bar mitzva, she secretly devoured twenty marzipan cookies. The hunger flew into a vengeful rage and threatened to leave her entirely, but she begged forgiveness and vomited. That time the hunger was appeased.

She was seventeen when she received the keys to her first home of her own. Even though it was little more than a closet and next to her parent's flat, she had the freedom to do whatever she pleased, and of course that terrified them. Of course she experimented some. She gave herself injections of Smirnoff in her thigh, using her friend's insulin syringe. Every now and then she got high with a couple of pals. A few times she engaged in some moderate shagging. But the hunger was most important and most dear to her. It fought with her like a trusted friend, against her enemies, until she made the mistake of her life and betrayed it. Because of a man.

The skinny woman knew she had atoned many times over for the betrayal of her youth. The hunger had returned to her after a series of reconciliation cycles, but in a way it still seemed somehow hurt, somehow . . . conditional. It always seemed to demand more of her; a day limited to five organic carrots was now an insignificant achievement to it—there were no thanks, no euphoria. Not to mention the dervish dance—the hunger remained silent as a mouse. Eventually she grew angry. Fine! She made a new pact. She promised to go farther than ever, farther than anyone had ever gone, just so long as she could return afterward. She would spend the rest of her life just thin enough, balanced on the rapt line between health and disease. Was that enough? And so they made their new agreement.

Then something happened. *Something* took the reins and decided for her, without her permission, to continue a trial she had already completed. She was thrown here, into this perfect white, with no instructions coming from anywhere. In one fell swoop, everything had been different. Even the hunger had disappeared without a trace, disappearing so completely that she didn't even think to miss it.

If in her initial shock she had thought to analyze her situation, perhaps she would have landed on the idea that she knew later, in hindsight, to tell Polina when she appeared, bewildered and sobbing. What she said to Polina went something like this: "At first it felt like I had just had the best sleep of my life. A deep, dreamless sleep." And then: "Gradually I felt lighter and lighter, and the pain that had been in my stomach for so long disappeared, and all my aches were gone; I felt like I was in seventh heaven." But alone in a place like this without another living soul—no one thinks that way then. She only noticed the pain and nausea were gone once her panicked mind had explored every other alternative and dead end.

Theory number one: Was she blind? This first thought upon opening her eyes is understandable. The whiteness all around is like a sickness, is like blindness, is like the conclusion: "So this is how I'll be punished." And this isn't a terrible theory since there are sicknesses in which the first, dramatic symptom can be a sudden loss of vision (for example, Horton's disease, also known as temporal arthritis, which generally strikes aging women).

However, the blindness theory fell apart quite quickly because she thought to look at herself, first at her hands, and there they were. A thin wrist peeked from the sleeve of her black caftan with the veins in the back of her hand shining bluer than ever. Long, slender fingers, long, red nails, joints like jewels, knuckles like the brass variety. She struggled up onto her stick-thin, bowed legs. Just a heave, a movement without air resistance, and suddenly she was up.

Theory number two: She was in some sort of building. Somewhere there had to be a surface that would expose the structure as a dome, a cube, or a sphere. At this point she began to feel a rage. *They* had really done this to her! It wasn't enough for *them* that she had her own things in order, that she had calculated everything going in and exiting her body down to the last calorie. That she had arranged—of course she had arranged—follow-up care for herself and made numerous backup plans. Nothing had been left to chance. She wasn't fooling around. But *they* had still just snapped her up and locked her up in . . . where?

She tried to walk but didn't get anywhere. Her legs moved, but whether she was making progress was impossible to say. She threw herself on her stomach and felt a light rocking in the pit of her stomach. She did not feel an impact or any pain, and she still couldn't see anything anywhere. There was no reference point. She squinted, looking for hidden cameras, motion detectors, something dark that might take shape against the background. Someone had to be watching her on a monitor. Things like this could happen—it was almost to be expected. She had heard the rumors about them: science abductions.

There it was, theory number three, the natural, logical jump from theory two. Nowadays information about human behavior was needed more urgently than ever. Real, brutal information, the kind that might not be available for collection following accepted ethical norms. And she had been the subject of enormous, undisguised interest. *They* simply wanted to know more. Would she survive? How had she survived up until now? And above all: how would she do now, in a controlled environment? What was her secret?

Triumphantly she stuck her finger into her shock of hair. She was convinced of the find she was about to make. The antennas. She dug deeper, tugging at the roots of her curls, nails scratching her scalp. Antennas, antennas. Even just one. However small. Is this? A scab. A microchip. Implanted deep. A mole? A small wound. Psoriasis. No! A device. Definitely something technological. The latest, nearly invisible technology that they were testing for the very first time.

She pulled at her hair. She removed her clothes, turning them inside out and inspecting them carefully, then turning them back and checking them again. She did things that would have looked strange and perhaps indecent if anyone had been looking; the analogy of a snake eating its own tail would not have been far off as she finally bent double to search for foreign devices inside herself.

Shlomith.

The thin woman extends her hand to Ulrike and introduces herself, adding a most important detail, a fact apparently meant to explain everything: *I was the first one here.* The other five women have come to sit next to her. They seem in reverent fear of Shlomith's austere statement, and of Shlomith herself, this offensively thin, ancient-looking woman. Now that her hair is not in the way any more, her face is visible in all its horror. Her skin is wrinkled and fragile, altogether paper-like, as if blowing on it would dislodge it. Her cheekbones are high and would cast enormous shadows below if the light were not so uniform. If she wished, Ulrike might describe her thus: old witch, chestnut hair, corkscrew curls, large eyes, glinting irises flashing brown. Enormous hypnotic belladonna eyes. A gaze slightly too intense, almost annoyingly unabashed, which is guaranteed not to look away first from anyone who dares to stare back. The leader. Of that there is no doubt. Shlomith is the Leader.

To repeat.

First, she herself, the very first: Shlomith.

Second: Polina.

Third: Rosa Imaculada.

Fourth: Nina (in her womb Little Antoine & Little Antoinette).

Fifth: a "W" drawn in the air (W as in Wlibgis).

Sixth: Maimuna.

They introduce themselves one at a time, each in her own way, and shake Ulrike's hand politely. Their arrival order appears to be a very important thing to them, because they each raise the appropriate number of fingers, as if by prior arrangement; this is their very own number of arrival. If this were to happen anywhere else, in a stadium where people had come to flee a hurricane, in a tent city where refugees were being assembled during a civil war, then Ulrike, who has entertained herself with dreams of catastrophe since she was a child, would burst into laughter. The women are so comical, so overly serious. Their arrival order number fingers are still in the air. A smile begins to tug at Ulrike's lips.

Suddenly Rosa Imaculada retracts her three extended fingers. She takes a step toward Ulrike, shaking her fist and launching into an explanation of something in a confusion of Portuguese and English. From here on, the performance is a familiar sight to everyone except Ulrike, who looks on in shock. They're always embarrassed when Rosa's show of panic begins. Lines appear on the women's faces, furrows of impatience characteristic to each face type, which depends not only on temperament but also age, skin quality, and fat percentage. Of course Shlomith's face is most creased of all. But Rosa pretends not to notice. Words burble out of her as her voice turns shrill and her hands move restlessly. Occasionally she crouches to pound the white below them with her fist. The pounding makes a hollow sound that starts out sharp but is instantly blunted, as if someone were striking a culvert with a metal rod covered in a woolen sock.

Ulrike begins to understand. Rosa Imaculada wants Ulrike to tell her something the others haven't been able to say. Rosa Imaculada taps her head with a finger and waits for a response, even though she must understand that this tearful wretch of a girl isn't capable of answering.

Ulrike gathers her courage and begins to rekindle her quenched anger. She opens her mouth and shouts at Shlomith in her high school English, with her high school pronunciation, with her high school vocabulary, with the high school impudence of a small, seventeen-year-old high school girl (with exactly the defiant self-assurance characteristic of young girls that can make some older men completely lose their wits); she screams at Shlomith and demands that she tell her everything, absolutely everything, because she knows that Shlomith knows. She has to know. She was the first one here, after all.

And this leaves Shlomith no alternative. She must tell, as she always must. Over and over she must tell, and now she must also expose some slightly more delicate matters. Why she stripped Ulrike's lower body bare (just now Ulrike realizes she should put her trousers back on), why Polina and Nina held her arms (shame rushes over Ulrike again: how has she been sitting here with her pussy bare?!), why Maimuna and Rosa Imaculada forced her legs apart (*Scheiße! Scheiße! Scheiße!*), why Wlibgis lifted her head on her knees and why she, Shlomith, the worst of all, stuck her tongue in Ulrike's most secret place.

THE CAMPFIRE

Come, Shlomith says to Ulrike, *let's move to the campfire*. And before Ulrike has time to understand what is going on, she finds herself gently lifted up. She stands, feeling dizzy (that expectant vertigo caused by the first proper lurch in one direction of a ride that moves back and forth, such as an amusement park Viking ship or a traditional Scandinavian yard swing). Ulrike stands and instinctively spreads her arms, trying to find her balance and momentarily closing her eyes. Then she opens them again and looks down, at her feet that is, and tries to jump up, but she fails. The women standing around her remain where they are.

She didn't rise a single millimeter.

Maimuna can't resist the temptation any more. Crouching, she pushes off and whooshes high into the air, her bent knees reaching the level of Ulrike's neck. What is even more confusing, she stays there as if imprisoned in a perfect photograph (a model dressed in sporting gear bounces on a trampoline in a garishly lit studio, *just do it*, in the background is a bright, monochrome but decidedly flashy backdrop, *just do it*, the model jumps, jumps, jumps but doesn't sweat, *do it, do it, do it*, she jumps and is immortalized in the air and will never age again).

Shlomith glares in irritation at Maimuna, who obediently begins to descend without any further antics. Yes, Maimuna descends, or, in other words, kneels down low and begins to screw herself down by placing her arms tightly against her sides and thrusting her upper body in quick, sharp movements from left to right. The descent is jerky. Maimuna falls gradually, twist by twist, to the others' level, and finally she is on her knees before Ulrike, in feigned humility, and then Shlomith turns her back, motioning impatiently with a hand and beginning to walk. As one might say, Shlomith begins to move forward.

DYING IS GOD'S REVENGE. In that moment when Shlomith turned her back, that thought, precisely that thought and no other, flashed across Ulrike's mind. Fear filled her being because she wasn't in the habit of thinking about God. God, one might say, did not speak to her. God was not a joke, not an injunction, not a subject for argument, not anything at all except an event on the calendar. God definitely was that—a magic something that was utterly invisible but could stop every business in a country when necessary. That was how God was. God radiated his liturgical light on holidays, on evenings when even the non-God-fearing but sufficiently tradition-reverencing portion of the Austrian citizenry made its way to Mass because that was the way. There was some sort of God there, or at least a picture of the Son of God and the Virgin Mary, and if there is a mother and a child, there must also be a father, even if he is an absentee. At Mass you could kneel (it was good for the soul!), so long as your knees weren't too bad (then you could stand in good conscience), you could sing and shake hands with your neighbors and then finally take communion. But no one ever required belief.

God did not exist *in persona* for Ulrike and her family. In some distant branch of the family tree was one aunt who prayed earnestly, went to church, and regretted all the sins she committed and the sins she hadn't committed but which she made the mistake of thinking of, because her God saw all, every thought, and every possible thought behind the thought, and every association lurking at the root of every thought. In the end that aunt landed in the loony bin.

But now, out of nowhere, this claim pops into Ulrike's mind: DYING IS GOD'S REVENGE. Suddenly everything is oppressive, impending thunder, heaviness, terrible heaviness. Or maybe: a brain jam. This was the term Ulrike used for her state of mind after a test, the minutes that started when she returned the math exam to the front of the room and placed it in the teacher's hand, walked out the door into the hall and maybe all the way to the schoolyard: it wasn't a mood of relief, even though she had no doubt a good grade was on its way, presumably the best in the class. Numbers and vectors continued to zoom around maliciously in her consciousness until at least her third cigarette. Her head really wasn't a normal head. She had a tendency to think thoughts that made her sick.

Ulrike strains to pull her mind together: there is no God to take revenge by dying. God does not exist. Ulrike squeezes her eyes shut tight and strains some more: *click* says the Colt lighter. A flame emerges (this is the best moment) to suck into the Lucky Strike cigarette. Lungs fill, her whole body tingles, a gust of wind blows through her head, and God disappears. There!

Ulrike opens her eyes and decides to focus on movement so she can keep up with Shlomith, who has already moved away. Shlomith has clearly become smaller than the others (not thinner, thank goodness, just smaller—this is called perspective, a phenomenon that even the congenitally blind know, so it isn't just a convention; Picasso was wrong: perspective is more real than any god or goddess).

So Ulrike takes her first step.

If someone were to describe that step, say by comparing it to Neil Armstrong's great (for the human race) small (for himself) bounce on the surface of the moon, they would be lying. Ulrike does not bounce. And Ulrike's step also does not resemble the first, tentative, sideways thrust of a foot by a ten-month-old baby (which is usually followed by a fall, then crying, then another attempt), because Ulrike steps right after Shlomith without faltering. But it is also not a normal step. Because although Ulrike's right foot moves sixty centimeters away from her left foot (which is a perfectly common "now I need to hurry" stride for her 159-centimeter frame) and although Ulrike pulls her left foot after the right (or, rather, in front of the right, as is the way in walking), she does not progress. She does not move away from the others. Dumbfounded, she turns her gaze to Maimuna, who has risen and is now standing again. But Maimuna only smiles mischievously and starts walking after her leader, without offering a single gesture of instruction to the helpless newcomer.

Nina and Polina are the ones to come to her aid. Purposefully they take Ulrike by the arms, one on either side. First step in place. *Think about a swamp*. Polina suggests this, but she soon realizes that Ulrike probably doesn't have any experience with swamps, unlike her. She recently read a long, stunningly illustrated article about the peat bogs of Western Siberia. And she has no time to ask Ulrike about possible excursions she might have taken on the banks of the Danube before Ulrike is slogging away almost perfectly. She mimicks Nina and Polina's walking extremely skillfully. It is like kneading dough with one's legs—you have to *think* more weight into them, you have to think the resistance. Ulrike will soon hear that each woman has her very own resistance: Polina has swamp, Wlibgis has snow, Rosa Imaculada has a slightly waterlogged feather pillow, Nina has swimming floats (the orange arm floats for children sold in every discount store, *la bouée pour les enfants à partir de 12 mois*) placed on her feet in the deep end of a pool, and Maimuna has one thousand and one thoughts. She can do all manner of bizarre tricks in this white material, Ulrike has already noticed, and it is a result (although neither Ulrike nor anyone else knows it) of her not thinking of any resistance at all when she moves. Shlomith, on the contrary, thinks of food. Ultimately for her the hardest thing to bear is that she can't even abstain from food. She is accustomed to abstinence, which triggers deep feelings of joy in her with near Pavlovian consistency. This is why at one moment in her mind she might be treading a square kilometer carpet of roasted marshmallows, in the next stomping sugary potato pudding, or then (if for one reason or another she wants to spur herself to especially quick movement) wading in her favorite food, a vat of miso soup filled to brimming with tofu cubes.

Motion and thought. It is so simple. Ulrike thinks of Hanno's parents' water bed, where screwing had always been unreasonably difficult. The rhythm was too different, and it made it all far too embarrassing.

Thus they finally get moving. Ulrike, Nina, and Polina walking in a line, Rosa Imaculada and Wlibgis treading behind them. Each in her own way. Presumably as a result of this first, somewhat traumatic image, Ulrike's style becomes *flamenco furioso*, a banging rhythm executed with an exaggerated straight back: see how with each kick the tips and heels of the shoes gradually wear through the double-laminated vinyl surface ... Bring on the flood ... Let them all drown ...

Ahead, beyond Shlomith's narrow frame, something red suddenly flashes. For a moment it disappears behind Shlomith and then appears again, a tiny red spot that grows, disappears, then comes into view again a little larger. Some sort of shape begins to take form. It isn't a blotch or a hole but a separate thing like Ulrike herself and the other women. Something that could be touched. Clearly it could be touched, but what is it? Red, rippling. It seems to be a little higher than them, and the closer they trudge to it, the more clearly above it is. And then: they are beneath it. Ulrike bends her head and looks into it. A hollow cage like a calabash gourd, with red hair fanning all around as if floating in water but completely motionless.

Now Ulrike is forced to learn another new skill, the skill of rising upward. Maimuna has already dived to the surface: the red hair has become the level relative to which everything else is defined. Everyone is going there, to the level of the hair, and Ulrike must rise too, but once again: how?

Maimuna had raised her hands like a diver, squeezing her head between her long arms (plug your ears!) and clenching her right thumb in her left fist (hold tight!), and then she pushed off, and now she is there. Polina of the Swamp grabs something with her hands (peat moss, tormentil roots, bog star stems, sawgrass blades?) and heaves herself up little by little, with some backsliding. Wlibgis of the Snow simply digs herself a tunnel to crawl through. Rosa of the Feather Pillow licks her hands and then squeezes and rotates the nothingness to make small, apparently rock-hard balls she can place as steps. Nina of the Waterwings thrashes and falls and lurches up, and Shlomith of the Miso Soup launches into a series of movements that look like vomiting. Throwing herself back-first with the force of the retching, she moves in fits right up to the hair.

Ulrike thinks of a flood. She thinks of Hanno lying naked on his stomach at the bottom of the empty water-bed frame, drowned. She thinks of her shoes and the shreds of PVC fabric stuck to her heels. She thinks of Hanno's parents' bedroom and the stains on the ugly brown antique wallpaper. She begins to fall. Slowly she begins to float farther away from the women and the red hair. Instinctively she lifts her hands toward them, like a child asking to be picked up; she kicks and pushes but only continues to move away. She screams like she is drowning (actually people who are drowning don't scream), and as she shrieks she senses how the sound disappears somewhere, as if it has never left her throat. She hears her cry for help, her echoless, impotent wail, and still it seems to come from somewhere else. She waves her arms and sinks, until she feels Maimuna's firm grip under her armpits. *Do not think bad things*, Maimuna whispers to her, *only good things*, and in her panic, Ulrike thinks of cyclamen. *Eyes shut!* Maimuna orders, and Ulrike obediently closes her eyes and curls up in the middle of a meadow of cyclamen. The sun shines, birds sing, and a butterfly lands on her arm as they begin to rise.

This is their campfire. Their gathering place. Whenever they wish to speak about something together, Shlomith says, they come here to Wlibgis's wig. *It was veeeery kind of her,* Shlomith drawls—that Wlibgis donated her beautiful, artificial hair for this use. Although, privately, Shlomith really thinks that Wlibgis's wig is rather second-rate. And that one could only get truly beautiful wigs that actually looked genuine from the Hasidic Jews in Borough Park, who covered their married women's hair not with scarves but with hair creations, each more lavish than the last. Women who covered their hair with *sheitels* were always well groomed, with an enviable polish that rivaled that of manikins; *bad hair day* was not in their vocabulary. When a mother of a family she knew came down with cancer and started chemotherapy, she immediately demanded to go to Borough Park. Her Hasidic wig had been more beautiful and natural than her own hair ever was. The cancer took the woman, but the family didn't want to give up the wig. They set it on a beige velvet display head and the display head on a dresser in the living room, and told everyone who visited that some day, if one was very lucky, cheerful vanity might catch the fear of death in a headlock.

Ulrike glances at Wlibgis, at her misshapen, lumpy head, flat at the back; her whole head actually looks like a pickle. The sacrifice has undeniably been great. Or maybe not. Perhaps it hasn't been a sacrifice at all. Do things like hair, clothing, or hygiene mean anything any more at this stage? On the spur of the moment, Ulrike lifts her hand and sniffs her armpit. She smells nothing. Nothing bad and nothing good, not sweat and not the *Angel* by Thierry Mugler she had undoubtedly sprayed there in the morning as she left for work. It had been a pathetic gift from Hanno. She had wanted perfume but received deodorant.

We don't stink any more, Shlomith says, noticing Ulrike's gesture, *because we might not be alive any more*. There. Now they are getting to the point. This was Shlomith's style. At times she could be rather un-American and spit things out without any warmup laps, and this is why they had come to the wig now: to explain the situation to Ulrike.

Originally the wig campfire had been Nina's idea. Into Nina's cute little head had popped the thought that they needed some reference point, some common place of refuge, so why on earth shouldn't they create one for themselves? Whipping her arms about and slurring her R's, Nina explained her idea. Polina was the first one to understand what Nina was actually saying: Nina was talking about the wig on Wlibgis's head. About the unnaturally red artificial hair that suited the cancer-ravaged woman so surprisingly well. Nina glanced at it constantly but didn't dare to say out loud that Wlibgis would have to give up her hair now. That it was what she wanted to use to make them a homey little fire, a place to gather and chat. Because weren't all the world's stories told around campfires once? Like about how the world was born from an egg, the horse from the sand, the foal from the foam of the sea. The wolf from a coupling of virgin and wind, iron from breasts of motherless nymphs, frost from a serpent that gave suck with no teats. Agony from stones of suffering ground against a mountain of pain. Tumors from a golden ball dragged to shore by the fox. Death from arrows carved from splinters of the World Tree. And Summer

Boy brought blood! Later, when everyone has settled in properly, the noses have been blown, and the tears cried, and everyone gathers around the comforting crackle of the fireplace, the confessions begin. It's now or never: Mom, I'm pregnant. Son, I don't have long to live. Dad, I'm moving to Sicily. Dearest daughter, I've never liked women that way, not even your mother. Best friend, I've done something terrible, something I can't take back. I've been living a lie all these years. I don't love you any more. I love someone else. I emptied our retirement account and invested the money in stocks that crashed today . . .

Polina had stopped listening to Nina's clumsy coaxing ages ago. She stared at Wlibgis's hair. The tangled fibers were hypnotic, concealing an endless supply of new, blazing filaments, new burning secrets. Confessions it might be nice to listen to as a fly on the wall! Polina couldn't imagine herself confessing, telling the others her personal business; she didn't really have any, but she could see from the others that they did. Polina saw Shlomith explaining the reasons for her anorexia; the brutal image of femininity that had locked the poor woman in her decades-long prison. She saw Nina dishing the dirt on her relationship troubles, and Rosa Imaculada crying about the violence she had experienced. And someone had probably mistreated Maimuna too. Hadn't they all been hurt somehow? In Polina's vision, even mute Wlibgis burst into speech. Wlibgis, if anyone, looked like a victim, and it had nothing to do with her illness. It welled from her gaze. Polina had looked into the eyes of the dying, had seen grandeur in those eyes, resilience and self-respect, but Wlibgis's gaze was like her dying mother's gaze had been during her final weeks: servile, false, just playing for time. If you just visit me every day, death will stay away! That was what her mother's gaze had communicated to her, and it was a lie.

Polina couldn't restrain herself any more. She grabbed Wlibgis's hair and snatched the wig from her head. *There now! There's our fire to sit around and talk!* Polina thrust the wig down with all her might, and as if by magic the hair spread and began to fall slowly, drifting slightly to one side, finally coming to rest about half a meter below the soles of Polina's feet, as handsome as a lion's mane.

This was how, through the application of a little violence, their campfire was lit. Of course Wlibgis didn't like the change. The others were also shocked. How could Polina act that way! And so suddenly! However, the wig was enchanting nonetheless. When they stared at it, peace spread through their minds, and concentrating was easier. The entire group began to try to appease Wlibgis as she sulked. She wouldn't have to look at her own bald head here, Nina said. Instead, now she could see her fabulous hair in all its glory whenever she pleased, Shlomith exclaimed. Maimuna said *Oooooh!* and dropped to her knees to press her cheek to the hair, and Rosa Imaculada followed suit, letting out a sigh of *Beleza!* but did not, despite the visible bending of her knees, succeed in dropping down next to the hair.

Wlbigis looked at her choices. Either she would kick Maimuna in the head, shove her bodily away from the hair then take Nina's hands, which were already on the wig, straightening and fluffing it, shake them loose and make herself altogether difficult, or she would give in. She decided to give in.

Ulrike lifts her nose from her armpit and looks at Shlomith, who does not avoid the girl's bewildered gaze. On the contrary, Shlomith stares greedily at Ulrike, practically salivating for a reaction. Shock? Disbelief? A hoot of laughter? She's already experienced it all. Everything except calm acceptance, the kind that might be expressed in a nod: fair enough, we might not be alive any more.

Ulrike looks in turn at each woman gathered around Shlomith. Did they understand what that grotesque woman had suggested to them? That they were here but that they weren't after all? *Verdammt!* Was that how this bag of bones explained all of this?

That was one explanation, yes. One possible theory. Not invented by Shlomith but by arrival number two, Polina. When arrival number five, Wlibgis, appeared and in rapture mouthed the words, *I'm alive! No more pain!*—at that moment the matter became as clear as day to Polina. Her final doubts disappeared. They were all as dead as rocks. They could go without food and drink. They had no need for sleep (privacy, yes, and then they closed their eyes). They had no need for any of the other normal, daily bodily functions, such as urination or defecation, for example. No one even missed the movements and gestures associated with urinating and defecating. No one mimed them just for the pleasure of miming them, unlike the choreography of eating (although they soon tired of that as well). Only Maimuna's bowels had worked here, once. This occurred around the time of her arrival, soon after she had rolled out prone and materialized from the white. She squatted and squeezed a small, dry turd out of her anus. Then everyone had gathered to admire and wonder at it (it didn't smell, which they noticed), and that was that. The only known shit in the whole place. Things like that simply stopped existing—the feeling of pressure on the bladder, grumbling intestines, heaviness in the anus, sphincter contractions, the rhythm of holding in and release.

Of course Maimuna's excrement existed. It existed so strongly, so disturbingly, that with one accord they decided to move away from it. The shit didn't actually disgust anyone as such, its presence simply confused them. It was something at once too familiar and too strange: the Last Time embodied in shit. And that was why it began to signify things they didn't want to remember yet. The condemned do not enjoy their final meals either, do they? (According to one former prison cook, a cheeseburger and French fries were the most popular last meal. He prepared 220 last meals in Texas from 1991–2003 while serving a fourteen-year sentence for kidnapping his brother-in-law and raping his ex-wife. In a way, it's sad that the average murderer in Texas headed for a lethal injection wants to eat that specific variation of the hamburger invented in the United States in 1935, and not, for example, a double cheeseburger or a bacon cheeseburger, not to mention any other foods. Why didn't anyone ever order *vorschmack*, for instance? Fortunately some had the sense to cut loose. They ate until they were so bloated that death must have felt like a relief rather than a punishment.)

Or when a person has sex for the last time with their beloved (or with anyone)—isn't that sad too? At least it's *something*. It's strange and significant. The last intercourse before the car crash that takes a spouse. Or the more common case: the last intercourse after which

intercourse simply stops. Too old. Can't or won't. Not interested. The
last sex was five years ago on the sixth of April, at home in the bed as
usual, in the usual way, a bit limp, a bit dry, prodding but well inten-
tioned, and then—that was that. All the sex you would ever have.

And there is always a last time, Shlomith says, breaking the silence
and drawing together every possible incomplete thought that might
be spinning in the new arrival's head. The last time of all last times.
And because in these exceptional circumstances it is possible to
experience that specific last time (fortunately Ulrike had been very
gifted in this regard), there was no reason to skip the intervention.
Simply put: Shlomith licked Ulrike down there because soon she
wouldn't be able to experience anything like that any more. No physical pleasure and no pain. She licked Ulrike down there because
every woman present—Shlomith, Polina, Rosa, Nina, Wlibgis, and
Maimuna—desired pleasure (each in her own way), or at least just
touch. She licked Ulrike instead of, for example, beating her, because
these women weren't sadists, and if they were, they didn't have any
room here for sudden, inordinate bursts of violence. They knew
without saying it that now was not a time to rock the boat. The mere
thought of violence felt more improper here than in that other world,
where there were police, law books, trials, judges, fines, prisons, and
in some countries even capital punishment. Here there was nothing.
Presumably the target of the attack wouldn't even be injured, at least
not permanently. Again, this was one of their hypotheses, and they
had even done some cautious tests a little before Ulrike's arrival by
pinching each other. Each found that the pinching felt the same as
squeezing or scratching an arm that has gone to sleep under a pillow.
It felt like nothing. They saw it with their eyes, but the skin on the
arm didn't react, and they started to laugh. There they sat next to
each other, scratching and pinching and squeezing each other.
Nothing that held true before held true any more. That was what they
wanted to demonstrate to each other with the pinching, even though
none of them knew what to do with this fact. Or did this fact comfort
them? Did it fill them with faith, did it give them a reason to go on?
And what did going on mean? What the hell would they do after they

stopped pinching each other? None of them knew, and that was why
they were all laughing.

They laughed until Shlomith noticed a bundle resembling a human
figure lying somewhere in the distance, a figure who later turned out
to be none other than Ulrike. When they set off, moving toward the
bundle, they decided to try to satisfy the being, whether it was a
woman or a man (of course, with a child they would have given up
their plan). Shlomith, still excited about the pinching, came up with
the idea, which almost all of the women thought was excellent, nour-
ished as they were by their laughter. The women decided that
Shlomith would lick and suck the erogenous zones of the being they
found until it came, assuming it still had the ability to experience
pleasure. It would be a double welcome gift, a gift to the new member
of the group and a gift to them all: to see arousal, orgasm, sweat in the
hollows of the knees, and remember, if only distantly.

Thank you, Ulrike, Nina says and strokes her round belly. *Thank
you*, Shlomith says. *Thank you so very much, liebe Ulrike*, Polina says
tenderly. *Obrigado!* Rosa Imaculada says. *Merrrrrci!* Maimuna says,
gaily rolling her R. Wlibgis smiles sadly, nods her bald head, and
strokes the red artificial fire, her very own poor hair, which at least is
permanent unlike some teenage girl's orgasm—and a feeling resembling stale jealousy wells up in Wlibgis's mind. No one had ever
granted her pleasure. If she had ever panted—and she had, she had
given birth to a son an eternity ago—she had gasped with pain and
fear, she had panted from the agony, the tearing, and the blows, and
after the blows she continued panting. More of them were to come,
and she gasped over and over again out of sheer disbelief. How many
times does a person have to be hit before she believes that she's really
being hit? That it isn't a bad dream? The same boy who had ripped
her open as he pushed his way out had hit her later in so many ways
and in so many tender places that she had lost count. Gradually she
had given in and allowed herself to become a woman to whom much
evil had been done, who would receive atonement only at the Final
Judgement. Was that where she was going now?

Wlibgis's fingers disappear into the wig. What did that little girl think she knew about life? Ha! But here she was too, beyond the reach of any aid. Gaunt, fleshless schadenfreude fills Wlibgis's mind.

There is other undeniable evidence for the death theory. Shlomith is doing quite well even though she, like Wlibgis, should be as dead as a doornail. *So it's just beyond dispute!* Polina was completely sure and she had said so directly during the stage when only six of them were there, when Ulrike had yet to appear, before they had burst out laughing during the pinch test and Nina hadn't had the idea about the campfire wig.

It isn't possible you're alive, Shlomith, Polina had said. *You aren't morbidly thin; you're something much worse.*

Of course that caused a fight. For Shlomith, thinness wasn't "something much worse": it was part of an experiment, an extreme yet controlled test that she had come out of as the conqueror. She had survived, she remembered, and the memory was as sharp as a postcard, a postcard crammed full of words in a fit of emotion. The applause in the auditorium of the Jewish Museum had begun cautiously, probingly, as people had glanced at each other in shock: is it even appropriate to clap now, or should we gather our things and leave quietly as one does after a church service, eyes meekly cast down? But then someone burst out in furious applause and someone else, a man, shouted a choked "Bravo! Bravissimo!" and suddenly the entire packed hall began to tremble at the joints as dozens and dozens of hands came together, sucking up the surrounding oxygen. The air turned thick, too overpowering. Shlomith retreated and sat on a wooden stool. The stool had been placed behind her on the stage as a precaution in case she was unable to stand after all. But it was now, as she accepted her ovation, that she needed the chair. She sat on it in a half-unconscious state. A red cushion had been placed on the stool so her hollow hindquarters would not be damaged by the hard wood (she already had enough bruises). Sitting on the red cushion wearing only panties, she had gulped in the plaudits, the dense, oppressive air that few people ever get to enjoy, and then her mummy-like, parchment-dry body began to react. A cramp doubled her over, and the cry that struggled out of her folded her against her knees, forcing her flat, body part against body part, face against knees, sharp nose between sharp kneecaps. It was no final aria rising from the base of her diaphragm. It was shriveling, huddling, and it had to happen. She had to collapse for all to see, and she allowed herself to finally collapse. Her hardness, the edge (which some have and others don't) that she had developed over decades, began to crumble. And the more Shlomith crumbled, the more the audience cheered, because everyone in the auditorium knew that Shlomith's life mission was now complete. Shlomith had said it herself a moment earlier: "This is the last performance I will give. When I recover, I will organize my archives and donate them to a museum. Initial discussions have already taken place. After that I will begin to enjoy life. In a healthy way." The ambulance stood ready in front of the museum. A place had been reserved for Shlomith in a private hospital where she could gather her strength in peace and regain her lost weight. No calls, no emails, no visitors. She would cease to be an attraction. She would learn to be a human first, then a woman, and finally perhaps even a mother again.

In that beautiful auditorium, in the building the rich Jewish widow Frieda Schiff Warburg had donated to the museum in the fateful year of 1944, Shlomith howled with her bone-hard nose between her bone-hard knees. For the first time in thirty years she shed great, hot tears that tasted the same as the tears in the Kibbutz Methuselah communal kitchen: salty, crushing, but still cautiously foreshadowing a new beginning. Shlomith crouched on the red cushion, amidst the ear-splitting storm of applause, as the waves of thirty years of sorrow and at least as great an amount of loneliness battered her, and not just her but also every soul who sat in the hall, nearly all of whom had now risen to their feet. For there is no creature alive who does not have a secret sorrow to mourn, no one who in her inner parts is not waiting for permission to release her cares.

The final, spontaneous and unscripted climax of Shlomith's work, the cathartic mass weeping that had overtaken the crowd, which a few cynical head shakes and a couple of people marching out in open irritation could not repress, began to change shape after surging for some time. One after another people began to collect themselves when they noticed that Shlomith had lifted her head from her knees and raised her eyes. Someone stopped clapping and began to rustle his clothing as a sign he intended to move, and his neighbor did the same, and somewhere else in the auditorium someone else also started to move, and those around her did the same, and then the people next to them, and soon the whole hall was moving. But people did not press for the doors. Instead they formed a line before the artist just as spontaneously as they had burst into tears a moment ago. They wanted to hug her, each in his or her own way to say THANK YOU and to wish her a productive recovery. As they dried the corners of their eyes, one or two wondered to themselves how they would live without her. Who would channel their emotions after Shlomith had retired?

So when Polina said to Shlomith, with Nina, Wlibgis, Maimuna, and Rosa listening, that she couldn't *be alive* any more than Wlibgis could be alive, Shlomith became terribly angry. Even though Polina immediately added that by the same token she couldn't be alive either, any more than Nina, Maimuna, or Rosa were alive, Shlomith began to rage. Polina's claim was downright offensive. Of course she was alive! She was more alive than she had ever been. She had begun to recover. She knew it because she no longer felt pain. Her thoughts were clearer now than they'd been in many years, and the dead didn't have thoughts anyway. How do you know? Polina asked. I know, replied Shlomith, because everyone knows that. Has someone come back from the dead to tell you? asked Polina. The dead don't speak, Shlomith said angrily. The dead have no brain activity. But what if we don't continue our existence as physical beings? Polina continued. What if that something in us that science can't measure never dies? But here I am, and you and all of us, just as alive as can be. We can see it with our own eyes! Shlomith shouted. Where the hell is "here"? Polina bellowed, spreading her arms theatrically. We aren't anywhere! God help us, we aren't anywhere or anything except this stupid fight and all these empty words!

Polina could have continued to talk for much longer, because she

had a dogmatic certainty about her cause. Talking doesn't stop even
when everything else stops. Laughing and quarreling don't stop, even
when the bodily functions stop, one by one, even as the senses fade
by degrees. This is death, Polina would have liked to cry. Something
larger than the person continues to operate, using the person's shell,
drawing power from the person's empty gestures; that Something
needs this delayed destruction for something. That Something places
the helpless creature torn from its life to struggle in a small society,
and that society is made up of similarly helpless creatures torn from
their lives. Survival depends entirely on good will. Does that exist or
doesn't it? Yes or no?

Polina had stopped arguing. They had to cooperate, they had to
forget their dispute. Polina closed her eyes and swallowed what she
had just meant to lob into the air: that *they* were the evidence of the
existence of death, that *this was the world* no one had come to tell the
living about, because the ones who have seen the light at the end of
the tunnel, who have watched the sepia-toned filmstrip of their lives
sped up in reverse in the waiting room of death, never make it this far.

Polina leaned back, farther away from Shlomith's threatening forefinger. She was just on the verge of understanding something that she
would have immediately written down if she had had pen and paper:

- THE HUMAN VOICE —> REACHES BEYOND DEATH

- WE GRADUALLY LOSE THE ABILITY TO TOUCH, WE BEGIN TO DESTROY

- SOCIETY IS <u>ALWAYS</u> IN DANGER!!!

- SEIZE UPON THE LEAST COMMON DENOMINATOR WHEN EVERYTHING
  BEGINS TO FALL APART

Dear God, they were right at the heart of things now, these women
sitting in a ring gaping at each other! If she had known about the
existence of this world earlier, back when she was still with her

own . . . If she could have seen this in advance . . . If she could have known the right words to use . . .

Polina stopped. This was pointless navel gazing. Her own only would have thought she was even more crazy. One of them in particular, Maruska, her coworker at Zlom, the Moscow Central Agency for the Dramatic Arts, who was always preened down to the last hair, would have been certain to call over her doctor husband at some opening night reception where, after a few drinks, Polina had perhaps built up the courage to share her insight: "Serjoža! Serjoža!" Maruska would have shouted and gesticulated, and Serjoža would have rushed over to them from the furthest corner of the hall. If they were one centimeter larger, his protruding ears would have flapped, and his tail, if he'd had one, would have wagged—a truncheon tail, like a Rottweiler's, that's what he would have had: a stiff, black wagging tail. "Serjoža, my dear Serjoža, Polina is talking nonsense again. She thinks that we continue existing after death. In little groups! In emptiness! And we gradually lose our senses. But not our ability to communicate, especially not our ability to quarrel! I think Polina must have been reading some crazy philosopher's books too much again . . ." That's how Maruska would have chirped, and she wouldn't have stopped until she had said, "Tell Polina about that patient you treated, the young man who thought he was dead. Go on! Polina likes macabre stories!"

DEATH REHEARSAL NUMBER 1
(COTARD'S DELUSION WITH A DASH OF TIBETAN BUDDHISM)

Serjoža would have escorted Polina to the sofa group and offered her something to smoke. These stories were the kinds of stories you couldn't listen to (let alone tell) without cognac and cherry cigars. Serjoža was happy to tell his friends stories about his clients (which is why people liked him). All of his patients, regardless of sex, were named Pyotr, and the most unbelievable things always happened to them. Otherwise they wouldn't have been Serjoža's clients.

This specific Pyotr suffered from a very rare disease named

Cotard's Delusion. The name came from French neurologist Jules Cotard, who began his career under Professor Jean-Martin Charcot at Pitié-Salpêtrière Hospital. In the 1870s, Cotard moved to a small city near Paris, Vanves, which nowadays is one of the most densely populated places in Europe, where he died fifteen years later from diphtheria acquired from his daughter.

Cotard's Delusion, which the neurologist described as a new form of melancholia comprising restlessness and agitation, saw the light of day in 1880. Its typical symptoms include "the delirium of negation" (*délire des négations*): depression accompanied by delusions related to one's own body. Anxiety and guilt afflict some who suffer from the syndrome, along with hypochondria, auditory hallucinations, and, paradoxically enough, delusions of immortality.

Serjoža's Pyotr was a unique case in many regards. He had read a Russian translation of *The Tibetan Book of the Dead* immediately prior to falling ill—this topic, death, had gripped him long before the appearance of his actual delusions. When he was brought to Serjoža's clinic, he was convinced that his mother had failed miserably in her most important duty: she hadn't known how to assist his consciousness to launch out of his body in the instant before his breathing stopped.

Pyotr had a photographic memory of the situation in which he believed he died. Yes, a photographic memory: as if death hadn't been enough, to top it all off he had separated from his body. He had watched events unfold from the ceiling, and now he gave Serjoža a voluminous account of what he had seen. So he lay lifeless in his bed. Before that he had pushed himself up on his elbows and shouted to his mother in terror as he felt his spirit leaving. He had hoped his mother would come in time to help him, that his mother would have a chance to read aloud certain important lines from a book that was on his nightstand. But when his mother arrived, it was too late. Pyotr had already managed to move, or rather had been dragged, up to the ceiling.

The arrival at his lifeless body of his father and little sister, who had run in spurred by his mother's cries, did not change the situation at all. And because his father's bald head was right below him, so

Pyotr had related to Serjoža, he thought he could take the grandfather clock weight from high atop the cabinet, where it had been
placed to await the clocksmith, and drop it on his father's head. He
wanted to see his father's skull break. He was convinced his father
had slipped thallium into the water he had been drinking. Pyotr
claimed that his father had long been looking for an opportunity to
take his son's life. That was why, for months, Pyotr had been buying
his food and drink exclusively in cheap restaurants and refusing any
family dinners, despite his mother's beseeching and tears.

But now his father had won. He had found the rucksack Pyotr had
hidden under his bed and the unopened bottle of spring water in it.
As he slept, his father had opened the top and crumbled a full gram
of thallium powder into the water. And then Pyotr had unsuspect-
ingly drunk the water in the morning. And now he had died, and all
of his precautions had gone to waste.

Serjoža didn't ask whether Pyotr had experienced sudden stomach pains, diarrhea, and vomiting, which were the first symptoms of
thallium poisoning. Instead he let Pyotr continue, and Pyotr pressed
on, telling him that the clock weight hadn't budged no matter how he
tried to tug on it as he floated, stretched out horizontally. His father
had disappeared from beneath him, leaving the room with a
concerned sigh—faking, of course, Pyotr added—to call the doctor.
His little sister had burst into tears, and all his mother could do was
stroke poor Pyotr's forehead as it cooled.

Serjoža listened to his patient in all seriousness, not allowing even
the hint of a smile to reach his lips. And he wouldn't laugh when he
passed the case on later. That was part of his professional ethic: seriousness no matter how insane the story might be, and no matter how
his listeners might double over in laughter, holding their stomachs
and drying tears of mirth.

But there was one feature in Pyotr's story that to his knowledge
had received no mention in the literature on Cotard's Delusion,
and from which Serjoža might derive a marvelous peer-reviewed
article which could receive hundreds if not thousands of citations
in the future. The Tibetan Book of the Dead. The question of how a

written work can influence the onset of delusions in a mind susceptible to delusions. Pyotr would be Serjoža's key to international
success!

Pyotr sat slumped before Serjoža, overcome with grief. He
hadn't managed to tell his mother, whom he trusted implicitly and
loved boundlessly, that at the moment when he felt his spirit leaving, she should have quickly picked up the book next to his bed on
the nightstand, opened it at the bookmark to page fifty-six, and
read:

*O child of noble family, Pyotr, the time has come for you to choose
a path. After your breath stops, the basic luminosity of the first
bardo, which your guru has already shown you, will appear to
you. This is the dharmatā, empty and open like space, a luminous
void, pure, naked mind with neither center nor circumference.
Recognize then, and remain in that state, and I will show you at
the same time.*

Pyotr's mother was supposed to read these lines in Pyotr's ear as he
died, so long as he continued to breathe, so long as her son maintained contact with the material world. And when Pyotr had stopped
breathing, when his arteries had ceased to throb, he should have
been turned to rest on his right side with his right hand at his head
with the palm against his cheek. This was the position in which
Gautama Buddha died, the position from which Gautama Buddha
passed immediately and directly into the final resting place of the
soul, parinirvāṇa

Now, Pyotr complained to Serjoža, he would be relegated to wade
through hallucinations of his memories alone, without a guide. He
would always fear losing his way, because the bardo was full of false
allurements, which came from his very own consciousness, from his
projections, fears, and desires. How would he be able to keep his
wandering thoughts in check without his mother guiding him, without his mother reading in his ear:

O child of noble family, death has now arrived, and so you should adopt this attitude: "I have arrived at the time of death, so now, through this death, I will adopt the attitude of the enlightened state of mind, of friendliness and compassion . . ."

Pyotr wept bitterly, because he had not recognized the "basic luminosity of the first bardo", the pure, immaterial, colorless, unfettered, gleaming, and shimmering brightness, nor the secondary luminosity of the second bardo. For this reason he was forced to walk, so he shouted at Serjoža, toward the terrifying karmic illusions, toward the horrors of the Lords of Death, toward the deceitful colored light and frightening sounds of the false kingdom of the bardo of dharmatā. Right now, as they spoke, he walked there, and he was afraid because no one could help him. No one was there to tell him: *This is the natural sound of your own dharmatā, so do not be afraid or bewildered.* And no one whispered in his ear: *You have no physical body of flesh and blood, so whatever sounds, colors, and rays of light occur, they cannot hurt you and you cannot die.* And his mother did not assure him that: *It is enough simply to recognize them as your projections.* And he would never receive instructions for closing the door to the womb in the bardo of becoming. He would be eternally alone, wandering in the muddy swamp of samsāra, as the living dead, separated from his loved ones, his mother and his sister, who would now have to survive alone under his father's tyranny.

At this point in the story, Serjoža would have tapped the ash from his cherry cigar and enjoyed his first shot of cognac. He would have looked at Polina carefully, observing the effect of Pyotr's patient history on her. Then he would have looked at his wife, Maruska, as she purred like a cat, only to nod gently to indicate that now it would be her turn, that now it would be her job to guide Polina back to good sense and away from these follies that would only bring Polina to grief. "Dear Polina," Maruska would begin to warble, "these are the kinds of stories madmen tell. They're an amusing distraction, aren't they! But I'll tell you now that no matter what you invent, Serjoža will always be able to give you one better.

And he doesn't even have to use his imagination. Being a doctor is enough for him!"

°
°

But *here* Polina was more sensible than many others, for example Shlomith, whose bony finger began to look ridiculous as it wagged. Surely they all understood by now that when you're dead, you can't die any more—or kill anyone else. Did Shlomith really want to grab her by the neck (that's how it looked) and strangle her only to see that she couldn't be strangled any more? Only to be forced to admit defeat, to admit that their inviolability and immortality offered final proof of the claim she had just made that *de facto* they were dead? Polina waved in the direction of Shlomith's finger and gave an irritable hiss.

And in that moment, right on the heels of that hiss, which seemed to echo around the women, apparently only due to the suppressed anger with which Polina ejected it, Nina began to talk about the place. The point of reference, the safe harbor, the fireplace, the camp-fire—the wig. Peace be to you, Shlomith and Polina! No fighting. We're all grown women!

Thankfully adults also have permission to play. Especially around a campfire. Shlomith was the one who came up with it, as she watched Nina crouching to fluff the wig and saw her belly protruding like a ball bursting with life from beneath her black maternity shirt, a counter-point to everything Polina had said, an exclamation point affirming life. *Let's play dead!* Shlomith decided to make a game of it: *OK. Let's pretend we aren't in the land of the living any more. It might be fun, a little like reading a mystery where each of us dies in turn, Polina, Nina, Maimuna, Wlibgis, Shlomith, and Rosa. It might put a little excitement in our . . . this, whatever we want to call this, it's all the same.*

Both Polina and Nina eagerly joined in the game, relieved that the quarrel was past, as did Maimuna when Nina was good enough to promise to translate between French and English. Rosa Imaculada also would have had a tale to tell, perhaps the wildest tale of all, but the time for that was not yet, not in this place, not around this campfire. Here it came out of Rosa's mouth in a confusion of languages fit for Babel, and no one could catch hold of the plot. Rosa grew frustrated and tried again and got flustered and finally began to irritate everyone. The others began to hope, secretly, or less than secretly, exposed in the slightest expressions and gestures, that Rosa would be quiet. That Rosa would content herself with listening. Maybe Rosa would gradually learn to express herself better. Listen and learn instead of constantly getting so wound up.

And poor Wlibgis. With no voice, with no words.

But Shlomith, Polina, Nina, and Maimuna began to play murderer for their own enjoyment and to entertain the rest. Someone (or something) had rubbed them out, had knocked them off; someone (or something) had wanted to get rid of them so suddenly that they hadn't even noticed where their enemy was, who (or what) was hounding them, or who had a motive.

SMALL CINNAMON-BUN-SHAPED STORIES

Shlomith said:

As you know, I am an artist. I do performances, and my work takes me to extremes that are unpleasant and even dangerous. But I never hurt anyone other than myself at most. The world is full of violence, but that wouldn't diminish even if I blew up shopping centers full of trash produced in immoral working conditions. I shake people up, but I never violate anyone's person or free will. If someone is hurt, that's a matter of interpretation, that I've hit a tender spot, metaphorically speaking. Is everything clear so far?

My final memory relates to a performance I did in my home city of New York, in the Scheuer Auditorium at the Jewish Museum. I've just given a presentation on the connections between anorexia and Jewishness—I use my religion and my culture as material for my performances. I've finished, and I'm standing in my underwear behind the microphone, waiting for the audience reaction. Even though I've only been telling the truth, conveying simple, cold facts, and even though I've stated that I take full responsibility for myself and my work, in some people I awaken a primitive rage. I'm prepared for rotten fruit, eggs, water bottles, even small pebbles. Nothing truly dangerous could come flying from the audience because the security screening has been even more strict than usual. Everyone walked through metal detectors, all bags were opened, and no large backpacks were allowed in the auditorium at all. Just to be safe, my assistant, the indispensable Katie McKeen, is ready in the wings just behind the red curtain. We have agreed that if anything starts raining on the stage, she'll come and get me. She'll open a large black umbrella, and we'll walk together under cover to a back room where no outsiders are allowed.

Two armed guards stand at the door. In the restricted courtyard behind the museum a car waits for me, an ambulance. I can see that this astonishes a few of you. The deliberateness, ribaldry even, that unavoidably attends this performance. But let's not talk about that now. All I did was go on an expedition into my culture, which in a roundabout way is the culture every one of us self-righteous bastards shares. I harnessed my body completely, as I always do in my art, for use in my research. I made it into an instrument, which I cared for with great love. Vitamins, trace minerals, fatty acids, all carefully calculated and controlled; nutrition therapy was instrumental. My goal was not to starve myself to death, but of course I dropped my energy intake relative to consumption very low. I shot for a body mass index of twelve, met it, and even went a bit below. I knew the risks. I'm not stupid.

My motives? When I start something, I go all in. Nothing less is possible. I've been sick for years, assuming you want to call voluntarily abstaining from food a sickness in this world. Ultimately I wanted to gaze into the soul of my sickness—and not just for selfish personal reasons but for cultural research. Because in the final analysis, this is a sickness we all share. This sickness and its different variations have a soul, and it is the Jewish soul, the landscape of the Semitic spirit. This is my argument, and this is the soul I believe I succeeded in revealing.

And I received enormous applause for this service. No rotten fruit or stinking eggs. Those would have been thrown by neo-Nazis, Haredi Jews, or Christian extremists who had infiltrated the crowd, because they all have one common enemy, and I am it. Polina, there's no use staring at me that way. I'm not boasting. This is simply a fact! During my career, I've received death threats, I've been stalked, and once someone tried to run me down with a car. But I've never retreated: the call of art has been stronger than fear. I have an obsession with honesty, and I don't give up, even if my honesty might drive some with weak nerves to insanity.

But now *they* succeeded after all. Let's just agree on that if we really are dead. *They* killed me, let's just say, and pretend that you're right, Polina. Let's assume that it happened in the following way. The performance is done, the applause has been given, and people are lining up to greet me. They thank me, and everyone wants to exchange a few words. Believe it or not, many people cried! They cried because my example gave them permission to cry. Wait, Polina, let me continue! You're thinking that I suffer from megalomania. But that isn't so. To put it simply: people want to be led. When that happens in a safe place, like in a museum or in a gallery, and they all receive the same conduit, which in this case is me, at the same time, they surrender. I call it intermental metabolism. It does the audience good, and ultimately it makes all of society healthier. I wouldn't do my art if I didn't believe in this. But this all has a dark side too.

So the performance is done, and everyone has given their hugs, their thanks, their tears. The auditorium begins to empty. The guards are friendly as they usher the audience out the door, and I watch them all like one might watch an anthill or the draining of a bath full of water. I am empty. I drain as the people flow out of the room, approaching complete emptiness of thought. I register movement but no movers. The people are vertical lines, multicolored hairs, backs, and bottoms, each dressed differently, being sucked by the door to the other side. Very soon they will be gone.

I am exhausted. I could fall asleep on my stool, but suddenly I snap awake. My attention focuses on the final person leaving the hall, who has stopped. A disturbance in the landscape. He turns and reveals his face. A middle-aged man with glasses, perfectly normal, or so you might suppose if you saw him on the street walking with everyone else. Suit jacket on top, relaxed jeans below, slender, obviously in good shape. Maybe he's a marathoner, since something in him seems tenacious that way. There is determination in his movements, with a dash of compulsion, which is needed to carry out the plan he has been nursing for so many years in his mind.

He has the wiry stride of a long-distance runner, but now he isn't in his own element, out in the fresh air. The hall stinks of a mass ecstasy whose causes he can only understand one way. In front of the crammed door, he makes a small, restless turn and finally lifts his eyes to me. I see in his gaze that he is looking at Satan himself.

He has hung behind to the last in order to ensure being noticed, so I will see his significant gaze, which is meant only for me. Then he slips out the door. In that very moment I realize I am in great danger. He isn't working alone! There are several of *them* here. A moment ago I had seen that same look in the queue that formed in front of me. I remember a young man whose body language was similar, made tense by a stubborn vehemence; behind him walked a young woman, and I remember her too. They came together. Neither of them cried. Neither of them looked for comfort in my eyes. Their eyes were full of something they had brought into the auditorium themselves and which they took with them when they left. And I thought they were upset! How blind a person can be. They were full of hate and nothing else.

The young woman wordlessly slipped a piece of paper into my hand, and I placed it on the stool under my rear end to wait. More people were coming, and I tried to brighten my face for each of them, to be unique for each of them for one moment.

Once the marathoner is gone, I pick up the scrap of paper and unfold it. BITCH YOU'RE AN INSTRUMENT OF SATAN YOU OUGHT TO DIE!!! The message is written in block capitals with a black marker, and after it are three exclamation points: a vertical line and a dot, a vertical line and a dot, a vertical line and a dot. Any less would not have been sufficient. Sensible, vigorous Katie McKeen comes from behind the curtain now. She just waves when I show her the paper. "It's a wonder there weren't more of those crazies this time," she says. She just wants to get me to the ambulance. "You aren't going to die in my arms," she adds. I love her black humor.

Katie drapes a caftan over me and hands me my favorite slippers, these silly fuzzy ones. From one side of the stage we can walk downstairs to the basement, to a cluttered dressing-slash-storage room, and from there outside. I can walk under my own power, supported by Katie. I'm at my thinnest point and the uttermost limit of my strength, and that was exactly how it was supposed to be.

Katie forces me to sit in a wheelchair, which had been left in the corridor for this very moment. I can't be allowed to walk another foot so I won't needlessly lose any energy. We start moving. Katie pushes me, occasionally reaching ahead to open a door with an electronic key, which she has on loan from the museum caretaker. This is surprisingly laborious: there are a lot of doors, at least six, and we are deep in the bowels of the museum. The corridor is only a little wider than the wheelchair, so Katie has to stand on her tiptoes and suck in her belly to reach over the chair and open the door; she's a bit plump, and her belly is large. The doors have no mechanism to keep them open, so they start closing as soon as she lets go of them. So Katie uses her rear end to hold the door open and pulls me by the leg to get the chair through. When I cautiously suggest that I might walk myself, she snorts, wipes her brow, and says, "Sit down, Shlomith."

God I miss her . . .

Then something happens that neither of us expected. One of the doors refuses to open. Katie presses the keycard in its leather cover against the reader over and over again, and the green light flashes. She pushes the door and jerks the handle, but the door doesn't budge. Is this a technical glitch or sabotage? It's as if something heavy is in front of the door on the other side. Katie lets out a groan and curses. She tries to call the caretaker, but she doesn't have any bars in the basement. "Shlomith," she says with false vivacity to cover her exhaustion, "I'm afraid we're going to have to go back." "Yeah, Mama," I mutter and close my eyes. I feel Katie's soft stomach against my arm as she squeezes by to the other side of the wheelchair. Katie is a safe woman. I could sleep every night in her arms. She's so forgiving and round, while I'm hard, too hard even for myself. If I sleep on my side without a pillow between my knees, in the morning my legs are covered in bruises. But Katie can't be by my side every night. "You hurt me, dear Shlomith. Do you understand? I can't get any sleep because you're so sharp you injure me." Katie has spent so many nights helping me fall asleep before returning to her own home. She has stroked me gently under the thick duvets. Yes, I am the pea, and she is the princess. She is beautiful, vibrant, and real. I long for her constantly.

She can't turn the wheelchair around, but Katie still doesn't dare to flout the doctor's order and suggest walking. She decides to pull me backward to the small room we started from. "We'll go out through the main floor of the museum," she says. "The ambulance can meet us there. Besides, the museum will be closing soon, so we'll be able to move around without curious stares."

Katie has moved behind me. She is just grabbing the handles to pull me back when the stuck door in front of us suddenly opens. In the door, in the bright light, stands a bespectacled man; I recognize him from his athletic posture and wiry physique. He is tense, trembling, ready to dash away . . . but first he has a task to complete. He lifts his hand . . . Polina, will you please make up the rest.

Polina continues:

Well . . . The marathoner stands before you. He lifts his hand. Maybe he's holding a heavy object wrapped in gray fabric? And he starts to beat you. His blows land where he intends . . . the forehead . . . and the temples. You lose consciousness. They are forceful, blunt blows that leave no external marks on your head. Numberless internal tissues rupture, causing your brain to swell. Your breathing slows. You will never regain consciousness. You die . . .

The murderer flees the scene. He leaves your assistant screaming next to your body slumped in the wheelchair. He knows a secret way out . . . Maybe he's in league with the museum caretaker. Maybe the caretaker thought you were evil incarnate. Maybe the caretaker had *that look* too . . .

Whatever lies behind it, you die, Shlomith. You die from your brain injuries, not malnourishment. Are you satisfied now?

And what about my death? Are we going there too? I've given it a lot of thought. I always return to the same point—a warmth, an all-encompassing, tingling warmth. That's my end. I sense a bright, yellow light, even though I keep my eyes shut. And the tingling . . . It doesn't focus on any specific location, like the skin. It's everywhere. Things like "skin", "head", "limbs", "pointer fingers", "little toes", no longer exist. Existing that way has ceased. I'm not lying much if I say that at the moment of my death I was at one with the universe. Do you understand what I'm talking about? I didn't accept the light like Saint Teresa of Ávila. Do you know the statue? Bernini's Teresa: mouth open, slumped uncomfortably, a cherub nearby threatening her with an arrow? It wasn't like that. First of all, I wasn't in any particular position.

And can you imagine divine love? No matter how I turn it over in my head, I can't come up with a better expression for what I felt. *Божественная Любовь*. It has to be said in Russian because no other language has words that penetrate this feeling in the same way. Listen: *BooŽEStvennaya LyuBOF*. That was how I felt, exactly how I felt. A bright yellow light that requires no eyes to perceive: *BooŽEStvennaya*. A tingling warmth that requires no body to feel: *lyuBOF*. Taste it. Taste those words!

All my earthly fears ceased in the moment when that celestial warmth filled me. The warmth came first. Yes, the warmth came first. I closed my eyes as if someone had whispered quietly in my ear: "Now you don't have to fight any more, Polina. No one is threatening you." As if someone had kissed my eyes closed: "Polina, *they* can't hurt you any more. Submit. Submit!" Then came the light. And I relaxed. I stopped fearing and died. Why, I don't know, but that's what happened. I wish I could return to that moment, but it's gone now.

What about you, Nina? What do you remember?

Nina said:

They stopped moving. Every now and then, Little Antoine and Little Antoinette stopped moving. As if by mutual agreement: "Haha, let's be really still and scare *Maman* . . ." Then they moved again. "Yoo-hoo, here we are! We tricked you!" It was OK. I got to know them. Their movements and when they didn't move. There was a certain logic to it. They slept when I moved and woke up when I lay down. They had a sort of rhythm like that. They were—how do you say?—*les noctambules* . . . like owls . . . yes, "night owls". They were night owls. Just like their father. Jean-Philippe often put his ear to my belly and listened. When he felt them kick, he would yell, "*Ça commence alors!*" Then he twisted one hand in the air as if he were swinging a rope, *le lasso*, yes, the lasso: "*La-la-la-la discoooooooo!*" Those moments were the best. We laughed a lot. Jean put a toilet roll tube against my belly, put his ear to it, and listened, taking one hand away and said "Shhhhh," and there they were, two hearts and their quick beating. He heard them.

Those were happy moments.

One night Jean-Philippe wasn't home. Actually there were many nights like that, but this one was bad. I went to bed and waited for them to start to rock out. But they didn't. I waited and waited, but they were perfectly still. I couldn't sleep. I called Jean many times, but he didn't answer. I grew angry. I got out of bed and tried to wake them up. I ate milk chocolate—sugar always drove them wild. I sang to them. I rubbed my stomach. I drank lemonade. I lay down again and pretended to sleep. That usually helps. When I want to feel that they're alive, I lie down and take deep breaths. Using your diaphragm, like they teach in yoga. That almost always wakes them up and starts their boxing and kicking practice.

I've always been a little worried, even when there were kicks, if they only come from one direction. They're very close, in a sort of "69" position: Little Antoine head down, Little Antoinette head up. I wonder if they're both still alive or if one of them is kicking for the other one. Or has one of them kicked the other to death? Smashed the other's head in with a foot? The doctor said that's impossible. The water protects them. And besides, this is the easiest kind of twin pregnancy. Fraternal. They each have their own pouch with their very own placentas. Technically they're completely separate. They can't even get tangled in each other's cords. And because they have their own placentas, no bad connections can form between them, no *vasculaire* things, shared blood vessels that one can suck too much blood through and swell while the other one loses blood and shrinks.

Little Antoinette is a little smaller, but that's because she's a girl, not because Little Antoine is sucking the life out of her.

But then came that horrible night. Jean-Philippe was gone. They stopped moving. For real. Both of them. One night. I sent Jean a text message, at least five, asking him to come home, saying I was afraid. Usually I'm very rational. I call the family doctor and ask my questions if I have anything to ask. It doesn't embarrass me at all. Stéphanie answers patiently, explaining as many times as necessary until I understand. But that night I didn't bother waking her. I called the hospital directly. "Are you having contractions?" they asked. "Is there any bleeding? What week are you? How long have you been feeling the pain?" But I didn't have any pain. The babies were quiet. That was all. "Monitor the situation," they said. "And if you're still worried in the morning, call again."

I can't describe that night. Occasionally I fell asleep and felt something moving inside of me, but as soon as I woke up, everything was still again. I also had a dream, or it wasn't a dream but a vision, because the whole time I knew I was lying in bed waiting for the morning and kept looking at the clock. So I was lying in bed and suddenly our doctor, Stéphanie, walks through the door. She walks up to me with a box of matches in her hand. Supposedly I'd given birth to the children or they'd been taken out of me somehow. And now they were sleeping in the matchbox! Stéphanie didn't say a word, she just handed me the box. I took it and pushed in one side. I saw Little Antoine's face, his skin transparent and his eyes black spots, like pinheads. *Salamandre blanche.* Sort of a human fish that had come out too soon. Then I pushed in the other side, and out came Little Antoinette's head, her face red and shriveled; but around her head was wonderful hair, like grain. The hair covered both babies and kept them warm. Stéphanie had put in cotton wool for their bed.

So there I was pushing the ends of the box back and forth: Little Antoine, and then in the other direction, Little Antoinette. Little Antoine. Little Antoinette. Monsieur Transparent and Mademoiselle Red.

I was sure I had gone *tout à fait folle*, but then the phone rang. I woke up. The matchbox disappeared. Jean-Philippe explained that he'd missed the last train. That he was staying in a hotel and would come first thing in the morning, and that everything was sure to be fine, *ma chère*.

I could have strangled that man. He was with some woman. I know that.

Well, so how did I die?

I survived until morning because I remember preparing to leave for the hospital. Alone. I remember crying and putting on these clothes, and I remember how difficult bending to tie my shoes was. I felt as if I was smashing them once and for all in there. Water isn't any protection. My burnt toast stank. The whole house stank, and I couldn't eat a single bite. I felt like vomiting. Finally I got the laces tied, and then—a blank. Did I take a taxi? Did I get to the hospital? I don't remember the reception, the hallway, the waiting room. I don't remember a doctor or an ultrasound. Did someone say, "I don't hear anything. There's no heartbeats"? I have no memory. I managed to tie my shoes, and that's it. Then comes the blank. And what if I did go *tout à fait folle*? I wanted these children so much! If they had really ceased to exist, then I might have done anything. I might have gone to the harbor and thrown myself into the sea. I might have traveled to Cassis, where we were married five years ago, climbed the limestone cliffs, and jumped. How should I know?

They're quiet now too.

Here, you can feel: nothing.

They're as dead as rocks, and I'm here.

Bof, on laisse ça alors.

Let's move on.

Maimuna said (with Nina translating from French to English):

I walk, I walk, I walk (I walk), and it's hot. I'm in the desert (I'm in the desert), and there is a terrible uproar. Someone pushes me with the barrel of a rifle, says, "Faster, faster," and I trip on this dress. (I'm in the desert, I'm pushed with a gun, and I fall to the ground.) My lip starts bleeding. There are two Europeans with me, Marcel and Mikael. "Are you alright?" asks Mikael. He's walking behind me and tries to stoop to help, but they won't let him help. "Forward, forward," they yell and push Mikael in the back. Mikael trips over me. His hand touches my back. Mikael and Marcel are good people. They're interested in buildings. They aren't *make-troubles*, but now they're in very bad trouble. And I am too. (There are two European men with me, and we're in trouble—so there are three of you?) Originally there were five of us. Samballa was with us, the quiet driver who brought us from Bamako, and Marcel and Mikael had a guide with them, Bonaventure from Cotonou in Benin. (There were five of us, we three and a guide and driver.) Marcel, Mikael, and Bonaventure began their journey from Cotonou thirteen days ago. They've traveled through Benin, through Burkina Faso, and ended up in Mali. They left early in the morning on a bus from Ouagadougou to Bamako and rode for twelve hours. It was dark when they arrived, and they took a room in a cheap hotel run by the nuns at the Mission Catholique. I'm also sleeping there. (I spend the night in the same cheap hotel as the European men and their guide.) Marcel, Mikael, and Bonaventure are very tired and hungry, and so am I. I've traveled the whole day and half the day before, a total of thirty-five cursed hours from Dakar to Bamako on Gana Transport (I've traveled thiry-five hours from Dakar to Bamako). The bus bench shakes, and I can't sleep. And if I do nod off, I have to wake up soon because of the customs officials. I'm afraid at every checkpoint, and I'm afraid of every government bastard. They make us stand in place for two hours and collect extra fees. They want all the luggage removed from the bus and put on the ground, and so all the luggage is removed from the bus and put on the ground. (The customs officials are assholes. They slow down the bus.) They don't touch me. I have a gris-gris around my neck, which they respect. I know that nothing bad will happen to me, but I can't help being afraid, and sweat drenches my waist. I feel the weight there. I feel the fabric of my dress glued to my skin, and I'm afraid they will show through. (Maimuna, you're afraid that what will show through?) I have . . .

little packages there. Finally they allow us to leave, but soon the bus gets stuck in the sand. All of the passengers have to get off again. The men start to push, and when the bus finally moves, we can't get on because the ground is too soft. The bus would get stuck again if we got on and made it heavy. So we walked behind the bus. We walk slowly since there are children and old women, and even older men with us. When I finally reach Bamako, I'm definitely more exhausted and hungrier than any men from Europe! They're enjoying themselves on the Mission Catholique terrace. They laugh and drink Castel, and when I walk past them, suddenly one of them says, 'You're beautiful,' and asks, 'what's your name?' But he says it very nicely. I stop. Then this Marcel wants to take a picture of me. He asks me to stand next to the wooden cross nailed to the wall and look wherever I like. He gives me three thousand céfa and invites me to eat dinner with them at the De la Paix restaurant next door. He's delighted when he hears I've come from Dakar. He visited there some years ago for work. I almost fall asleep in my spaghetti. (I finally reach Bamako, and I'm very tired. Marcel and Mikael invite me to eat with them. I order spaghetti.) When they hear where I'm going, they're even more delighted, and when I tell them that my ride will be coming directly to the hotel in the morning, they ask if there might be room for them too. They promise to pay. They may just want to stop in a few places. But they promise to pay a little extra. I call Moussa immediately and ask. (Where were you arranging for all of you to go, Maimuna? And who is Moussa?) Monsieur Moussa is my father's cousin. He arranged my journey from Dakar to Timbuktu and back. At first he sounds angry when I tell him about Marcel and Mikael, but he relents and says he'll call me back in a few minutes. He calls an hour later when I'm already in bed sleeping. The packages rub my skin and make me sweat, but I'm not allowed to take them off. (What packages? Why are they against your skin?) Wait, I'm coming to that part! Monsieur Moussa promises that Samballa can also drive Marcel and Mikael to Timbuktu. He's just arranged it with Samballa, and Bonaventure can also fit since no one else besides them will be in the car. Marcel and Mikael are still awake when I go to tell them the news. They're sitting on the terrace drinking Castel again and offer some to me. I linger for a few minutes to chat with them. They're excited about the three old mosques built of mud and wood in Timbuktu. They talk about attempts to protect the mosques but how hard it is: the desert is always coming closer and threatens to swallow them up, the northeasterly Harmattan blows sand on them, and they're in danger of crumbling. (We're all traveling to Timbuktu—Maimuna, why were you going there?) I have packages I'm supposed to deliver to a certain man. (I have packages I'm supposed to deliver—what was in the packages, Maimuna?) I don't know. That isn't my business. Monsieur Moussa convinced me to go on this journey. At a party I told his wife, Ndeye, about my dream, and apparently Ndeye told her husband, because one day Moussa came to talk to me: "You're beautiful, Maimuna. You could have opportunities there." He promised me enough money for a plane ticket if I did one big favor for him. (Mr. Moussa, my father's cousin, asked me to do him a favor and promised me money for an airplane ticket in return.) "I can't get away from my work right now," he said, "but this is a very important matter, and I'll lose a great deal of money if this isn't settled soon." "And what about Moustafa or Issa," his grown sons, I asked, "or Mamadou," my brother. But Monsieur Moussa needed his sons at the construction site. And he didn't trust Mamadou, unlike me. "Maimuna, you've never disappointed us," he said. So I agreed. Monsieur Moussa gave me five buckskin belts with flat, oblong packages sewn into them, which I was supposed to put on under my dress. "You can't take your dress off until you meet Mister Mecanico and give the belts to him," Moussa said, "and if something happens, you keep your mouth shut. You don't talk to anyone. Understand?" "How do I wash?" I asked. "You'll come up with a way," he said. I couldn't tell anyone I was leaving. "Not even mother?" I asked. "Not even her," Moussa said. (You received packages from your father's cousin that you were supposed to deliver to a man, and you couldn't talk to anyone about it, but you still went! Maimuna, are you crazy?) No! Our family has many secrets! My

father has four wives, and the youngest one, Fatoumata, disappeared. She probably ran away. "Fatoumata was no good," they said,
but that wasn't quite true. So I can have secrets too, can't I? And
besides, my father doesn't support my dream. He wants me to get
married, but I don't want to. At least not to the man my father chose
for me. He's rich but he's ancient. His breath smells bad. And he
doesn't even know how to read. Monsieur Moussa promised me a
plane ticket to Paris if I helped him. Moussa is a good man. Why
would he cheat me? We have a shared secret: I don't talk about
Timbuktu, and he doesn't talk about Paris. I promised to pay the
price of the plane ticket back as soon as I could support myself, and
why wouldn't I be able to support myself? Everyone says that I'm
much more beautiful than Penda Ly. I'm thinner, I'm more graceful, and I'm taller than her. My face is *noble*, one family friend said.
But Penda Ly looks more like a dolphin than an international star.
She may be Miss Senegal, but Penda Ly lacks style. And the compe-
tition organizers don't have any money. I'd rather go straight to the
source: Europe. Monsieur Moussa said he can arrange a contact for
me there. He has connections. He knows the press secretary for
Dakar Fashion Week. Believe me, these things will happen! *Femme
Africaine* magazine just had a long article about this. Alek Wek,
who's from Sudan, got into music videos for Tina Turner and Janet
Jackson, and made it to the top. Liya Kebede from Ethiopia was
discovered outside a high school. She made it to Paris and the cover
of *Vogue*, and they put her story in the magazine. Waris Dirie fled
Somalia as a teenager and had a great career as a model. And as a
defender of women's rights. And then there's Iman. Glorious Somali
Iman. I admire her so much too! An American photographer found
her in Kenya, at the University of Nairobi, and after that she
achieved everything a black woman can get in the world. And she
has done so much good for Africa. Especially for African children.
She's fought against AIDS. She made a big noise about those
diamonds . . . she . . . (Wait, hold on, Maimuna! I'm trying to translate this: Mr. Moussa promised me a trip to Paris if I take the
package to Timbuktu. In Paris I intend to find work as a model and

earn money—is that what you mean, Maimuna?) Yes. (I wanted to leave Senegal because I didn't want to marry the man my father chose.) Say that he doesn't even know how to read! (He doesn't even know how to read.) And that his breath smells bad! (Maimuna, is this really relevant?) Yes! He's disgusting, gap-toothed, and impotent. I hate him! (He's disgusting and impotent—so what happened in Timbuktu, Maimuna?)

A CERTAIN JOURNEY BEGINS

Maimuna, Mikael, Marcel, and Bonaventure departed Bamako for Timbuktu the next day. As arranged, Samballa drove up to the Mission Catholique Hotel in his red Mitsubishi Galant sedan at eight in the morning. Bonaventure took the passenger seat, and Marcel, Mikael, and Maimuna squeezed in the back, with Maimuna in the middle, even though Marcel was significantly smaller than her and had shorter legs. It was clear to everyone that Maimuna had to be in the center. Maimuna was a woman, so Maimuna was in the middle. She was Jeanne Moreau and they were Jules and Jim. Which was which Marcel didn't know, and he didn't intend to find out. Simply put, Maimuna was a fetching girl, and it was only right that they both have a small piece of her, if only the touch of a thigh, an arm, or her thick Afro. After this brief, gentle contact, their journey would continue on a flight from Timbuktu to Casablanca by way of Bamako.

Maimuna sat between the men and smiled. She was more exhausted than happy, but the nice cameras made her smile. The men snapped extremely beautiful pictures, especially Mikael, who knew how to use light and could catch her just as a smile appeared and make her look her most beautiful. Mikael had wanted to take a drowsy photograph of her in the evening against the turquoise wall of the De la Paix restaurant. The shot was incredible. She had never seen her face so languorous, so abandoned to the camera. What if they took more pictures of her? What if Mikael did? She could put together her modeling portfolio . . .

Maimuna wanted to get rid of the belts strapped beneath her dress as soon as possible. They pinched and made her sweat, and they

made her waist appear lumpy, if you knew to look. Had Mikael and
Marcel noticed? The dress was loose at the waist—she had borrowed
it from Ndeye, who was a little plump. Maimuna would have drowned
in the dress if Ndeye hadn't sewn a line of smocking under the breasts.
As soon as she met Mister Mecanico at the Amanar restaurant and
passed off the belts, she would be free. They could arrange a photo
shoot and linger at the edge of the desert for a little longer, looking
for the perfect dune to use as a backdrop. She would put on her other
dress, which was turquoise and tight-fitting. Mikael was sure to
agree. Why wouldn't he?

Mikael and Marcel weren't in a hurry to get anywhere. They
insisted that they wanted to go through Sévaré to Mopti, where there
were more mosques, which they never seemed to tire of photograph-
ing, and a building devoted to earthen architecture. How they
managed to be so excited about that she didn't understand. Mikael
and Marcel had slept well at the hotel. Nothing weighed them down,
and nothing was wrapped around their stomachs that chafed and
made them sweat. They could sleep stark naked under the hypnotic
whopping of the ceiling fan, and now they eagerly pressed against
her in the bouncing car. Each wanted to show her the pictures he had
taken on their journey. Look, Maimuna!

And she looked. She listened to Marcel's soft, flowing French, and
Mikael's tentative, rougher French. She felt Mikael's arm, clammy
with sweat against her skin, and she felt Marcel's arm, which was dry
despite the heat.

"Maimuna," Mikael said, "do you know the Batammariba people
of Benin and Togo?" Mikael showed her a photograph of a boy with
long, thin scars lined up across his face and began to speak. Marcel
came to his aid any time Mikael got stuck on a word. Maimuna sat
obediently between the men. It was a very good camera. A professional camera. If she could just not ruin this . . .

Maimuna?

Maimuna, you must have heard of them, the Batammaribas, who
as their name suggests are the real architects of the earth. They deco-
rate their faces with scar tattoos in parallel lines like the walls of their

mud houses. (No, she hadn't heard of them.) Surely you must know about their unique houses. (She didn't know.) They're called *takienta*. The houses are three stories and built according to the architecture of the human mind. Every house has a bottom floor, the dark, animal subconscious, a middle floor for the ego, and round granary attics protected by hats made of straw for the superego. (She didn't know, and she didn't understand, but she nodded and smiled.) The houses not only have the psyche of a person but also all of a person's body parts: eyes, nose, mouth, vagina, penis, anus . . . The buildings are constructed by the head village architect, the *otammali*, he-who-knows-how-to-build-from-earth. Here he is: such a happy man! We met him in the village we visited, and he allowed us to spend the night on the roof of his house . . . And now we've moved on to a Kassena village in Burkina Faso! Look at these amazing black and white geometric patterns. (She looked.) These triangles painted on the walls of the building represent broken gourds, which are a symbol of wealth. Another symbol of wealth are these cowry shells, which were once used as money. Look, Maimuna, at how the beautiful python design slithers around the wall of the chief's house! (She looked and thought it was childish, clumsy, and pretentious.) The python is one of the Kassenas' most important totem animals. The doors of their houses are like the openings of an igloo: round and very short. When you go inside, you have to bend down very low, maybe even crawl. Just imagine the problems I had with my long legs . . . (Mikael's legs really were quite long and slender. Compared to Mikael, Marcel was as small as a Pygmy, as nimble as a gazelle, and as supple as rubber. They were perfect opposites, one lanky and blond, the other dark-haired and muscular. Which one would she choose if she had to pick? Tall Mikael or short Marcel?) Immediately inside, a visitor runs into a threshold about forty centimeters high. Can you imagine a better defense? Brilliant! If an enemy tries to crawl in, knocking him over the head in the darkness of the entryway would be easy. Light filters in from a hole above, making the dark room a holy place. Do you know what, Maimuna? Our whole trip we've been surrounded by everyday truths. We've come to understand something fundamental about the deep secrets of humanity! We talked about this for hours on the bus. The human subconscious is also sacred, and light can flow into it . . . Do you know, Maimuna, that a person's head can literally open up during meditation? (No, she didn't know. Swallowing a yawn, she acrobatically turned it into a smile and asked Mikael to give her a drink from a water bottle.) A year ago we were on the Bandiagara Escarpment in the Sahel region, an area inhabited by the Dogons. We found clay houses there too, each with a soul, with eyes, a nose, and a mouth . . . houses that are images of humanity . . . The whole courtyard was laid out according to the parts of the body: head, arms, knees, and womb, yes, a womb, which was the place where the women prepared the food . . . They served us this wonderful spicy chicken and millet porridge . . . (Of course she would take Mikael. They would have beautiful, tall, slender children who would be much lighter than her . . .) Marcel, I've been mulling over this crazy idea for a while. I've been thinking about building a summer cottage for my family following a similar principle, taking conditions in Finland into account, of course. We can tear down the old, run-down place to make room. Of course I'll build it out of wood not mud. Reclaimed timber from Terijoki. I've heard there's still wonderful wood to be found there. The timbers of the abandoned villas are prime quality . . . Our property is in the Inkoo archipelago. You should come visit. You should come to Finland. How about next summer? (Maimuna leaned her head against Mikael's shoulder, utterly exhausted. They would be in Mopti soon, and she would stay by the car with Samballa to wait. She could nap in the shadow of a baobab tree. She would have a nice long rest, and then she would be a new person in Timbuktu . . .)

Maimuna clutched the pouch in her lap. A beautiful dress was waiting for her there, turquoise as the morning sky. It revealed her shoulders. She would pull it on as soon as she escaped her cargo, as soon as Mister Mecanico took the belts, as soon as she was free. Liya Kebede, Alek Wek, Waris Dirie, Iman – and soon Maimuna Mimi Mbegue, age twenty.

She had truckloads full of courage.

ULRIKE PLAYS DEAD

Let's play Dying! Shlomith yells excitedly, almost impatiently, now that they finally have a new playmate. Her voice has gone shrill like a child just about to receive permission from her parents to dive into the amusement park ball pit, or into the sea, into the frothing waves under a watchful eye, into turquoise water, which is warm and clear. Soon her tiny body would tremble from head to toe with the pleasure of it. And this excitement begins spreading to the other women too. What will happen now? No one has a clue yet about Ulrike's story. Shlomith, Nina, Polina, Maimuna, Wlibgis, and Rosa Imaculada all realize together that they are finally faced with something new, that for a moment they will no longer need to ladle the same thrice-reheated meal into their mouths. Ratatouille, moqueca, ceebu jën, bacon mashed potatoes, chicken soup with dumplings, stroganoff. Finally they will be served a surprise menu made from all fresh ingredients, and this makes them realize they are hungry, so terribly hungry. How long has it been since the last time? An eternity? One second? Maimuna was arrival number six, so they must have gone on her journey last. Yes, they have been in the desert, in Timbuktu. They have closed their eyes and each imagined as best she could dying with Maimuna in a hail of bullets. But how long has it been since then?

Shlomith can't wait any longer. She claps her hands. (Her fleshless hands slapping together makes a very strange, loud and splintering sound, which disappears without an echo almost as soon as it begins: *whim-whim-whim*. It is like a whip that never hits anything. It just swings and then the sound disappears.) *Let's play Dying!* Lightly Shlomith touches the girl's shoulder. *Ulrike, what happened before you woke up here? What happened before our first meeting? What is your last memory? Try to remember!*

Ulrike takes a contemplative position, sitting, legs crossed. She has already spent a few moments considering this question herself; for instance, when her legs finally found the furious, hacking rhythm she was able to use to move in the emptiness. The rhythm, which demanded focus and calm, began to fill her mind with a cloudy substance unfit as raw material for words, emotional states that briefly illuminated images, possible flashes of memory: a mountain, a home, a ravine, a conductor's purse, a flower, mother, father, an elevator, Hanno, a mountain, Ulrich B. Zinnemann's glass eye, a home, a ravine.

But the images soon went dark. No story stuck to them or bore them up. From the edges of the images, terrible flapping black tatters have sprouted, leading—no, practically tugging toward an all-consuming black hole that causes pain to even think about. So much pain that she has to seek safety in words after all, no matter how trivial what she spits out of her mouth might be.

All the other women already know that the final memories preceding the white space are not so simple to grasp. You have to lure them out, and group pressure strangely seems to help. Staring at Wlibgis's wig also has an effect that improves concentration now that it isn't on poor Wlibgis's head, now that her head isn't detracting from the brilliance of the artificial fibers any more. Polina has just crouched to fluff the fire, to straighten the fibers with her fingers, so the wig forms a complete and unbroken, calming circle. When she has finished she straightens her back and looks at Ulrike encouragingly.

In the name of truth, it must be said that all of the gazes focused on Ulrike are not equally encouraging. Some of the women stare at the girl meditating in the lotus position with unvarnished greed in their eyes, each observing something different: one the trembling of the girl's lips, another her deepening frown, a third the motion of her eyelids. (Ulrike has her own gaze fixed on the wig.) Some of them clearly expect somewhere in the recesses of their minds, hidden even from themselves, that the young, beautiful girl from Salzburg will begin to cry. No tears will fall from her eyes any more, but perhaps she will still make the face? Any strong emotion, even fear or sorrow, would be a pleasure to watch . . . And if she cries, they might be able to manage a sympathetic thought. Now it is difficult, since she seems so proud, almost impertinent. She shouldn't have any reason to show contempt for them. She is young. But what does that matter? They were all young once. Doesn't she realize she is the one who has lost more than anyone else here? She had her whole life ahead of her . . . unlike Maimuna, for example, who only had disease and misfortune to look forward to.

But Ulrike doesn't notice their gazes. She is struggling to think. Her thoughts keep unraveling. The transition from her previous state to this wasn't something that can be described, like giving a report of a bicycle trip, which would include departing home (around 10:30) and arriving at a destination, for example downtown Salzburg, perhaps the apartment building located at Rainerstraße 13 (around 11:05). Such an account might also include some description of what one might have thought along the way; the landscapes, and the moment when the industrial ugliness of the suburbs gives way to the beauty of the old world, Alpenstraße to Hellbrunnerstraße, and the Salzach River appears. The moment when you can abandon the dust and noise of the motorway and turn toward the river, onto the bicycle and pedestrian path, when you can momentarily switch to the hardest gear. When you can accelerate on the gentle downhill as fast as you've ever gone!

Ulrike rings her bell in irritation, cursing aloud: some moron is in her way again. And this is her way. The left bank of the Salzach, where she can see the familiar fussy cream-cake landscape that stinks of the time when they still lived on Herbert-von-Karajan Platz, before her father's clothing company went bankrupt. Where, on a hot summer day, horse shit assaults your nose. The shit of the horses that pull the carriages of tourists around. Shit ground into the asphalt, which the horse shit cleaners brush onto shit platforms welded to the front frames of their bicycles. Such positions did indeed exist in Salzburg: the professional guild of horse-drawn-carriage-following bicycle horse-shit cleaners.

But there is more in cream-cake Salzburg, especially on the left bank of the Salzach. There are windows with glass cases filled with bottles of Champagne seasoned with nuggets of twenty-three karat gold. And then there's the Mozart Santa Claus. He's the real one. There are chocolate Mozartkugel balls in enormous violin-shaped packages. There are Mozart masks. Mozart magnetic buttons. Mozart wigs. Wolfgang Amadeus Mozart: the powdered-wig freak Ulrike feared more than anything else as a child. Buskers dressed as Mozart terrified her. And of course this became a family joke that always made Ulrike cry. Be good or Mozart will come and get you! Be good or Mozart will come and play the "Turkish Rondo" over and over! Ulrike simply can't help riding along the left bank of the Salzach. Her entire classical Viennese childhood is there, a bright frenzied time kept moving by the wheels of wealth. Coins spin, bills crinkle, the bank card swishes, howls, and whines. A new fur muff for the winter for Mother, a posh car for Dad. Ulrike gets almost anything she can think of to want, until the bankruptcy comes, until they move away from Herbert-von-Karajan Platz.

Ulrike always rides to the Makartsteg. The bridge is covered with love locks, including Ulrike and Hanno's: *Ulrike ♥ Hanno 16.8.2012.* Together, hand in hand, they flung the key into the mud at the bottom of the Salzach, and then only a few months later Ulrike learned that she was a traitorous whore.

The Makartsteg Bridge is full of people. Ulrike walks her bike to the other side of the river, climbs back on the saddle and heads for the riding path. The newly serviced gears shift so well! And the man with the beard who fixed it a couple of days ago was so nice. He even gave her a little bag of valve stem caps for free. Not boring black ones, raucous red and white like polka dots . . . It's hot . . . her shirt is wet . . . her back is covered in sweat . . . She has to get in the shower, but Hanno wants to fuck . . . goddamn it, in the shower . . . Hanno wants to come in the shower with her . . . Hanno wants to fuck of all places in the bathroom with the orchid-patterned tiles . . . now, when her parents are away . . . otherwise he wouldn't dare . . . He can't get it up if her mother is running water in the kitchen . . . if her father is rustling the *Salzburger Nachrichten* in the living room . . . He wants to fuck standing up in the shower, even though it's so uncomfortable . . . Ulrike braces against the wall, rising on her tiptoes so their genitals will be almost at the same level . . . just so Hanno can calm down and get it over with . . . Damn it . . . Ulrike is slipping . . . Can Hanno hold her up if she falls, if her feet slip out from under her? . . . Is she falling? Is she hitting her head on the tile floor? . . . Is she breaking her neck . . . in the middle of fucking?!

Ulrike unfolds her legs from the lotus position and switches to sitting on her knees. She shakes Hanno and the apartment at Rainerstraße 13 out of her head, banishing from her mind the bathroom with the orchid tiles, and the water. Not like that. She didn't die like that! She'd spent so little time with Hanno lately. They'd tried to arrange a meeting, but had anything come of it? Not likely. If she inspected the situation from a probability standpoint, she had probably come here from Kehlsteinhaus, from her summer job in the Eagle's Nest, not from Salzburg, where nowadays she mostly only went to sleep away what was left of each night. Every morning she climbed onto articulated bus number 840 on Alpenstraße and, after finding a seat, closed her eyes for the next half hour. Almost always.

Ulrike closes her eyes.

She shifts her weight onto the floor and collapses on her side. Polina tries to help. She pushes her fingers into Ulrike's hair and touches her scalp: if only her thoughts would start moving.

If only she could remember her last moments!

°
°

Ulrike begins to relax. She feels drowsy, woken up too early, yet again. With her eyes closed she turns on her iPod, and the first song on the album, her favorite song, starts to play: Scott Walker's 'Farmer in the City'. Today is the Assumption of Mary, Thursday the fifteenth of August, 2013, the day when Ulrike dies, which of course Ulrike doesn't know yet. *Mariä Aufnahme in den Himmel.* People cram

into their cars and buses and trains, each wanting a moment away
from the noise of the city. They reserve a hotel room or a whole
house in the countryside. For example, in Berchtesgaden. They
want to roam the mountains, swim in the lakes, and enjoy the
susurrations of history. That means more work for Ulrike, as she is
forced to jog around the dining room at the Kehlsteinhaus restaurant from ten in the morning until six in the evening. But so what?
It just means more money.

Ulrike slips into a torpor at about Sankt Leonhard. The articulated bus trundles along with hisses and squeals, a mechanical
female voice announcing the stops, but Ulrike doesn't hear. She
hears other words, a story she doesn't understand but loves nonetheless, which she wants to hear over and over again. She is
enchanted in turn by each individual word Scott Walker's fateful
voice gives form to. Every word is overwhelming, full in itself; each
syllable passing Scott's vocal chords is worthy of singing, overflowing with emotion that grabs you and pushes you into a sweet
darkness you have no desire to leave. Ulrich B. Zinnemann intro-
duced her to this album. The song is based on Pier Paolo Pasolini's
poem "*Uno dei Tanti Epiloghi*"—"One of Many Epilogues"; U.B.Z.
told her this during a smoke break in July when they were finally
starting to get to know each other. The music led them from one
sentence to another, from question to answer, from cigarette to
cigarette. Ulrike learned new things, information that fitted into a
framework that was light years away from Hanno's infantile
thoughts. Such as this: Pasolini dedicated his poem to the amateur
actor Ninetto Davoli, his protégé, with whom the director began a
love affair when Ninetto was fifteen years old. Pier Paolo wrote the
poem around the time Ninetto entered the army at age twenty-one,
after which he was quickly returned to civilian life for being too
nonconformist.

Glass-eye U.B.Z. stubbed out his cigarette and looked Ulrike
sternly in the eyes. "Pasolini was one of the great film directors, but
only one. In contrast, there has never been a more ingenious musi-
cian than Scott Walker. Period."

Ulrike nods, half asleep, in the sweet darkness behind her Eye Mask DeLuxe. She amuses herself, imagining a roguish Ninetto and a handsome Pier Paolo making love. Slow, moose-like movements. Open mouths, gruff bellowing. How does a middle-aged man make love to an underage boy? Does he make love to the boy, or does the boy make love to him? Or does it really happen together, at one time, the man with the boy and the boy with the man? However it works, Ulrike enjoys their love. This time she decides to let Paulo lead. She is Ninetto, young fifteen-year-old wicked Ninetto, who submits, who allows the older man to mount his back once again . . .

Glass-eye U.B.Z. knows a lot of things. He tells stories, but he still doesn't reveal anything. Ulrike's new friend at the Eagle's Nest, Anke-Marie, is sure that U.B.Z makes up all of it. "It can't be true," Anke-Marie says. "Like the story about the eye. Come on!" Anke-Marie is skeptical. She frowns as if in disapproval of U.B.Z.'s stories, but she still enjoys them. Maybe Anke-Marie is a little infatuated with Ulrich? She smiles (her gums show) when Ulrich walks up to the kiosk in the courtyard of the Kehlsteinhaus during the shift change and buys a package of throat lozenges and cigarettes from her. The kiosk belongs to Anke-Marie's mother, but because her mother has to care for her own ailing mother in a gingerbread house in the valley of Berchtesgaden, Anke-Marie is spending this summer sitting on a tall barstool behind the kiosk window. Ulrike thinks Anke-Marie is the best thing at the Eagle's Nest, besides the salary. And besides Ulrich. When Anke-Marie explodes with laughter, the vultures in the mountain tops hear it too.

Ulrich B. Zinnemann is a unique case. None of the characters from any normal gallery of stereotypes fits his description. A forty-year-old man who lost his left eye in a duel! Ulrike and Anke-Marie have spent many a day considering the mystery of the unmoving, lifeless glass eye. Until one fine day, Anke-Marie goes and simply asks, "One of your eyes doesn't move, Ulrich. What happened to it?" The three of them were hanging around the kiosk. The Eagle's Nest was already closed, and Anke-Marie was locking up. "Is your left eye made of glass?"

Ulrike wanted to kick Anke-Marie in the shins, but U.B.Z. didn't seem to mind. He leaned on the counter, loudly sucking on a mint, and began to tell the story of his left eye: "There was a woman, a very beautiful woman, who had another man. I got in the way of a budding romance. The woman fell in love with me, and the other man couldn't get over it. He happened to have certain obsessions with the past, so he suggested a duel in accordance with the old ways. For some crazy reason, I accepted. I was young, stupid in love, reckless, and competitive. We arranged the time and the place, and invited seconds to witness. Then we dispatched the battle with rapiers. Neither of us died. He ended up gushing blood. I lost my eye, and all for nothing: the woman wasn't worth it."

Anke-Marie is right. It can't be true.

Ulrich B. Zinnemann works as a lift-boy at the Eagle's Nest. Temporary. Really he's a film director, but his projects are too uncompromising, too artistic, so finding sources of funding is difficult. Which is why he directs tourists into a shiny, golden time capsule that rockets them 124 meters up to the top, through a chasm quarried into the mountain. U.B.Z. counts the proper number of people, cuts off the queue at the right spot, and presses the button. Up above, he directs the people out of the lift and then takes on an appropriate number of people going down. Then he presses another button.

Sometimes someone asks something. U.B.Z. replies with a routine, cursory answer. Lift-boys are not allowed to speak out of turn. Tour guides distribute the necessary information, but they have also been instructed not to mention the Forbidden Name (unless it's absolutely unavoidable). They prefer to discuss the great arc of history, the Allies and the German Army, the movements of troops, and military strategies. The fact that the Kehlsteinhaus is actually a hideout, built as a fiftieth birthday present by the National Socialists for Him of the Forbidden Name—that doesn't actually mean anything. "You can easily hide that in an aside so it won't give anyone the chills," Ulrich B. Zinnemann whispers to Ulrike in the Eagle's Nest kitchen as they wolf down a quick standing lunch. "The

Kehlsteinhaus lacks any hint of the macabre, any of the eerie karma that tyrants leave on things they touch and in places they visit. And do you know why?" Ulrike nods but can't say anything because her mouth is full of spaghetti and she doesn't want to get any sauce on her blouse or spit mushroom bits in U.B.Z.'s face, which is very close to her own. "Because," Ulrich whispers, "the recipient of the gift wasn't able to appreciate the gift he received due to his fear of heights!"

Ulrike knows. During her downtime she's read all the Kehlsteinhaus tourist information plaques and listened to all the stories the guides tell. He of the Forbidden Name only visited the mountain about ten times and spent a maximum of half an hour there on each occasion. The visits were pure theatrics. He of the Forbidden Name didn't enjoy a second of it. And because he didn't enjoy it, the Allies didn't have to bomb the building to smithereens.

That was not the case, however, for the Berghof in Obersalzberg, He of the Forbidden Name's beloved vacation home, which had an entrance hall decorated with cactus plants in majolica pots. The ceiling of the dining room was paneled with expensive cembra pine, and the walls were covered with watercolors painted by He Himself. The British air force bombed the building to the ground and retreating SS troops lit the ruins ablaze. Nothing that He of the Forbidden—and becoming more Forbidden by the moment—Name had *really* and *truly* liked could be allowed to remain intact on the face of the earth. The imperceptible but inevitable transformation of it into a memorial had to be nipped in the bud.

Paulo and Ninetto have long since slipped into a deep post-coital sleep, and Ulrike dozes along with them. Not until the bus arrives at the Berchtesgaden Station does Ulrike-Ninetto start awake, with the taste of moss in her mouth and her tongue feeling hairy. Today, on the fifteenth of August, Ulrike is getting to the Eagle's Nest in Ulrich B. Zinnemann's Volkswagen. This is the first time she's climbing into Zinnemann's Volkswagen without Anke-Marie. No giggling. That much is obvious. Giggling doesn't work without Anke-Marie. Lots of things don't work without her, but one thing

might work now that the kiosk is closed. Anke-Marie has to be away
to help her mother, her mother who insists on taking her own dear
mother to Mass and then out to eat. Anke-Marie didn't think that
was a good idea. "Grandma Verona doesn't need to go to Mass any
more," Anke-Marie huffed as she shuttered the kiosk. "Yes, she
might very well need it," Anke-Marie said, mimicking her mother's
loud, shrill voice. "Grandma still understands the language of
music!" Then Anke-Marie put her hands on her hips like her mother
does, apparently, when she wants to tempt fate more than necessary: "We're going to put her in her dirndl, we're going to buy her
flowers at the door of the church, and we're going to wheel her to
the front row just like last year." At this point Anke-Marie lowered
her voice back to her own tone: "Really Grandma Verona will just
get tired and start to whimper." In the end Anke-Marie cleared her
throat and shouted louder than was necessary, and off key in the
way someone who doubts her own decision but is stifling those
doubts is wont to do: "Grandma is going to church and that's the
end of it! We're taking her to Assumption Mass every damn year as
long as she's alive!"

Ulrich is waiting for Ulrike outside the bus station. He waves and
opens the door for her. "Could you put on *The Drift*?" Ulrike asks as
soon as she sits down, and without a word, Ulrich puts Scott Walker's
thirteenth studio album in the CD player. The passenger seat is
Anke-Marie's seat, but Anke-Marie isn't here. "Is your left eye
glass?" God damn it! She would never dare ask that! But Anke-
Marie does, and in reward they get to hear all kinds of crazy stories.
Do you have any children? A wife? Oh, you live with your mother?
Isn't that a little . . . psycho? U.B.Z. always plays along. Anke-Marie
says something inappropriate and turns to look at Ulrike sitting in
the back seat. She laughs and her gums glitter. It's hard to resist.
Gradually Ulrike learns to relax, to laugh along with them. U.B.Z.
doesn't bite. U.B.Z. looks at her in the mirror and winks, with the
eye that moves, the right one. Ulrike smiles back, and U.B.Z. turns
serious. He glances at the road and then looks at her again. For just
a moment too long.

And now they're in the car together.

Ulrike's exhaustion is gone. That's an accomplishment. When she started at the Eagle's Nest in May, when she didn't know Anke-Marie yet, let alone Ulrich, she always slept whenever possible. She slept on the way to work, she slept coming home from work, and without enormous doses of caffeine, she would have slept at the Kehlsteinhaus too. She would have nodded off in her seat or passed out standing up like a horse. Yes, in an emergency she could have locked her knees like a horse and dozed on her feet, or even on one foot like a flamingo. That was how profound her exhaustion had been. But of course sleeping at work was not befitting. That would have meant getting the boot, and Ulrike couldn't afford that. She needed money. She needed to save for the coming year. For leaving Salzburg. Goodbye, horse-shit cream-cake city! Goodbye, Hanno! Goodbye, Mom and Dad! Living at home was simply too intolerable. The atmosphere was slimy. Whose fault that was, Ulrike didn't care to figure out any more, but two opposing truths existed. Her father thought they were victims of speculators. Her mother thought they were victims of her husband's obstinacy, since he had refused to sell his money-losing company in time and just let the Great Catastrophe happen. He had practically rolled out the red carpet for the Catastrophe despite all the warnings. But if that was the case, if her father really had made too many unforgivable mistakes, as her mother claimed, why on earth were they still married?

Goodness, how Ulrike could drink coffee! Sometimes black, sometimes with milk, sometimes as espresso from the espresso machine, sometimes instant from coffee granules—whatever happened to be within reach. And sometimes, for variety and refreshment, she drank lemonade. This was how Ulrike was able to offer her best service the whole long day through at the Kehlsteinhaus.

Tourists arrived at the parking lot in lines of buses that wound along the serpentine road, disembarked, and then moved in a queue to the tunnel carved in the mountain. Clumps of them then entered the polished brass lift, the buttons of which were pressed by the lift operators, among them Glass-eye Ulrich. The lift carried them and

their cameras and sun hats or ponchos and umbrellas or walking
sticks or binoculars or tightly packed backpacks and water bottles
and sunglasses on their foreheads, straight to the lobby of the Eagle's
Nest. Ulrike waited for them in the restaurant. She wore a picturesque if not rustic blouse with gathered sleeves, in a customer-friendly
and easily approachable white-and-violet checked fabric. Her right
hand was prepared to set a laminated menu on the red-and-white
checked tablecloth before the customer next to the artificial white
roses decorated with glass beads. *Ach so gemütlich!* On the belt of
her black work trousers, Ulrike carried a train conductor's wallet for
easy access to coins and bills, as well as a small notebook where she
could quickly check the orders. This summer she was Fräulein
Kehlsteinhaus, a diligent, eager, perhaps slightly hysterical, but all
the more lovely waitress.

Sometimes she got moving so fast the money belt swung all the
way around her hips to her behind. Ulrike strode from the dining
room to the kitchen delivering orders to the cook, and back from
the kitchen to the dining room carrying dishes to the hungry
customers. Weighed down by coins, the bouncing money pouch
lent her movements even more speed. This quick scatterbrain
wasn't the gloomy Ulrike of Salzburg; this was the light-footed,
sashaying Ulrike of Kehlsteinhaus. If she slouched around Salzburg
in combat boots and with her hair in her eyes, just for the sake of
contrast, here she had intentionally learned perfect grace as she
carried head cheese seasoned with oil and vinegar, Hungarian
goulash, Leberkäse buns, pork schnitzel and chips, hüttenwurst
and sauerkraut, spätzle, venison and red cabbage, salad, beer,
coffee, and apple strudel—with charm and swaying hips. Her
blokeish walk, where she moved her entire upper body as one
massive plate like a security guard, which appealed to Ulrike so
much because it matched so poorly with the natural movement of
her slender, somewhat girlish frame, did not belong in the Eagle's
Nest. In the Eagle's Nest she had to hurry with the cotton-wool
lightness of *Lepus timidus*, which leaves the beaded paw prints of a
fox as it flees.

The results of her walking practice at the Kehlsteinhaus were excellent. Now and then Ulrike ended up posing in front of the enormous, restored picture window with overly tanned American men drunk on beer who looked like Hugh Hefner. Their friends took pictures and then traded places. Ulrike might smile under the arm of as many as four Hefners at a time. She always got an excellent tip. The men were extremely generous. She also got a round, white bobtail between her buttocks and long rabbit ears on her head, which made returning to the packed dining room difficult. The ears always seemed to get in the way and made it hard to see as Ulrike weaved between the tables with a tray full of empty plates and tall beer glasses. The bunny tail swung under her legs and dangled like a poorly-seated tampon, and her mood didn't return to normal until her smoke break or even the ride home, when Ulrike, already half asleep, inserted her earbuds.

Ulrich B. Zinnemann turns up the CD. He rolls down the window of the car, shifts into fourth, and makes the tires of his Volkswagen squeal. Old, wise Scott is singing about Claretta Petacci, who demanded to die alongside her beloved Benito Mussolini. Ulrike learns, U.B.Z. makes sure, that women who fall in love with dictators are always like that. Poor Eva Braun married her Führer only a day before their double suicide. Death and love, violence and passion, sacrifice and victory—"Listen, listen carefully!" U.B.Z. says. And Ulrike listens.

Benito and Claretta were shot on April 28, 1945. The following day their bodies were carried to the Piazzale Loreto in Milan and hung upside down from the roof of an Esso petrol station. Their bodies were desecrated with much rage and rejoicing. Their bodies were mocked and abused. Their bodies were shot to pieces, BAM BAM. The tires of the Volkswagen wail a strange love song. Ulrike and Ulrich sing along with Scott Walker, their individual voices still coming through the melody. How thoroughly the nervousness has disappeared from Ulrike. She doesn't need Anke-Marie for this. She'll do fine. She'll do fine, BAM BAM, she'll do fine. Hefners, tails, and ears—BAM! Coffee cups beer glasses plates waiting above

—BAM! Notebooks coins banknotes lilac white gathered checked sleeved waitress blouses, BAA-AM! If the Volkswagen drove off the road right now . . .

Auf der Alm da gibt's ka Sünd . . .

They both know the mountain knows no sin, which is why Ulrich B. Zinnemann has the courage to make a proposition to Ulrike.

$\vdots$

Mountain, home, ravine, conductor's purse, flower, mother, father, elevator, Hanno, mountain, Ulrich B. Zinnemann's glass eye, purse, home, ravine, endlessly, endlessly, endlessly.

Ulrike opens her eyes and sees the women's expectant expressions. She rises up on her elbows and glances at the clothing she has on, gently worn corduroys and a Scott Walker T-shirt, still stiff from being new, with a young mop-headed Scott looking confidently and also very dramatically somewhere up and to one side, toward the sky, toward Ulrike. The digital display of her wristwatch stopped at 21:03. So that was how it must have been. She had died on August 15, around nine o'clock. Had she made it back home to Alpenstraße from the Kehlsteinhaus? Alone, of course alone, and on the bus. Not in the Volkswagen? No, not in the Volkswagen. No matter how hard Ulrike strains, she cannot recall Ulrich B. Zinnemann's face or touch or kiss. Had she turned tail like a coward? Or—a terrible presentiment suddenly forms a tight lump in Ulrike's throat, which she can still feel—had U.B.Z. changed his mind while they were at work?

Horrible shame rushes to Ulrike's ears. Just so. Yes, yes. Ulrich B. Zinnemann had succumbed to regret. The more openly Ulrike glanced at the elevator, the more he had berated himself: what had he gone and done? She was still a little girl. Every 124-meter ascent, every 124-meter descent had confirmed the understanding that chafed and grew within U.B.Z.: No, not like this. She's still a child.

Now Ulrike remembers the trembling of her legs, the sweat that formed in her armpits and on her back, even creating a tiny bead in the droplet-shaped cleft beneath her nose, the *philtrum*. Ulrich B.

Zinnemann had disgraced her. At the end of his shift he came, grinning, and took up a position along her route: the corridor between the kitchen and the dining room. She had walked with a stack of dirty dishes in her hand the way one walks toward the rising sun: eyes squinting, a bewildered expression on her face. She had walked right up to U.B.Z. and smiled knowingly at him, the way people do who share a secret smile at each other. She looked him straight in the right eye, ready to accept anything. But not this. "Can we go for a drink some other day, Ulrike? Sometime when Anke-Marie can come too?"

These words hit her in the temple like a nail gun. BAM!

Ulrike had been able to read between the lines in a thousandth of a second: *Ulrike, I'm really sorry, but I didn't realize before that you have these kinds of feelings for me. You're just a child still. I like you, and I also like Anke-Marie. Let's keep this as a bit of fun, this friendship of ours. Let's not mess it up with anything that doesn't fit with that.*

This was precisely what Ulrich B. Zinnemann said to her after her shift, amending his proposition from the morning, suggesting that they enjoy their drink together after work some other day, with Anke-Marie along, all three of them.

Ulrike had composed herself in a hundredth of a second. She had sung out a happy "OK!" and continued on her way as if she needed to rush. Then Ulrich had suddenly yelled to her, "Wait!" Ulrich had asked her to wait, and, heart pounding, she decided to turn to listen. "I can drive you to the bus station if you want. I can wait until your shift is done. I'm not in any rush."

Sometimes, when forced, you can arrange shreds of joy on your face even if your heart is rotting inside. Ulrike managed to reply lightly, even with a smile, "Thanks, Ulrich, but I don't need a ride. I think I'll walk today. Yes, I'll walk." Then she turned back to the kitchen and disappeared from Ulrich B. Zinnemann's gaze.

For the rest of the day, Ulrike remembers, she did her job without glancing around, as if any break in concentration could at any moment lay bare the feeling that pounded in her skull, protruding nastily in every direction.

Ulrike remembers, unfortunately. She shakes her head, but it doesn't help. It forces itself into her mind: lips rubbed raw by teeth. She had started descending from the Eagle's Nest by foot. She hadn't lied to Ulrich. She really intended to walk. From the parking lot she slid down to the gently inclined, paved walking path, and then she remembered: her lips.

In a panic she took a few running steps and did three squat jumps, so deep that the fabric of her corduroys painfully rubbed her labia. The FACT didn't give a hoot about that. It was practically overjoyed and began to do its worst. It tried to spread a burning heat through every nook and cranny of Ulrike's body, because it was a vengeful, exceptionally nasty FACT that had once failed to receive its dues.

It was a simple reality that on August 15, on the day of the Assumption of Mary into Heaven, the doors of the lift had opened at just the moment, around 13:20, when Ulrike had been walking from the kitchen toward the dining room. Ulrich B. Zinnemann stood behind the opening doors, mysterious and large, and their gazes met. After this Ulrike had spent the rest of the day biting her lips for good measure. In the back of the kitchen she had chafed her lips with dry paper towels and then broken the thin protective membrane with her teeth so they would swell, and then moistened them with her tongue. So they would be juicy and red on her pale doll's face.

o
o

The memory of that shame feels so terrible that Ulrike rolls on her back. She feels the need to roll down and down—if only there were a place you could say "down is that way"—that was where Ulrike wanted to roll now, away from the expectant gaze of other women, away from the tormenting thought: "U.B.Z. had begun to regret his suggestion" and the even more abhorrent corollary: "she had rubbed her lips raw".

Ulrike wants to destroy the whole Eagle's Nest. She wants to think of home, or at least her home street, Alpenstraße. This stifling feeling

that makes her ears burn needs a deep line scratched through it on
the page: ~~Ulrich B. Zinnemann.~~

Ulrike does it many times in her mind. She does it to everything
that rises steaming to the surface from it:

~~Ulrich B. Zinnemann.~~

~~Glass-eye-U.B.Z.!~~

~~Volkswagen.~~

███████

~~Auf der Alm da gibt's ka Sünd~~

~~Let's keep this as a bit of fun~~

~~This friendship of ours~~

~~Benito ♥ Claretta~~

~~BAM!~~

~~Pier Paolo ♥ Ninetto~~

████████████

~~BAM! BAM! BAM!~~

~~Aladobi! Goulash! Leberkäse!~~

~~BAM!~~

~~The elevator! Volkswagen?? The elevator!!!~~

██████████

~~BAM!~~

~~Apple strudel! Spätzle! Hüttenwurst!~~

~~. . . I like you . . .~~

~~. . . I like you . . .~~

~~. . . Anke-Marie . . .~~

~~BAM!~~

~~BAM! BAM!~~

~~BAM! ♥ BAM! ♥ BAM!~~

█████████████

Ulrike feels fingers on her temples. She opens her eyes and sees
Maimuna sitting behind her head. Maimuna smiles at her sweetly,
encouragingly, as if to say: You've arrived home, my dear. As if to ask:

What happened to you there?

And so finally Ulrike is safely on her home street. In gratitude she takes hold of Maimuna's gaze and continues her journey. Had she walked in front of a car after she exited the bus because she was so tired? Or had she gone to see Hanno for some incomprehensible reason after her long workday? To suggest a split?

Yes, that's it: she had taken her bicycle and careened down the Hellbrunner Allee toward death. "The sensation is less of flying through the air, more of being picked up and hurled, and when she comes to rest on the roadside verge with her face against the wet pavement, her first instinct is to look for her bicycle, which has somehow disappeared from beneath her." Is that how it happened? That's the way the heroine of a certain blithe novel dies, right in the middle of the book. At the beginning of the summer, Ulrike had read it on the articulated bus. At the moment of the accident that takes her life, the heroine first "thinks very distinctly of two things" and then, in the final sentence of the chapter, "dies, and everything that she thought or felt vanishes and is gone forever". And it wasn't even true! There they were in the book, her important thoughts and unique emotions, running to hundreds of pages.

Ulrike had spent the entire journey wondering about the author's trick. So it's that kind of death, is it? A real masterclass about death! Everything is left undone, just as it always is in life. And as a bonus, the dramatic, slow motion at the moment of death: the final thoughts of the dying. Let the reader gasp for oxygen in astonishment: Emma can't die, dash it all, Emma can't go and die! But Emma does die, and the book becomes a bestseller.

Is this how it goes?

No chance. Not like that.

No bicycle, no flight through the air, no crash in the bushes at the side of the road, and especially none of this at the edge of the sidewalk. No bruises of any kind are visible on Ulrike. Instinctively Ulrike raises her hand and touches her head to be sure. The women nod, smiling. It's fine, beautiful. Nina even flashes a thumbs-up and sighs: *Ulrike, you are just lovely!*

So could she have been inside during her last moments after all? Yes, she had ridden to Rainerstraße 13 and suggested to Hanno that they should call it quits. It was a doomed relationship, a teen romance that should have ended after a few red-wine-fueled fucking sessions. And then . . . Crazy, sick with jealousy, Hanno shoves her down on her parents' water bed . . . Because sometimes Hanno did shove. Sometimes Hanno became agitated and shoved her when they were walking on the street late at night having a fight. She staggered toward the wall of a building and hurt her hands. She screamed, I'LL REPORT YOU TO THE POLICE, and Hanno yelled, GO AHEAD. WHAT DO I CARE!

So Hanno shoves her down on her back on the water bed and starts to press an enormous pillow against her face . . . so that she can't breathe any more . . .

And just as Ulrike reaches those words, reaches Hanno, jealousy, and the pillow . . . just as she is saying *and so I couldn't breathe* and her listeners seem to hold their breaths in anticipation, just then she realizes: she *isn't* breathing. *No one* is breathing. Breathing is impossible. Breathing doesn't work, even when she stops talking and expands her chest and flares her nostrils, as she sometimes did on the overhangs of the Unterberg when the air was fresh with morning dew and dizzyingly full of oxygen, and in the distance mountains shone with dazzling white, and the clear waters of the Königssee— the cleanest water in Germany—sparkled at the foot of the hills. She still wanted to go there. She would suggest a picnic to Anke-Marie and Ulrich B. Zinnemann, and they would eat leftover hüttenwurst, leberkäse sandwiches, head cheese, and spätzle on a red-and-white checked tablecloth . . .

Ulrike isn't breathing.

Ulrike hadn't noticed she'd stopped breathing.

Ulrike can speak.

Ulrike can move.

Ulrike can think.

Five incompatible facts that require an immediate cessation of dying and a quick inquiry. This isn't a game any more. Everything else can wait now. Please be so kind as to explain. For God's sake do something!

As she attempts to breathe, Ulrike's body convulses hideously. Her eyes widen and widen. Nothing goes in, and nothing hurts. It isn't suffocating, it isn't drowning, and it definitely isn't dying. It is pure terror that eventually distills into a whisper like a sob, completely impossible in a physical sense, but still that's how it is, a real expression made by speech organs and audible to ears: *I can't breathe!*

A BRIEF LESSON ON
BREATHING

Breathing, also known as respiration, occurs as if by itself thanks to the respiratory center. Those unfortunates who suffer from Ondine's Curse, more properly a mutation of the PHOX2B gene, represent an exception. They must breathe consciously or otherwise they die. But there are very few of them in the world.

As we breathe, oxygen (O, oxygenium) moves with the air into the alveoli and from there through various molecular intermediaries to the cells. Carbon dioxide (CO_2) moves from the cells back into the air. Think of a funny little red car that drives around the body transporting back and forth Mr. Oxygen and Mrs. Carbon Dioxide, who, according to the script, can't decide where they want to be, inside or outside, because if they did that, decided and stopped inside or outside, then someone else would arrive—Death. Mr. Oxygen and Mrs. Carbon Dioxide also shouldn't travel in the wrong direction. People who breathe carbon dioxide are in grave danger. There have even been reports of near-death experiences caused by carbon dioxide.

So the act of breathing requires i) a breather who is well equipped in the physiological sense and ii) oxygen, which is the most significant component of air after nitrogen. Other more minor constituents of air include krypton and argon, but none of these are visible to the naked eye. Fundamental to the breathing process is that a properly equipped breather need not wonder whether he or she will bother breathing again and again and again.

As can be deduced from the preceding, suicide by holding one's breath is practically impossible. Diogenes of Sinope, the founder of the Cynical school of philosophy, succeeded, as did Girolamo, who was hopelessly in love with Silvestra in the eighth story of the fourth day of the *Decameron*. Others have needed the assistance of a plastic bag.

The diaphragm is located below the lungs. Shove your finger in there, and you might cause a cramp. Below the diaphragm are the liver and the stomach. During inhalation, the diaphragm contracts, descending and thus expanding the chest cavity in the direction of the belly. This creates negative pressure, and air begins to flow. As they contract, the external intercostal muscles spread the thoracic cavity forward and to the sides. Exhalation, on the other hand, happens more or less by itself as the aforementioned muscles cease contracting.

It should be noted that if we were in a near-perfect vacuum, such as in space, we could not breathe. In space we also cannot speak without auxiliary instruments. Sound cannot travel through a vacuum because there is nothing to transmit it. Although to prove this one would need an ear and a mouth in space, because otherwise the question is completely theoretical.

Let us return to respiration, or more precisely to the vital function called "lung ventilation". Don't bother thinking of an open door on a French balcony unless you can also think of a volume measurement gauge near the door. During a twenty-four hour period, a well-equipped breather breathes approximately ten thousand liters of air. The volume of a single breath is about one half liter. An experienced yogi can circulate as many as five liters through his body at once. So the air can be measured in liters, like strawberries or peas. This can be a little difficult to understand, but just try blowing in a plastic bag sometime.

There are various opinions about how many times a breather who is sufficiently well equipped and in a state of rest breathes in the space of one minute. Some say fourteen to sixteen times, while others claim eight to eighteen times. This divergence of opinion stems from the fact that the concept of "state of rest" is very much open to interpretation, let alone how many matters of interpretation are involved when referring to "sufficiently well equipped" breathers. There is also reason to point out that when scholars utter figures, talking about liters or times, in their minds they picture the average adult male, not children, women, infants, the elderly, the sick, yogis, elite athletes, or wind instrumentalists.

The pseudostratified epithelium covers the respiratory tract. The cilia of the pseudostratified epithelium sway in waves during respiration. Mucus moves around on them, among other things. The cells are covered in mucus. Now imagine a mucus car, perhaps also red, moving toward the throat. The swallowing reflex carries the mucus car to the stomach. Moving along the pseudostratified epithelium with quite a sense of direction, the mucus car carries microbes from the airways, but they meet a miserable end as they are broken down more or less completely in the stomach. As an aside, the air we breathe is never clean.

HEART, OH HEART!

Rosa Imaculada manages to calm Ulrike. Rosa Imaculada, who has a tendency to hysterical reactions, is as cool as a cucumber this time. Astutely, Rosa goes and sits next to Ulrike and wraps her arm around the girl. She is not even startled when she barely feels Ulrike's slim figure as she hugs her. Ulrike is softer than cotton to her, and soon she won't even be that, Rosa has finally realized. Soon she won't be able to feel anyone. She won't even be able to touch herself with so much as the brush of a feather.

Then, as if some divine wisdom has descended in the form of a tiny fairy on the lips of that normally hot-headed woman, Rosa begins to explain, in cheerful Portuguese-laced English, an idea that she has obviously been bouncing around in her head for more than a few moments. The idea runs more or less along these lines: not breathing is just as normal *here* as breathing was *there*. While *before* we breathed and didn't think about breathing, *now* we don't breathe and we don't think about not breathing. *Cês entendem, né?* This material around us, *esta substância maldita*, is some sort of cursed substance that influences us in a very strange way. If we could take a piece of it with us in the moment we're snatched back to where we came from—at this point Rosa Imaculada gives a wink that assures victory—the learning of the entire earth would be overturned. All of science would have to be rewritten!

Rosa Imaculada's eyes gleam. She sees the sparkle of flashbulbs and jostling crowds of reporters as they all, all seven, step back into the world. She sees it as clearly as if she were watching the television news. She sees them appear, one by one, on the surface of the earth like the thirty-two Chilean miners trapped in the San José copper-gold mine (along with one Bolivian), whose rescue operation she had watched unceasingly, as she lay in her bed awaiting death or salvation. In order to save those thirty-three legendary heroes, an unearthly, demanding drilling operation was carried out—and at this point Rosa Imaculada's gaze suddenly begins to blur. Of course *they* wouldn't be drilled out, since they weren't below ground. Where would they come from then? And where in the world would they pop out?

The beautiful picture begins to fade. The women, she along with the others, fade somewhere into the background like fluttering astral beings. In the foreground, a massive shuttle-shaped rescue capsule appears, which one by one disgorges dirty men stained by the dark underworld, to thunderous applause.

Rosa strains to see the women coming back. Shoo, away, you miners! This welcome is for her and those six others! They would come one at a time, in order of arrival, a happy smile on their lips: first skeleton-thin Shlomith (not Florencio Ávalos), then one-shoed Polina (not Mario Sepúlveda), then she herself (not Juan Illanes), Nina with her baby belly (not Carlos Mamani), and after Nina, poor mute, bald Wlibgis (not Jimmy Sánchez). After Wlibgis, graceful Maimuna would appear (not Osmán Araya), and finally beautiful Ulrike (not José Ojeda).

And they begin to come, and unfortunately, it looks ridiculous. They don't glide smoothly to the ground, they fall headlong, collapsing on each other like rag dolls thrown angrily in the air. There are no hurrahs or clapping. Instead they are laughed at. Pictures are taken of them, and it will only be a matter of time before they are published on the cover of a tabloid.

Rosa shakes her head in irritation: NOT LIKE THAT! Hesitancy begins to draw ugly creases in her face—how in the world will they come back to earth?

But then, as if the tiny invisible fairy had whispered the answer in her ear, she understands: they will materialize! This insight shakes Rosa, and joy spreads across her face once more, the wrinkles smoothing and a glint returning to her eyes. Why didn't she realize this before? There will be no flopping. They will simply appear. They will materialize out of thin air. That is exactly how they will return to the old world!

Rosa already possesses an abundance of knowledge about these things. In a certain telenovela, there had been a medium who began excreting ectoplasm after a sitting. The clear goop took the shape of a hand that could write! The ectoplasm excreted by the medium covered an invisible hand that had an important message for a woman participating in the séance who had been crushed by grief. Thereza was her name, and her son had died from a police bullet in the previous episode. She wanted to tell her son, I love you, *você tá no meu coração*: you will always be in my heart. And so the medium's ectoplasm hand wrote the son's response: *Go home, open the linen closet, and spread out the bottom sheet.* And the woman did so. And in the folds of the sheet she found half a million in one hundred Brazilian *real* bills!

Rosa Imaculada rocks Ulrike in her arms and forgets everything. She forgets the glare of the flashes and the reporters swarming around with their mouths opening with questions. She forgets the miners, the Florencios, the Marios, and the Juans, who at least had a place even if it was located seven hundred meters underground, a place they could come from and a place from which others wanted them to emerge. A place where supplies to meet their desires were sent. Well, not alcohol of course, but food, drink, medicine, tobacco, and all sorts of harmless entertainments. *Amazing Chilean Babe Named Bianca Bends Over!* Because the most important thing was that those industrious men stayed healthy and didn't go crazy in that enclosed space. Every measure possible was taken to care for them during those months. Even underground they were able to be men. *Chilean Girl Bianca Gets Done Right!* Masculinity kept them together. Their desires were known. Those above knew that more than anything else they wanted to return to the surface to their wives and girlfriends and children and babies. *Chilean Bianca Dagger Fucked Hard by Her Boss!* That's how life was. Men fought, beneath the earth and above.

The whole world kept its eyes glued to the rescue operation, which dragged on for months, from the August Thursday collapse to the middle of October. Rosa Imaculada was there too, watching. At the time, in the fall of 2010, she was waiting for a brand new heart muscle to replace her worn out one. Like the entire world throbbing with tension, it pounded as best it was able on behalf of the miners. If they survive this, I will survive too, Rosa swore. I will get a new heart and survive it. Do we have an agreement, God? Can we shake on it, Lula?

Rosa Imaculada received a new heart and survived it.

Rosa Imaculada also received much more than a new heart, and that she did not survive.

But now Rosa rocks Ulrike in her lap like a rocking chair on a spring, lost in entirely other thoughts. What lovely things Thereza had done with the five hundred thousand *reais* her son had left her through the medium!

The gall of bitterness wells within Rosa. If *she* had found half a million *reais* in her sheets, she wouldn't be in this fix right now, that was for sure. She would be at home with her son and grandmother, recovering from major surgery, and she wouldn't have had to worry for a moment about her income. She would have been able to recover in peace. The operation itself had gone remarkably well, and Rosa hadn't suffered from any rejection symptoms. On the contrary: the new heart had pretended to become a seamless part of her. It hadn't just taken the place of the removed heart, it had taken over everything. It began to pump strange thoughts into her body. And then things started happening. Bad things. Because of money problems.

If Rosa Imaculada had had half a million *reais*, she never would have opened the door of her home to Estêvão Santoro again. She would have stood tall and in a resolute voice said, "Enough. Dear Estêvão Santoro, my words are insufficient to say how grateful I am to you and your son Murilo, whose heart now beats in my chest. I can never express how sorry I am for his death and your loss. But dear, good Mr. Estêvão Santoro, now you must seek help for your sorrow elsewhere. I must focus on recovering and on my little son. These are the most important things in my life right now."

But Rosa Imaculada never said those words to Estêvão Santoro. She didn't have half a million reais, so she opened the door of her home to this father who had lost his son. This father who was the grandson of a rubber baron and who was swimming in cash. She opened her door, and she opened it so many times that she lost count.

If only she'd had money wrapped in a sheet . . .

Because Ulrike has calmed down and because Rosa's eyes have stopped glittering, Shlomith sees fit to open her mouth. Let Rosa tell her moving story about her heart now. She is clearly in an amenable mood. Let Rosa tell about her death and about Esteban Santiago, or whatever the man's name was, the man whose name Rosa repeats in her fits of madness and who has clearly done her much evil.

It is obvious that no matter what direction Rosa Imaculada's story takes, she will become so thoroughly emotional about her own tale that calming her down will take the "rest of the day". The thought of that feels, as theoretical as it is, somehow comforting, and comfort is what Shlomith longs for now more than anything else. In order to receive comfort herself, she is prepared to comfort her afterworldly sister as she convulses with no tears. In fact she practically longs for Rosa's grief, which might go dry in time as well. Like tears, secretions, pain and ecstasy went dry. She waits with more anticipation for Rosa's grief than for perhaps any of the scraps of story she has heard, which quite frankly she could never understand in the least. Even Nina didn't understand Rosa's stories, despite having practiced "a little *fado*" for her "own enjoyment" long ago (or so Nina claimed, although she would never agree to sing a single line for them). Rosa's torrent of words only left behind snatches of detail that never joined together in any imaginable way, and two names which repeated persistently, little Davi and this Esteban or Eduardo, who, as Shlomith understands it, knocked at Rosa's door over and over and who, of this Shlomith is more or less sure, bought something with his cold, hard cash that she didn't ultimately want to sell to him.

THE STORY OF THE HEART

The heart located and working on the left side of Rosa Imaculada's rib cage was, in principle, when viewed superficially, almost normal: two atria, two ventricles, valves, veins, arteries, and aorta. But it wasn't an entirely normal heart, because for some unknown reason, the left ventricle began to expand, and the heart muscle couldn't pump blood at its previous efficiency. That was where Rosa's troubles started.

The woman who surrounded the heart was at least as extraordinary as her recalcitrant organ. At first glance she too could have been almost anyone. She was not particularly striking or of sufficient visual caliber to attract many lingering stares, but she was also not insignificant. Definitely not that. Rosa was fleshy without being slack. Black hair plaited in innumerable small braids framed a face that had an undeniable lack of symmetry. Her nose was a little too large, and if you wanted big, you just had to look at her lips. Her ears and cheeks protruded sharply and crookedly, as if someone had shaped her face with a hatchet sharpened only on one side, perhaps during a cigarette break, ignoring the final sanding; Rosa's cheeks also bore pockmarks. However, there were times when Rosa's eyes sparkled with a wild, provocative glow of adventure in the offing, and in such moments those eyes might have been the only thing in the world.

Rosa lived with her son, Davi, in a small house located on a mountainside in a favela of twenty thousand residents. Rosa's grandmother lived upstairs, and in the last, most decrepit shack on the road lived blind old Gustavo with his three chickens. Then the street ended at a wall with a slope beyond so steep it was impossible to

traverse. Unless you had the nimbleness and strength and courage
of an acrobat. But the agile children of the neighborhood had grown
big. These days they had other things to do than climb on the mountain. They had become quick, dexterous, and extremely perishable.
Only a few of them returned from roaming out in the world, with
hard faces and gold chains around their necks. The ones born after
them were still too small and too afraid. They were either sucking at
the breast or chasing balls in the street, and the mountain slope
could be at peace, likewise the tin roof of Gustavo's house, which
was the best place to start onto the slope if you wanted to go there
for some reason.

With all her miserable heart Rosa Imaculada loved her small son,
who had come into being almost virginally, during Carnival. Now or
never, Rosa had thought. I want a husband and a family! So Rosa
made herself up. She glowed and shimmered, giving off a lovely,
provocative scent of carnations, which made the stray dogs howl as
she waddled past them in her sequined high heels.

And things went as intended. A certain Caio (or was it Flávio?) let
her take his hand as the axé music played, as the drums beat, as the
wild, howling whistle blared the chorus and the güiro grated rolling,
enticing rhythms in the air. Caio (or Flávio or João or Fernando or
Antônio) was driven mad by this woman who smelled of carnations
and shook her buttocks properly in time with the music, who whispered in his left ear that she was a respectable woman and then
immediately murmured in his right ear that yes, she was a woman—a
woman who needed love, and for once the planets were in alignment.
Vamos, vamos, let's go!

Rosa and the man rollicked in the throng. They danced and kissed
each other with lips wet with sweet maracujá juice and strong cachaça
and nearly swooned. Finally, as the drums still beat, they slipped
from the press of the crowd into a dark alley and joined, quickly and
intensely, in the first doorway they found by fumbling with their
hands.

That was how Davi came to be.

She never heard from the man again. The phone number he left

Rosa was fake. But the boy born of his seed was healthy and fat, breathtakingly beautiful and hair-raisingly loud, and above all Rosa's very own. Davi would not disappear. Rosa would see to that. She would raise her son into a man, not a rat in the shape of one. Davi clearly agreed. He cried day and night, those cries filling the small house and his mother's heart, the heart which began to act up even worse after the child's birth.

It was April. Rosa was rocking her six-month-old son in her arms when suddenly her heart skipped a beat and then only weakly returned to operation. Rosa sat down on the floor and couldn't get up under her own power any more. The baby screamed and Rosa couldn't lift him to her breast. The whole house and street filled with ear-splitting bawling that didn't end until the grandmother finally arrived, snatched up the boy, who was sweltering from his cries, and ran three blocks down as fast as her legs would carry her to pound on the door of the largest and tallest house and yell, "Mr. Rogerio, come help!"

And so old Doctor Rogerio struggled up the hillside after the grandmother, up the same hillside that Rosa Imaculada hadn't been able to climb for ages without becoming winded. When she was expecting Davi she had been forced to take long breaks, during which she traded gossip with the women who came by on the street, as much as she could amidst her fits of coughing. She thought that the panting was all part of pregnancy at the comfortably plump age of thirty-five. She thought that the cough that troubled her, especially during physical exertion, was caused by dust. She hadn't had the energy to clean her home, and there was dust at work too. The Salão de beleza Alessandra, where she styled, was full of hair and chemicals that smelled nice but irritated the lining of her throat. She was more sensitive and that was normal, all the women said. Irritants simply bothered you more when you were pregnant.

But this time they were wrong. Most wrong of all was Rosa Imaculada, who knew within her, in a place that someone less knowledgeable might call the heart, that all was not well. But the desire to have a child was great, and the fear of losing that child was even greater. Just as human brains often do, erroneously, when threatened with danger, so Rosa's brain forced into her consciousness the command, *Flee!* And Rosa didn't know how to interpret the command other than in the way that was natural to her: she buried her head in the sand.

Rosa reeled. Rosa gasped. Rosa endured a frailty that began to be more miserable than her eighty-year-old grandmother's infirmity, at its worst making her short of breath from simply talking on the phone, and Rosa was a master at much talking. She could talk after the other person had run out of things to say, and even after she herself had run out of them too. She talked about television series or the newest nail polish innovations, like the phosphorescent party enamels they had just received a box of at the salon. They had become a hit in Rio too, and now the São Salvador girlboys sent messages to each other in the darkness of the night with their glowing fingers in a new phosphor language . . .

Rosa blamed her other symptoms on the pregnancy as well. Like the swelling. Salts and fluid began collecting in her body. She worked as much as she could. She curled and blow-dried and dyed and cut, and did manicures and pedicures and was very conscientious about her job, and talkative, a veritable windbag, except when her lungs bothered her. Then she was quiet. And as she bustled about, her lower limbs began to swell into shapeless lumps. If she pressed on the swollen area, a strange pit remained in her skin for a moment, and then the pit filled with fluid, and the leg was ugly and enormous again. They all wondered at this, she and the other women in the salon, Leticia, Raquel, and Alessandra. "It'll pass when you have the baby," Raquel said, and gave Rosa a jar of cooling foot cream made of horse chestnuts and peppermint.

However, edema was the most harmless of Rosa's new ailments. Her eyes clouded over more and more often. Sometimes her heart skipped a beat, as they say, and the beat ended in a flutter. After a quick but terrifying series of incidents like this, Rosa was so tired that she couldn't lift her scissors even if she sat on a stool. Then her lovely coworkers took over her clients for her. They would hustle

Rosa into the back room to rest on the couch. She had to be careful. She wasn't a young woman having her first child!

Davi was born, but Rosa's condition did not improve. On the contrary. When wise old Rogerio walked in and looked at poor Rosa sitting on the floor, swollen and panting, he saw immediately that this was serious. He checked her pulse, which was one hundred and twenty, and listened to her chest with a stethoscope to hear her delicate heart ticking away amidst the wheezing. Rogerio sent the grandmother to the nearest pharmacy to fetch nitros and diuretics, and shook his head. "Rosa, go to the hospital, soon, before it's too late!"

The fetus developing in her womb had not weakened her; it was her heart, her very own heart, which was her downfall. The fact was that secretly, as it seemed to pump away relatively irreproachably, Rosa's heart had deteriorated to the point that it was mostly just a liability. And so the sick heart within Rosa Imaculada, along with Rosa herself, ended up in Hospital Geral Roberto Santos, where everyone, including the indigent-like Rosa, was given the best possible treatment. The equipment at the hospital may not have been quite as flash as the miraculous instruments at the private sanatoriums on the north side of the city, but it still provided test results, and by her third visit, Rosa Imaculada's diagnosis was clear: *dilated cardiomyopathy.*

And thus, Rosa Imaculada's heart received a new name. This muscle throbbing for its life turned into the lair of a monster called dilated cardiomyopathy. Whatever that meant. The young doctor attempted to explain. Rosa, my dear, your heart is dying. The left chamber is expanding like outer space and growing brittle like parchment, and your heart muscle isn't as efficient as it used to be. Actually, your heart is drowning in blood. It can't pump it any more. Do you understand? Even with the drugs, you're going to get more tired and out of breath. You're on a whole battery of pills, and even so the pumping strength, the "ejection fraction", is incredibly low at only fifteen percent. We can't give you any more medicine. And you're still having atrial fibrillation attacks. Rosa, I have to ask you one important question now. Are you motivated to live? Are you ready to go on a journey? I'm speaking both metaphorically and literally now. Because—and now I'm going to be very blunt—with this heart you have less than a year to live. Absolutely no more than that.

At this point Rosa could only sleep in a sitting position; she couldn't breathe lying down. And there was no question of her going to work or caring for Davi, whom the women in the neighborhood were taking turns looking after (the grandmother's health had declined dramatically just from worry). It was unambiguously clear that Rosa wanted to live. She wanted that more than ever. The surge of adrenaline that accompanies the will to live is a familiar feeling to anyone who has ever been in real danger. The faintness you feel from voluntarily standing on a mountain cliff is only distantly related. Rosa wanted to see her son grow up. Only that mattered. "I'm ready for anything," she whispered to the doctor, "for anything that will give me more years to live!"

And so Rosa first became a transplant candidate and then, after passing the tests, number thirteen on the national heart transplant list. She was an emergency case, but not the only one by any means. The doctor wrote a heartrending statement about her to the Foundation of the Sisters of Saint Angela, which helped "poor women of good repu- tation with the cost of treatment for serious illnesses", as the foundation's bylaws stated. Mothers received first priority. With the help of three guarantors—the angelic Leticia, Raquel, and Alessandra—Rosa was also able to acquire a low-interest loan from the foundation, which she meant to use to cover the rest of the expenses. These included everything she had to pay, after donations: for the tests and the doctor, the medicine and the care both before and after the operation, the operation itself, the new heart, and her stay in Federal University of Ceará Hospital, ward eight, in the city of Fortaleza on the northeast coast of Brazil. Those were minimal costs compared to the astronomi- cal fees for private hospitals, but Rosa had no savings. The loan felt big to her, almost impossible ever to repay. And she had even voted for Lula! She had believed the former nut merchant would build a society for the poor that would help citizens when they were in need. On the wall of her home was a photograph of a laughing Luiz Inácio Lula da Silva with gray hair, with which she sometimes held secret council, because Lula was second only to God, and he actually had a face to talk to. And now she was in this bind: with her life on the line, she was taking a giant loan from a charity, which would crash down on her beloved coworkers if she couldn't pay it back.

"Rosa," Lula's picture whispered from the bedroom wall, "everything will be fine. I promise you. You will get a new, strong heart, and after that you will be a new person." "But, Lula," Rosa whispered as she packed her bag with clothing, nice-smelling skin oil, and a stack of thin magazines to cheer her up, including two-year old copies of *Claudia* (*orgasmo inesquecível!*), last year's *Ana Marias* (*12 kg em 1 mês!*), and an ancient *Uma* (*Horóscopo 2007: amor, saúde, dinheiro, sucesso, amigos!*), "it's so much money, eight thousand *reais*! What if I die? What will happen to Davi? What will happen to Leticia, Raquel, and Alessandra?" "Dear Rosa," Lula said with a smile, "don't worry. Seize the moment. You have to save your life. That is your duty as a mother. You'll find the money!"

Rosa Imaculada pressed her lips to Lula's glass-covered paper lips, locked the door of her home, and left with her son and grandmother on the bus for Fortaleza, for the apartment of her cousin's husband's brother's friend's wife, where they would be able to live in one room for a small fee until a new heart was found.

Not a single person on the road died during the bus trip, and so Rosa and her family ended up in her cousin's husband's friend's wife's apartment waiting for someone else to pass away. Those were dark, hazy days, with nights that were even more full of impending death, and, what was worse, chillingly lonely, because Davi (thankfully) slept and Grandmother—now, there was sleeping! Each woozy exhalation hissed as an interlude to a growling snore. The whole building shook. The whole city trembled to the random rhythm of those croaking jerks of breath. But Rosa couldn't sleep. Rosa had nightmares with her eyes open.

Rosa had already waited 138 fear-filled days, punctuated by visits to the Ceará University Hospital for additional tests and mandatory stupid walks to keep up her health, which Rosa did obediently on doctor's orders, even though taking any steps felt bad, and every swing of her leg felt as though it sapped strength from her pump. The panting began when Rosa got out of bed, which was where she preferred to spend her time. She didn't have the energy to read any more, and even women's magazines felt heavy in her hands. Rosa wanted noise around to cover the feeling of her heart, and that was why all day every day she kept the flickering television that was bolted to the wall turned on, watching everything that came from it, from reruns to new telenovelas, each more suspenseful than the last. She watched a serial named *The Chilean Mine Disaster*, which happened on precisely the same day (it must have meant something!) that she was placed on the heart waiting list. The bouncing flesh of her arms, legs, and backside had started to sag. Her skin had begun to turn gray, and her magnificent breasts had turned to dozing bats, mournful, empty leather bags. Her entire body felt like a strange, angry accessory that was welded to a separate headlike thing built of heavy stone. Time just passed and passed but never revealed its bottom, the end of the waiting, and day by day Rosa became increasingly sure that she wouldn't get a new heart in time. Until, on the twentieth of December, she finally received the good news: a donor had been found!

Anesthesia. Cleaning of the skin of the chest. Crack open sternum. Affix rib spreader. Attach heart-lung machine and switch on. Begin external blood circulation. Blood is oxygenated, temperature control carefully monitored. Blood back into patient. Ribs spread apart. Rubber-gloved hands grip stopped heart. An incision in the pericardium surrounding the heart. Heart disconnected from arteries and veins. Heart removed. Say goodbye to heart: Bye, bye, heart. New heart positioned, skillfully sutured to veins and arteries. Does it work? Yes, it works. Is it pumping? Yes, it's starting to pump! Heart-lung machine turned off. Tubes inserted in the thoracic cavity to allow fluid to drain. Tubes set to exit skin at an appropriate point. Set spread ribs back in place. Stitch split sternum back together with wire. Sew skin tissue back together nicely. All done— there you go, Rosa Imaculada!

* * *

Rosa woke up after the more than three-hour operation pleasantly high. The doctor had two faces and eight arms. The nurse's voice welled out of a hollow cavern in varying octaves, her words echoing like a church choir belting "Ave Maria". Somewhere on the ceiling Lula floated and hummed a familiar lullaby: *Nigue, nigue, ninhas . . .* Lula's beard had grown, and it tickled Rosa's nose, prickling her sides, her toes, the insides of her thighs . . . Then Lula's head descended onto the doctor's shoulders and the long beard flicked under his arm like the tail of a fox. A warm, soft fur began to grow around the hospital bed, wrapping tightly, hair by hair, around Rosa's body. At the same moment, many small orange suns sparkled into life along Rosa's skin. Rays of light shone through the fur. It was bloody hot. Steam rose toward the ceiling. Rosa opened her mouth and tried to ask for water but didn't remember the words. Rosa closed her eyes and fell back asleep in her fox-fur-beard bed. Lula bowed so solemnly that the doctor's back nearly broke, clapped his hands, and took Rosa back under the blue duvet into a deep morphine dream.

When Rosa woke up the next time, Lula was gone. There was no sign of foxes or suns. There was the familiar strange body with seven hoses coming out of it. The upper body was supported tightly with pillows, and thin, transparent plastic tubes protruded from it. Two drips were connected to the left arm, one dosing medication, the other providing nutrient fluid. The chest was attached by wires to a monitor with the new heart's ECG, like a hyperactive green-light creature running on a mountain range.

So somewhere under the blankets and wires *it* was beating. The grotesque, anticipated interloper. Because of which the body's immune defenses had to be destroyed. Because of which the entire system had to be filled with immunosuppressants. They even stole from other species. Some of the antibodies came from bunnies. In order to negotiate a permanent peace between the transplant and its new mistress.

So a warm welcome to worms, parasites, viruses, and fungi. Welcome to shaking, numbness, convulsive attacks of chills, hair loss, and headaches. Come right on in, most honored guests: diabetes, osteoporosis, renal deterioration, and cancer. Come in, come in, even the least of you, shingles and painful cold sores that spread all the way to the esophagus. Because a transplant will never learn to behave without making its homecoming comfortable! This is a small price for a new life, is it not, Rosa Imaculada?

"Rosa, you've had your operation now," the doctor said and patted Rosa's arm. "Everything went very well, and now you need to start focusing on your recovery." And so Rosa did. She listened to how her body felt. Despite the powerful pain medicine, she felt as if the new heart beat somehow more deeply and more on the left than the previous resident of her chest. Where the old one ticked, the new one hammered, galloping so fast she felt she might fall off. Was it even a human heart? What if it was from a lion! How could she treasure up her secrets in it then? It would instantly make mincemeat of them! A terrible, insatiable thirst tormented her. The heart demanded to eat fresh fruit flesh. Mango papaya kiwi kumquat. Give me carambola. Peel an orange. Rosa opened her mouth and mumbled. The feeling of thirst made her feel sick. The nurse gave her water mixed with honey. Rosa opened her mouth and tried to ask but couldn't form the words.

Is death gone now for sure? Can someone promise me?

ESTÊVÃO SANTORO COMES
CALLING

Death did indeed stay away. But Rosa Imaculada was warned: death will always be hard on your heels now. It will be like a violent ex-husband who wants to come to visit despite the restraining order, who flops down on the couch and casually asks for a beer, and, after drinking his beer, says like a punch to the gut: "I'm coming back, baby . . ." But you can't let it move in! You can't even let it get to the door. You have to keep death at a distance, and you probably can get it to stay far enough away with a few simple precautions, which you should follow for at least the next six months: avoid crowds; stay away from public events; no herds of children; hygiene; carry disinfectant with you at all times. And you can forget about working in the salon for a while.

All of this Rosa recorded obediently in her mind. But where would she get money to live? The loan was running out, and everything had been more expensive than she ever could have known. As she lay in her bedroom, Rosa glanced questioningly at Lula, but Lula just smiled his gray-bearded senior smile and didn't say anything.

But then one day, when Rosa was padding around the house in sandals and a red and white striped negligee, occasionally going to stir her palm oil and orange bean stew, which Davi was waiting for, drumming his spoon on the table, a knock came at their door. Three times.

Rosa turned the heat on the stove down and went to answer. At the door was a sturdy man who was strangely hunched for his size, who filled the entire doorway but still seemed to shrink into his legs. If you had to choose a fruit, you might say his face resembled a pear; his jaw was robust and his cheeks round, but his forehead was a significantly less impressive sight. He wore a vermilion BOW TIE. Red, of course, Rosa realized later. The silk tie practically blazed against his creamy white shirt. In the left pocket of his saffron-yellow double-breasted suit was a rust-red silk handkerchief folded in a triangle and wet with sweat, and, it must be said, without that startling, flirtatiously feline BOW TIE and slightly clumsily matched rust-red pocket triangle, he would have looked like a perfectly normal gentleman with an appreciation for old-world style, but that vermilion BOW TIE and the conservative handkerchief that emphasized the jauntiness of the BOW TIE with the *saffron-yellow* and *double-breasted* suit coat made for a very eccentric overall impression. Based on his outfit, the large, hunched man looked if not like a cockscomb at least like someone seeking to be peculiar, who was nevertheless strangely embarrassed by his choice of dress, like a woman dressed too boldly for her temperament might regret the fripperies she has on once she's already on the street and late for a meeting she's been looking forward to with excessive enthusiasm: she went crazy with a miniskirt (which wouldn't stay put), fishnet stockings (which would snag), and a crimson frilly shirt that exposes a generous cleavage— but the man standing at the door filling the opening even as he shrank within the frame was an even more pitiable sight, completely lacking the loitering frivolity, the shockingly bold, waxed-mustache flirtatiousness, and the playful ruby-red cufflinks that would have made him what the choice of outfit claimed he was: a nonconformist, a dandy, a man of the world with a wink to match. When you looked at him more closely, no ambiguity remained: this man was at rock bottom. He hadn't come to sell perfume, skin cream, or fruit slicers. His business was—serious.

The conversation that the strangely dressed gentleman had with Rosa Imaculada is reproduced below in full:

ESTÊVÃO SANTORO: Are you Rosa Imaculada Araújo?
ROSA IMACULADA: Yes.

ESTÊVÃO SANTORO: I am Estêvão Santoro. I received a letter from you three months ago.

Rosa realizes immediately what letter the man is speaking of.

ESTÊVÃO SANTORO: I mean this letter.

Mr. Santoro produces a wrinkled paper from his pocket and unfolds it for Rosa to see. Rosa wrote the letter on the day she left Ceará Hospital, the fifteenth of January. The hospital promised to deliver the letter to the family of the donor, strictly anonymously: anything else would be bad manners, unethical, and altogether impossible. Rosa signed the letter "Someone who received a new life", but then—out of some damned vanity? self-importance? childish hope for contact, for understanding, for love?—she crossed out that line and inserted her name:

Dear Family,

I want to tell you how thankful I am. I now have your son's heart. I don't know anything about him except that he was eighteen years old. His death must have been a tragedy for you. I mourn that too. I would be dead without your son's heart. I weep with emotion and gratitude when I think about this. You are in my heart even though I can never meet you. God bless you!

~~Someone who received a new life~~

Rosa Imaculada Araújo, Bahia

ROSA IMACULADA (*embarrassed*): Yes. I wrote this letter.

ESTÊVÃO SANTORO: I'm happy I found you. (*He does not look happy.*) The heart donor was my youngest son. May I come in for a moment?

Davi walks up to his mother, pushes his head through the door opening, and begins to bang on the door jamb with his spoon.

ROSA IMACULADA: Yes, of course. Please come in! How rude of me to leave you standing there. Come in. (*She bustles about, leading her guest to the couch to sit.*) Would you like grapefruit, pineapple, or mango juice? Coffee? There's stew simmering in the pot. Are you hungry . . . ? Oh yes, this is my son, Davi. Say hello to the gentleman,

Davi. (*She picks the boy up, who begins to wail.*) There, there, so grumpy. He's hungry . . .

ESTÊVÃO SANTORO: A glass of grapefruit juice will be fine, thank you. I'm in no hurry, so please take your time feeding your son.

Grandmother comes down from upstairs. Rosa rushes to the door and whispers so the whole street echoes: "Guess-who's-sitting-on-my-couch! My-new-heart's-father!" Grandmother hobbles down with her cane to see. Estêvão Santoro stands up and walks over to greet Grandmother. They shake hands. "God bless you, dear man," Grandmother says in a hoarse voice overcome with emotion, unable to tear her gaze from the BOW TIE that protrudes from the man's collar like an overripe rose. "My daughter has been saved thanks to your generosity. God is good, amen." Estêvão Santoro nods and warmly squeezes the old woman's hand, and can't help noticing that her face has the same rough, statuesque quality as her granddaughter's. Grandmother clumsily retreats into the kitchen, making a hurried I'll-feed-the-boy gesture and pulling the child, who is now bawling a full-on I've-been-abandoned howl, along with her. Rosa brings a pitcher of juice and two glasses from the kitchen, closes the door, and sits on an uncomfortable-looking wooden stool a couple of meters from the couch. The boy's cry carries perfectly through the door.

ROSA IMACULADA: Tell me. What made you come?

ESTÊVÃO SANTORO: I wanted to meet the person in whom a small part of my son still lives. (*His voice cracks. A short pause.*) Do you know, my son Murilo intended to go to university soon. He wasn't stupid at all, just a little lost. He was interested in technical things, and I think he could have become an excellent wood-manufacturing engineer. He participated in boxing and swimming and all sorts of young people's games, and of course women (*a snort with a hint of fatherly pride*), he also "participated" in women. On the morning of his death, Murilo was just on his way to visit one of his "partici-pants" . . . (*long pause*) He was all dressed up and kept poking at his hair in front of the mirror, changing how it looked, and nothing seemed to be quite right . . . That made me think it was serious . . . But he wouldn't even tell me her name . . . He just got irritated when I pressed too hard . . . (*pause*) And then he went and drove his motor-cycle into a bridge girder.

Rosa only grunts because she is too horrified to scream and, as often happens, immediately realizes that this grunt is nowhere near enough, even realizes that the grunt might be interpreted as a signal of indiffer-ence: "What of it. People die. That's a typical way for a young man to go. Really it was predictable. Is that what you came to tell me, that an idiot with a hard-on screwing around with his motorcycle ran into a concrete pole . . . ?" Rosa coughs and fashions two words appropriate to the situation.

ROSA IMACULADA: How terrible!

ESTÊVÃO SANTORO: He lay in a coma for three days. Then it was over. I had to start organizing the funeral.

ROSA IMACULADA: Dreadful! (*Sighs in shock and reflexively places her hand over her heart.*)

ESTÊVÃO SANTORO: We left so many things unsaid. Murilo was so quick-tempered. He flew off the handle whenever you asked him something at the wrong moment, if you questioned how he wasted his money, or if you just suggested a discussion about decisions for the future. (*Raises his gaze to the ceiling, where a fan with a crooked blade flutters.*) I thought that he would calm down as he grew up. That he would find the right woman and so forth . . .

ROSA IMACULADA: And then when the right woman did come along, his motorcycle went out of control . . .

ESTÊVÃO SANTORO: Yes. But really, how can I know she was the love of his life? I don't actually know anything about my son. He was handsome. Look. (*Produces a photograph with bent corners from his breast pocket: a bronzed young man in Honolulu-style shorts smiles next to his motorcycle in a slightly affected contrapposto to ensure that the bulging muscle of his left bicep is visible, so his washboard abs will show, so—and now some painfully pleasurable, irrational feeling of familiarity scrabbles at Rosa in the pit of her stomach—his protruding penis in the leg of his shorts will be obvious; and from somewhere very close, Rosa realizes a moment later, from the night, out of a dream pops an image of a mysterious lover, a dazzlingly beautiful, barely full-grown angel whom Murilo is going on his motorcycle to visit . . . And to her shock, Rosa feels how the tiny head of her flower stiffens and sweat forms on her inner thighs . . . but it isn't from Murilo's picture . . . It's caused by Murilo's girl . . .*)

ROSA IMACULADA (*clears throat*): Very . . . pleasant-looking. Yes.

ESTÊVÃO SANTORO (*contentedly notes Rosa's confusion*): Ayayay, women had such a weakness for Murilo! (*Thinks of his son's lifeless body and grows dark again. Looks for a way out of the situation. Finds her face and makes a surprising move.*) Excuse me if I ask directly, but do you have mestizo blood?

ROSA IMACULADA (*even more confused by the sudden shift in conversation; becomes alarmed; perhaps he noticed her sudden arousal?*): D-d-do I have . . . (*straightens up*) My grandmother is half apinajé. Do you mean my facial features? (*Estêvão Santoro nods in relief.*) My grandmother's face? If only you had met my mother. It was very pronounced in her . . .

ESTÊVÃO SANTORO: And your mother . . . ?

ROSA IMACULADA: She's dead.

ESTÊVÃO SANTORO: My condolences.

ROSA IMACULADA: I was small when it happened.

ESTÊVÃO SANTORO: How sad.

ROSA IMACULADA: My father left. It broke my mother's heart.

ESTÊVÃO SANTORO: You have . . . sort of a hereditary taint . . . ?

ROSA IMACULADA: I imagine we do.

A warm, plaintive silence, about five seconds, which is a long pause in a fast-moving conversation, believe it or not. During this silence, Estêvão Santoro finally forgives the woman who has benefited from his son's death. (Of course—how else?—Murilo's parents had agreed to the organ donation, rationalizing that this is not a zero sum game—they couldn't get their son back no matter what they did, so let the heart go to someone who needed it. But feelings are feelings, and beneath all the confusion, Estêvão Santoro also felt a repellent, disgusting anger that he couldn't dispel with reason and which only disappeared when he thought of little Rosa's poor dead mother and the orphan girl left to her grandmother's care: they were both victims: now the situation was finally even.)

ESTÊVÃO SANTORO: Now tell me your story.

ROSA IMACULADA (*delighted by the request*): Do you know that the most horrible and most beautiful things in my life happened at the same time! I became pregnant with Davi and then came this heart trouble. My health collapsed. At first I thought it was (*a terrible amount of gentleness in her voice*) the flipping fetus that was sucking the strength from me, my growing belly. Davi was enormous. But it only got worse after the birth. And then suddenly everything was in a shambles. The doctor said I would die if I didn't get a new heart. Dear God, what a diagnosis! I had to move to Fortaleza to wait for the new heart. The waiting lasted and lasted and las— (*interrupts sentence, realizing that it is utterly inappropriate to complain about this in front of Estêvão Santoro*), well, yes, I mean, my son and Grandma were with me . . . I'm sure you can imagine how many times we all almost went crazy there . . . Our friend's wife, who we were living with, was so kind and so flexible . . . Davi would cry and this one (*points at herself*) didn't have the energy even to hold him properly . . . Grandma would get tired too, and our friend's wife would have to help with child care . . . (*shakes head*) and this one couldn't even promise that she would survive . . . that the whole circus was worth the trouble . . . I might just slip away despite it all . . . just die . . . in the middle of everything . . .

ESTÊVÃO SANTORO (*in a determined but not at all bitter tone*): And then Murilo died.

ROSA IMACULADA: Yes. Your son died, and now I'm here.

ESTÊVÃO SANTORO: How do you feel?

ROSA IMACULADA (*even more cheered by this question about her well-being*): Much better, thank you! But do you know, my immune system is weak, the doctors say. I can't live a normal life right now. I have to be very, very careful all the time. I still can't even go back to work at the beauty salon . . . The customers can have all kinds of germs, and I have to protect myself . . . But the doctor promised that if I survive the first six months, my prognosis starts to be quite good . . .

ESTÊVÃO SANTORO (*interrupts fervently*): Tell me how *it* feels!

ROSA IMACULADA (*taken aback*): Excuse me?

ESTÊVÃO SANTORO (*impatiently*): Tell me how the new heart feels.

And this is the critical moment, although neither knows it yet, the moment that could have been nothing more than one small, strange twist in a discussion, the content of which has otherwise been more light small talk than emotional confessions, which is more than desirable in these unique circumstances: a certain safe superficiality, a distance . . . acknowledge the facts . . . respect each other's grief and understand each other's relief . . . Rosa could have responded with something vague such as "Well, it's in there pumping away," or "It's big, but I'm already used to it," or "Sometimes I forget the whole thing happened," (although this might have been an insulting response in this situation) but no, Rosa didn't evade the question. Instead of politely sidestepping it, she approached it head on. For a long time she was quiet, observing an entire spectrum of expressions on Estêvão Santoro's face, impatience turning to curiosity, curiosity turning back to annoyance, annoyance to embarrassment, and embarrassment to empty horror (an expression that anyone who has lost a loved one tragically recognizes on the faces of her companions in misfortune but outsiders usually interpret as arrogance or rejection), and, this has been proven time and time again, empty horror is only a short journey from remorse, which can reach the level of "I wish I had never been born." But Rosa did not allow Mr. Santoro to fall to the bottom of the well of remorse. Instead she made a move that changed EVERYTHING.

ROSA IMACULADA: Would you like to touch it?

ESTÊVÃO SANTORO: Excuse me?

ROSA IMACULADA: You can place your hand on it.

Rosa moves her stool closer to the couch, and Estêvão Santoro mechanically extends his hand toward Rosa's chest. Rosa grabs his hand and guides it to the right place.

ESTÊVÃO SANTORO (*in an almost piping, little boy's voice*): I don't feel anything . . .

ROSA IMACULADA: Put your hand under the shirt. No reason to be shy.

Estêvão Santoro obediently slips his hand under Rosa's red and white striped negligée shirt. The hand is large and clammy. When Santoro's hand is in the right place, Rosa presses her own hand on top of it. On Murilo's heart. Yes: Murilo's heart, not hers. Rosa is sure of that now. The new heart has been sewn into her chest and there it is, a kind and compliant creature, because it doesn't reject her, but something is still wrong. The heart is becoming part of her in a way no one told her about before the surgery . . . There are things Rosa has never told anyone. Not the doctors, not her friends, and not her grandmother—least of all her. Every once in a while, the new heart plays nasty tricks on her. It sort of sends messages. Not like Lula (Lula doesn't talk to her any more) but in a very different way. Not with words but with actions. It makes her think about things she'd prefer not to think about. It forces her to feel strange feelings. Example No. 1: For many nights she has been having a dream of an extremely beautiful girl who lives in a large, white house behind a wall. She's come to visit the girl. She climbs the winding stairs to the girl's room, and they exchange a few insignificant pleasantries ("Hello", "How are you?", "Did you miss me?" and so forth). Then, without further discussion, she tumbles the girl on the violet-colored silk sheets and slips her finger under her panties into her wet, nearly ready pussy. With her other hand she removes her shorts, climbs onto the girl, and after pushing into her begins a rapid series of movements. She thrusts, rams, and twists herself inside the girl, lithely rotating her sporty rump. She nibbles the girl's lips with her teeth and sucks on her neck with her lips and pulls the girl to sit on top of her. She wets her thumb with her own saliva and shoves it in the girl's anus so deep that she reaches the wall between the vagina and the rectum. With her first two fingers she massages the girl's perineum, rotating the thumb against the rectal wall at the place she can feel her own organ doing its piston motion . . . Her penis swells even more, grinding brutally against the thumb as if wanting to push it away, but the thumb only presses more violently back . . . and so the thumb and forefinger and middle finger and the whole hand squeeze and knead and rock the now dripping almost-woman lost in abandon in her lap . . . And every time, at exactly this spot, the girl completely goes off the rails. She screams and rises and pushes down and rises and pushes down and rises and crashes down and moans and comes, and at that moment she wakes up to her own orgasm with her lower abdomen wet, her whole body hot and sweaty and pulsating, and she doesn't understand, truly doesn't understand, not until NOW, now that she has seen Murilo's photograph, her own nocturnal self . . .

ROSA IMACULADA: Can you feel the pulse?

ESTÊVÃO SANTORO: Sort of . . .

Suddenly Rosa pushes the man's hand away and pulls her shirt off.

ROSA IMACULADA: Put your ear against my breast. Then you'll hear it.

Estêvão Santoro does as ordered and hears the sound, TuTUM, tuTum, TUtum, tuTUM, and begins to sob. Rosa strokes his hair.

ESTÊVÃO SANTORO (*sobbing*): What is it like . . . now that it's there?

ROSA IMACULADA (*in a quiet, calm voice*): It's big, bigger than my own was. They had to put it in deeper, and that's why it felt strange at first, kind of heavy and occupying too much space. At first I was afraid of it . . . That it would turn me to mincemeat . . . But it didn't. It does something else. (*Pause.*) This may be hard to understand, but I think that in some strange way Murilo is . . . working inside of me.

Estêvão Santoro jerks his head away.

ESTÊVÃO SANTORO: What do you mean?

ROSA IMACULADA: I have dreams of Murilo with his girlfriend. I just realized it. It's him, definitely him. We have . . . I'm sure you can guess what. (*Rosa begins to pull her shirt back on.*)

ESTÊVÃO SANTORO: You can't be serious!

ROSA IMACULADA: The girl has long, shiny brown hair. She's really cute. From a rich family. The house is so splendid. In the dream I climb a spiral staircase. The steps are marble. The railing is like gold. The girl lives with her parents. She has her own room on the top floor, a fine four-poster bed, and violet silk sheets . . . And, don't misunderstand, I don't like women that way.

Estêvão Santoro stares at Rosa with an incredulous look on his face.

ROSA IMACULADA: And that isn't all. I have new, strange desires. I crave chargrilled chicken skin . . .

ESTÊVÃO SANTORO: I don't believe you! That was Murilo's favorite!

ROSA IMACULADA: . . . which I couldn't eat before. Anything burned tasted horrible to me. And what about this: grunge rock, like

Autoramas. Before I detested it; now I like it. Beer. Football. And the most incomprehensible of all: Marmite. I hadn't even heard of it before, and now I could eat it straight out of the jar with a spoon.

Estêvão Santoro collapses deep in the corner of the sofa, his red BOW TIE now askew. His shocked expression confirms that each item Rosa listed was correct: chicken, rock music, beer, football, Marmite—bingo! Santoro takes the rust-colored handkerchief from his jacket pocket and dabs his brow. Rosa feels tired, at once heavy and light. She has said out loud the thing that has been bothering her for months. She has also received an explanation, and that brings on a faintness, making her afraid and disgusted, and (as even the most crushing diagnosis also comforts with the knowledge of where the tormenting symptoms are coming from) it also calms her: it will never just be "her", Rosa Imaculada, again. Always and forever it will be "they", Rosa and Murilo . . .

ESTÊVÃO SANTORO: Rosa—may I call you Rosa? (*Rosa nods*)—I have to go rest. I'm sure you'll understand how shocked I am. But I want to hear more. (*Begins digging in his pants pocket.*) Take this money; no, don't object, Rosa dear, I know that you need it. I want to . . . Somehow I want to make up for this . . . and the conversations we will have . . . You have information about my son . . . that I need . . . you understand . . . I want to know more about him . . .

Rosa nods. Both stand up, shake hands, laugh nervously, and hug. Rosa escorts Estêvão Santoro to the door.

ROSA IMACULADA: Please do come again. Where are you staying?

ESTÊVÃO SANTORO: Near Pelourinho. In a hotel named Beija Flor. Here's my card with my number if you want to call and talk.

ROSA IMACULADA: Wait a moment.

Rosa turns away, rips the white order coupon off the back of a Claudia *magazine sitting on the table, and writes her own phone number on it.*

ROSA IMACULADA: I'm usually home, but it would be a good idea to make sure. Goodbye.

ESTÊVÃO SANTORO: Goodbye, Rosa. Remember to take good care of yourself.

ONEIRON: THE FIRST VICTIM

Oooon . . . ei-ron!

The women stare at Rosa Imaculada, whose eyes gape wide as she says the strange word. They didn't expect this. They had imagined, and with good reason, that Rosa was trying to tell them about her heart operation again, about her child, about that strange man who invaded her home. Some of the women had even been ready with questions to give the story a direction. (Nina: What did he want from you in the end? Shlomith: Did I understand correctly that he was related to the organ donor? Polina: So was it him who blackmailed you?) Rosa had looked so intently focused, as if she were struggling to find precise words from her limited vocabulary, something savage to start with that would capture her listeners' interest. And now this was the word that came out: *Oooon . . . ei-ron!*

Or was it three words? If it was one word, then Rosa had pronounced it oddly, staring into space: she drew out the beginning and then divided the end with an emphasis on the syllable boundary. The EI jumped out like a scream or a hiccup between the slightly mumbled beginning and the final growl, RON, which for all its gruffness was amazingly snappy. And then again: *Oooon . . . ei-ron!*

And if it was three words, they still couldn't make any sense of it. The way that Rosa growled the end, RON, was particularly strange: the R didn't roll sensually in her throat, and it didn't soften into an uvular fricative—it was at its most revolting and impossible, an aggressive AR trilled with the tip of the tongue.

What did you say?
What is it?

What?!

Rosa Imaculada's gaze is utterly empty. Her eyes don't flutter even though Nina, who sits next to her, waves her hand in front of Rosa's face. Before anyone can do anything, Rosa moves, but not like a person moves when she shifts position, say by fixing her posture vertebra by vertebra, or by stretching her arms, by flexing her legs. Rosa doesn't do anything like that. She trembles all over like an aspen leaf in the wind. Or, since she isn't particularly slender, since her body lacks the long petiole characteristic of aspen leaves that makes the aspen quake perhaps more elegantly than any other tree in the world—an effect that is heightened in the fall when the colors have changed (the entire tree seems to transform into dancing, tremulous, join-us! nuggets of gold whose collective siren allure makes a smile appear on even the most hardened nature-hater's lips)—since no part of Rosa's body resembles an aspen leaf in any respect, but more like, if we continue searching for a metaphor from botany, a hand-shaped, palmately veined maple leaf that, having separated from its stem, thuds to the ground after a brief, zigzag glide (whereas an aspen leaf can easily end up spiraling), Rosa's body trembles, first and foremost, as if someone were shaking an empty tin box with both hands: violently, through and through, ever so slightly sideward, and without a sound. It is frightening. The work of a demon, one of the women easily could have said (presumably Maimuna, because she had used the word "demon" a couple of times before; ça c'est un travail du démon!), but no one makes the slightest sound. They only stare, mouths more or less open.

What happens next surprises everyone. For, you see, Rosa begins to sink. But not down. Rosa remains in exactly the same place she had been. She does not recede or shrink but also does not stay the same. In some way she begins to . . . fade? To lose her features? As if light snow were falling over her. Or as if very thin, nearly transparent ice were forming and covering her. Or is it more like gauze? Or a clouded glass surface, or a sarcophagus made of thick, transparent plastic that slightly distorts the features inside? However, there does not appear to be anything *in between*. Shlomith is the one who checks, boldly sticking her osteoporotic, bony hand (which could have been broken with one quick snap) toward Rosa but touching nothing, and let it be emphasized: nothing. She encounters no ice or snow or gauze or glass or plastic, nothing of the sort, and nothing of any other sort, not even Rosa, although Shlomith pushes her hand deeper and deeper. And yet Rosa is there! Like a pillar of salt, frozen but real. Very close. Shlomith continues pushing, and her arm keeps sinking. Everyone sees it, the hand, and everyone also sees faded Rosa, the hand and Rosa at the same time, and it isn't possible, but nevertheless it is.

Can you feel her?

Shlomith answers Polina's whispered question with a shake of her head and pulls her hand away: Rosa Imaculada's form hasn't caused so much as a tickle against the skin of her arm.

So there they sit around Rosa, as if horrified by the carcass of a hare crushed on the road, silent, unable to avert their eyes, unable to leave the scene of the accident, because there is a feeling that this is far from over. No one knows how to act in a situation like this. Should they mourn? Should they organize a small devotional? Light a candle (in their minds), bring flowers (in their thoughts)? And more generally—is it so horrible now? Is Rosa Imaculada's vanishing, fading, partial disappearance something to cry over at all?

There are a number of facts they have to hold onto. So says Polina suddenly. The women give a start when they hear her voice. They had each sunk into their own slack, unfocused thoughts, thoughtlessness, a state that wasn't ultimately that bad to be in, where they could have perfectly well remained, staring dumbly at pale Rosa. But Polina wanted to begin collecting thoughts. They can't stay here! They have already begun to move away, haven't they? Have they begun to grow pale too? To cloud over? Is it only a matter of time before the next one's turn? Does the word Rosa said have the power to destroy them as well?

It is a fact, Polina says solemnly, that Rosa Imaculada's pigmentation has suddenly begun to fade. The strident magenta of her piqué shirt first changed to a gentle flamingo red, then to a washed-out porcine pink, and then to white. The same had happened to Rosa's red lips. Her black hair, on the other hand, had gone gray by way of dark brown, light brown, and the color of a field of grain, and the darkish, pockmarked skin of her face had gone pale. Her beige shorts had gone white all at once, while the red fabric belt threaded through the loops had lost its redness the same way as the shirt and the lips: magenta, flamingo red, piggy pink, and white. It is also a fact, Polina continues, that this change occurred after Rosa said a word which she had never said before, which no one here has ever to their knowledge said, a word whose meaning will remain an eternal mystery since Rosa is no longer able to give any answers.

They can't be sure of anything else. Rosa has become unattainable, closed-off, displaced. Perhaps the most dead of all the dead or maybe returned to life. Who knows?

Ulrike moves like an insect awoken from dormancy: with an almost imperceptible flinch. With helium lightness she remembers the horror that waking up to not breathing had caused in her before Rosa began to fade. She remembers the cursed matter of which Rosa had tried to speak. She remembers being in Rosa's lap, the comfort of Rosa's feather-light embrace around her body. And then: the feeling of horror had disappeared. She had found comfort in the strange woman's arms as she listened to her confused explanations. That did not fit the image Ulrike had of herself. She was not easily comforted. Even as a child she had cried inconsolably if she was ever injured, if someone had caused her distress. And it was not, as others imagined, demonstrative weeping. If it had been that, she would have enjoyed it when whoever had wronged her came begging for forgiveness. But the more the people who had offended her asked forgiveness, the more deeply she sank into disconsolation. And no one else could join her there. Sorrow flooded in, then receded a little, but only temporarily, only in order to build up speed, to gush back even stronger. All that worked was a 10 mg diazepam, or two. She had been given the prescription when she was fifteen years old.

Now Ulrike remembers her inability to breathe, like you remember your grandmother's birthday: you splash some rosewater on a card, put it in an envelope, drop the envelope in the nearest postbox, and there's your happy birthday *liebe Bettina*! Something very strange

is happening. Rosa, obviously, has bodily reached the heart of the
mystery. Like a plaster statue, Rosa the White is still visible against
the white background if you look carefully. She seems to stare at
them calmly, devoid of any panic. From her eyes they can tell that
consciousness remains behind her apparent stasis.

Rosa really is now one with the substance surrounding them!

Ulrike decides to take a risk. What does she have to lose? If she
could choose—and why can't she, since she still has her own free
will?—she would much rather be with tranquil Rosa than these other
women. So Ulrike opens her mouth. She feels how, by only the force
of will, with no air current, sound comes out, her very own voice,
now metallic, electrical:

Oooon . . .

And instantly there is a terrible, nearly simultaneous wave of
horror around her:

No!

Non!

Non, s'il te plaît, non!

Нельзя!

But why not? There is no reason why not! They can each finally
move on. Suddenly Ulrike has no fear. It is the courage of Fräulein
Kehlsteinhaus, a madcap, hysterical bravado that everyone loved
(except for bitter old maids). So why not indeed? Like a dung beetle,
her lack of fear rolls a growing, hardening feeling beneath articulated
legs, a knowledge that however she has done it, Rosa Imaculada has
moved forward. Rosa has reached enlightenment. The calm of her
death-mask expression conceals within itself everything that matters.
Her waxwork face closes the gate of knowledge before them. Ulrike
is sure of that. Ulrike knows that Rosa is traveling somewhere. She
can see Rosa grinning at them through her matt membrane: Come
with me if you dare! But no. They prefer to stand here, gawping at
each other. Soon they will go back to fiddling with the wig, apathetic
as wilted rutabagas. God, it is exasperating!

Ulrike opens her mouth again and utters the most obvious fact that
separates Rosa Imaculada from the other women: *Rosa really showed*

her feelings! Rosa shouted when she felt like shouting, smiled when she felt like smiling, showed her fears without restraint and her joys without calculation. Rosa had let it rip even though it had often been irritating for the other women to watch. Was this Rosa Imaculada's secret? Was this why she had been allowed to escape this place?

Or had Rosa's transition been a prize for the best acting? Her gesticulation must have been at least partially theatrical, because big feelings shrank here. Ulrike had already experienced that personally. Her own horror had shriveled and vanished too quickly. And her lack of fear, her Fräulein Kehlsteinhaus bravado was just a nimble creature with segmented legs. It wasn't her own, like the horror and inconsolability were. It just appeared from somewhere, from outside, and started rolling things up underneath itself. It was lacking in history. Empty of big emotions. And besides, it only knew command words: Go. Do. Say. Be direct.

A sudden longing for Rosa strikes Ulrike. Rosa had held her in her arms. Rosa had pressed her against herself, very instinctively, just as mothers who love their children do. Some mothers. Not all. Not the ones who are jealous of their daughters instead of loving them. Some mothers are sowers of discord. Some mothers are worn out and cantankerous. Some mothers are simply unable to discuss anything rationally with a toxic wave of envy washing over them. How small they are then! When she mentioned the name Ulrich B. Zinnemann at home, when she told her parents about U.B.Z.'s ambitious, uncompleted film project, when she told them about Scott Walker, who created music by beating his fists against raw meat, her mother, her very own mother, standing at the sink, wrinkled her nose. She slumped as if someone had pressed down on her shoulders. And as if the bitter lemon expression weren't enough, her mother also had to give a snort and huff: "Oh, so your new coworker at the Eagle's Nest is an aaaartiste." And as if the huff weren't enough, her mother had to go on huffing: "Just be careful, little girl. Aaaartistes, especially failed aaaartistes, can be unpredictable!"

It didn't help things at all that her father took her side, as fathers often do, because it is the duty of fathers to defend their beautiful daughters when mothers attempt to put them down. That was why Ulrike's father pulled out of the mothballs of his mind a tidbit of information: Ulrich B. Zinnemann's fifteen-year-old film *War Painting*, which received an award at the Chicago International Film Festival. It was a marvelous directorial debut! A strong showing from a first-timer. U.B.Z. had given statements to every German-language paper, and there had even been talk of a collaboration with Werner Herzog. What ever happened to that project? Had Herr Zinnemann told Ulrike anything about it?

Those mothers who don't want to pull together with their daughters completely lose their minds when they discover their spouse choosing a side that isn't their side, instead the opposing side, the disobedient daughter's side. The girl's enthusiasm needed crushing not fanning! Didn't he see that? An ugly fact had been shoved under their noses: their daughter was going to end up being used. Why on earth would a man who was nearly thirty years her senior devote so much time to a scatterbrained teenager? What drives failed aaaartistes who press elevator buttons for a living? Tell me that!

The mother, Ulrike's very own bitter mother, sent a scowl scorched in the flames of rage at her husband as he sat at the kitchen table. He had dodged the situation yet again. His resigned grunt made the mother fling her dishrag into the sink and let out a sound that was either a yowl of pleasure or disgust, the orgiastic cry of someone in the right, or the bellow of a spurned truth-teller. And the thrower of the dishrag likely didn't know herself, screaming because that was the best she could manage, because out of sheer bovinity she had married a slob who drove his company into the ground, who had hidden his true nature, his spineless tapewormness, quite skillfully for several money-saturated years.

Rosa Imaculada never would have played her hand so miserably. Ulrike is sure of that. If Rosa were concerned about the safety and welfare of her child, she wouldn't have schemed, and she definitely wouldn't have plotted. She would have shed a theatrical tear and then, voice cracking, screamed her cares to the world. She would have warned her child of the Big Bad Wolf, she would have given a colorful lecture on the full spectrum of male treachery, and finally she would have slapped a package of condoms in her hand.

Aaaartistes, Ulrike whispers without a sound, her mouth twisting in anger as this memory of her mother pops unexpectedly into her mind. Had that been her last interaction with her mother?

Ulrike slumps, even though her posture doesn't change. Something inside her snaps, something stops supporting her. She looks at Rosa in the distance, her outlines just barely visible: mouth, a sort of a smile, the bump of her nose, plump breasts. There beyond reach are the arms where Ulrike had just been, the arms that do not exist any more. There is no stopping it. Her mother, her very own mother from years ago, pops back into her mind. The memory rolls over her like the terror before, completely and everywhere, but still different, because her mother from years ago was warm, her mother from years ago was beautiful, her mother from years ago was something completely different than the moooooother it was impossible to live with in the same flat, the same city, the same world. Her mother from years ago had smelled of an expensive nightgown woven by silk worms, soft and sweet. Her mother from years ago wrapped Ulrike under the covers, snuggled up next to her, and, in a voice that smelled of peppermint, hummed "*Schlafe, meine prinzessin, schlafe . . .*"

Out of old habit, Ulrike begins to sob. No tears come any more, so the weeping resembles vomiting on an empty stomach, without the pain caused by the bile. It is acrobatics for the face. Ugly, or at least far from beautiful. Embarrassing, not at all sympathetic. But what does it matter! Like Rosa, she also knows how to feel. And, like Rosa, she will be gone soon too. These women who dangle the dim lamp of reason in their dead fingers can continue developing their theories until the end of the world for all she cares.

Shlomith, Wlibgis, Nina, Polina, and Maimuna stare in fear as Ulrike's face contorts. There are differences of degree in their fear. There is a dash of irritation (Polina), a pinch of confusion (Nina), and a smidgen of curiosity (Shlomith). There is perhaps one stare in which no fear can be found: Maimuna's empty look of *Ça va bien*, which seems to underline the meaninglessness of it all. There is

Wlibgis's gaze, which contains bucket-loads of suffering, which admittedly could have been caused by her sickness, not the situation currently underway. Wlibgis had learned to be a person in suffering no later than in the hospital bed where she knew she would stay and which she had no chance of leaving healthy. And besides, suffering can become a second skin, a hardened leather, a mask that no longer even requires an illness. All that's needed is one lifelong disappointment . . . and repeated violence. And you can't just take off that mask. Not even if everyone around you yells in chorus, "Start LIVING, dear woman!" Suffering is better than emptiness, a pillow with a musty smell you can discern at a distance, and still you bury your face in it to stifle your sobs.

Ulrike has stopped crying.

Her mother from years ago hadn't existed for ages. So why waste the tears? Ulrike stiffens. The women stare at her like cows at an open pasture. Is it time to leave? Is the way open? And what if the "Oooon . . . " Ulrike had uttered had been enough, what if the change had already begun in her? What if she was about to begin to rock, to shake, to zigzag, then to sink, to sink *and* to fade?

Shlomith acts first. She lifts her hand and places it against Ulrike's, and it looks exactly as it should look, like hand holding, and that is enough. In this situation, that could be enough. Nodding, Shlomith encourages the others to follow after her: Let's form a circle.

So Maimuna clasps Ulrike's other, if possible even stiffer hand, Polina slaps her fingers against Maimuna's digits, Nina snatches Polina's arm, Wlibgis slides between Nina and Shlomith, and then the circle is closed around Rosa Imaculada's pale body.

Now each of them is stiff, tense like a bow. Shlomith glances at Ulrike: Yes? The others glance at Ulrike and Shlomith: Well? Ulrike nods and in a low voice begins to murmur *Oooo*, just as a yoga teacher murmurs "Oooo" as she begins to call the holy Pranava symbol with her larynx, with that Highest Holy Syllable vibrating the entire universe, the world soul, and Truth—in a word, Brahman—as she, with the students sitting before her also murmuring, awakens every slumbering corner of the bodily existence.

Except for Wlibgis, all of the women join in the utterance, one eagerly huffing, another more cautiously, voice cracking. Finally, they are doing something! Something like joy begins to bubble in one and all: perhaps they will soon be on Rosa Imaculada's heels!

Oooo . . . nnnnn . . .

But then no more: no "EI-ron". The end of the word simply won't spurt from them. No yell, no hiccup, no final syllable catching in the throat, no R vibrating softly or harshly. The women's lips remain rounded, as if someone has just snatched a sucker out of their mouths.

Plop.

And as if there wasn't enough to endure in all of this, a much greater PLOP crashes down, an end-of-the-world sort of PLOP, a PLOP that all women trying to become mothers feel inside if heart-breaking tragedy decides, for one reason or another, to activate its screeching machinery. Suddenly Nina rips her hands free of Polina and Wlibgis, and folds up. Not out of pain but out of knowledge, knowledge like the intuitive flash that pierces all expectant mothers when Things Are Not Right. That information comes straight from where every creature comes into the world and will continue to come. It comes from the incorruptible core of womanhood.

Nina knows, inside and out, through the darkest realms of consciousness: Little Antoine & Little Antoinette are no longer inside her.

TEN REASONS
WHY NINA WOULD HAVE BEEN AN
EXCELLENT MOTHER

Nº1. Pragmatism. Nina was usually a very pragmatic woman. Not at all melodramatic. A melodramatic woman would cut up all her husband's ties if she suspected him of cheating on her. A melodramatic woman would bake the shreds of tie into a loaf of bread and serve it to her husband. She would write a threatening message in nail polish on the bathroom tiles at precisely the height she anticipated his eyes landing in the morning when he staggered in to piss. She would get on the train and spend the night in an idyllic hotel in a nearby village. She would let her phone ring. She would pretend to be missing, maybe even dead. She would set her phone on silent and watch, nauseated and weeping even as she enjoyed seeing JEAN-PHILIPPE appear with his cheater face over and over on the display, obviously insane with worry. The hotel's pillow would soak through. The ring would come off her finger and fly in an arc from the balcony over the hotel entrance and into the decorative pond in front of the entrance. With the accuracy of a dart thrower, the ring would land in the middle of the waterlily arrangement, directly on the stone frog's outstretched waterfall tongue. *Touché!* But that melodramatic woman is not Nina. That woman is Jean-Philippe's former fiancé, who never would have become the mother of Jean-Philippe's children.

Nina was different. Of course she noticed all the same things women tend to notice. She was five months pregnant when she happened to catch a glimpse of an email whose content could be ambiguous, or maybe not. She packed a bag and traveled to her parent's house one hundred kilometers away, leaving a note on the table: *Deal with this and then tell me when the situation is under control again.* Nina knew how to keep a cool head at the right times. She focused on solutions.

N°2. Facing facts. Dear Jean-Philippe Pignard, the ball is entirely in your court. If you want a divorce, say so. Just one word and I'll start looking for a new flat. Jean-Philippe didn't want a divorce, though. Yet again. This was one of Nina's bravuras: through imperceptible moves, without making any noise, she got everything she wanted. Her tactics were not based on manipulation, psychological games, or blackmail. On the contrary, she only dealt in facts. Nina was a strong-willed woman from a family of strong-willed women. Facing facts took women in her family only milliseconds. If an ugly word was the most appropriate, they said it (e.g. her grandmother when Grandfather's love child turned up), calmly and without raising their voices (e.g. her aunt when the repulsive reason for her divorce had to be stated out loud in court); they listened to what others had to say and tried to summarize (e.g. the cousin when cases of chlamydia revealed utterly inappropriate cross-shagging in her group of friends); they didn't provoke or become provoked (e.g. her mother when her old, demented father began berating his daughter as a skinflint and a closet drunk—the latter accusation was also baseless). That was what the women in her family were like, and that was how she was too.

Which was why Nina boldly opened her mouth and let her mother, her grandmother, her aunt and her cousin do the talking: "Dear Jean-Philippe Pignard, the ball is entirely in your court," they all said in unison.

Jean-Philippe obediently cleaned up the mess he had caused. He picked up the phone and invited his wife, who was carrying Little Antoine & Little Antoinette, back home. Nina came, because these children were supposed to have a father, and their father was supposed to have a wife, and their mother was supposed to have a husband, and they were all supposed to have one flat bought with the

husband's family money on a linden-lined street five minutes walk
from a market square, where one could buy the world's best organic
marmalade made from White Transparent apples.

N°3. Apt situational assessments. When Nina appeared in fourth
position in the place which did not at that time have a name but
which everyone later, due to Polina's harangues, began to call, more
or less seriously, with joyful resignation or crushing gloom, "the
hereafter", she recognized quite quickly, after recovering from her
initial shock, that now, if ever, her organizational skills were needed.
In all her (dyed, but that isn't relevant now) platinum blond glory she
had popped up right in front of Shlomith and Polina, in the middle
of a heated argument, which was interrupted momentarily due to her
appearance. The women burst into spontaneous hurrahs as if the
Mother of God herself had descended into their midst, but their
enthusiasm quickly ebbed because Nina was as bemused as they
were. The arrival clearly had her own problems: she held her belly
with both hands while muttering something, *Il faut aller à l'hôpital,
vite, vite*, but this didn't interest the women in the slightest. There
were no hospitals or nurses here. Whatever the arrival had needed a
moment ago was irrelevant. It no longer had any significance.

So the interrupted argument began to perturb Shlomith again.
They hadn't belabored it completely, and unbelabored arguments
tended to return to the scene of the crime even more charged than
before, practically snapping their suspenders; you couldn't simply
spit them away along the road. Especially not here.

Nina didn't understand the slightest bit of the content of the
argument. The women's expressions were terrible. Shlomith and
Polina were entirely focused on each other. They would have made
low growls at one another if they hadn't had words to use. They
would have rushed at each other's throats like mongrel dogs if their
words had failed. But they didn't fail. English blasted from both of
their mouths, with a Slavic accent and without. Nina quickly understood that *she* was not the subject, had not been and would not be,
that *her* situation did not interest anyone, that no one would ever
help *her* again.

At this point our maternal candidate revealed another aspect of herself that was found on the list of Characteristics of Excellent Mothers: she was able to make quick situational assessments and change course. So Nina removed her hands from her stomach bulge and shook off her confusion and terror. She shook them off as naturally as a lifelong smoker taps ash from the end of a burning cigarette (Nina didn't smoke), like someone leaving for a party inconspicuously brushes the dandruff from the shoulder of a black blazer (Nina didn't have dandruff). She strained her senses to understand what these two enraged women's problem was. And, sure enough, they did have a problem, an extremely concrete problem, and the problem had a name: Rosa Imaculada.

Nina bent to one side, finally bringing into her field of vision the third woman, who had been behind the two adversaries. Arrival number three sat with legs bent, arms around her legs, face pressed to her knees. In a strained voice she muttered something like a lullaby and rocked back and forth like a lunatic. Nina called to the woman, but she didn't lift her eyes and only continued stubbornly rocking.

So was this the problem? How to stop the poor woman rocking? How to make eye contact with her, how to get her to quiet down?

And then, apparently not for the first time, Shlomith snapped: *ShutTHEfuckUPPPPPHHH!!!* And Nina wasn't sure, and Shlomith likely wasn't either, at whom that shout was directed: the Russian arguing for a soft approach and arguing aggressively against violence, or the Brazilian, who had unilaterally abandoned all contact with the outside world and chosen wailing as her method of communication. Perhaps Shlomith was bellowing at them both, perhaps also at herself, perhaps at the entire situation, which was, in a word, agonizing.

In any case, Shlomith's shout hung heavily over them like a wet sleeping bag with a school of dead herring rotting inside. Soon it would start to stink. Soon everything would be ruined for good. Soon Shlomith wouldn't be able to restrain herself any more and would begin shaking Rosa Imaculada by the shoulders, force her onto her back, and press her foot to her neck, and then nothing would be the same again.

Nina decided to act. Maternally. She pushed aside her own questions—their time would come—and the panic simmering in her
breast, which in Nina's case was also the type that can be pushed
aside: a convenient, compact panic, a pre-prepared microwave
dinner. Nina stood up and walked with the force of will of the women
of her family straight to Rosa. (Later, after the situation relaxed, Nina
realized that walking hadn't been quite so easy, that unfortunately
one had to learn to do it again here, like many other things.) Without
asking her leave, Nina's fingers began deftly to braid Rosa Imaculada's
enormous head of hair, and Rosa calmed down like a child calms
down when her mother's loving fingers stroke her scalp.

Shlomith and Polina glanced at each other in embarrassment.
Finally, as Nina was working on a seventh plait the thickness of her
pinkie finger, Shlomith straightened up and found her missing lead-
ership qualities: *We're so sorry you had to get involved in this dreadful
situation. What's your name, dear?*

N°4. The ability to melt with tenderness. Nina absolutely
looooved children! **N°5. Health.** There were no known hereditary
diseases in Nina's family line. **N°6. Secure finances.** Nina had understood to marry a man with money, old dignified money not new,
tipsy money, not Lamborghini money, and not even Chevrolet Bel
Air money, but more like Citroën Déesse money (and even that
sympathetic jalopy spent most of its time in the garage). In his youth,
Jean-Philippe had liked to hitchhike. Jean-Philippe gazed at the sun
while others like him fixated on Rolexes and Raymond Weils.
Wristwatches depressed Jean-Philippe. He did have one brand new
luxury watch called a Brighella, part of the Italian luxury brand
Bulgari's Commedia dell'Arte series. His parents had given it to Jean-
Philippe as a fortieth birthday present. It was partly a joke, but they
were thirty-five percent completely serious. They had decided that
their son had to have a watch, and they believed that this unique
contraption with its €370,000 price tag was sufficiently extraordinary
for their extraordinary first-born son.

"My son," Jean-Philippe's father intoned at the dinner table on the
sixth of January as he handed the leather watch box to the birthday

boy, "as you may remember from theatre history class, Brighella is a layabout who only works when his money runs out. Brighella loves to swindle people stupider than himself, amuse women, and play as much music as he can. Perhaps you recognize yourself in him?" Jean-Philippe's father burst into laughter, which his mother dutifully joined in on, and then grew serious again. "Each detail of the watch face was painted by hand using a microscope. After each layer of different colored paint, the face was placed in an oven to enamel. This watch may have been in the oven as many as fifty times! Every single tiny piece was made by hand, without regard for the labor time. And that isn't all. You can also bring the watch face to life by pulling this lever on the left. Look!" The father reached over the table and grabbed the watch from his son's hand. "You can make Brighella and his friends dance the polka, heh heee!"

The hero at the center of the watch, Brighella, in a white suit sitting at the base of a set of stairs, jerkily raised his hand, which held the bow of a violin. A shrill jingling began. Brighella began shaking the violin back and forth, lifting it closer to his chin and then lowering it again. A woman in a white dress sitting higher up on the steps began to pluck a harp. In the right lower corner of the clock face sat a man, also in white clothing. He began nodding his head and counting time with his hand. Between the harpist and the timekeeper crouched a strange oddity resembling a turtle with a harlequin checked cape on its hunched back. The turtle man twitched his head in a nod, chin up, chin down. Those were all the clock face's animated parts, three hands and two heads in jerky motion.

Masks covered the upper parts of the faces. Everyone wore foolish headgear, like collapsed chef's hats or crumpled nightcaps. The only woman in the group bore a sort of Valkyrie helmet on her locks. Really, when you thought about it carefully, the characters looked more like *Star Wars* heroes than commedia dell'arte figures. They were situated on the imposing white steps of a Renaissance-style mansion, but the view out the window was an entirely different, almost futuristic scene, some kind of space station with rockets prepared to lift off. The numbers on the watch face didn't follow normal watch face logic (so much for practicality and usability!), instead resembling more a countdown. Along the left edge of the watch face near Brighella's lifted violin bow snaked the number series 60, 50, 40, 30, 20, 10, 00. Did this thing only measure one minute?

The watch was butt ugly. Even uglier was its six-figure price, which is worth mentioning again: €370,000. For that you could have bought 190 water tanks (at 8,000 liters a piece) for use in an emergency. Or 1,947 family tents (at 16 m²). Or 74,000 warm blankets. Or 411,111 measles vaccinations. "There are a total of twenty-four Commedia dell'Arte watches in existence, one of which now belongs to you, Jean-Philippe," the birthday boy's father said in conclusion. Then he winked. "Now you can't miss the last train any more! In future you'll always be able to make it home in time to your little Ninjuška!"

N°7. Optimal body structure. Nina had ideal birthing hips, which also appealed to most hetero men. In Jean-Philippe's words: *Plus que fantastique!* N°8. Efficiency. Nina could operate on four to six hours of sleep even if she only enjoyed them in two-hour stretches. N°9. Imagination. Without this you can't be a Good Mother. At most you can be middling but more likely bad. In the modern multiple choice world, an unimaginative mother is no better than a chain-smoking mother, a boozer mother, an absentee mother, a mother who uses the belt, a profligate mother, or, worst of all, a scene-scripting drama queen mother (which Jean-Philippe's previous fiancé doubtless would have become), who believes her home is a stage and her children paying customers, expecting to receive applause and roses after every show. An unimaginative mother fails to offer her children *the best opportunities*. She operates on autopilot. She glides along in one rut, blinded by the speed, and never sticks her head out the window.

Nina had a singular imagination that always activated in difficult situations. It was a minor miracle, at least if you consider her first and third characteristics, Nos. 1 ("pragmatism") and 3 ("apt situational assessments"), which are counterforces to imagination. Imagination springs from disorganization and failed situational assessments. Life doesn't conform to the ideal and heaps obstacles in the wanderer's way. Imagination is an adaptation. As the species improves, it will disappear. In three hundred thousand years, no one will remember Proust, Nerval, Pascal, Brecht, Luther, Puccini, Rosa Luxemburg, Wittgenstein, Louise Bourgeois, Paganini, or Sappho. They simply aren't needed. In the future, all scientific and artistic struggling will only weaken the species.

Nina was an almost perfect woman. All of her sharp edges had been smoothed away. However, the world around her was not on the same level with her perfection. It was illogical and capricious, cruel, and sometimes even ugly. Nina's mild temperament and maternally oriented, well-incubated Words of Sense simply weren't enough in all situations.

Now and then, to everyone's surprise, Nina's hibernating imagination awoke and lifted its drowsy head from beneath the covers. It found focus. It found the solution that no one else had thought of. Take one example. Let us return to the series of events currently underway. Nina is doubled over, holding her belly with both hands, bellowing like a lioness. The women have gathered around her. They flail frantically without a clue as to what to do. Now Nina collapses on her back. Now Nina whimpers. Now Nina is in such a bad state that she must be helped instantly!

Surprisingly, Wlibgis makes the first move. She has a son herself, a thirty-year-old good-for-nothing, so she knows something about pregnancy and childbearing too. From being in the hospital, she's also used to the idea of turning and tugging and rolling a person during washing; lifting them from bed to bed using a sheet, or easing them to the side when the bedpan needs to be changed. Wlibgis doesn't hesitate to take hold of Nina's stylish maternity shirt, which has smocking around the stomach region. Unapologetically she reaches and makes a modicum of contact with the fabric. The stretchy rayon moves. She flexes her fingers and begins to pull. Nina's shirt hem rises, revealing as it does the white mound of her belly, which is adorned with an out-turned belly button and the exploding purple lightning of stretch marks. Based on this quick examination, nothing appears amiss. This is how a pregnant woman's belly looks. A big raw bun.

Wlibgis waves Ulrike over closer, points to Nina's turquoise trousers, and makes off-off gestures. Ulrike understands: it's her turn. With her fingers, which have retained slightly more feeling than the others', she takes hold of the luxury fabric, the cotton satin, and begins with two hands to roll down the front panel, which is made of sturdy stretch jersey. When the trousers are at her ankles, Maimuna comes and on her own initiative lifts and bends Nina's legs. She grabs the pure white panties and pulls: Mamabel Basic Maxi, in the gusset a panty liner, on the panty liner a tiny rust yellow stain. Nothing else.

Nina's vulva is also very clean. No bloody mucus and no one coming out either, head or toes first. Her inner labia fold nicely, slightly asymmetrically. The clitoris is covered by a small hood with a slightly teasing lift, and a halo of fine hair covers the mons veneris. Wlibgis, Shlomith, and Polina stare, wistful at the sight. But Ulrike can't take her eyes from Nina's stomach. A skin-colored mound like that attached to a human, and it's supposed to be natural! Where does it all go once the birth is done? Does it collapse like a soufflé, its dreams disturbed by opening the oven door at the wrong time . . . ?

Shlomith carefully places her gaunt hand on Nina's belly and smiles. The other women nod, murmuring encouragingly: the babies are absolutely safe. But they're wrong. Nina knows better. She's stopped wailing, because that's the kind of person she is. In Nina's head, someone has already pressed Rewind, then Play.

And so it went: they took each other by the hand and tried to recite the magic word together, but they couldn't reach the end. Their mouths were open in confusion, and just at that moment some power inside of Nina shifted slightly. It was no normal physical sensation, no complaint of the internal organs: her stomach, lungs, and heart had all long been silent. The babies had been quiet too, but she could almost bear that, because Nina believed (ultimately perhaps stronger than anyone) in the theory called "death". That was the only sensible explanation when she inspected the issue from a sufficient number of viewpoints. However, the babies had still been inside her. Of that she was sure. She was their tomb. That thought was macabre but also strangely bewitching. They were all of the same substance, one and the same after-worldly dust, and even so something continued—death did not mark the end of EVERYTHING.

The rainbow shimmering soap bubble burst when that power, which only made itself known by moving, shifted inside Nina. It was as if it lurched to the side, leaving in its place an emptiness, the most phantom of phantom pain. Then Nina knew: Little Antoine and Little Antoinette were gone. She had ceased to carry them.

Nina's imagination burst into flower amidst that catastrophic crisis following the babies' alleged disappearance. The women stare at Nina, almost angrily. This woman with the distended belly is insisting adamantly that her babies are gone. Are they supposed to believe that? At this, their whole miserable world, stitched together with assiduous chatter and good will, begins to crumble. There are far too many unanswered questions—above all, why? Why are they here, why has Rosa Imaculada faded away from them, and how can fetuses simply disappear from a womb? Why hasn't the prospective mother surrounding the babies disappeared with her children? In general: where are the boundaries of transition and dislocation? If they are dead, they are strangely untouched, uninjured. They are wearing their clothes (or at least some of them), and nothing much else. And when they really start thinking about all of this . . .

Shlomith lets her tongue sing again. Why, for example, hadn't the bed the dead person had been lying on come with her, the white mattress the corpse lay on, with its purple-red knee joints, its blotches, its livid palms? Why not the floor that touched the bed where the small, withered body lay, the corpse with the purple back and its purple knee joints? Why not the whole building connected seamlessly to the floor, first one wall, then the second, then the third, and finally the fourth, the ceiling, the corridors, the other levels, and the stairs? Why not the whole hospital where all the incurable patients are brought, the ones for whom nothing more can be done? Why not all the sick? Why not the whole city, the whole country, for example Holland (for some reason, mute Wlibgis is Shlomith's favorite example)? Why not the whole continent, Europe, and the waters that led to America? Why not the whole world?

Why? Why? Why?

Nina is unique in that she has never surrendered to that line of thought or anything similar. Not even out of peer pressure. Just as she doesn't laugh if she isn't really amused, she also doesn't go hysterical if she doesn't see any cause for hysteria.

Nina knows that too much thinking is harmful. That simplicity is beautiful. The way to calm a rebellious child howling over the agony of existence and tormenting her parents with whys is through creative diversion. And this is the method that Nina now intuitively adopts to soothe her afterworldly sisters as they approach the brink of mass hysteria. Suddenly, interrupting everything, she says, *We're going to build a world. Right now. Right here.*

With the eyes of her soul, that gifted platinum blond *fée blanche* saw in a vision how they would all soon be living in a cute little house where it would be spring outside on a lane lined with linden trees. Or cherries! Why not cherries? If someone wanted a seaside boulevard, that was available too. All they needed was a dash of imagination. Let each make her world as she saw fit!

And it isn't long before all the women are hard at work building their home. Peace and good will reign over the land, once again thanks to Nina. Mothers, especially *excellent mothers*, have a special talent for sweeping big questions under the rug and redirecting the attention of children confused by too much asking. At this task they are more imaginative than anyone else in the world.

N°10. The gift of love. At times it seemed that Jean-Philippe loved his old leather jacket, with the holes worn in the elbows, more than his wife. His feelings toward people were of a combustible nature, alternating between flames and ashes. Symptomatic of this was the way Jean-Philippe took it as his right to enjoy freedom more than was appropriate to his class. However, far-seeing Nina understood that it was best to give her husband a long leash, to a certain point. That point, which was frequently tested, was located unambiguously in the genital area.

Despite it all, Nina loved her husband, for better or for worse. She had a gift for loving that not all do, just as not all have perfect pitch or a poker face. Nina sensed that the gift of love would burst into full flower after her children were born, and so she, with ant-like diligence and determination, arranged the surrounding conditions to be as favorable as possible for the maternal love that awaited her. Nina and Jean-Philippe had an excellent marital contract. They had 220 affectionately decorated square meters in an awfully beautiful house on a lane lined with lindens, and ten thousand euros of IVF babies on the way—love was one thing they wouldn't have lacked.

THEN THEY MADE A HOME

Nina was right. They need a home and walls around them as protection. Space is unbearable. White causes blindness. White will drive you mad. Another person can also drive you mad, even if there are more than two people, even if there are seven people, six for each to look at in turn. So they need a kitchen. The heart of a home. Sitting around the campfire is beginning to feel insecure; walls behind their backs would do them good.

But where will they get walls? What will be the construction materials? Each has her clothes but not much else. Nothing beyond the odd little thing that happened to come with them when they left; something forgotten in the bottom of a pocket. So they start with the easiest thing and empty their pockets. They all have pockets except for Wlibgis, who is wearing ugly, green hospital pajamas. The pajamas have faded to barely discernible vertical stripes. Really they are prison pajamas. Wlibgis had harbored a bitter hatred for the hospital pajamas when she'd had time to hate, when thinking the garments were dreadful and the buttons most dreadful of all made sense. Yes, those big, white pancakes with their four holes were the worst. Was anything more tasteless than hospital pajama buttons? Sitting on her hospital bed, Wlibgis had obediently fastened them from the bottom up, obediently but angry. "Is this the best they can do?" As if the designer had intentionally made the ugliest possible poison-green clothing so the patients wouldn't begin to think too much of themselves, secretly becoming prideful and growing lazy as a result of the high-quality, tender care they received.

On the day she arrived at hospital, Wlibgis folded her jeans, sweater, and socks into a nice pile, which was placed in a cabinet with her purse, wallet, and house keys, along with her pocket calendar that contained a picture of her good-for-nothing son's charming daughter, Melinda, age five. Once the flowers stopped coming, she asked for that picture to be placed on her table. (Have the rest of you noticed this? People bring you flowers if you're just visiting, if you're on the mend and returning to the land of the living. And they bring flowers to graves and for caskets. But never for the dying. Whenever a person is dying, as we all are when it comes right down to it, and ceases simply to convalesce, when she begins actively, sometimes even hurriedly, to die, she stops receiving flowers. Flowers suddenly become obscene. *Memento mori*—that is their nature, being of the same withering substance as the loved one who has now become, to use one popular euphemism, a *fighter to the end*.) "Would you like to go home?" came the cautious question. Do you want to go home to die? But Wlibgis didn't; she didn't want to die alone. She didn't want to die at all! But she had to die. The cancer was everywhere.

At that point the green hospital pajamas stopped bothering her. They just were, like things just are: the moon and the sun in the sky, worms in the ground, and birds in the air or on the branches of trees or attacking a meat pasty dropped on the ground. The pajamas were swapped for identical, clean ones as needed. The nurses did the buttons, because Wlibgis couldn't any more, and they always fastened the middle one first. It was the hub, positioned into its stitched, oval hole before tackling the others. It was the central switch, a touch of which closed the patient into her shirt, just so, and then the two below and the two above.

There was Wlibgis with her cancer, properly buttoned and enclosed and well off in every way. Secretly the nurses hoped that the juice splashing would stop, that Ms. Wlibgis would carefully sip her drink with a straw and swallow everything she sipped, that trails of juice wouldn't run down her chin onto her shirt, that Ms. Wlibgis would urinate in her diaper, that Ms. Wlibgis would have as little diarrhea as possible. They hoped she would sleep. That the morphine would

help. That death would take her away. Because at this point, life was
only suffering! And that cute little child, Melinda. She came with her
blue-ish mother to visit her grandmama. In her reedy voice the girl
sang "*Aan d'oever van de snelle vliet*" to her grandmother, and why
not? Singing is never wasted in the terminal ward.

But Wlibgis doesn't have pockets in her hospital pajamas.
Everything, absolutely everything she had once owned had been left
in that other world, in the cabinet at the hospital, in her home, or her
useless son's home—some of her things were there too. Although
truthfully they usually only spent a short time there before continuing
their journey. One rather valuable pocket watch did just such a disappearing trick. Her son had threatened to take it to a pawn shop if she
didn't give him a "loan". And so she had given him a "loan". If some
memory of her father remained, just one, it could be this beautiful
pocket watch with its patina of time, which her father had always
taken from his suit pocket to check the time, to ensure that the watch
was running, that he himself was on time. That masterwork of antique
craftsmanship was, let it be said, a complete contrast to Jean-Philippe's
idiotic Brighella watch, which remained, quite understandably, in its
leather box (put simply, Jean-Philippe was ashamed of it). Wlibgis's
father's watch was old enough, however, that each day it lost about
fifteen minutes. Her father was perfectly capable of living with this
fact, though. In all aspects of his life he took it into account, standing
with his shoes on when others were still eating breakfast.

Wlibgis never saw the watch again.

In her own opinion, Wlibgis has given all she is going to give for
the construction of the house. She has given her orange fire-wig,
which will of course also become the heart of the new home. That is
enough. And the dying games can end now too! Wlibgis is utterly fed
up with them. Certainly she participated, listening and nodding,
pretending to be interested, but really the whole thing disgusted her.
What sense was there in making that sullen teenager gloat over her
own end? Was it a big surprise that the girl wanted to believe she was
killed out of jealousy? Me, I alone, me, the center of the world. Men
mad with passion around every finger!

Wlibgis had never been in a relationship. A man's stiff cock had entered her a total of three times. Each time it had happened with a different piece of equipment, and none of them had been an experience she would have felt like boasting about afterwards. By accident the last one led to a son, and that was where the game ended, the role play in which she was encouraged to engage by a certain feminist group that proclaimed carnivalistic love. She had participated in some lectures a few times in the early 1980s at the urging of one of her friends at the time. The game proceeded according to a specific pattern. Wlibgis got mildly drunk, alone, and then put on clothes that would make her own mother not recognize her, or, as Wlibgis said to her reflection in the mirror, "If Mom saw me now, she'd roll over in her grave." Wlibgis was embarrassed. She felt like a transvestite, a lump that had fallen to earth from outer space, with flirty lips and fluttery eyelashes painted on it. She put polish on the squarish nails of her fingers with their swollen joints, and after each smeared, roughly nail-shaped blood-red stroke she took a swig of cognac and allowed the color to dry, until all ten fingers glittered like the flames of hell, and then she was ready to go.

Wlibgis's lugubrious mien, leaning against the bar sipping a dry martini, miraculously enough aroused a few representatives of the opposite sex. The melancholy emanating from her, the garish clown make-up and appropriately muzzy, uncritical gaze actually drew several contestants. Perhaps it is not completely wrong to say that on these three occasions, when Wlibgis forced herself to go on the hunt, she had her pick of men.

The role play ended, and then came the punishment, the worst possible: a son who hated his mother and a mother who hated her son. And as if Wlibgis had angered all the powers of the cosmos and upset the balance of the entire universe—to top it all off, a cancer grew in her throat.

And what was she left with? An orange-red wig that she doesn't even get to use any more because these women need a campfire, god damn it, these women need a "heart" for their home. Without a wig, with her pickle-shaped head, her lashless eyes, and her hairless brows, she looks so depressing that it is a veritable miracle that only Rosa Imaculada has thought to dissolve away.

When Wlibgis chose her wig, she truly had no idea what it would end up being used for. But had the wig salesperson sensed it? When Wlibgis lost her own thick, auburn hair (it fell out soon after the chemotherapy began), with a scarf on her head she slipped into a shop whose address she had received from a nurse. The shop had a unique feel. It wasn't on account of the numerous plastic heads or the false hair on them, and it wasn't because of the slightly musty, herbal scent (sage? thyme?)—it was due solely to the owner of the shop, who was an altogether extraordinary lady. First of all she was the kind of woman whose age was nearly impossible to guess. Forty or sixty, it was hard to say. Her skin was smooth and clear but simultaneously ancient in some way that was difficult to define. Her black hair looked plastic, her bangs were short, and she had no eyebrows, or they had been completely plucked away; thin violet lines had been drawn in their place. Her eyes were large, and the Cupid's bow of her lips was painted with exaggerated sharpness; it matched the sharp, narrow line of her jaw and the violet eyebrows. A face like that should have had a plumb frame beneath it, a body with military bearing, but no, the thin (of course thin!), nearly gaunt woman was not at all august. Her body was not particularly worthy of her unique face. She stood slouching before her counter, or, if you considered it from another angle, that slouching demeanor completed her face, strained and ready to bolt, providing it with an appropriate counterweight. Maybe one of her legs was shorter than the other. When she walked up to Wlibgis from behind the counter, she walked unevenly, limping, slightly dragging one leg.

Let us call her "Owner K". Owner K. looked Wlibgis straight in the eyes, which darted nervously under the scarf that surrounded her pale face, and said, "Did you come for this?" Then she pointed back and up to the left, where the orange-red hair sat coquettishly on a mannequin head with heavy make-up. "No-o," Wlibgis managed to say. She had just had her first throat operation, and the radiation had destroyed her salivary glands, but she still had her vocal chords and was able to utter that dry, gravelly "no-o"; actually a very distressed "no-o". No orange wig! Did she, a fifty-eight-year-old woman, look like she was going to run down the street with an orange wig billowing in the wind?

Wlibgis irritably, almost demonstratively, began trying on other wigs. First her own color, an auburn bob cut. Strangely, it didn't suit her at all. She looked like she had a bowl cut. Blond curls made her look like an old wino, black hair like a witch, the various shades of brown: all just as unnatural and ugly. The hair was high quality, Owner K. assured her, skillfully handmade, which was why the prices were so high, but there was a wig for each head, and she could see that now was a time for setting aside prejudices and trying that orange. Holding back her tears, Wlibgis took the wig being offered and put it on her pickle-shaped head.

And behold: it fitted as if it were made for her. And it even made her gray skin glow! Her lashless eyes were no longer pale, they were steely; they had a depth they'd never had before, and Wlibgis knew: this wig was hers. She took ten seconds to poll her attitude. Should she allow those three incidents of fornication and the shameful details surrounding them to spill out into the open: the smudged mascara, the smeared lipstick, and the scratchy stubble? Should she allow those shoving penises to come and shove into her, in her memories, again and again . . . ? Or was this wig something different? Was it just a beautiful red, well-fitting wig, and nothing more?

Wlibgis gave in. Joy filled her when she turned in front of the large mirror with a smaller mirror in her hand, looking from the side and back and every angle. She smiled. She simply couldn't help smiling. "I knew it instantly," Owner K. exclaimed but not at all in a scolding way. She was overjoyed too. She had a professional eye for this sort of thing, and she saw as soon as this woman stepped through the door that she needed a wig for her sorrows. The agony that lay in her face was the sort that one could only survive with a healthy dose of bright orange.

Owner K. was satisfied. For once, a customer consented to see the truth about herself! It was a good sign. A sign of life. Some, you see, couldn't give up their illusions even with advanced cancer. They had decided that a white cloud of curls suited them, even though they weren't rosy-cheeked princesses any more; they were pale, too thin, or too swollen mortals. They spent a fortune on the wrong hair and vowed to themselves that they would get used to it and were almost hurt when Owner K. told them that the hair should feel like their own instantly. They didn't believe it. Injured pride shone in their eyes as they asked Owner K. in cold, tense tones to box up the wrong wig for them. They would pull their hat or scarf or hood tight on their bald or almost hairless head and slip out—KLING!—and decide not to practice with their new hair until they got home. But some of them came again. And Owner K. was kind enough to allow them to trade the wrong wig for the right one.

Owner K. congratulated Wlibgis heartily for her correct choice: "It's like it was made for you, even if you didn't believe it at first. You know, a person's face really does change when they experience a tragedy. It leaves marks that anyone who looks carefully can see. I saw them immediately on you. I could see that you need color. Color won't hurt you; it'll make you a woman again. If you'll allow me to say so, you sparkled. Ten hard years fell away all at once."

Wlibgis paid and wasn't the slightest bit offended by Owner K.'s words, which in some other situation might have sounded intrusive, and so they were. But Owner K. knew she spoke the truth, as always, and she also knew that her customer understood this time. So Wlibgis tripped lightly out of the shop—KLING!—and couldn't help but twirl her new orange hair one more time in front of the window—goodbye!

Wlibgis's fire wig becomes the heart of the kitchen. A wordless decision, Shlomith's gentle nod: *This is our kitchen.* Polina dramatically removes her sable fur: *Let this be the couch.* After this each woman dumps out the contents of her pockets. Total: two crumpled tissues, a silver ring that Hanno had bought for Ulrike, a ring that didn't quite fit (Hanno imagined Ulrike's fingers were more slender than they are—they are slender, but not *that* slender; her ring finger diameter is seventeen and a half millimeters), a frayed piece of string, a two-euro coin, three ten-cent coins, one fifty cent, one dollar, one greatcoat button, a lighter and some shreds of tobacco (Ulrike tries to strike the lighter wheel, but it only scrapes without sparking, and no flame appears even though the reservoir is still halfway full); a mobile phone (also Ulrike's, from the large back pocket of her corduroy trousers)—"1 missed call", but the buttons don't work, the phone won't do anything no matter what she pushes, and the phone clock has also stopped at the same mysterious moment as Ulrike's watch: 21:03—a wine cork that is red on one side, which is Polina's, along with lip balm, a slightly rusted flat snake forged of iron, which is Maimuna's totem animal, and a colorful superball you can fit in your fist, which is Shlomith's. The pockets of Shlomith's long black caftan are like the pouch of a Tasmanian tiger or the beak of a pelican: you can find all sorts of things in them; in theory, half the world could have fitted in there, but now all they find are the super ball, a measuring tape, and a small pipette bottle. Was that what poor Shlomith had used to eat her daily meal, one drip into her mouth at a time? And what would it have been, tepid broth or only water?

The women donate their possessions to the common pile next to the wig and the sable fur sofa. *Do I need to give away my gold teeth?* Shlomith mutters, but only Polina understands the joke, and it doesn't amuse her in the slightest. Wlibgis smiles in satisfaction and waits for even bigger sacrifices: disrobing. Soon she won't be the only one who has been forced to give up something too personal, something that has functioned as a cover for something esthetically indecorous. Few women pranced around in society with their heads shaved completely bald. There was that beautiful Irish singer, who had a symmetrical face, doe eyes, and a perfectly shaped skull, and there was that athletic actor who killed space creatures. But most of them needed hair much more than breasts. Without their hair, eyelashes, and eyebrows, they looked like death's own. People averted their gazes and wished they didn't exist. And soon they wouldn't. Soon they would all die. All except her, Wlibgis. She hadn't died. Of all the miserable denizens of the terminal ward, she alone had avoided death. She had been promised a deep, blue sleep and eternal peace, and what had she received? A bright, white endlessness, constant arguing and hullabaloo. Where was her death?

Wlibgis's downturned lower lip, the smothering of her initial good mood under a somber blanket of disappointment, goes unnoticed by everyone. Nina is caught up in her work, and everyone else is enjoying watching her. She places all the objects in a half circle in front of the wig like a fireguard. Even the used tissues she sets out with care, because everything has value. Then it is time for the base layer. *Clothing off!* Nina cries. The clothes are to become the walls, the boundaries of the rooms, and boundaries are what they need now, because without boundaries a person becomes a panoply of pirouetting panic. Like a child who gets everything she wants. For whom no verbal edifice of opposition is erected.

Wlibgis, who now stares at Nina's belly as she kneels, had known even before her son was born how *not* to act with children. The lines have to be drawn clearly. She raised her son with this knowledge as her guide, although Wlibgis found it was difficult on her own. Without a companion she had to say NO with the force of two people. She had to set herself (sometimes quite literally) crosswise to the little hoodlum. You *do not* go there. You *do not* touch this. You *do not* do that. The prohibitions never had any effect. Wlibgis screamed herself hoarse yelling NO NO NO, and her son just threw himself against her with all the force of a little boy, then of a larger, sixty-kilo youth, and then a young, gangly adult. What had gone wrong? Her ancient, now rather hoarse NO worked even more poorly in the final years than when the boy had been two, three, five, seven, eleven, fifteen, and twenty years old. Wlibgis didn't know how to say a "no" as a suggestion to another adult who was as stupid as could be and utterly at the mercy of evil. He just continued crossing all the lines, and she got the bruises. His requests for money were accompanied by a twist of her arm. When he went to prison, all she felt was an astonishingly deep sense of relief.

But because Wlibgis was from an upstanding family, the boy must have taken after his father. Whom Wlibgis didn't know at all. What kind of profile could she draw of a man who had wanted to lick the soles of her feet? Who had wanted to take her in the bath after being urinated on?

When her son was in prison, Wlibgis gradually worked up the courage to go out in the yard to smoke. The move from the corner of the stove, out from under the range hood, first to the kitchen window, then to the balcony, and finally out under the maple, took time. But in the spring, when she finally stood under the nearly leafless branches, under bursting flower clusters, utterly ignorant of the exceptional versatility of this noble tree, she felt a wondrous triumph. (Everyone knows about maple syrup, but how many have tried maple soap? This palmatisect deciduous tree is now considered, for good reason, to belong to the family *Sapindaceae*, the soapberry trees. So in addition to sweet latex, or sap, the maple also produces bitter, frothing sponids, which in accordance with their name are excellent saponificants, soaping reaction agents.) Although unfortunately her son didn't receive a life sentence, she would have at least half a year to puff away out in the fresh air.

So Wlibgis stood under the maple and smoked her menthol cigarette with pleasure. The skin around her lips had turned into a wrinkled meat pie, and her mouth had tapered to match the kiss of a cigarette filter; without a cigarette her mouth was utterly orphaned.

And then a deadly cancer grew in her throat. She had one operation, then another, and yet a third. First they destroyed her salivary glands, then she lost her vocal chords, and finally most of her larynx was taken out. They made a repulsive hole in her throat, and Wlibgis was given a speech prosthetic, a big black tube that resembled a giant dog whistle. The prosthesis was connected to a black cotton string that slid around her neck, and then supposedly she would be able to talk again just so long as she took the time to practice patiently with the device.

At first Wlibgis thought she wouldn't bother. She didn't want to speak another word. Was she going to talk to Lisbet next door? Lisbet often imposed herself on Wlibgis under the maple tree, coming to "trade news" as the saying went. But they never traded anything, because without exception Lisbet always just launched into the same

long, meandering sentence about her own wonderful son and
Wlibgis's terrible one. Let's call them "Nicholas" and "Petrus". When
Lisbet opened her mouth, Nicholas and Petrus seemed to neutralize
each other, so dreadful was the former, so marvelous was the latter.
Once Lisbet had squeezed out her sentence, nothing was left for
Wlibgis to say. She completely agreed with Lisbet about her own son.
But what of it? She already knew that Petrus, who had the same
appealing good looks as the late politician Pim Fortuyn, never made
a ruckus in the stairwell and never screamed through the mail slot so
loud that the whole corridor echoed.

"My son is in prison now," Wlibgis once tried to say, but Lisbet,
unsurprisingly, took this in a different direction than Wlibgis had
hoped. "When your son comes back, he'll be even more dangerous
than before," Lisbet said with a sigh and then sucked on her cigarette.
"I'll have to talk to Petrus about this. He can come help us." And what
would Petrus do? Run Nicholas off with his belt? Slam the junkie up
against the wall of the building by his collar? Drag him down to the
cellar and kill him?

They stubbed out their cigarettes, turned around, walked to the
stairwell, and squeezed into the same small lift. No, Lisbet was no
reason for Wlibgis to want to learn to use the speech prosthesis.

But there was little Melinda. Lovely, bright-eyed Melinda with her
hare-brained imagination and her W's she said in place of R's.
Melinda's stories could always make Wlibgis's wrinkled meat-pie
mouth spread in a smile, and she would shed tears of joy as she
laughed hoarsely. Then Melinda would giggle too since Grandmama
had blessed her silly idea with her laugh. Perky ears, tiny pink glasses
absurdly askew, freckled pug nose, face so plump you could eat it up.
To her, Wlibgis still wanted to be able to say, "Oh, you dear silly
sugarplum," and all the love-filled variations of this theme: "bitsy-
boo", "doodlekins", "honey giggle-bunny".

Really, if you looked at the situation from the perspective of Fate,
the girl was *her* real child. Melinda was meant just for her in every
way. The girl's mother had to give birth to her, of course, and Wlibgis's
son was a necessary intermediary as well, whose gene map carried

Melinda's assembly instructions from the start. Without him, there would be no Melinda, and so Wlibgis could more or less tolerate his existence. Fortunately he had the good sense to stay far away from Melinda. In his typical traitorous style, he left the girl to her mother, who at least tried to stay clean. And because of Melinda, Wlibgis wanted to help her mother. Wasn't this enough reason to fight? Wasn't this sufficient grounds to practice with that stupid dog whistle?

Thank God she could still sputter through that hole in her throat, through the speech prosthesis, syllable by syllable, letter by letter, her reedy, wavering, jerky robot sentence, *G-r-a-n-d-m-a-m-m-a. l-o-v-e-s. y-o-u. s-o. m-u-c-h. l-i-t-t-l-e. M-e-l-i-n-d-a.* It came out misshapen, interrupted by phlegmy intakes of breath, and completely exhausted Wlibgis, but regardless of the technical performance, it was as true as true could be.

Nina finishes arranging the objects. The fireguard is handsome, with all manner of shapes. There is a ball, a ring, and a cylinder. There are rectangles, creases, and shapelessness. Nina shoots upright and begins resolutely to undress. The women obediently follow her example, all except Wlibgis, who believes that the order to disrobe does not apply to her.

Showing no shyness at all, Maimuna simply pulls her yellow dress off in one motion. The dress has frills on the bodice and the hem, and under the breast is a beautiful series of pleats; but at the waist and seat the fabric is too loose, almost shapeless, until it falls with its flowing frills toward the ankles. Then slender Maimuna is in her underwear. Suddenly she places her hands modestly over her vulva, although it isn't even bare, and waits for the others.

Shlomith slithers out of her caftan in a series of complicated motions. First she pulls both arms inside the dress and then begins to scrape the garment off from within. She crouches and disappears completely, including her head, into the recesses of the fabric, but her limbs continue their work. The fabric bulges here and there, quite ominously, as she moves. No one can help wondering what will appear from the black sack once she is done. The wizened wrists that peeked through the sleeves and the thin neck that protruded from the top didn't bode well, not to mention the legs, a withered horse collar.

Finally Shlomith slowly begins to roll up the caftan from the hem. Everyone stares. No hint of discretion. There are the hip bones protruding, the bottom like a serving tray, no buttocks at all. The genital region under the panties is sunken. The kneecaps form two asymmetric lumps, from which the stick-like thighs grow diagonally up like stalks from a tuber, leaving between them a gap a throwing hammer could pass through. The shins fall straight down like boiled spaghetti.

Now, when the whole body is visible, the feet look like enormous caricatures, just like the large fingers and shovel hands that straighten the dress. On the left wrist is an amorphous, black tattoo. Blue veins marble the entirety of the delicate, white skin, and fuzz covers it like the chick of a sandwich tern. All bones out, on display like an educational model, Mrs. Skin & Bones constructed with anatomical precision.

Shlomith is only a hanging display that has stayed upright through sheer strength of will. Or stayed and stayed. And now she is here too. She probably dieted her heart away. In the hospital, Wlibgis had seen other carcasses like this. In ward six, and in the hospital cafe. Tremulous specters, all owl eyes and wispy hair. A fleshless nose, two gaping nostrils, dried craters under cheek bones. But the mouth was the most dreadful. It was disproportionately large compared to the rest of the face, a brazenly useless hole. It was ghastly to watch as they tried to gnaw the pieces of bread they bought to accompany their coffee, as they rolled the crumbs around endlessly in their mouths, and finally, after losing the battle once again, spat the dough plug into a serviette.

Hunger might go away but not the need for nourishment. When the women (they were usually women) stopped eating, their bodies ate away at their muscles, brains, and thoughts. And what was left of them? An empty gaze. Slow, lethargic movements and careful sitting (since they easily broke themselves on benches, tables, and even their own bones). That was what was left of them. If they didn't know how to stop, they finally broke down under the breast and to the left. So it goes: the resting pulse slows, the heart sometimes pumping below fifty beats per minute: bradycardia. Blood flow decreases, blood pressure falls, the heart muscles contract. Starvation and dehydration lowers mineral levels in the body and decreases body fluid flows, which has a devastating effect on blood sodium values. Vital minerals—calcium, magnesium, potassium, and phosphate—dissolve poorly, leading to an electrolyte imbalance. The body's internal electrical currents go wrong, disturbing the heart's normal rhythm. The heart stops. Death arrives.

Heart, oh heart! You are the last to betray us, but when you do, we've reached the end!

According to all logic, Shlomith has now reached paradise, a place where she can never gain a gram. So is she happy? She doesn't look that way. There she is straightening her caftan, buried in her big cloud of curls, folded like a pocketknife, occasionally glancing around suspiciously as if to ensure that the other women are concentrating on their own clothing, not her disfigured body.

Wlibgis, who has been staring at Shlomith greedily, quickly averts her eyes, slightly embarrassed. She sweeps from her mind the skeletal princesses of ward six and the incomprehensibility that some maniac would put herself in that state on purpose. Instead she looks to Nina and lets her gaze rest there for a turn.

Nina has already been undressed once when her enormous, supposedly babyless stomach and lower half were inspected. Now she is almost naked, in her Mamabel Basic Maxi panties and sturdy, but not at all marmish bra. At first Nina had thought the bra and panties could stay on, but because Shlomith doesn't have a bra (or breasts), along with Maimuna and presumably Wlibgis (who still stands sullenly in her hospital clothing; why doesn't she begin undressing like the others?), having everyone go without begins to seem like the more equitable option. And besides, the bras will provide more building material, 70–85 cm of wall depending on the bust measurement, Nina calculated in her head, and because three of them appear to have bras, that will give them approximately . . . 240 cm!

Reassuringly Nina lowers her bra, black smocked maternity shirt and turquoise cotton satin trousers next to Shlomith's clothing pile. And socks (high quality, thin) and trainers (meant more for walking than running). The shoes could be door hinges, if nothing else, or room corners. Shlomith had come here with soft, fuzzy slippers, Wlibgis has loose, white hospital socks covering her feet (*merde*, start undressing already!), and Maimuna has sandals, no socks. Polina has, as noted, only one shoe, a heavy, knee-length winter boot, worn, bright-red woolen socks, thick brown tights, black form-fitting slacks, a snappy, expensive, pink polo shirt, and instead of a suit coat to match the slacks, a dark blue cashmere jacket that is much too big for her and buttoned askew, and—where did she come from, Siberia?!—then the ankle-length sable fur, which has just become the couch. (Ulrike refuses to sit on it, don't you know: *FUR? I'd rather go naked!*)

Ulrike and Polina are also almost naked. Ulrike has on a charming sunshine-yellow A-cup lace bra and Polina, somewhat surprisingly, a red satin bra, which doesn't at all match her large, powder-colored underpants. They modestly cover her ample backside, coming up almost apologetically over her round belly all the way to her navel. But what about Wlibgis? She doesn't show any intention of casting off her hospital pajamas. Is she shy? What is the problem? There are all sorts of bodies here—she can see that. This is no beauty contest!

Nina, who has taken on the role of supervisor, encourages Wlibgis in a friendly tone to disrobe. Wlibgis looks at Nina as if she were an idiot and points at the wig lying at her feet. No one makes a move.

Generally when a person can't get her message across in the normal way—that is by speaking, by stating her business out loud to the other person, the person from whom she wants something—she begins to gesticulate. She raises her voice. Then she tenses, goes momentarily mute, and then suddenly releases an uncontrollable stream that collects whatever words happen to be there in the way of the stream, in the crevices of her teeth and on her tongue. Those words are hard. It can also happen that the other person, the one from whom something is wanted, can't answer. That the other person can do nothing but cower, raise his arms to shield his head, and retreat into the corner of the room, then slip out of the door to disappear down a dark alleyway or into another's arms, from where he may never return again.

Wlibgis has abundant experience with running out of options. But what do you do if your son uses the final resort, his fist, as his first resort? Talking to a fist is inordinately difficult. A fist is deaf, dumb, and blind, but it can find its target easily enough, because it smells fear.

Her son wasn't the only one. There were many who wanted to prod Wlibgis a bit, although using more delicate methods. Lisbet ("Petrus is a TEETOTALER . . ."), her doctor ("Listen, we've reached the end . . ."), her boss at the cleaning company when she used to work (" . . . *you* of all people going behind my back . . ."). In the face of these assaults, Wlibgis crumbled time after time, because she didn't know how to fight even when she really tried.

When Wlibgis lost her ability to speak, she also lost the last of her rights. People talked over her. Sometimes they expected nods or shakes of her head, sometimes not. Sometimes they didn't even look at her. Sometimes they pretended to look deep into her eyes, but they didn't want to know anything about how she felt and even less about her thoughts. They just drilled in deep to make sure that if they stared long enough it would come, that nod, that gentle approval, whether they were offering bland porridge or a needle in the arm.

Now Wlibgis attempts to utilize the tool that had been taken from her in the operation. And why not? If Shlomith is alive, even though she is obviously dead, if Nina's babies have disappeared even though they are obviously in her womb, why can't she, who lost her power of speech, begin to talk again? Why can't she use that confident voice she practiced so many times in front of the mirror to say that giving up the wig is enough? That she has already given her all!

Wlibgis lowers her clenched fists and straightens her throat like a rooster preparing to crow. From the bottom muck of her memory she dredges up the English equivalents of her thoughts. What is "clothing"? And what about the word for "wig"? How about *fake hair . . .* Quickly now, with a finger raised in emphasis, say: *My fake hair is there. I give you no more!*

And then Wlibgis opens her mouth.

Not even a hiss comes from her mutilated throat. Wlibgis opens her mouth like a fish tossed ashore: nothing, nothing. Putting her hands under the scarf tied around her neck, she feels for the hole and presses it with her first two fingers. Nothing. Not a single scrap of sound!

Can't Wlibgis imagine the current of air that in normal situations forces through the vocal chords to make them vibrate? She can imagine moving and can travel about in whichever direction she wants, just like everyone else here. But what kind of crazy person thinks about air currents when she talks? No one. Speech seems to come from the other women with ease; they just move their lips and the words are at the ready in their mouths. Sound comes out. The empty space gives the words a metallic tinge, but each voice is still recognizable. Why didn't speaking work for this one woman?

Shlomith is becoming impatient with Wlibgis's dithering. Just like on a nudist beach, the rules are the same for everyone here. Either you lose your clothes or you take a hike!

Wlibgis understands. Shlomith's gaze is compelling. There is no point resisting. Everyone else is already in their underwear, and when she thinks about it for a moment—and Wlibgis does think; for a fleeting moment she thinks so hard her brain hurts: take the injury, fight, or give up?—it is clear that she also has to undress. In her hospital pajamas she would be different. Someone the others wouldn't be able to stand being with. She would be isolated in the same way a strike agitator is isolated when the plans go awry and a scapegoat becomes necessary. She would become air again. She would cease to exist. Wlibgis humbles herself and begins to take off her clothes.

As it happens, Wlibgis does it with style. Theatrically she takes off her light-green silk scarf, ceremoniously revealing the opening in her throat: Look and be horrified! The other women watch the performance in satisfaction, taking in the totality, but Ulrike stares at the red hole as if hypnotized. The edges of it are ragged. Ulrike looks unblinking into the hole, at the interior of the trachea. Then she moves her gaze back to the ragged red edges, from there to the waxen, wrinkled neck, and finally past the jaw to the thin, almost gray lips, which part and form a word. Did Wlibgis whisper *cigarette*? Is that the short story of this hole?

Wlibgis has dropped the scarf. She begins undoing the flat buttons of the pajamas from the top and pulls her arms through the sleeves. She stands before them shirtless. Her upper body is a hunched sack, breasts hanging empty. On her gray skin there is something yellow and violet, splotchy, a runny sort of smudging, bruises with indistinct boundaries, like in a small child's watercolor painting where the edges of the paper have come too soon. By squatting clumsily, Wlibgis throws off her trousers. In her enormous underpants is a large diaper. Wlibgis points between her legs and raises her eyebrows in a question. Nina quickly shakes her head: No-no-no, keep your diaper on, we don't need that as building materials!

Thus peace returns again to the land.

Nina looks in satisfaction at the pile of clothes. Picking up the topmost piece, she spreads it out flat and then takes the next, spreading it and smoothing it. Then she signals for the others to help. And so they get to work on their togs, building a long, straight line. Nina walks behind, perfectionist that she is, straightening corners and patting crinkles flat.

Finally Nina takes the measuring tape that came from Shlomith's pocket and measures: yellow lace bra (70 cm), red satin bra (85 cm), white maternity bra (80 cm); long black caftan dress (132 cm), hospital shirt (55 cm), black smocked maternity blouse (65 cm), pink polo shirt (68 cm), black-and-white Scott Walker T-shirt (56 cm), large dark-blue cardigan (75 cm; also with belt, 100 cm); suit trousers (85 cm; spread in the "splits" 158 cm), turquoise cotton satin trousers with stretch jersey front panel (93 cm; spread in the "splits" 159 cm), hospital trousers (78 cm; spread in the "splits" 141 cm), brown corduroys (95 cm; spread in the "splits" 178 cm), yellow dress (135 cm); thin black socks (34 cm x 2), thin white hospital socks (30 cm x 2), bright-red woolen socks (40 cm x 2), furry slippers (38 cm x 2), thick brown tights (73 cm; spread in the "splits" 110 cm); light green scarf (70 cm); green trainers (size 41, 27 cm x 2), brown sandals (size 40, 25 cm x 2), blue trainers (size 36, 21 cm x 2), and one winter boot (size 37, laid flat 40 cm).

Total: 22 meters, 7 centimeters. Which would yield about 30 square meters.

Nina lifts the sleeves of the long-sleeved shirts. They will add a few dozen more centimeters.

Next they have to make a decision: one larger room or two smaller ones? They want one big room. The kitchen. It is simpler to be either outdoors or in. Movements between rooms could be problematic: Why did she go in there, with her, and what did it mean? What did a second room signify in general? Could it belong to someone? The thought of two rooms arouses so much concern that no one wants to take the risk, even though there would be undeniable benefits to a two-room version. Dividing rooms (kitchen + bedroom, for example) would have provided the possibility for some amusing routines. They could sit and imagine a delicious, candlelit dinner. Afterwards they could all go sleep on the floor, closing their eyes and imagining a shared dream. But if they used the rooms wrong . . . If cliques formed . . . If two nations formed . . . If a war started . . .

The women begin to arrange the clothing in a rectangle around the sable couch and the wig fireplace. Then Polina thinks to ask whether they should change the couch to a long bench, since kitchens didn't have couches, at least not her kitchen in Moscow. The others are not enthused by the idea. Long benches are hard and the fur is soft, regardless of whether they feel its softness or not. They can see the softness all the same—the sable fur is fluffy in a way that a bench could never be, so the thought is impossible, period.

But Polina doesn't give up so easily. Could the fur be a rug then? It could be an *oriental* rug! Or a flying carpet! A flying carpet in the kitchen. Polina doesn't think there is anything strange about that, unlike a couch, which doesn't belong in a kitchen, period.

No one reacts to Polina's suggestion. *Let's vote*, Nina exclaims, clearly worried about the increasing discord. *Who wants the fur to be a couch?* (Everyone except Polina and Ulrike raises their hands.) *Who wants the fur to be a rug?* (Only Polina raises her hand.)

And what about that fireplace? There aren't fireplaces in kitchens! They can have old-fashioned wood-burning stove tops or baking ovens. But not fireplaces! Polina is angry. *Why don't we make a living room then,* she screams, *if you don't want to turn the couch into a rug and the fireplace into an oven? A couch and a fireplace belong in a living room!*

Nina, who wants to complete her brilliant idea, places her hand calmingly on Polina's shoulder. *Would it be OK,* she asks in as gentle a tone as possible, *for each of us to think of this room exactly as we please? For some,* she continues, *like me, the idea of a kitchen is extremely important.* Extremely *important. And in my kitchen under these exceptional circumstances there can be a couch and a fireplace. I've already become used to them, and so I'd prefer to hold onto them. Anyone who's bothered by this can imagine a living room instead of a kitchen. Would that work for everyone?*

Polina grits her teeth and accepts Nina's suggestion. Defiantly she decides to think of a flying carpet, only and exclusively that. To hell with rooms.

But building continues. And the farther construction proceeds, the greater their joy grows. Nina and Shlomith look at each other and smile. Hostilities could be suppressed after all. Fangs could be sucked back into gums. It was as if morning had been waiting for them somewhere. A gentle, bright morning that wakes sleepers with light. Morning, the scheduled beginning to the day: was it the walls that did it? Did walls make it feel as if they could almost rise from their beds, brush their teeth, and jump in the shower? That if they turned, they might find the breakfast table set behind them? Coffee, juice, toast, eggs, and marmalade . . . A newspaper, sensible sentences concerning the world . . . *Le Monde, The New York Times, Komsomolskaja pravda. Salzburger Nachrichten. Le Soleil, De Telegraaf.* A world full of real problems, but what did that matter when they were inside. They were safe! At home!

The bustling continues within the clothing foundation. Each labors in her own spot, on her knees, straightening and flattening

the trousers and shirts to increase the room area as much as possible. The three full pairs of shoes make excellent corners when placed
in Chaplin position. The fourth corner is made of Shlomith's fuzzy
slippers. Polina's orphaned boot receives a place of honor as the
door. The tapered tip of the boot is the clasp that locks the door.
Once it is set in its proper place, no one outside has any business
coming in any more.

It feels better, Nina says repeatedly, and to the rhythm of this slogan
they make themselves at home. Maimuna sits on the sable fur couch,
Polina on the flying carpet. Nina, Ulrike, and Shlomith sit down in
front of them. Wlibgis lies in front of the fireplace and sets her head
right next to the wig. There is enough rebellious spirit in her that she
uses her fingers to put the ends of the wig on her forehead. They don't
feel like anything, not on her fingers or her forehead, but she manages
to prod the wig until the orange fibers fall over her field of vision.

Wlibgis closes her eyes. She sees herself in the spring on a muddy
street in the center of Zwolle. She walks with determination, bright
and ablaze. She feels herself walking a few centimeters above the
surface of the ground, and no wonder, because she is hurrying toward
her greatest love. The girl is waiting for her a few blocks away, her
plump hand in her mother's gaunt one. The girl will soon receive her
first ice cream of the spring, and in the meantime her mother can get
her weekly dose of buprenorphine. Vanilla, chocolate, pistachios;
cherries, a paper umbrella, and whipped cream; sprinkles, chocolate
chips, strawberry sauce; whatever Melinda can think of to ask her
grandmother.

POLINA'S LIQUOR WINDOW

The women barely have time to get comfortable and each stray into her own thoughts when with no warning a story begins on the flying carpet. No one is prepared, and no one expected it. *Well, I'm Polina,* Polina suddenly says (confusing everyone, because of course they already know), *and I'm an alcoholic.*

No one had known this. They didn't know what Polina had been like. Polina talked a lot but not about herself, except once. Once she had talked about herself. She had briefly related how her dying mother had refused to die right up to the end, how her mother had taken her final, suffocating breath with a look of shock on her face, and how at that moment Polina had decided to settle her accounts with life. But she had said little to broaden the fundamental impression of a woman who devoured books. She was just Polina, who had worked as chief accountant at Zlom, the Moscow Central Agency for the Dramatic Arts. Although she said her work wasn't always pleasant. There had been a lot of gossiping behind her back that she'd had to treat with a maternal but slightly restrained attitude. So Polina had told them. She said she had to remember that this had nothing to do with her *in persona*, that it only had to do with her role at work. (She had lied, but the women didn't know that either.)

Now, inside this brand-new clothing house, on a sable-fur couch that had turned into a flying carpet, but which for some is still a couch, Polina reveals something entirely new about herself. This is Polina *in persona*, and she is an alcoholic.

What Polina does not say is that she was uttering this statement for the first time in order to try out how the admission felt when it no longer had any consequences. She doesn't feel like drinking here. Here there is nothing to drink and no reason to drink. In order to drink she needs certain props, which were found in the old world, in her home in fact. There it was possible to drink *properly*. More than the drinks, Polina misses a place to drink where she had everything she needed within reach. She had acquired an armchair for this specific purpose. A deep, soft armchair with a graceful three-legged table next to it. What was atop the table varied: a grog glass, a wine carafe, one night's serving. There she sat, sipping and sitting, and all the bad things stopped. Day-Polina went away and Night-Polina flooded into her place with every drink.

In her own home, Polina believed she was free and independent. Someone else might have disagreed, but no other thinking beings were inside the flat (her cat, Begemot, did not count, although he must have thought in his own feline way). Polina told herself she was relaxing. "I'm relaxing, because otherwise I can't shut off and I'll go crazy. Otherwise I'd be doing salary calculations, shadow budgets, reports, tax plans, and bookkeeping at ten at night at Zlom. At three in the morning I'd still be sitting on the sixth floor. I might even be there when the others came to work in the morning. Before long I'd end up on sick leave, and that wouldn't do. There has to be more in life than numbers!"

In theory, Polina's method worked. Each week she drank enough that she could go to work in the morning without agony. Half a bottle or as much as a bottle of decent wine, a couple of glasses of cognac, herbal liqueur if her throat was sore, raspberry liqueur if she felt like something sweet.

Polina lived in a fourteen-story yellow-brick building on the top floor, at the place where Pokrovsky Boulevard turned to Yauzsky Boulevard. The bedroom window and balcony gave a handsome view of the city, dominated by Stalin's Tooth, one of the seven architectural wonders of Moscow built by Stalin. Those Seven Sisters, as the buildings were called, slightly resembled the skyscrapers of Manhattan, but they were too rambling and lonely. Their towers made them medieval, or neoclassical, or maybe, perhaps, baroque?

During the day, with clear weather and binoculars, from the window of Polina's home one could catch a glimpse behind Stalin's Tooth of the roof of Zlom and the red banner flapping there with the embroidered injunction, *Love the art in yourself not yourself in the art*, which could not be seen unless the wind was stiff and more or less in one direction, so that the flag flew straight as an arrow.

There was Polina's daily life: a kilometer from Yauzsky Boulevard to the other side of Stalin's Tooth and from behind Stalin's Tooth one kilometer back to Yauzsky Boulevard. Polina enjoyed walking. Now and then in the mornings, when she glanced at her reflection in a display window (yes, she did that too, all people do), she didn't check her hair or posture. No single detail interested her. She was only checking that she was there, more or less complete; that she had legs, arms, and a head, even if it didn't feel like it. Unfortunately she needed all of these things to be out among people.

There was also another kind of window, one that didn't open from Polina's flat, not from the kitchen, the living room, or the bedroom, which all faced different directions and offered views and details for spotting through binoculars but which Polina had already grown tired of. Her very own secret window opened when an alcoholic beverage was poured into a glass. The first snifter of cognac, the tilt of the glass, the strong, brown liquid flowing into her mouth and beginning to work there. Polina breathed through her nose while the liquid was still in the concave dish of her tongue, and then, abracadabra, her whole body filled with fresh air, with an otherworldly gust, with promises and expectation. This was her *real* life. She had permission to take up her books when this window opened. She had permission for anything for a moment, to be a philosopher, a mass murderer, a princess, or maybe even a horse. Without a glass the books were mute to her, and that was a bad thing, because she loved books. She just had to open them first, and to open them she needed a special torsion arm, one that cranked her up out of the endless circle of numbers, from the addition, subtraction, and multiplication. She liked that too, but in a very finite way. Business was dealt with on the sixth floor of the Agency for Dramatic Arts without the agony of creativity, which she encountered almost every day in the canteen downstairs. There was always some Dimitri or Vladimir shouting, some wounded artist with visage downcast, and it was amusing to watch. Especially when the production was rubbish, in no imaginable way worth all that shouting and sulking. At those moments Polina felt a malicious schadenfreude. She would walk out of opening night at intermission smiling from ear to ear even though she knew the production would cause losses for the theatre.

Yes, numbers were good. Nodding acquaintances but not lovers. Only books were lovers. But it was a long journey to them, much longer than from Yauzsky Boulevard to the other side of Stalin's Tooth, and Polina's mind did not open to the words printed on the paper through only the power of perambulation.

Polina usually came home after seven o'clock, ate, and settled in for the night. She didn't turn to a book until everything else was ready, when nothing else stood out in the wrong place. Even the tassels of the oriental rug had to be straight. "Begemot, my kitty, come to Mamotška's lap and let's read," Polina said. The cat also liked books, or at least being in her lap. All the distractions and bustling were done for the day. The lady of the house took to her reading chair and extended her hand toward the graceful three-legged table, where the day's estimated serving was at the ready, which could be refreshed if necessary, and usually was. But there were reasons for that. Polina wanted the books to really mean something. Otherwise reading them was pointless. She didn't read frivolous books, the kind you could talk about at work to make yourself approachable. She only read the crème de la crème, and only when intoxicated.

Polina read for herself. She was not, for example, waiting for the man of her life, into whose ear she would pour whispers of the honey of her sophistication, because she knew well enough that in Russia there were roughly ten million more women than men and that the best had already been skimmed off the top. She had abundant empirical evidence of this fact. She wasn't just looking for Anyone. No drunk, unemployed losers, dependent carrion crows, abusers, or thieves. She read for her own sake just as some women really do dress up only for themselves. They brush on mascara first thing in the morning after polishing their faces, even if they don't intend to step outside all day or let anyone else inside. Polina at least didn't intend to let anyone inside. No one was coming. She also never, EVER, approached the Dimitris and Vladimirs to share her thoughts—what would she have said to them? She preferred to socialize with liqueurs, cognac, and wine. Each beverage type had its own place in the bar cabinet. The liqueurs were on top, the cognacs in the middle, and the horizontal, symmetrical hollows were reserved for the wines. There was also the decanter, which Polina used assiduously and filled on her wine nights. On cognac nights there was a moka pot full of espresso next to her, and with sweet liqueurs she would have a few salt biscuits to ward off the sugar high. Alcohol did not fatigue Polina, except when she gave it permission to fatigue her. She drank either to be inspired or to fall asleep, and the god in the glass usually obeyed her commands. She had a notebook where she sometimes scratched ideas that the texts she read aroused, because perhaps one day . . . one fine day . . . in retirement . . . ? Well, perhaps in few years . . . The great synthesis of her erudition! The book she would pour her whole self into!

Polina didn't feel much guilt over her drinking. She'd gained amazing knowledge that she would have missed without it. The books wouldn't have sung to her without this wondrous secret window, which sometimes nearly flew off its hinges. That was worth any side effects. The moment when a book began its raging storm. When it began to surrender in a silken symphony, when all the voices of all the instruments were individually and collectively audible: the French horn, the oboe, the contrabass; irony, context, intertextuality. If only she could share this some day . . .

It wasn't as if Polina had *never* talked about what she read with anyone. There had been situations in her life, parties for example, where people chatted in a way she experienced as meaningful. Not just trivial tongue-wagging or, even worse, flirtation concealed as conversation, which could begin out of nowhere, on any topic, even Chekhov. The rules of that game were not at all clear to Polina. Once at a premier she'd stood dressed to the nines with a glass of champagne in her hand along with the rest of the audience, in the company of a man she knew a little and a woman who was a complete stranger, and imagined that they were talking about *The Cherry Orchard*. But the conversation wasn't really about *The Cherry Orchard*.

Apparently she was supposed to realize this and then immediately excuse herself with a bow before retreating to another corner of the hall and slipping out of the party, but she had frozen in place, as always. She made the mistake of thinking the moment would pass—that was what an ignoramus she was—believing that soon the conversation would return to the way it had been. There they had been just a moment ago, the man, the woman, and her, and Chekhov in all his glory. She had actually begun to warm to the conversation, and her cheeks had burned with excitement as she returned to the adaptation they had seen on stage two hours before, to the blackness lit by only a sea of candles. Candles as snow-white cherry trees in bloom and buckets of tears, of weeping, such deep sorrow that it couldn't help infecting the audience . . . And then suddenly the woman and the man weren't there any more. Some strange membrane had appeared between her and the two of them. They didn't even see her.

Was the fault in her? Had she said something foolish? Did her breath smell bad? The man and woman spoke to each other, quoting the play from memory. "Did you eat the frogs?" "I had crocodile." It was absurd. "It smells of patchouli here." How did they suddenly decide to repeat all the lines about smells? "Who here stinks of herring?" It was irritating, but they seemed to be endlessly amused. "Go, my dear man, you reek of chicken,"—were they mocking her? They sang to each other like birds, chirp, chirp, *fiuuuu-druip-druip-druip*, and she found she couldn't move any more. "I can smell the cognac on you, my darling," "my little cucumber," and her cheeks began to burn with shame.

Fortunately there was plenty of champagne served at these parties.

At another, more high-brow frolic she managed to take the baton. An emeritus professor of history from Nantes University in France gave her a tip. "Read Swedenborg," he suggested as they discussed Christianity and mysticism. Polina took his advice and read. That could have turned into something if another event the gentleman said he would attend hadn't been canceled due to a hostage crisis that occurred in the House of Culture of State Ball-Bearing Plant Number 1.

Polina was left quite alone with her Swedenborg. She never saw the French gentleman again. She had completely forgotten his name (you know how little names mean when a conversation is flowing), and no one in her circle of acquaintance seemed to know whom she meant when she went fishing for information afterwards. No one knew whom she was talking about when she described a man who looked disconcertingly like an old Jean-Louis Trintignant with a red scarf around his neck—could she have invented him entirely? In any case, Polina had a sticky question for him about Swedenborg that it now appeared would go permanently unanswered.

Here in the new home, sitting on the flying carpet, Polina knows she has finally found a suitable audience, an audience who won't initiate any brazen, erotic merrymaking before her eyes, who won't retreat into the washroom or disappear without a trace because of an unlucky terrorist attack. Polina knows she could try anything, so she decides to give it her best. She tosses out a slightly more precise sentence than before: *My name is Polina Yurievna Solovyeva, and I am an alcoholic.* After the final word she snaps her mouth shut in satisfaction, like a cat who's just licked the last drop of cream from a plate. She just didn't lick her lips.

Oh, the confusion her confession arouses! Everyone is as quiet as a mouse. They stare, appearing to wait for her to continue. Polina, who sprawls imposing and lumpy next to trim, thin-legged Maimuna, knows that her moment has come. She has taken control of the situation. Soon every one of these women will be eating out of her hand.

The silence continues. Polina surrenders to the pleasure of savoring a moment of a sort no one had ever really allowed her before, so quick people were to trade words, first one sentence, soon another, and instantly a third, regardless of the content, just so long as the speech continued and a wicked glint remained in their eyes. But here Polina makes a mistake. She hasn't given a moment's thought to how her story will continue, to what she actually wants to say. That she liked drinking wine, cognac, and liqueur at home in the evening?

Polina's silence has unpredictable consequences. There are silences, and then there are *silences*. This silence, which gradually spread through space like fire, was of the latter sort. It destroyed the nub of her story, burning it to ashes, despite how appetizing the subject was. Too late Polina realizes that the pleasure of expectation cannot be dragged on forever.

Here on the other side, however, measuring the length of silences is impossible. A minute or a year—who is to know? When nothing around changes, when the sun doesn't rise or fall, when nothing within any of them moves or makes a sound, when no heartbeat counts pace and no breathing raises their chests, what would they do with time? There is no such thing. It is only a word. A stomach complaining of hunger is a clock. A pulse is a clock. Pain is a clock. Now everything else is gone, everything except words. Conversation, no matter how clumsy it is, no matter how loaded with misunder-standing, maintains time, nurturing them, helping them remain people in some incomprehensible way. Talking, prattling, even argu-ing: it isn't a question of entertainment. Words offer them safe chains, something to keep them afloat, causes and effects, although not yesterdays or tomorrows, which have become meaningless expres-sions, but continuums, continuums all the same: that is what speech gives them. The evergreen groves of memory, from which they can draw both the feeling of the past and the expectation of the future. And if anyone can't keep up, at least she has the melodies: Shlomith's deep, somewhat hoarse tones; Ulrike's bright, sharp voice; Polina's squeaky, nasal speech; Nina's soft, slightly childish elocution; and Maimuna's eager, gushing, and quickly ebbing energy.

Why doesn't anyone ask Polina anything?

Polina, what triggered your need to drink?

How much did you really drink?

When did you realize drinking is a problem for you?

Did you lose your job?

Did you die of drink?

Silence, this particular *silence*, is eerie, although no one except Polina seems to notice it. Apparently the others think there is something arresting in this silence, in these mute, dead calm moments that have escaped the orbit of time. Something they want to throw themselves into, despite the fact that with a few small follow-up questions they could turn all of this into the best, most realistic, most tragic, and gut-wrenching story ever told here.

So is the issue, once again, with Polina? Had Polina's opening, even in these conditions, been too heavy, too dumbfounding?

Polina lets her gaze move from one woman to the next. Wlibgis dozing under her wig, Maimuna hidden under the arm of the sable fur, Nina nodding behind her mound of flesh, Shlomith meditating in the lotus position, Ulrike lying on her side . . . How impolite they are! Good manners mean saying something, even just sighing sympathetically, when someone offers up a confession like this. It is downright indecent that they have all gone silent at once like this, with their eyes closed no less!

Polina feels a familiar gate begin to open. How, with trembling legs, offense shoves its muzzle through the hole, pushes it wide open, and, shaking its numb limbs, joyfully strides onto the flat spring pasture. This isn't about her alcoholism. This is, once again, about her *in persona*! A beautiful woman can lob whatever sleaze she wants into the world. "I'm Ulrike from Salzburg, and I've been mainlining heroin for five years." People want to listen to beautiful women, without exception. "I'm Maimuna from Senegal, and I've been selling my body since I was sixteen years old." For the first time in this otherworldly emptiness, a feeling resembling bitterness flickers within Polina. For Ulrike and Maimuna everything is still possible. Even death hasn't made them equal.

Death.

Death?

Shlomith, Wlibgis, Nina, Ulrike, and Maimuna are all strangely frozen, unusually absent. What if it isn't that this has anything to do with her, with Polina? Could this all, somehow, be about something much, much more . . . fatal? And what if the women are traveling right now? If their souls have gone wandering? And soon they'll be gone entirely—like Rosa Imaculada!

Polina makes a lightning-fast decision. She doesn't want to be alone. She closes her eyes. Not lightly but squeezes shut hard, because instinct tells her to keep them open. But what does she care about instinct? She wants to be where the others are. She doesn't want to be left to watch them disappear!

Then something begins to appear on Polina's closed eyelids that deviates from the normal light-gray opacity. It is a yellow color, as if the sun had risen. As if light were coming from somewhere, as if day had dawned, as if summer had begun within her eyes. If you place your hands cupped over your closed eyes, if you turn toward a bright light and then drop your hands, you can get some sense of what began to happen on Polina's eyelids. When your closed eyelids are turned toward the bright light, at first a yellow glimmer appears, then red splotches, then small, black, oily moving circles. Or even more peculiar things if you rub your eyes. (Eye doctors always warn against this: "Don't rub your eyes! You can do permanent damage!" But they never tell you what can happen. What would break, what could never be made whole again? In fact, the eye doctors are lying. Eyes are made of exceptionally flexible material: you can even poke your fingers in an attacker's eyes—this is one of the first self-defense techniques women learn—and you won't end up in court because your attacker's injured eye will be sure to heal. Unfortunately. Your attacker will still be able to watch his future victims: you, your sister, your mother, your daughter, your best friend; your attacker will still be able to follow the next woman he chooses and wait for her to reach the darkest part of the underpass . . . wait for the moment when you are, when your sister is, when your mother, your daughter, or your best friend is most vulnerable . . . And then: the attack: the assault: the rape: remember the perpetrator's eyes then!) If, despite your doctor's warnings, you still decide to rub your eyes, it's possible to see almost anything: a sunny yellow that thickens to orange and blood red, great, dark, moving blobs; Rorschach blots, thunderclouds and lightning. Wasp nests, helium balloons released into the air. Rainbows. Tremulous bullets. Gyrating hex nuts. The entire universe, your worst nightmares, all on the safety of your very own eyelid silver screen!

To Polina's surprise, the bright yellow begins to crumble after blazing momentarily. Like a smashed mirror in slow motion. Broken shards billow about as if they've been shaken hard in a closed box, zigzag, zigzag, and then they begin to settle, to settle like powder.

Suddenly Polina feels as if someone has pulled the rug from beneath her feet. As if something has turned upside down under her. Or is she herself hurtling toward something, toward . . . grains of sand? Is she lying on her face in sand?

Polina begins to make out bulges and hollows, wind-formed waves, dunes. She lifts her head a little more and sees a vast expanse of sand shimmering in the heat, which should burn her cheeks, her hands, her chest, her stomach, her thighs. Cautiously, as if testing whether her vertebrae work, she begins to turn her head to the left. She doesn't feel her neck move but, led by some unknown force, she finds her gaze focusing to the side, up and back.

At that moment the whining of a motor begins to reach Polina's ears, as though someone had pressed the volume button of a muted television set. She notices a beat-up jeep stuck in the sand behind her. The vehicle's tires spin as the engine revs. It howls, then croaks, then gathering strength again it utters another tortured howl.

Polina gets up on her knees. Next to the jeep stand men with rifles, scarves covering their faces and shoulders tense with rage. Two men crouch on the ground, hands clasped behind their heads. Before them lies Maimuna, with her familiar yellow dress rolled up to her buttocks. Five buckskin belts are spread out on the sand. One of the men wearing a scarf has the barrel of his rifle buried in the curls of Maimuna's hair.

It is like a pose. The press photo of the year.

And then. The women! Wlibgis, Shlomith, Nina, Ulrike, and— Rosa Imaculada! And Maimuna! Maimuna too, not just on the ground, her dress rolled up, but also in the air, once again in her underwear! All are in their panties except Rosa, lucky Rosa in her modest clothes, her magenta pique shirt and beige shorts. There they stand, next to the jeep, like any old guardian angels. They stand but don't stand. They float a few dozen centimeters above the surface of the ground, a little crooked, swaying somewhere around the rear bumper at the level of the exhaust pipe. They are somehow disconnected from the image, as if under cellophane, flickering, without any depth.

Rosa Imaculada begins to gesture eagerly at Polina. Nina gives an embarrassed smile, Ulrike looks tense, and Shlomith seems to tap her foot impatiently. Wlibgis leans on the spare tire bolted to the back of the jeep, though without touching it. The Maimuna in the air is calm. The Maimuna in the air looks at the Maimuna on the ground.

Polina feels a desire to join the others. She stands up, already seeing herself as a continuation of the line, next to Rosa, who stands farthest from the jeep, perhaps even arm-in-arm with the Brazilian . . . And then, and then—what then? What will happen when she stands beside the other women?

DEATH REHEARSAL NUMBER 2
(ACCORDING TO SWEDENBORG)

Polina's eyes snap open. The desert disappears. Once again everything is harsh, shadowless, painfully white. Maimuna still sprawls the way she did a moment ago, face under the sleeve of the sable fur. Wlibgis lies on her back with the wig's bangs on her forehead. Ulrike, Nina, and Shlomith each sit in their own familiar style in front of her. The women's eyes are still shut tight, but their mouths are all open a crack. Even Wlibgis has her lips parted.

Oooon . . .

Slowly, vibrating like a meditative om-syllable, that frightening word begins to form in the women's mouths. Soon, it is clear, they will all disappear. They will move, in one way or another, perhaps in stages like Rosa, perhaps all at once, to the desert by the jeep to escort

Maimuna over the frontier, to witness Maimuna's death. All except her, Polina Yurievna Solovyeva. She isn't going anywhere!

As the R is rolling on the women's tongues, Polina opens her mouth and screams, screams as only a person can scream when the train hurtling at her has to be stopped, or an airplane rushing at the ground has to be lifted back into flight; like you have to scream to wake up from the nightmare, when bullets whistling through the air have to be forced to change direction. Polina screams the scream of a person falling, a wordless, rising cry. She wants to stop death. It can't be Maimuna's time yet!

Polina's scream has an effect. The dormant women's eyes snap open like automatons that have been recently serviced, almost at exactly the same time, right after hearing her voice. They seem astonished, maybe even a little startled, all except Maimuna, who lifts her head from under the sleeve of the fur and looks annoyed, perhaps even angry. Quickly she shuts her eyes again in protest, but Polina doesn't care. She has just saved the ingrate from certain destruction! At least she has postponed the girl's final moments, if that's what this is about, if a person really can die twice.

Wild thoughts besiege Polina's mind. What would Swedenborg, with his obsession with visions of heaven, say about all of this? If only the professor from Nantes, her very own Jean-Louis Trintignant, had been her companion for longer!

Listen up, ladies! Once there was a mystic . . . Polina begins, because she wants to put the world back on track, and the best way to do that is by talking. The possibility that by opening her eyes and shouting she has prevented something important, perhaps even essential from happening, didn't even cross her mind. Swedenborg now leads Polina like a ram on a rope, and she spares not a thought for the possibility that her act might have slowed some sort of progression.

Polina didn't allow questions of this kind into her mind. As perspicacious as she was, she succeeded surprisingly often in avoiding what was most essential; in losing track of the crux of what she had been on the cusp of discovering, of what could have begun leading her to the light. She circled her prey, peeling the onion layer by layer, but then something would happen in the heat of the moment and she would get lost, straying into detours she took for shortcuts.

Alcohol could have played a role. Polina, if anyone, should have known that in the final analysis, truth is a very simple thing. She wouldn't have needed to search for it in all those hundreds of books if she had had the patience to take a moment to focus, for example, on her cat, if she had abandoned herself with all her heart to playing with it for a while. Then she would have learned indispensable things. But Begemot was left to purr his deep secrets alone. His mistress certainly cooed at him but was probably speaking more to herself than her cat. When she stroked her pet, she was really stroking and nurturing herself. Begemot was terribly dear to Polina, as warm as cognac, as homey as liqueur, as irresistible as a medium-dry Shampanskoye. He was a sweet fellow, but he could have been so much more: a four-legged lesson on the Essential Things of Life. If Polina had stopped to listen occasionally to what Begemot had to tell her, she could have poured her drink down the drain and remained in the book of the living a little longer.

"Listen up! Once upon a time there was a mystic who was also sometimes called a philosopher," Polina says in her squeaky voice after clearing her throat. "He described the afterlife in a way that *slightly* resembles where we are now. Yes, well. Ehem." Polina pauses, confused. She has thrown out the hook, and the bait dangles on said hook, this, their so-called *situation*. The women sharpen up, becoming more alert, just as she had anticipated. Well, they aren't quite licking their lips with excitement, but a feeling of expectation is palpable. With a cough, Polina opens her throat and lets the words flow.

"Emanuel Swedenborg, a wise, mad penitent, lived a respectably long life for his age, in total eighty-four years. He was, depending on one's perspective, a mystic, a philosopher, or an occultist; an eccentric, an epileptic, or an erotomaniac; a hypochondriac, hysterical, or schizophrenic; the Great Dreamer, a flatulist, or, in Balzac's words, the Buddha of the North—a beloved child has many names. This baroque, rambling character was born in 1688 in Stockholm and died in London in March of 1772. As an amusing detail let it be mentioned that Swedenborg's skull, like the skull of Descartes before him, was lost for a short time subsequent to his death. The skull was found, don't ask me where, and the earthly remains of the mystic were moved in 1908, with much ceremony, to his final resting place in Uppsala Cathedral.

"Before we move on to the actual subject, i.e. Swedenborg's visions of heaven, which are the main topic of our lesson, we ought to review a few facts. The reputation of Emanuel Swedenborg is, undeniably, dubious. Following his death, the poor man was left to the mercy of many stripes of lunatic: somnambulists, mesmerists, illuminati; practitioners of animal magnetism, Rosicrucians, alchemists, and kabbalists . . . And let us not forget the Freemasons. Even though he was a scientist. Who, in truth, it must be admitted, didn't care much for the empirical and preferred to socialize with angels. That was more or less how he described his own field in the preface to one of his latter works, *Arcana Caelestia* . . . "

It is important to know one thing about Polina that has remained hidden until now, namely that she had a photographic memory. When her mind was sharp, she could recall a very detailed picture of any page of a book she had read if the book had touched her in the slightest, and most books she read did. The citrus bitterness of Cointreau, *l'eau-de-vie* V.S.O.P. aged in oak barrels, or a sweet muscat helped impress the pages on her mind. Begemot had listened to many lectures delivered from memory in his mistress's lap. Unlike human beings, the cat clearly enjoyed the voice she used to tell him things. Polina's voice was individual; indeed, her whole self was very individual. Begemot's poor mistress didn't know how to approach most situations other than by carrying on, by taking up space in a style that was far too original given most people's limited tolerance. When Polina joined a group of people and opened her mouth, that was almost always the end of everything. Either she was silenced by a sly change in topic, or she was simply left out entirely. Everyone suddenly had somewhere else to be, and the cluster of people scattered, leaving Polina alone with herself again.

Polina was an entirely insufferable person. She happened to have a
few special abilities, for example this cursed photographic memory,
which would have been useful in a magic act but not in an office and
not even in the world of creative people, because the creative world,
like any other socioeconomic stratum, is full to overflowing with
carefully polished posturing. Fortunately Polina had her cat, her bar
cabinet, and her books. Or should things be arranged differently in
the name of truthfulness: bar cabinet, books, and cat? The significance of the cat was great, though. Every morning Begemot meowed
and butted his drowsy mistress into a good mood, *meooow!* His
lovely shining black coat and the slender, strong frame that slid
beneath (he mainly ate raw entrails like liver) felt *so good* under a
crapulous hand, *so very good.* Yes, her cat was dear to Polina, the
dearest of all, so the final order is this: cat, bar cabinet, and books.
The bar cabinet has to be put there in the middle because there were
no books without alcohol, as we know, although we also know that if
Polina had been forced to put a tick mark next to either the bar cabinet or books in a multiple choice questionnaire, concerning the most
significant things in her life, of course she would have ticked the
books, since they had intrinsic value, and alcohol only had significance as part of her reading ritual.

Let this introduction suffice for Polina's special gift, her monstrous
photographic memory, of which we receive the following indisputable evidence:

"'It may therefore be stated in advance that of the Lord's Divine
mercy it has been granted me now for some years to be constantly and
uninterruptedly in company with spirits and angels, hearing them
speak and in turn speaking with them. In this way it has been given me
to hear and see wonderful things in the other life which have never
before come to the knowledge of any man, nor into his idea.' Thus wrote
Swedenborg in the introduction to his *Arcana*, a work of which only
four copies were sold during his lifetime, one of which was purchased
by Immanuel Kant. Kant read the book and was deeply disappointed,
because he did not find any evidence of the spirit world in it. A hypochondriac wind raging in a delirious mystic was Kant's evaluation.

"So was Swedenborg insane? Or was he a great, misunderstood poet? Due to his high social status, he wasn't shut up in an asylum, although apparently that option did receive serious consideration. I, on the other hand, would say that we, dear women, are in a unique position among the critics of Swedenborg's celestial visions. So I propose that once I've given you a basic overview of his ideas, we vote as we just did about the couch and the flying carpet, about whether Swedenborg was right or wrong when he wrote about the afterlife. What do you say?"

Should Polina have become a teacher? Damn it to hell, she knew how to talk! Had she made the mistake of her life when she made the safe choice of business education, which had only led her to a fair-weather camaraderie with pleasantly incorruptible yet depressingly emotionless numbers? Perhaps she should have worked with children! Polina clearly had a talent for engaging an audience, assuming the audience was primed before her, as it now is (and as well-bred students are).

What Polina hasn't noticed is that she is talking about Swedenborg in her own language, not English. And everyone seems to understand although no one else knows a word of Russian. Nina nods, and soon all the others are nodding; Polina's suggestion of a vote is an idea they could support. Wlibgis has sat up from under her wig, and Maimuna has opened her eyes again and doesn't look at all angry now. There the women sit, gawking like obedient little girls eager to learn. All that is missing from the picture are partings running down the middle of their heads, tight plaits, and bright red bows.

"Emanuel, eldest son of the chaplain Jesper Svedberg and Sara Behm, got along famously in the company of the royal family," Polina continues self-confidently, downright beaming, "and he even competed in philosophy with his friend Charles XII. So Queen Ulrika Eleonora elevated Swedenborg, not forgetting his sisters and brothers, to the nobility in 1719. That was how Svedberg became Swedenborg. The family had mining interests, which Emanuel inherited when he was thirty-two, after which he no longer had any financial worries. Quite a nice starting point for erecting the architecture of the heavens, wouldn't you say!

"Swedenborg was a product of the University of Uppsala, and his colleagues included Carl von Linné (the king of taxonomy!) and Anders Celsius (the thermometer!). So you could say that he matured intellectually in extremely elevated company. His own subjects were geometry, metals, and chemistry, but of course he practiced other skills such as mechanics, mathematics, and astronomy. He advanced the understanding of hydrology and attempted to solve the hottest scientific problem of the day, how to determine longitude at sea. He didn't get anywhere near a solution but, proud as he was, refused to admit his failure.

"Swedenborg's skill and especially the subjects of his interest were not insignificant. He bound books, ground lenses, did clever engravings, made furniture, and even tried his hand at clock making. Fourteen inventions can also be credited to him, including a universal musical instrument, a notable flying machine design, and a less notable submarine design. In my opinion his most fascinating invention was the analytical method he developed for 'predicting desires and emotions'. Unfortunately little record of this bright pearl of thought was preserved for future generations, and so Mr. Sigmund Freud later swept the board."

Polina pauses briefly, as if she wishes to say something about Mr. Freud. (She doesn't like Mr. Freud very much.) Will is more important than understanding, Polina had always believed, and with this thought she catapulted centuries back, leaving behind the muddy present and the pathetic onion-like model of the soul dismembered by too much talk and endless stinging discoveries. Her soul was not an onion. And she also wasn't a ruminant. If human will was as tortuous as the human walnut brain with its endless folds, nothing would ever come of anything.

And nothing ever did come of anything! There were an unfortunate number of cautionary examples. Once long ago at an evening gathering, Polina had wished to recite a poem from memory to delight the other revelers. Her voice was practically made for intoning hundred-year-old verse. She wanted to give herself, her whole aspic-like body, to the service of the poem, humbly and selflessly.

Unlike the others, she didn't imagine she was special. That one of her loathsome personal secrets, whatever it might be, could be an interesting topic of conversation. None of them were. But neither were anyone else's secrets! Every explanation of a motive pressed into service as a blithe amusement—*I only meant to wound him*, that loud but oh-so-primitive way of speaking, *I went looking for attention and I got it, believe you me, I got it with interest*—sent shudders through her body. It irritated, scandalized, and shocked her. The direction of the conversation was always so depressingly predictable. Surely she wasn't the only one to be disgusted by the exhibitionists? The admiring gazes and encouraging nods the confider received were just theatre. Right?

There Polina had stood and seized, as they say, the moment. "Mmmmm, do you know, I just read . . ." As a rebuke to the confider and in order to delight the others, she began to recite from memory an old poem that lacked any hint of the onion soul, that had a stately rhythm and a bright, uncomplicated will. Each line resounded in the hall, and, entranced by her own voice, Polina added volume. Everyone within ten meters froze to listen.

And then—silence. Someone snickered. The circle dispersed. Someone, perhaps in the corner with the fireplace, lobbed a feeble effort, doomed to failure, at building a swaying suspension bridge: ". . . that someone still knows how to do that in the age of copy and paste . . ."

That Sigmund Freud, not Swedenborg, received the glory for developing a method for analyzing desires and emotions was only a small, repulsive fact, though. Polina quickly brushes both of her ample, sagging breasts with her hands as if wanting to shake something off them. Then out of old habit she straightens her back (as she had done with her cat in her lap: her back hunched from reading, she would continue scratching and petting with her right hand as she straightened up, so as not to interrupt Begemot's purring and cause him to misinterpret her change in position and jump off her lap, because, Begemot soon learned, now began the best stage of the evening, when his mistress would begin a trance-like oration, during

which her touch would become almost supernaturally gentle). A
bright, clear voice begins to rise from Polina's erect frame.

"Swedenborg practiced his more customary scientific skills by
founding a vernacular publication, *Daedalus Hyperboreus*, and serving as its editor. He was also a keen economic thinker, adamantly
opposing limits on trade, such as customs laws and navigation acts.
He placed society above the individual, the fatherland above society,
and the church above the fatherland. Well. Ehem. Perhaps this is
sufficient background on the temporal interests of Mr. Swedenborg?"

Instead of waiting for a reply, Polina continues, sliding forward
like a slippery herring, like a shuttle in a loom, because she is in
motion now, in her element; she is in a seraphic mood.

"So let us move on to Swedenborg's literary output; here also we
have reason to detour through his early writing in order to avoid
misrepresenting his achievements. *Regnum subterraneum*, 'The
Underground Empire', became one of Swedenborg's most notable
scientific works from his period of activity in the mining industry.
Especially the sections on iron and copper, '*De ferro*' and '*De cupro*',
which offered an excellent general treatment of the subject even for
encyclopedists. Swedenborg adopted his conception of reality from
Descartes, who believed in the fullness of the universe, not Newton,
who defended void theory. We know that he should have listened to
the latter ideas, at least if we're approaching the matter from a scientific perspective. But poetic souls may find more inspiration in
Swedenborg's speculations. At least I find them both uplifting and
diverting!

"According to Swedenborg, reality is made from small bubbles or
bullae. The space between these bullae is filled with even smaller,
finer bubbles, aether particles. The smaller the bubble, the more
durable and quick moving it is. And things certainly have a habit of
moving in this world! Nothing remains stationary for even a moment.
Either movement arises internal to the bubble, tremulation (vibra-
tions), or externally, that is motion caused by the bubble, known as
undulation. Let me see if I remember how it went . . . 'The atmosphere, whether the ethereal atmosphere, or the aërial, is a lower aura,

and with this also the angels are compared; and the human animus, to which the affections or passions are attributed, is a similar spirit or genius.' Yes, that was it!

"Gradually Swedenborg developed more interest in the human body, the kingdom of the soul. He became fascinated with the circulation of blood and especially the anatomy of the brain. Open a brain cell, Swedenborg said, and you will find small spheres within that give birth to material ideas. Continue opening, peel back one more small sphere, and you find new small vortices, namely intellectual ideas . . . According to Swedenborg, the soul is created and limited, bound by the body, one of the natural parts of the body, but, by the grace of God, immortal. It is a point. The extreme point of finitude, beyond which begins the divine, the infinite, which the soul, being on the boundary, brushes up against. Thus, the soul is not located in the epiphysis, as Descartes claimed, but rather flows through the whole body. *Ergo influxus gloria!* Therefore we all have direct contact with the divine!"

Perhaps Polina should have become a poet after all. Her mind clearly yearned for poetic heights. If Polina had not been so utterly misunderstood in her work community, which at the very least failed to encourage her to pursue her strengths, and if she hadn't been so bibulous and died before her time, she might have written anything. For example, perhaps an ode to the beautiful Nadezhda Tolokonnikova, like this:

ODE TO A BUTTERFLY

Spark of life, oh thou, bright and colorful,
amidst the tattooed crowd you walk,
but paint yourself with marks as well,
you dance, wild, and burst into song,
     guileless, innocent child,
      whose merit, whose success
is to play with flowers beneath the trees!

Your nature is to be like the butterfly: free,
a winged flower that soil cannot mire,
who may, and can, and wishes to find,
to search the garden's corners and boundaries!
        Fly, fly away now,
        reject the root, the ground,
nimble, flee far with the winds and squalls!

For only a moment you can endure, Nadezhda,
thus must your brilliance burn bright
like the red dying of the day
to color the sky and land,
        you too, bold girl,
        will conquer the choir of men,
despite their wish to silence your sound!

Nor would you devour the offerings of your garden,
although you reveled until you were old,
since even a drop of honey suffices you:
a second would daze your delicate frame!
        Here is the virtue of your feast,
        although you do not bow to the snare,
nor laws restrain or hold you back!

Even laws are made to remind us
of will, of desire surrendered,
of power to prescribe oneself alone,
what we will surrender for peace,
        but we remember still
        what true freedom is like:
your game, frenzied, riotous, bright, innocent!

The ode would have been published in *Novyi Mir*, and Polina would
have become famous. No one would have dared question her unique-
ness any more. No one would have laughed at her. She would have

been a woman equal to her poem, equal to all the poems she wrote, equal even to all the poems she might one day come to write. She would be big and magnificent and soon greater than Akhmatova herself!

"Despite his poetic ideas, Swedenborg's works were left rather incomplete. *Œconomia regni animalis*, 'The Economy of the Kingdom of the Soul', was a hastily patched together book, and only three installments of the planned seventeen ever appeared of the *Regnum animale*, 'The Kingdom of the Soul' series. It may be that Swedenborg preferred thinking and reading to writing his ideas down. It may be that he preferred dreaming to writing . . ."

Out of habit, Polina slips back into her book-reading stoop, into the posture she assumed when scanning the words that throbbed on the paper. Thoughts born of words soaked into her with ease, becoming her thoughts, her knowledge, growing her larger and larger, making her a giant. But why was talking about those ideas so hard? As soon as she tried something, disturbances cropped up, circuits shorted. Maybe Emanuel was the same. The mystic closed his eyes, saw angels around him, and that was enough for him. Then when he tried to write out of a sense of duty, the visions didn't bend so easily to words, the words didn't melt into sentences, and the angelic nature of the angels didn't appear on the paper at all. The ideas became dead, rotting things, little more than poor maxims. "He that is deficient in mind and spirits, is also deficient in life and intelligence; he is a dead man, a stock, a carcass," Swedenborg wrote.

Just then a melancholy enters Polina's mind, somewhat similar to that in her fourteenth-story flat on Yauzsky Boulevard, in those moments when she thought of her French professor, the Swedenborg scholar with the beautiful soul. He had given an assignment to her and only her: "Read Swedenborg. Even though he may be a complete wacko from a modern perspective, I found myself identifying deeply with him as I studied his ideas. I don't know why. Perhaps I'm going crazy myself. My wife already lives somewhere in the world of the angels. She smiles into emptiness and doesn't even recognize me. But, to return to the point, it would be interesting to hear what you think of Swedenborg as a layperson. Does he arouse any feelings in you . . . for example a protective instinct?"

The professor had cast Polina a significant look, and Polina returned it. A long, burning silence ensued, an electricity between them, and *snap*, Polina received a shock on her fingers when she happened to touch the man's red scarf. They both burst out laughing in relief, after which they leaned on each other. The wine was better than ever. And soon they would meet again.

But then the world built a barrier between them. The House of Culture of State Ball-Bearing Plant Number 1 was occupied, people were killed, and the world observed a moment of silence for the deceased. The timing was perfectly wrong for Polina. It was nothing but the snot-faced mockery of a sadistic fate. Polina was left alone with her Swedenborg. For a long time, a full six months, she believed that things would work out, that fate would yet deliver a surprising, joyous reunion. Because it couldn't be a coincidence that a man like that, speaking words like those, with glances like his, appeared before her—could it?

Polina read, waiting and pining. Her heartache was salty, manifesting as sweat in the folds of her knees and on her back, palpable as a burning in her face. Begemot was gracious. He didn't judge her as she lolled in her cognac, wine, or liqueur chair after a few glasses, her office skirt rolled up to her waist, her stockings down to her ankles, her fingers where lonely virile women's fingers sometimes are. Terrible perspiration, estrus sweat, menopause encroaching; salt, amino acids, phosphates, potassium chloride . . . Her very own Jean-Louis Trintignant was inside of her, whispering in her ear, "Read Swedenborg," and full to overflowing with pent-up passion from caring for his ailing wife.

Here was her Swedenborg: erotic longing, unfulfilled promises, which she felt like indulging, in which she wanted to wallow. Her personal pleasure-taking couldn't hurt anyone, could it?

But Polina was wrong. It hurt her. Her longing grew. It became a great, iron-hard feeling, which gradually formed an obstacle to normal life. Polina began having more trouble opening her liquor window each night. No more sensuous gales, no more revels, no more soaring thoughts. It was as if several meters of snow had fallen in front of the window, first soft, then hard, and finally freezing to ice, which wouldn't melt no matter how much mulled wine she poured in her glass, how much hot punch, anything warm, fortified tea, straight burning clear vodka poured down her throat . . . There was only the longing. Nothing else. Suddenly she had no taste for books, and her drinking became poisonous intoxication, sleep from which her alarm clock did not wake her. She even received one verbal warning, which the director of the Agency for Damatic Arts came to give Polina personally: "Dear Polina, this can't continue."

That was the final straw for Polina. She took her Swedenborg to a second-hand bookshop and bought books written by women instead, by Erica Jong, by Marguerite Duras. She shut her French gentleman and his intense gaze out of her mind. He had returned to his demented wife, and that was right. Polina kept her fingers in check, and that helped. Normal life resumed, and her liquor window opened and began operating in the desired fashion: just enough fresh air in, just enough books, and just enough sleep.

Here on the other side, a gentle nostalgia hovers over Swedenborg, not a deadly thirst, and so Polina once again straightens her back. She shakes her trivial notions from her mind and rushes to the place where all her intellectual groundwork has led her and her listeners in such a spiral fashion, whirling like a falling leaf. And we will allow Polina to continue without interruption, won't we? In order for us finally to get to vote?

"On one April afternoon in 1745, something happened that completely changed the direction of Swedenborg's life. The scene is a certain London tavern, and our main character is fifty-seven years old. Imagine yourself in a dimly lit, rather common watering hole. Before you is a large slice of hot, steaming liver pie you've just tucked into. You're eating leisurely, chewing contentedly, when suddenly a fog, similar to the river mist that hangs over the Thames each morning, fills the entire room. It rises steadily, insidiously, spreading everywhere, not just from one or two corners. The fog is thin enough, however, that you can see in front of you, at least to your feet. The floor is covered in reptiles: snakes, lizards, crocodiles, and all sorts of god-forsaken creatures cloaked in scales. Instinctively you lift your feet onto the bench you're sitting on. When the fog begins to clear, you see a man on the other side of the room bathed in light. He speaks to you, saying, 'Don't eat so much.' This strange, parenthetical statement may explain Swedenborg's ascetic diet, because according to the story, after this vision often all he would eat each day was a single bun dipped in milk with an enormous amount of coffee.

"The apparition disappeared, and the tavern returned to its previous state, but the customers and staff didn't seem to have noticed anything special. But beginning from that moment, Swedenborg knew that he had been chosen to unpeel the hidden heart of the Bible. And so he decided to become a guide to heaven and hell.

"Could Swedenborg's vision be explained by his circumstances? If Swedenborg had strayed from the way of tea to the beer streets of London, or farther to the gin lane of the proletariat? *Drunk for a penny, dead drunk for two pence, clean straw for nothing!* At the time of Swedenborg's visions, wine and beer were consumed in abundance in London, but the Gin Craze formed a veritable epidemic. Sixteen gallons of gin was distilled per resident of the city. Genever or Madame Geneva or Mother Gin was the favorite of the soldiers and sailors, cheap firewater distilled from barley and rye, with juniper berries mixed in for flavor. Men and women drank it, and even children received some. People died of it, of course, but it was a patriotic death, because the state supported the distillation of domestic grain. Processing taxes were reduced, since the government wanted to support the large agricultural producers, and they didn't want French brandy being imported. Drinking that was like an act of treason. So could the scholar from Uppsala have been under the influence of spirits?

"Whatever the case, just as Swedenborg was on the verge of finding the human soul, he experienced the mystical revelation, as described, and permanently abandoned science. The theory of correspondences Swedenborg had developed earlier meshed naturally with his celestial visions.

"Correspondence theory means that all things in existence have three meanings within each other: natural, spiritual, and celestial. There are the senses, then the thoughts, and finally heaven; and everything correlates with its own correspondences. Swedenborg was convinced that ancient primitive man knew the secrets of correspondences and that in the ancient world all books were also written in the language of correspondences. This was the original perfect universal tongue, *verbum vetustum*, which humanity unfortunately lost after they became too wise . . . They forgot the words . . . which Swedenborg spent years searching for . . . In human bodies and bodily functions he found codes, which would lead to the truth . . . The complete revealing of the correspondences . . . The understanding of symbols and metaphors . . ."

(We don't have anything to add to this. Continue, Polina, do not allow your train of thought to derail!)

"Swedenborg also deduced that because God had created man in his own image, the universe and all its levels, as well as the afterlife, are in the shape of a man. If this is the case, then we must be located on the milky-white sclera of the eye, although the veins must have been removed! Swedenborg carefully studied every growl of his gut and burble of his bowels, because through them he believed he could access ultimate reality. He himself, of course, was a link in the chain of correspondences . . .

"According to modern conceptions, Swedenborg is the first modern architect of heaven. He divided the afterlife into three parts, heaven, hell, and some sort of intermediate space, the spirit world, a place where the dead go first. There is no time in the spirit world of the dead. In the afterlife, changes in spiritual state correspond to differences in time.

"In Swedenborg's heaven people work, go to school, and improve themselves. They eat, drink, and make love—although marriage in the afterlife means a melding into one mind. Swedenborg says it this way: 'In the spiritual world, love is conjunction. Wherefore, when all act thus, then from many, yea from innumerable individuals consociated according to the form of heaven, unanimity exists, and they

become as one.' Do you follow? And what do you say of this: 'The
spirit of man after the death of the body appears in the spiritual world
in a human form, in every respect as in the world. He enjoys the
faculty of seeing, of hearing, of speaking, and of feeling, as in the
world; and he is endowed with every faculty of thinking, of willing,
and of acting, as in the world; in a word, he is a man as to each and
every thing, except that he is not encompassed with the gross body
which he had in the world.'

"Well now, dear women. Based on this, can you say where we are
now if we even believe a part of Swedenborg's teachings?"

"In hell."

Shlomith's reply comes as easily as from a druggist's shelf. At least
she had listened carefully to Polina's speech.

"Good," Polina said, taking up Shlomith's response without missing a beat. "Let's assume we're in hell. That's fine with me. But in the
meantime we must have been in the world of the spirits, and I at
least have no memory of that. In the spirit world, everyone who has
ever lived is arranged orderly in groups. The hallmark of each group
is a special fondness for something or a peculiar quality of life—and
I still haven't been able to figure out what might connect the seven
of us."

So maybe they are in hell. At least they are hopelessly far away
from the normal world and the bustle of normal people, far from
Moscow, Zwolle, Salzburg, New York, Dakar, and Marseilles. But
Ulrike looks alert now. Her mouth is open a crack, and she clearly
has something on her mind, but she waits.

No, they aren't in the waiting room between heaven and hell, in
the spirit world, looking forward to their final placement, which will
be an absolutely just judgement. The surroundings should look
different. It should resemble the world of the living. "Or, to be more
precise, it doesn't resemble life, it *is* life," Polina says, as if she is reading Ulrike's thoughts. "It's a life more real than life. The 'spiritual
substance' of the spirit world is the first, primordial substance, which
the world of the living only reflects. Do you understand? Swedenborg
was an arch Platonist!"

Ulrike nods enthusiastically. She likes philosophy, and she especially likes Plato's cave, which her teacher, Frau Schwartz, talked about
before the summer holidays: she saw herself on the floor of the cave
stoking the fire, the Fire of Truth, which threw terrible shadows onto
the black rock walls. The distorted, almost unrecognizable silhouettes
of all the stupid, doomed beings rampaged there: Elfride the prima
donna with a smoking Lucky Strike in her hand, loud-mouth Felda
and her constant powder mirror, Timberlake-oh-Timberlake Trixi
waving her brand new mobile phone camera—Ulrike smoked all of
them to death in the cave, all their lies and stupidity and loathsome-
ness. Thank God *they* aren't here!

"If we assume we're dead," Ulrike says, also not noticing that she is
speaking her own language, which everyone simply just understands
without a second thought as everyone had understood Polina's
Russian, "and if we imagine that we're Swedenborg's spirit beings,
then what primordial state have we entered? What does the emptiness around us tell us about the world we lived in before? That
everything, absolutely everything, is an illusion and a fiction?"

Polina takes up the challenge. She positively waxes poetical as she
describes the Swedenborgian death, a space that in terms of sensory
perceptions was one-to-one with the world of the living. Flowers and
trees, meadows and fields, asphalt and weeds growing from the
cracks in the asphalt, sparrows, eagles, rattlesnakes, parking structures, cement foundations, saffron milk caps and all the other
mushrooms; simply put, *everything* is exactly the same in both
worlds. Both for the living and the recently deceased. When you
mistake the sole of a boot thrown on the shoulder of the road for a
crouching cat, or a paper tissue dropped on the pavement for a dead
bird, you could be either living or dead. Even illusions don't disappear when you die! Because the dead, Swedenborg believed, Polina
argues vehemently, the dead first step into the state of the external
mind. Which is exactly the same kind of state as the state in the world
of the living, so the dead can't even know they're dead! The next step,
Swedenborg claimed, says Polina, the next step in dying signifies a
transition to the state of the inner parts. The dead become their own

thoughts and their own will, and the body ceases to be an impediment. And pretending isn't possible any more.

"Hey, now I understand!" Ulrike suddenly exclaims. "We died long before we ever came here! We just thought we were still alive. We were wandering around the world like that guy Bruce Willis played, you know, in that horror movie . . ."

Polina's mouth hangs open in surprise. She didn't see this transition coming. Even Ulrike hasn't pondered it; the realization just flares within her, and the words come instantly. Ulrike searches for the name of the film, and a brightness resembling remembrance is somewhere near, but not in her; something definitive and sure drips with surging power toward her from just a step away . . . from Nina. Yes. Something floods from Nina toward Ulrike, something which at first is difficult to grasp, something delicate and strange, but then, suddenly, *snap*, utterly personal and bright and sure: "It was *The Sixth Sense*. Now I remember, and Bruce Willis played a shrink who's dead but doesn't realize it! It's the perfect Swedenborgian film! Or *The Others*, the one with Nicole Kidman . . . The mother, her light-sensitive children, and the whole horrible tragedy, and the viewer doesn't realize they're dead any more than they do!"

Ulrike goes silent, sinking into thought. So when did she start to be dead? Did she remember any situations where others couldn't see her? Did people see through her on the street? Did she go home without trading news with anyone? Did she wander around the Eagle's Nest in front of customers with blank expressions in a strange silence? Did dishes, coffee cups, and cakes rise into the air in her dead grasp . . . ?

"Well," Polina says, waking Ulrike from her reverie, "what if we vote now? Can we explain our current state using Swedenborg's celestial doctrine? Let me give a brief review: we died, we unknowingly passed through an intermediate stage, which was a place like the world of the living, and now we are in the 'state of the inner self', we have become our own thoughts and our own wills, and our bodies have ceased to hinder us. Shlomith suggested that we're in hell. On the other hand, we've been very quick to learn and very industrious here. We built this house around us and started a fire in the fireplace. So why couldn't we also be in heaven? Left hands up everyone who believes the hell hypothesis! Right, if you believe we're in heaven. And if you think Emanuel's visions are just the ravings of a deranged mind, don't raise your hands at all."

There it is. The straw. The magic has gone. She shouldn't have said that. "Don't raise your hands at all." *Of course* Emanuel was a crazy head. *Of course* his visions were ravings. *Of course* they have wasted their time, whatever that might be here now. All the enthusiasm and attentiveness has gone to waste because of one poorly chosen phrase: "Don't raise your hands at all." Polina realized her error the instant she said that last word, but it was too late. Would the curse never end? Everything had been so beautiful, so like a dream. She had shone, and now she, she alone, had deflated the dream. A sullen, unwelcoming expression appears on the women's faces, the resentful, wrinkled mug of a small child who's been cheated in such a way to injure her down to her very heartstrings. In hell, in heaven: all a sham.

And not a single hand goes up.

SHLOMITH'S EXPERIMENTAL LIFE

"In hell." That was how Shlomith answered Polina's question before the spell faded, and it was her firm opinion, not a joke or a game: they were in hell and that was that. However, it is necessary to stop at this point, because, as is well known, there is no direct reference to heaven or hell in the Pentateuch, and it is not easy to find a Jewish scholar these days who believes in messianic redemption, resurrection, or any otherworldly inventions—no, not if you should search all the synagogues of the world. Although Shlomith had been a passionate atheist since the age of sixteen, she knew her background like her own pockets, and she never made accidental mistakes. She dug out the dogma and placed it on the table and made contact with it; she dug out the belief and mocked it as necessary, but she didn't make mistakes. That was not her style. The older she became, the greater her longing for nuance grew. She loved contradictions, and she didn't fear conflict. She stood before humanity and placed her art on display, her culture, the most important raw material for her art, from which she drew compulsively some said, shamelessly and blasphemously said the orthodox. They hated her and organized protests in front of the museums and galleries, the places where she performed. They infiltrated the art-hungry crowd and pelted her with rotten eggs, but the eggs weren't enough. Those white, sulphuric bombs were only a prelude, because Shlomith also began to receive death threats. The first one came in 1979 and was a ludicrous pasting together of letters from newspaper headlines: BITCH YOU'RE AN INSTRUMENT OF SATAN YOU OUGHT TO DIE!!! Shlomith smirked at this, almost feeling pride. She had now reached this point and joined those privileged few who were doomed to die for their art. She used the folded sheet of paper, which was stiff with glue, as part of her next performance, in which she burned certain books in a kiln constructed in the gallery space from red bricks. The death threat went into the fire, along with everything else as soon as she had read it aloud. It was the last piece of paper to go into the kiln during the performance, which we will return to because it became a turning point in Shlomith's rising career—after this, the heavens opened, as the saying goes. Four more death threats came, and Shlomith didn't smirk any more. The police classified two as serious enough that Shlomith was forced to hire a bodyguard for the next eighteen months. Although it began as a contractual relationship, this "experiment", as Shlomith later described it in an interview, led to some unique situations; among other things, Shlomith found herself carrying her bodyguard's child. She had an abortion and used the material (*experiential* material, not the aborted fetus!) in a performance named *Kaddish for an Unborn Child*, and never accepted that the novel by the same name published ten years later by the Hungarian author Imre Kertész had *anything* to do with her work. Shlomith was a pioneer in her field, and she knew it. People followed her work, something of which she was also aware. And that was precisely why she approached her material so seriously. Being in the avant-garde creates certain obligations, and she couldn't give murderous religious fanatics even the slightest justification to throw stones. Now they could have a chance to swallow the strangeness of their religion down to the last bone, as she had done. But let them leave her in peace, Elokim save them, let them leave her alive! Because she, if anyone, didn't make mistakes and that was that, and that was precisely why Shlomith absolutely could never be let off the hook so easily. "In hell": where exactly did Shlomith think they were?

It's unfortunate if our thirst for civilization and above all our desire to unearth information causes disgust in two groups of people: in those who love adventure and quick progress and in those who already know everything, perhaps even more than us (which is hardly possible). But Shlomith must be held to account. We must explain how seriously her art should be taken (she herself took it deadly seriously). We must ask whether her art holds up to time or whether it was only born of a desire to shock. Of course we don't doubt her intentions *a priori*. Surely no one would care to provoke, just for the sake of provocation, for forty years on end. Surely a person could find something better to do in all that time. Shlomith could have, for example (and this is only a suggestion), rebuilt her burned bridges. She could, if she wanted to, have devoted all her strength to finding some new connection to her two children, Malka and Moti, a connection which she had ruined by her own hand (one could also say: out of her sheer stupidity). But that is also another story. Now we simply want an answer to our question: where is a Jew when she's in hell?

The written Torah, which God delivered to Moses on Mount Sinai, does not know heaven or hell. "But Gehenna!" some will shout with tremulous voice, "but Gehenna!" Yes, there is Gehenna, but it wasn't located on the other side of the veil, it was just on the south side of ancient Jerusalem. From the beginning it was a profane, miserable place, a rocky valley where innocent children were sacrificed to Moloch and the Canaanite god Baal, or Baal-sebub, who later, among believers, became Beelzebub, as you may know: the Evil One, Old Scratch, the Father of Lies, the Horned God. It was rabbis studying the cryptic language of the Old Testament who invented heaven, naming it *Gan Eden*, and hell, which they called (and yes, the connection to the place of slaughter mentioned above is clear) *Gehinnom*. They invented heaven because, despite his promises, Yahweh didn't remain by his chosen people's side. He seemed to be doing something else entirely (sleeping? demurely averting his eyes?) and allowing his people to suffer, allowing the children of Israel to be enslaved through no fault of their own, to be tortured and killed, even though they were willing with one accord to follow literally each and every one of God's 613 commandments and injunctions; or had someone gone AWOL after all? The irrational, unexplainable suffering simply began to exceed the human capacity to understand, so God a) was a sadist, or b) didn't exist, or c) had something better in store for his chosen people. And so that had to be it. He had reserved something better for them in another world. Not in some ancient, murky underworld but above, in a bright heaven. The first two options were out of the question. Contemplating them wasn't even permitted, at least not out loud. Those were ideas you couldn't even taste with your lips, even if you left the thought silent, even if your lips only brushed by the words (out of some incomprehensible defiance) and even if you uttered the words all alone, with your whole body facing the corner: *God is a sadist, God does not exist*. It's impossible. "For there is not a word in my tongue, but, lo, O Lord, thou knowest it altogether." And thinking about points a) and b) might lead to that place we shall soon reach, the Jewish hell, which no one actually believes in any more these days, and probably never believed anciently either. Jews have always been practically minded. Heaven and hell were just the result of frantic digging by rabbis in the post-biblical period using a big, rusty shovel to fill holes in the Bible. One might wonder whether a dose of narcotic herbs might have been necessary to invent them, or perhaps the human imagination was significantly more prone to megalomania in ancient times than today. Whatever the case, hell had to be invented. There was no other option. Otherwise the atheists and all the other soulless degenerates might get out like a dog from its cage, and often they seemed to: Yahweh didn't cast brimstone down on their heads; instead He let them become wealthy as their waists spread and necks grew thick, while He left his previous lambs, his most faithful bleaters, to the hands of their tormentors. And for this reason and no other reason, the rabbis' brains began to tick, TICK-TICK-TICK; they ticked so loudly that God's very angels heard the sound. Everything would be made right on the other side: it was better to die and wake up in heaven: Q.E.D.

And so it was. For centuries proud Jews who knew their worth and held tight to their religion fought against the oppressor at the sacrifice of their own lives, *Kiddush ha-Shem*: they sanctified the divine name by killing their stoic selves, remaining clean, becoming martyrs, floating like angels in a weightless state of bliss. This strategy was followed beginning with the Maccabean Revolt, and using this technique—we apologize for the macabre choice of words—one could escape almost anything: Christian crusaders, the Inquisition.

And then back to hell. *Gehinnom*. The rabbis believed that hell was a structure divided into seven parts, each section of which, whether you chose to move horizontally or vertically, required three hundred years to traverse from end to end. And every segment of hell was sliced into seven subsegments, through each of which ran seven rivers of fire and seven of snow, their paths guided by the Angels of Destruction. In each compartment of hell were seven thousand caves, each of which had seven thousand cracks, each of which had seven thousand scorpions. And each scorpion had three hundred rings, in each of which were seven thousand poison sacs, from which flowed seven deadly poisonous rivers. (Wait a moment, so there are now a total of three types of rivers, right?) With flaming whips the Angels of Destruction lashed sinners, meaning those who had broken the commandments of the Torah, insofar as the angels could spare their time from guiding the rivers. For Moses, at least, is said to have taken a guided tour with the angels through hell, like the Christian Durante degli Alighieri, alias Dante, did.

On his journey, Moses saw sinners hung up by their eyelids, their ears, their hands, and their tongues, and women by their breasts and hair, each according to his or her crime, according to what body part had been active in committing the sin. In a place named Aluka, sinners were hung upside down by their feet. Long black worms squirmed on their skin. They had sworn false oaths, they had desecrated Shabbat, they had mocked the wise, and they had defamed their neighbors and done evil to both orphans and widows. Elsewhere, sinners were tormented by two thousand scorpions, each with seventy thousand heads, each with seventy thousand mouths, each with seventy thousand poison barbs, each with seventy thousand poison sacs. The scorpions struck with their tails, stung with their stingers, and in every conceivable way tortured those who had robbed their own kinsmen and abandoned them to heretics, those who had publicly dishonored their neighbors and denied the Torah. To top it all off, those who ended up getting the scorpion treatment had claimed during their lives that God wasn't the creator of the earth!

In Tit ha-Yawen, Moses saw sinners up to their navels in mud. The Angels of Destruction whipped them with fiery chains—they had time for that too—and hung glowing stones from their teeth. These wretches had eaten forbidden food, given money to usurers to loan, and stolen pennies from their fellows. They had used false weights, they had written the name of God on infidel amulets, and they had eaten on Yom Kippur, and, logically, they had also drunk blood.

Finally Moses arrived at the level of hell named Avadon. There sinners were burned: one half of their bodies were submerged in fire and the other half in snow, and at the same time worms generated from their own flesh crawled all over them. The Angels of Destruction abused them without cease. These sinners were the worst of the worst. They had committed incest, they had murdered and called themselves gods, they had cursed their parents and teachers, and— well, that's pretty much it.

Then the bewildered Moses was delivered back to the surface of the earth, where in a daze he continued guiding his people away from the hands of their enemies. And the wretches didn't under- stand to be thankful, instead grumbling constantly, "Because there were no graves in Egypt, hast thou taken us away to die in the wilderness?"

Of course there are also detailed accounts of the Jewish heaven, but as all who have read their *Divina Commedia* know (regardless of whether the book was read in the original language or only in trans- lation), no one is interested in heaven. The rays of Beatrice's smile are just as boring as lukewarm bath water whose rose extracts have stopped giving off their fragrance. Hell is what stirs people up! Hell makes your skin tingle and your heart race. And that's why we will pass over the blooming trees of life and luxurious rooms paneled in olive wood (and also because the architecture of the Jewish heaven wasn't on the list of things to be explained in the first place, of course) and conclude that the hell Shlomith referenced in answer to Polina's question meant something other than the blood and thunder

Gehinnom of the rabbis, where fiery chains flail and scorpions work their tortures.

Perhaps when she said hell Shlomith meant other people, as a certain French intellectual wrote in his famous play set in the afterlife. The play was performed for the first time in May, 1944—note: the German collaborator Marshal Pétain was still in power then; Paris was not liberated until August—at a place named the Théâtre du Vieux-Colombier, and ever since the interpretation of the phrase "*L'enfer, c'est les autres*" has, well, gone all to hell. Not *all* people, always and everywhere, are synonymous with hell. Some of us at least sometimes are sublimely lovable. Just so long as it remains possible to get away from us for a while, if we can be missed and longed for, if we can be approached and retreated from, then, and only then, there is a particle of divine lovability in us.

But our women in white have been connected to each other like bulls mired in tar: Shlomith a prisoner in Polina, Polina in Shlomith, Nina in them all and all of them in Nina, and likewise Maimuna, Wlibgis, and Ulrike prisoners in each and each in them, all prisoners except Rosa Imaculada, who had known to flee.

This was most likely the kind of hell Shlomith meant when she snorted her response at Polina.

This idea is supported by a certain fact, which most who followed Polina's Swedenborg lecture closely may have overlooked entirely. If someone had happened to glance at Shlomith, they might have noticed a slightly downturned mouth, a jaw slack with disgust, belladonna eyes which had ceased watching Polina as she talked. Oh, so there's love in the spirit world, and that love is oneness, those scintillating eyes said. And the six of us here form a divinely harmonious mind? Ha! I, Shlomith, beginning with S and ending with H, have lived purely on argument, and argument is what I've come here to bring. That's my nature! Even when I loved, really loved, as I loved my husband Dovid, even then waves of dissatisfaction roiled and crashed within me, and I started arguments; yes, I was the one who usually started them, just like here. Just to indulge my frustration. So we're in hell. You're my hell, and I'm your hell, and that's right for me and it's right for you. So there!

And this was how Shlomith got out of the fix we'd put her in, out of our pure malice and inconsolableness, because unfortunately we're here too.

It may already be clear that when Shlomith was at the zenith of her fame as an artist, she didn't believe in anything but herself (in her best moments). She trusted herself and her material, which she viewed with a strange mixture of reverence and abhorrence. Yes, her *material*. It was like food you could put in your mouth and not be sure immediately whether it was good or awful. You can't tell whether you can eat a lot of it or none at all. But Shlomith wouldn't have been Shlomith if she hadn't continued taking more. She had to go on ladling it in for the simple reason that she was Shlomith-Shkhina, more intimately Sh-Sh; she had also tattooed this letter combination on her left wrist. That stage name and the abbreviation formed from it was known not only by every friend of the arts on the east coast but also by every hater of the arts; even those who had little interest in high culture and its highest form, performance, recognized it superficially if they read newspapers with the slight-est regularity. Because Shlomith-Shkhina had regularly appeared in almost all of them beginning in the early 1980s: *The Times, The New Yorker, The New York Times, Newsweek, Rolling Stone* . . . In honor of her sixtieth birthday in October, 2006, a cover story appeared in *Vanity Fair*: "Why Do We Drool Over Shlomith-Shkhina?" The author of the article, a young man early in a promising career as a journalist, had gone completely weak in the knees before the goddess he admired. Her desiccated body radiated a presence often called "charisma" but which was better captured by the phrase "Zen-Stoic grandness balanced with mania, impudence, uncon-sciousness, and erotic electricity". Shlomith's eyes bored straight into the viewer's and from the eyes into the farthest reaches of the mind; she gave herself fully even to this insignificant aspiring reporter dressed in a silly, pink anorak and one shade pinker Converse high tops, this thin wisp of a boy with horseshoe-shaped acne scars on his beautiful face, concealed with expensive cover cream. Shlomith-Shkhina was present for him too. For the entire hour and a half the interview lasted, she gave herself to this boy, without reservation but at the same time protectively, tastefully but not at all intrusively.

Shlomith-Shkhina as scapegoat

The article turned out wonderfully. In it Shlomith-Shkhina's most important work was reviewed, of course, including a piece named *I Shall Fear No Evil for Thou Art with Me*. That was an insult performance from 1979 that caused a terrible commotion. The audience was invited to pull out anti-Semitic slurs Shlomith had written in black art pen marker on slips of handmade washi paper from a willow basket covered in black fabric. The audience had a *duty* to come read the contents of the paper they had drawn before Shlomith-Shkhina. Otherwise the performance would have fizzled and the painful catharsis would have gone unfelt.

Shlomith-Shkhina sat half dressed in an uncomfortable position, on her knees, on an Ionic column one hundred and fifty centimeters tall, a column on the cap of which spiraled twisted scrolls like ram's horns. On her own head Shlomith-Shkhina wore large, heavy goat horns, which she had carved herself for this specific performance from Eastern poplar with the aid of a sculptor friend. Can it be said any more plainly: Shlomith-Shkhina was a scapegoat. She was suffering for her tribe's entire agonizing history. Many cried hot tears as they slandered her, weeping before Shlomith-Shkhina's gentle yet deeply mournful eyes, stammering as they read their papers and asking forgiveness with their whole beings. More than every tenth (by Shlomith's count) simply collapsed: they fell to their knees and extended their hands in agony toward the stylite. They wished they could come and embrace Shlomith-Shkhina, wished they could wipe away the tears that had begun to run down her cheeks as well. But a rope divided the audience from the artist. DO NOT TOUCH! was written in large Gothic script on the shaft of the column. A guard with a truncheon stood at the door so nothing truly bad could happen. Most of the people who entered the gallery were friends of the arts, but every once in a while the wrong people would come in, and Shlomith always recognized them instantly. "It was OK," she said to the *Vanity Fair* interviewer. "I knew they would come, and I was even prepared for a scuffle; I wouldn't have fallen far." The Neo-Nazis laughed as they read their slips of paper, stinking of beer, and then added their own significantly more derogatory comments, most of which dealt with Shlomith-Shkhina's half-dressed, rail-thin femininity (although at that point she wasn't thin enough to turn any heads, as had been the case before and would be again; at the time, her 164-centimeter body pressed toward the earth with forty kilograms of muscle and bone and liquid and the tissues that held her together; she was just "very Twiggy", and no worse.)

Believers shook their fists at Shlomith-Shkhina and read passages from the Bible. "You'll burn in hell!" they might shout in chorus, rhythmically, pounding their feet on the floor of the gallery. But Shlomith-Shkhina let all of them approach. She didn't draw the line anywhere, except, this time, around her physical integrity.

At this point unfortunately we need to turn back to the performance we mentioned a moment ago in passing, unfortunately because it may still agitate some. It agitates us anyway. Under no circumstances do we intend to rehash Shlomith's entire curriculum vitae, which would be inexpedient since there are simply too many performances. Including some (especially from the early stage of her career) which are less deserving of trumpeting. For example, the rolling about in food. But perhaps we can share a little about this after all? There was a milk basin and a basin full of roasted lamb shanks, and between them a large hourglass and Shlomith, who wasn't Shkhina yet. Shlomith dipped herself, naked of course, in the milk, submerging herself in the sweet, white liquid up to her hair and greedily sucking it in. Then she moved to the hourglass. With both hands she rotated the hourglass on its axle, and the hourglass began to drizzle the sand of Jerusalem through its funnel. The sand took twenty long minutes to flow out, during which time willow-switch slender Shlomith shivered with cold, covered in milk, bones protruding cruelly through her thin skin as she stood near the axle. When the sand had all drained out, Shlomith moved to the lamb shank basin and burrowed in under the meat. She nibbled and she licked, but she was significantly more restrained than she had been slurping the milk before. This continued for six hours, which was how long *Food Meditation* (1976) lasted. This performance (which we've now ended up describing in its essentials) and a few others (which we promise not to tell about) were mostly "fumbling" by an emerging artist coming out of such obscurity that hardly anyone attended them. But of course they were recorded. Shlomith knew her value from the start and sensed, we presume, the future appreciation she would enjoy. And we agree with this principle: you should always remember to record everything. Everything! Every newspaper clipping someone has ever written, all the photographs, the letters, and the postcards must be collected and organized in a scrapbook. Diaries must be kept, feelings must be written down, because does anything else exist once all is said and done?

Shlomith-Shkhina and God's 614th commandment

The development of Shlomith's career was finally sealed by a performance in 1983 that dealt with the genocide of the Jews. In the performance, Shlomith read excerpts of "Jewish theorists' post-Shoah attempts to explain the will of God", as she summarized the event in *Vanity Fair*. Many saw the presentation as pure blasphemy, not so much because Shlomith-Shkhina read the texts nude (she really did prefer not to wear clothing!), but more because she wasn't completely naked. She had decorated her body with clothes pins, hanging them from certain painful protuberances such as her nipples and labia. And that wasn't all: she had pierced her stomach with safety pins, her back was covered in red stripes from being whipped, and to cap it off she had been beaten; the bruises on her legs and arms were genuine. So there she was reading parts of these books, which are difficult even for us to repeat now because (we're sorry, don't attack us, this isn't something we invented!) they reveal a certain masochism that injected itself into Semitic culture at some point.

In her bruised hand, Shlomith first lifted a work by Eliezer Berkovits called *Faith after the Holocaust*, and began to read to herself in a steady, slightly monotone voice, autocratically changing "him" to "me", standing before a live audience bruised, legs slightly spread; there Shlomith read without expression, adding emphasis to not a single word, beginning from page eighty-one, changing one pronoun on the fly. Like this: "'I am alone—with my God. And God is silent, and God is hiding his face. God has abandoned me. Now I am truly alone. If at this moment I am able to accept my radical abandonment by God as a gift from God that enables me to love my God with all my soul . . . I have achieved the highest form of *Kiddush ha-Shem*.'"

The more monotonous Shlomith's recitation became, the more clearly and slowly she articulated, the more quiet the space around her became, the less the audience dared to rustle their clothing, to shift their weight from one leg to another. "'My radical abandonment is the great moment for which I have been waiting all my life. For no one can so completely surrender to Him as the one who is completely forsaken by Him.'" Did people really understand what Shlomith read to them? Did they understand that they had just been told that the Shoah meant the ecstatic fulfillment of a lifelong anticipation of surrender? That the greatest evil was actually the greatest good? That the deepest debasement of the soul gave birth to its highest ascension? Never again, but fortunately at least this one time?

When Shlomith had quoted enough of Mr. Berkovits's ideas, she picked up the most controversial book of her performance, Ignaz Maybaum's *The Face of God after Auschwitz*, and began to read from page sixty-one without changing a word:

"'The *churban* is an operation in which God, like a surgeon, cuts out a past from the body of mankind . . .'" Shlomith continued reading, and after reaching page sixty-four, she asked in Maybaum's words: "'Are we to say: the *churban* created this progress?! How terrible that we paid for this progress with the death of six million martyrs. Can you understand it? I cannot. You cannot. It is not for us to understand. For us it remains to praise the works of God. *Ma'asei Eloheinu*.'"

Auschwitz-Birkenau and all the other labor and concentration and extermination camps, prison camps, assembly camps, and pass-through camps: A as in Amersfoort, B as in Bełzec or Bergen-Belsen or Buchenwald, C as in Chełmno, D as in Dachau, now we jump around, F as in Flossenbürg, we jump and shout M as in Murderer, M as in Majdanek, M as in Mauthausen-Gusen, now picking at random, S as in Sobibór, S as in SS, T as in Treblinka, and that isn't the end, W as in Warsaw and Westerbork, and then back to the middle, N as in *Nacht und Nebel*, N as in Niederhagen, N as in *Nuit et Brouillard* . . . There's never any end. All the camps, the destroyed ghettos, the broken windows, the razed shops, all of them were part of GOD'S INTERVENTION as Ignaz Maybaum claimed and emptied his pipe bowl of ash. This wasn't a matter of punishment, it was a sacrificial offering. God used his chosen people as an instrument of creative destruction. All out of love. This is the meaning of the Hebrew word *churban*, a moment of massive destruction, in Maybaum's interpretation.

A small lesson on Maybaum may be in order to facilitate a better grasp of this plot stub. The story goes this way: when Jerusalem was destroyed in 586 BCE, the Jewish diaspora began, thanks to which knowledge of God and His laws spread across the world. This was the first historical *churban*. When the Romans destroyed the second temple in Jerusalem in the year 70, the synagogue was born, animal sacrifice ended, and religious study and prayer began, which elevated the system of Judaism to a higher level: this was the second *churban*. The third *churban*, as you can guess, was the Holocaust, which most Jews prefer to call the Shoah, but not Maybaum, not he, and began the modernization of Jewish culture. Regressive medieval traditions inherited from the feudal system, which people tended to follow in the ghettos of Eastern Europe and among Sephardic Jews, were destroyed along with the ghettos. Traditionally-minded Jews were "exterminated", as the sophisticated expression has it in this series of events, and "Their death purged Western civilization." Thus Maybaum wrote, and then began gently to clean his pipe with a bristle cleaner.

His remaining coreligionists, already cosmopolitans who had

opened their minds to progressive ideas (you may have heard talk of a Jewish enlightenment ideology named *haskala*) avoided destruction by moving to other countries, mainly the United States and Israel. Maybaum's God stood at the gates and chose carefully whom he would send on the ships to the New World or to the arrow-head-shaped strip of shore between the Jordan River and the Mediterranean, and whom he would shove in trains and barracks and gas chambers and then, finally, crematoria hidden in the shadows of the forest. In Maybaum's sketch, God's divine face bears a strong resemblance to an Obersturmbannführer. It might be handsome, kind, and even bear an affectionate smile, because carrying out great plans can make anyone beautiful, or at least a momentarily sparkling pulsar. According to Maybaum's God, purity, progress, shiny surfaces, and speed ran rings around cobblestones, smoky alleyways, and strange traditions whose origins the followers of those traditions didn't even attempt to trace.

Maybaum listened carefully to the whisperings of his God, acknowledging that they were logical in their own special way and recording his thoughts. His thoughts or God's thoughts, it made no matter—presumably they developed in a collegial spirit. After he finished writing, Maybaum filled his pipe with high-quality tobacco, lit the bowl, and inhaled with the utmost pleasure. A nauseating, suffocating smoke enveloped the room like a veil of mourning. Ignaz Maybaum wrapped his pages in brown kraft paper and sent his manuscript to his publisher.

Shlomith read Maybaum's book kneeling. Her monotonous, exaggeratedly calm voice resembled a speech simulator. And when she had read enough of the book ("enough" in the sense that our artist couldn't stand to read any more and began to trip over the words and nod off over the book, on the verge of passing out), she set it on the floor and began tearing out pages. With disgust she loved those densely printed pages, because (this was clear to Shlomith by the third day she presented the piece, on the day *The New York Times* published a halfpage review of it, which included, for the first time, a small sidebar about Shlomith-Shkhina) reading this specific scandalous book out loud clinched her reputation. The other books were actually props, just warm-ups for Maybaum. To be perfectly clear: it was largely thanks to Maybaum that Shlomith became an artist to be reckoned with. What a grotesque twist!

Fortunately there were specialists in tortuous twists in ideology who pounced the instant they smelled an Important Topic floating on the air. Performance art researchers came from as far away as Australia to watch Shlomith, and Shlomith did her best. In a frenzy she tore the pages of the book, wallowing in the white shreds, biting the paper and gnawing on the cover, and finally she put what was left of the book named *The Face of God after Auschwitz* in an incinerator build out of red bricks. Within the incinerator waited a large pile of paper shreds. During the debut performance, which was on the fifteenth of January, Shlomith ended her reading with the death threat she had received: BITCH YOU'RE AN INSTRUMENT OF SATAN YOU OUGHT TO DIE!!! She lit the sheet of paper with slow, ritualistic movements and shoved the burning threat into the oven, setting alight the other paper. Champagne glasses in hand, the invited guests with their geometric hairdos and garish lipstick clapped furiously.

The performance, which was named *The 614th Commandment*, by no means ended after one or two or even three days of reading and tearing and burning. Shlomith had collected an appalling number of Maybaum's books from every bookstore and second-hand shop she could find. She had sacrificed a small fortune in order to get her hands on every one it was possible to get. And the audience lasted as long as the books: all the way until May. (As a result of this, Maybaum's work is extremely difficult to find anywhere. You have to shell out $147 for a ragged, used paperback version if you can even find one.)

A certain Andrea Dworkin also came to see *The 614th Commandment*, on a day when Shlomith was particularly bruised (who beat her into performance condition and where, that Shlomith wished to keep secret to the end). In Andrea's opinion, the presentation was only *disgusting*, and she wrote an angry essay in the *New York Post*: "Anorexic-Masochist, the Wanna-Be Messiah."

Shlomith-Shkhina betrays feminists and Jewish women, imagining herself a reborn Simone Weil, *how embarrassing*! And Andrea wasn't just anyone shouting from the bushes—she was a passionately worshiped and deeply despised belligerent, a militant feminist who had eaten herself into enormity, who thought that Zionism produced macho wife beaters and oppressors of Palestinians. And copulation was the same as rape, which was the same as the Holocaust of the Jews. And men were fundamentally evil. And women were supposed to be on each other's side. Why on earth was a well-off woman like Shlomith playing victim again? Why was she using her slender body to repeat the wrongs the Jews had suffered? Were there no limits to her narcissism? Didn't she understand she was damaging the cause she defended?

"I'm not a lawyer, I'm an artist," Shlomith replied to Andrea in the next edition of the *New York Post*. "I show, I don't argue or defend. Everything else is interpretation."

Soon after this, Shlomith and Andrea were at Rockefeller Center for a taping of the *Today Show*. They glared at each other angrily from opposite ends of a curved sofa, hunched over uncomfortably. Between them the host sat straight as a board—the peacemaker, her long, beautiful legs smartly tilted to one side; that posture came naturally when you worked in TV, when you had to look, if not beautiful, then at least impeccable: no varicose veins on the legs and no runs in the stockings, and the camera could never, ever, under any circumstances, record even a *promise* of opening shins; the skimpy suit skirt had to stay on the thighs as if it was glued there; the slender kneecaps had to stay together as if they were sewn; the shins had to look more like plastic than flesh, and then you also had to be unaffected, from head to toe one hundred percent natural.

The host's mahogany-colored hair was teased skywards, and her eyelids were weighed down by heavy arcs of turquoise that could have extended farther but for the thinly plucked eyebrows. But this make-up served, strangely enough, the impression of naturalness, because on television everything was different from the outside world. If you were naturally natural on television, all was lost. And besides, the host's whimsical appearance calmed the picture frame, forming as it were a vertical divider between the spaces the two peppery women occupied. Without her, Shlomith and Andrea probably would have attacked each other, or at least that was the feeling that had been created in the studio. (We can only stand in silent admiration of the skill of the *Today Show*'s crew.)

There they were, the stars of the night, Lady Negative and Lady Positive: Shlomith, thin with curly hair and Andrea, fat with curly hair. One wore all-black overalls, held tight around her waist by a gold sequined belt but bulging loosely elsewhere, the other a mournful dark brown kaftan, brightened by an enormous Inca-style poplin vest. The conversation immediately went off the rails:

"My body is a transit place for the audience's pent up feelings of anger."

"Well, that certainly is pompous . . . Can we stop the bullshit? You do to your body exactly what you decide to do to it. You may not have heard but the battlefield is somewhere else entirely . . ."

"Of course I make my own decisions about my body! Pain is an important element in my work. I take possession of pain the same way I take possession of history: through my body. And you do the same thing: you take possession of something through your body . . ."

"Yeah, yeah, the personal is political . . ."

"Yes, the personal is political! I think you've eaten too much rugelach . . ."

"A few rugelach might do you good too, *darling*. All I can say is that it's significantly easier to think when you've eaten properly. Hunger also shrinks the brain, if you didn't know. It narrows the perspective . . ."

And so on and so forth. The talk show didn't give a terribly flattering image of either zealot. And besides, they looked comically identical, with the only difference being that one was thick and one was thin. What else could they do but fight! They obediently played their roles. It was a masterstroke of casting . . . They taunted each other's appearance, even though they were supposed to talk about the painful spots in Jewish culture. Maybe one of the production assistants sparred with them behind the scenes to bring out their worst sides? Maybe before the broadcast they were goaded into losing their composure and through their composure their self-respect? At least the viewers got the sensationalism they were hungry for. And the cartoonists. For the next week the papers were full of pictures, each more grotesque than the last: Shlomith and Andrea in a boxing ring, on a wrestling mat, brandishing swords. Shlomith and Andrea sitting at a banquet table, throwing cake, pies, and fruit at each other. "Shlomith and Andrea, Andrea and Shlomith, it seemed like it would never end," Shlomith said to the *Vanity Fair* interviewer, who had tilted his head empathetically. "It was a miscalculation for both of us. We made peace after a few years, but no one bothered writing headlines about that."

But now the interviewer wanted to move forward, or, more precisely, backward. "Since we've already discussed *The 614th Commandment* and your other significant performances, I wonder whether this might be a good moment to shift to a period of your life you haven't spoken about much in public. I mean the time you spent in Israel, at the kibbutz. When you were in your twenties. What happened then? At least your name, 'Shlomith', is from that period, as I understand, and it isn't your birth name. Why did you leave the United States, and why did you decide to return?" The interviewer poured Shlomith more oolong tea in her gold-rimmed porcelain cup and waited.

Sheila the drummer, adrift in Park Slope

So, what happened? What happened was a chain reaction, whose intermediate stages and flash points can be described in many divergent ways. Everything depends on which party one happens to ask about the series of events (which at the time they occurred weren't yet a *series*, nicely ordered in a line, canned and bundled, labeled and shoved in their box, like shoes are arranged on cleaning day, or jars in the refrigerator on jam-making day, or like the endless wires and connectors that build up behind the television crammed in a cable

organizer: in a word, tamed, because the nature of wires and connectors is to be tangled like a nest of snakes, and the same thing goes for
events; wires and connectors—and shoes!—collect dirt, dust, fuzz,
fluff, hair, lint, rocks, just like events collect shocks, changes in direction, hesitations, ruptures, pastilles down the wrong pipe, and, with
unfortunate regularity, terrible amounts of anger, which has a hard
time finding a target: objects fly, hands are raised, almost striking,
screaming penetrates all the surfaces, the walls, the floors, the earth,
and space, the cerebral cortex and that heart and the kidneys, which
specialize in waste treatment. All those disturbances ultimately end
up hidden, like the refuse that disappears under a snake nest of cords
and connectors, and under rubber shoe soles, in the grooves of the
tread pattern; that is the treacherous nature of refuse and disturbances, and even so—breathe, breathe, breathe!—all that distracting,
disgusting, difficult, depressing and indeterminate stuff has to be
picked up, like apples fallen in the garden; all of them, apples and
problems, need saucing and bottling like cables need bundling and
shoes need arranging in a row. And if you place a label on the side of
the jar, you know immediately what's inside: BREAKING UP, LOVE,
INFATUATION, COMING TO YOUR SENSES, BREAKING UP. A
beautiful series, no?)

In any case, the facts are as follows: the year was 1963 and Shlomith,
who at the time was not Shlomith, let alone Shlomith-Shkhina, but
rather Sheila, was seventeen years old. She lived in a small studio
apartment separated by a thin wall from her parents' apartment in
Park Slope on Carroll Street, and she was in bad shape. Before
Shlomith lived in the studio, and before Sheila, it had been cousin
Benjamin's temporary residence, but Benjamin had found the love of
his life and moved away. Soon after this, Sheila—we apologize that
we have to use, temporarily of course, this previously unfamiliar
name, which may be troublesome to commit to memory, but try to
remember: Shlomith is (to some degree) the same as Sheila, and
Sheila is (to some degree) the same as Shlomith (Sh is Sh is Sh:
Shlomith, Sheila, Shlomith, Sheila)—began to pester to have the
apartment for herself. She was fifteen years old. She had had enough

of sitting together at the dinner table. She didn't want to see her mother's face, withdrawn in her martyr's bitterness, which occasionally blew out an accusation, some sort of muffled exclamation, like a black cloud of spores from an old puffball fungus (*Lycoperdon perlatum*) that has seen better days. Sheila was bored and depressed, and that was why she was so insanely thin.

Finally, as a seventeenth birthday present, Sheila received her very own keys to "the practice apartment", as her mother, Miriam, referred to it. Miriam had demanded that a hole resembling a cat flap be built in the wall, near the floor, so she could send food to her daughter, who was incomprehensibly uninterested in preparing her own, even though the flat had such a nice little "practice kitchen", where Benjamin's then-girlfriend, now-wife, Raizy had enjoyed making food, including challenging baked goods, which everyone on both sides of the wall had relished—all except Sheila. No, Miriam's daughter was definitely not moving to the other side of the wall without this rescue hatch!

Sheila didn't have any alternative. So she pushed a chest of drawers she had inherited from her grandmother in front of the hatch, and her father cut a hole in the oak back. This way she could choose for herself when she opened the drawer to accept the food her mother had shoved in, or the messages; all vital dispatches. However, now her mother couldn't peek through the hole whenever she wanted. And Miriam definitely would have. Sheila could easily imagine her mother mopping the floor on her side of the hole, where something difficult to clean had supposedly fallen, something that had supposedly almost spread to the other side of the wall, so that she had to stick her head through and make sure nothing was left on the floor on Sheila's side, because (now Sheila heard her mother's feigned concern in her ears) if liquid gets in the chinks in an old wood floor (of course the substance that had spilled was "liquid"), nothing could save the floor, and they would have to replace a large swath of boards so they wouldn't warp over time and ruin the entire apartment.

Contrary to her mother's fervent hopes, Sheila lost even more weight after the move. They had unwillingly given their daughter "her own space", 21 x 21 feet, and a "chance to become independent", as Miriam's psychoanalyst friend had recommended. And what did she do? She took the delicacies her mother packed in cardboard out of the chest of drawers and threw them away! In a black trash sack on the side of the road, Miriam found a heap of untouched spinach pies, which she unquestionably recognized as her own handiwork. They had carefully pinched edges, the kind no one makes any more, except her. She would know her symmetric puff pastry pleats with her eyes closed. But her daughter refused to eat them. This caused a terrible row, after which a week passed before Sheila agreed to open the drawer again.

Sheila waited for the *deus ex machina* of her life and with increasing determination continued to leave the meals packed in cardboard uneaten. And then god appeared, but a very different god than she had imagined. Sheila had imagined herself being *caught up* into the next world by accident as a result of her dieting hobby. But no, she didn't swoon and fall to the stage (soon we'll get to why she was on stage so much during that period) and no ambulance came to fetch her. She didn't end up being operated on by people in white coats with stethoscopes, and her disfigured *oh my god!!!* body didn't stop functioning after all. Not yet anyway. (With what pleasure Sheila had looked forward to her own funeral! Her mother, her father, her siblings, her uncles, her aunts, her friends, especially a certain Penny, all blubbering because of her, finally able to understand how hard things had been for her; standing around the grave they would regret that they hadn't known how to help, that they had just nagged and shouted and judged and forced advice on her that she really didn't need—what do you say now?) And then, suddenly and without warning, god appeared before her in the form of a man from Poland.

Dovid had left his home, completely, eternally. (That's also a long and complicated story, with more than enough anger and disgust and disappointment; we trust that things will become clear with time what kind of man this Dovid was and from what kind of ragged hole his determination, which ultimately quelled Sheila's anorexia, welled.) Dovid traveled from Łódź first to London and then to the

Big Apple, and there, at a certain experimental club, which novice Fluxus pioneers favored, he ran into Sheila. Sheila played drums, and for that reason she was often on stage. She played drums before The Velvet Underground's Maureen Tucker! (Shlomith remembered to mention this in the *Vanity Fair* interview.) The band's name was Entropy and in the wake of Shlomith-Shkhina's rise it later gained cult status. Even John Cage was known to have attended one of their shows. In certain circles the band was called a "pacesetter", and there was actually a grain of truth in that. These days the band's only published EP (and a few muffled bootlegs) costs a tidy sum, by no means because of the lead singer, Penny, who in the mid-seventies decided she'd had her fill of messing about, became a jurist, and gave birth to three well-behaved girls, but rather because of Shlomith, crazy, genius Shlomith-Shkhina. But of course Sheila couldn't dream of any of that at the time: everything was shit, shit, shit, shit.

It would be fun to describe Entropy's music in more detail, but our competence is insufficient. To our ears, it was mostly buzzing and squeaking and onomatopoeic wailing. Sweating profusely, Sheila pounded a steady beat on the bass drum, adding violent drum fills that resembled landslides, but at what point these came we don't know because the music sounded like a chaotic avalanche and the fills seemed to join the mix unexpectedly. But the music wasn't random because, as if by a stroke of magic, with complete control, the orchestra stopped producing its croaking, beating, acid-hacking wall of sound. Silence. Shhhhh!

The spotlight falls on the singer, sunken-cheeked Penny in her tight T-shirt decorated with the letters L.H.O.O.Q., who plays a special role in Sheila's funeral fantasies. (Penny falls to her knees on the floor of the synagogue, crushed by guilt as soon as the reading of the first psalm begins.) Then the drumming begins again, *puduTum*, *puduTum-Tum*, *pudupudutratatatataTUM*, and Penny starts howling through the mouthpiece of a soprano saxophone she has brought to her lips. It is the agony of a tortured small animal, and Sheila's tom-toms torment the whimpering creature more. The saxophone creature bellows and moans louder, the bellows and moans convulsing the pit of the listener's stomach, causing an intense nausea (at least in anyone who had eaten too little before coming to the show and had drunk a couple of pints on an empty stomach). And then. Silence. Shhhhh! Once again seemingly at random. Penny and Sheila don't even glance at each other, apparently sensing when the right moment comes (people with the capacity for improvisation have a sixth, even a seventh or eighth sense), and so Penny gently lowers the saxophone to the floor and lies down next to it.

But the bliss doesn't last long. Suddenly Penny wakes up and attacks the saxophone, straddling it and beginning to spread her legs. She does a graceful spiral, like a gymnast, and finally bends her upper body with surprising flexibility over the metal instrument. Then Sheila starts pounding the bass drum pedal again. The bassist and guitarist join in, howling, whining, and banging their instruments. And Penny begins to sing. Lying on the floor, she sings in a trans-rational language that lashes its sensual message straight into the heart, as the critic at the *Village Voice* wrote in his two-column review of the show on March 16, 1965. "Penny McQueen is one of the most charismatic and unique female artists of the decade on the East Coast," was the ending of the short article, without a single word about the drummer! At least the critic wrote about the band, since Entropy was something different from the hippie and acid lineups, singer-songwriter combos, and folk artists who sang God only knew what childishness. Oh, how Sheila detested those do-gooders walking around with guitars on their backs! Penny and she had agreed on this point: *We will never write lyrics like that.* Freewheelin' Dylan was good, there was no point denying it, but most of them were unspeakable. They just bummed around Washington Square Park, sitting on the edge of the fountain and strumming their off-key balalaikas. Entropy wasn't like *them*.

At least someone saw the value in this originality, this out-of-step Dadaism, but that was no thanks to Penny, one of the most charismatic and unique female artists on the East Coast. No, it didn't go that way. That was simply wrong, because Sheila, not Penny, was mostly behind the original ideas. Sheila had asked Penny to meow into the microphone like a cat, and it had instantly sounded fantastic. Penny was actually *her* instrument, but of course no one realized it. Not even Penny. Least of all Penny.

It looked exactly how it shouldn't have: like Penny, her little marionette Penny, was the wellspring of Entropy's originality, that Penny with her sallow cheeks rampaging in ecstasy on the stage was the one who made everything work. Sheila was hidden behind her drums, even though she was the BRAIN and BACKBONE of the band, and also a phenomenal spectacle, at least in the same class as the singer! And besides, there was something extra in her that there would never be in cryptobourgeois Penny from her middle-class home: Sheila was in mortal danger.

What you might imagine happened did. In that moment of blessing by the *Village Voice*, Penny became the biggest bitch on Bleecker Street. She loafed around the streets carrying her soprano saxophone like a shoulder bag and made clear to everyone with only the position of her head that it was due to her that Entropy's gigs began to be so crowded, that people were coming to see her specifically, and that this meant she had to start giving them more. That was why she wanted a tail made of peacock feathers for her leather trousers. That was the final straw for Sheila. Oh, so Penny wants a peacock ass, does she!

The internecine rows and melodramatic disappearances began. First Penny was offended and didn't show up for band practice for days, and then Sheila began seething with rage and went missing. We don't know where Penny was, but Sheila was jogging in Prospect Park. When the anger didn't subside, she defiantly started running in Green-Wood Cemetery, on narrow lanes lined by pure-white tombs and massive family mausoleums, despite the guards' angrily driving her away, time after time. *Have some respect for the departed, miss!*

All this turbulence resulted in embarrassingly weak performances, bungled rhythms, and public crying fits, which were followed by even more appalling fights: recriminations, insults, thrown drum sticks, and one split lower lip, which almost ended up in court. "I would have ended up dead if Dovid hadn't showed up on the scene,"

Shlomith said in a tremulous voice to the *Vanity Fair* interviewer, who was so spellbound by Entropy's story that he could hear the drums pounding in his ears and see the bony arms with veined biceps swollen like apples from beating the drums in his eyes: in the interviewer's imagination the arm that worked the hi-hat was an impressive sight with its muscles outlined in almost anatomical relief, although in reality during those years Sheila's arm was only brutally thin and ugly. "I would have died sooner or later," Shlomith repeated, swallowing dramatically, wiping tears from the corners of her eyes, "if Dovid hadn't approached me at that bar and just blurted out what he saw: 'Girl, you aren't healthy.'"

Dovid decides to heal Sheila—and has a brilliant idea

Dovid bought haggard Sheila a Bloody Mary. This man had such power that he was able to get Sheila to drink it even though she hated the tomato juice, the equivocation of the drink, and how spicy it was; it all felt excessive in her mouth. Very quickly they fell in love. "You have to heal," Dovid said as he fed Sheila pudding with a spoon; "Have a meatball of love," he said as he speared one and filled Sheila's cheeks.

Dovid had the same black curly hair as Sheila, only shorter. He was twenty centimeters taller than her and ruggedly handsome, and that was how Sheila wanted to be too, but she was more rugged than handsome; she was a withered promise, 35 kg, and something had to be done about it quickly. And it wasn't long before a brilliant idea struck Dovid. He wanted to take Sheila away from New York, where there was too much of a "pathological atmosphere"; where madness was preferred, where unhealthy stunts were practically encouraged. Sheila also wanted out of her home city, out of Penny's increasingly capricious and egotistical circle of influence. She wanted away from the people standing by the front of the stage, whose stares changed the moment their gazes shifted from the singer to her behind the drum kit. Time and time again when she wasn't pounding her drums, blind with rage, she saw something twist painfully in those gazes: the unreserved admiration burning in people's eyes gave way to an expression of struggle between that and disgust. For a person who loved contradiction, it wouldn't have been any problem, but Sheila was still in the initial phase of her journey—she was not yet Shlomith-Shkhina. Sheila was unsure (Shlomith-Shkhina rarely felt such feelings). Sheila was scared to death that her *message* would be misinterpreted, that people would see her as sick.

So what did she want to communicate with her conspicuous thinness, someone might have asked, although people talked about such things significantly less then than now. Presumably Sheila would have said that at least she wasn't looking for sympathy. She wanted to do art "on the edge". (This was also an idea that was dear to Shlomith-Shkhina later.) She wanted to show her strength, not by lifting weights but by dropping weight. It was precision work, which the more or less fat people behind the gazes would at least respect. If something irreversible happened, that would also be her own choice: a creative leap over the line.

And besides, in addition to everything else, this was her back door. When an evening ended in dizziness, when the bed seemed to spin, when she felt that familiar chill, she knew that everything was alright, that her weight in the morning would be about the same, that her input and output were both under control. One teensy-weensy shift and she would be permanently on the other side of the line. Where no one could touch her. At least it was good for her mother to know this. To wit, her mouth was no hole in the back of a chest of drawers, one more hatch in an endless row of hatches, a hatch which her mother could open whenever she wanted, into which her mother could shove as much pie and porridge as she wished. Her mother had to be very careful with her. Because she had the power, all the power over everything.

Hunger narrows perspectives: on that point Andrea Dworkin was exactly right. Taken to a certain point, hunger refreshes, sharpens, electrifies, and clears the mind, as anyone who has fasted knows, but as the fast continues, the lack of nutrients clouds and slows the thoughts. So it may be that in this enervating process of flagellation, "the universe" shrivels from the vast expanse of space to take on the size, appearance, and feel of the withering person herself—from the perspective of space to an insignificant grotesqueness.

Sheila, Shlomith, and Shlomith-Shkhina disagreed with this at nearly every point of their life (in order to save time, we'll overlook a few moments of crushing doubt). And because talking sense didn't help then and doesn't help now, let the bed spin and Sheila along with it. Let life continue until life ends. But Sheila couldn't understand this idea any more. To live or to die? This was the question. She constantly had to choose. This is why Sheila lived in an intermediate space. She saw herself choosing during each bite of food, each kilometer she ran, each push-up she did, *to be or not to be.*

"Deep inside, every anorexic wants to rebuild the Oedipal theater of her childhood," Sheila's mother's psychoanalyst friend said, "but now the arc of the drama is slightly different. The child refusing to eat—let's ignore that in this case she's already on the verge of adulthood—sets up her mother to be guilty for her starvation. Even though the acute battles are mostly fought between mother and daughter, the anorexic's fundamental message is directed at the father: 'Save me from that harpy.' The less flesh there is on the child, the less the evil mother can enjoy her. You know the story of Hansel and Gretel, right? So you'll do well to give your daughter more space. Let her become more independent. When no one is metaphorically threatening her any more, eating up her living space, she'll find her own body and gradually learn to enjoy it. Believe me, Miriam, Sheila will get better if you just give her a looser leash."

Who would have guessed that in the end, right at the last moment, Dovid would find Sheila's abandoned body. Sheila's family viewed Dovid's motives with suspicion, to put it mildly, but this attitude only bound the lovers closer together. "YouR motheR is cRazy," Dovid whispered to his future wife on the evening after his third visit, in a cute accent that bounced on the R's and finally convinced Sheila: her mother *was* crazy, not Sheila, so she had to get away. Far away. To a place where she could be a little (not a lot but a little) plumper. Because in New York Sheila had no intention of giving in. That would be the act of a traitor. Was she going to fatten up and admit that her parents had been right and now she was going to fall back in line? Never.

Dovid's idea sounded more than promising. It sounded like life after death, with the difference that now Sheila didn't need to die. Moving to Kibbutz Methuselah sufficed. Honest work close to the earth. A healthy society. Everything shared, everyone honest. Submission to the land, the dirt, the sun, manual toil, and a purposeful walk. If this wasn't paradise, then what was?

Sheila fought and fought and finally decided: Let's do it. The two of us are going on the run like Bonnie and Clyde, exiting the stage with flare. Goodbye, worm-eaten Apple! And besides, another's embrace felt better with more flesh, spooning at night; ten more kilos and her bony knees would stop leaving bruises on her bowed thighs. "They aren't very beautiful, dear," Dovid said gently, as he placed his hand on the bruises. The xylophone of ribs, the clavicle crossbones, and the shoulder-blade platters that protruded from her skin also weren't beautiful. "But *you* are beautiful," Dovid said, "and we'll find you again in there once you fill out a little." Then Dovid baked Sheila a honey cake. "You have to build your strength so you have the energy to work in Israel."

The interviewer from *Vanity Fair* could barely stay in his skin. The details of the story that was beginning now had never been told anywhere. This stage of her life (or lie?) had always felt to Shlomith if not shameful then at least too private for public consumption, but now the situation was different. Surely a lauded and controversial sixty-year-old artist could give her admirers (and haters) a slice of her failed kibbutz experience. It was part of the jagged picture of her life, and it was also the story of her name. Keeping silent wasn't going to change it, so Shlomith decided: Let's do it.

The story (one of them) begins: breaking up, love, infatuation

Dovid and Sheila began to prepare for their big move. By day Dovid slogged away in the Herald Square Macy's men's

department and saved money for plane tickets. Sheila left the band
with a joyous slamming of doors and began to study Hebrew under
the tutelage of Rabbi Noam Aurbach at the temple on Eighth
Avenue, where members of the Reform Congregation Beth Elohim
worshipped. "You don't need God, but you need Hebrew," Dovid
said, and so Sheila obediently began beating the language into her
head. She already knew the basics, just like any Jewish girl who
had celebrated her Bat Mitzvah, but otherwise she hadn't used the
language. In her family, as in many of the families they knew,
Jewishness was more of a curiosity than a living religion. Her
family was Jewish because the family's ancestors had been Jews,
and their ancestors had suffered because they had been Jews, and
that was why they suffered too, because they were Jews. But no one
ever said that out loud. It was "unexperienced trauma", as Sheila
later expressed it with Shlomith-Shkhina's mouth. Tradition, and
the wrongs experienced by their ancestors lived among them, even
though little apparent attention was given to either, and because of
this they began to take on increasingly strange forms, worming
their way under their skins and running amok there; they were all
its victims. All except her, Shlomith-Shkhina, who forty years later
would shed her false flesh and force the world to see the truth, the
suffering from which it was possible to be freed through catharsis.
(But it isn't time for these themes yet, not until Shlomith is sixty-
one years old and deathly ill.)

Sheila and Dovid spent their evenings in the closet on Carroll
Street. Dovid made Sheila delicious food and, leading her by the
hand, taught her to eat and enjoy. He praised his beloved after each
bite, and he also rewarded her with a kiss, because love was the same
as food, and they had no lack of either. Dovid first placed a piece of
puff pastry pie in his own mouth, between his lips, knelt before Sheila
sitting at the table, and then kissed the piece of pie into her mouth.
"My little bird," Dovid cooed, and Sheila chewed and ground the
piece with her teeth until the saliva did its job, making the pie soft
and ready for swallowing, and then Sheila swallowed, and her
strength grew day by day.

No more food appeared in the chest of drawers. Dovid had asked Miriam to keep herself in check. Dovid had said to Miriam, "Don't you understand you're part of the problem?" which offended Miriam to the depths of her soul, even though her psychoanalyst friend had said basically the same thing. (But in a different way! That's critical. Over a glass of wine, reassuringly and with much encouragement, while that Polack came into her own home to accuse her and make her feel bad, backing her into a corner and making her force her daughter to choose between her and that urchin, and even as she shouted, "Choose him or me!" she knew the answer, that her daughter would choose the meddler; her daughter, whom she had brought into the world and fought tooth and nail to keep in the world, would laugh and turn her back, as if nothing that had happened up to that point meant anything. She would leave with that insane demagogue, and Miriam couldn't do a thing about it.)

Sheila's weight increased, and despite her indignation her mother had to admit, watching through the window as her daughter walked to her lessons with Noam Aurbach, that this apparent recovery delighted her even as it aroused painful questions with no answers, even though it also aroused fear: what was ultimately behind the improvement? She was still angry, hurt, and bewildered, and shaken to her core that some man had that kind of power over her daughter. But there was no getting around the fact that Sheila was filling out. Sheila alternated between horror and delight, delight and horror about her increasing weight, but even in her horror she continued chewing and grinding and swallowing, because Dovid was by her side. Dovid loved her exactly as she was, even her digestion and flatulence.

In the evenings, once they had eaten and regained their strength, they lounged on their bed they had made on the floor. Dovid told Sheila kibbutz stories that his father's older brother Zachariasz had recounted in his letters. Zachariasz was, excuse our choice of words, completely shiftless. In the late 1920s, his bosom friend had moved to a kibbutz named Degania, which was located on the shores of the Sea of Galilee, near the Golan Heights, and was the best place in the world, a paradise Zachariasz had to get to as well. Then the war came, and the Germans occupied Łódź. Zachariasz did the only non-shift-less thing in his life: as the Litzmannstadt ghetto was being set up, he slipped away to Israel. His mother gave him money for the journey, because dear Zachariasz was the best of the boys, better than Izajasz, Dovid's future father, who on the verge of this catastrophe was focused on his future wife, the picture-perfect beauty Agnieszka, and refused to heed any warnings. If someone had to be saved, then let it be Zachariasz, Mama proclaimed in rage, and so Zachariasz was sent away to Degania.

When the war was over, the old house was bleak: the only people living there were thirteen-year-old Dovid and his mother, who with her newborn son squeezed tight in her arms had succeeded by some miracle in escaping during the confusion of the Sobibór uprising and subsequent mass escape. She was no longer a picture-perfect beauty, for how could anyone be picturesque when her own family and her dear Izajasz and Izajasz's mother and all his family except for one miserable brother had been killed, when her dreams had been killed, when her future languished in Dovid's broken stare? Agnieszka closed her mouth up tight. Sobibór, where Dovid had been born and which they had both almost incomprehensibly escaped through a series of coincidences, ceased to exist.

But the promised land existed. Degania, Israel's first kibbutz, which the locals called the *kvutza*, bordered a 166-square-kilometre freshwater lake, which Dovid referenced in the same longing way as Zachariasz by the name Kinneret. Kinneret as in *kinor*, a violin: the dulcet lapping of the water reminded everyone who stood on its shores of that noble stringed instrument.

"Close your eyes, and I'll tell you," Dovid said to Sheila and kissed her closed eyelids. Sheila's full stomach gurgled melodiously as her carefully chewed food worked through her intestines, which were used to emptiness but now eagerly delighted in their new work, and squeezed the food rhythmically forward, compressing it into an ever tighter mass free of liquid, into the poop that was soon to come. But first this tale, this bedtime story, then evacuation and copulation, their evening routine, then kissing and more kissing, until sweet sleep came and rocked them toward the next day, once more a little closer to paradise.

Kibbutz Methuselah: coming to her senses & breaking up (one of the stories ends)

"Malka. Is. Not. Going. To. The. Babies'. House . . . Tonight!"

Thus shouts Sheila, red in the face and now Shlomith, but not yet Shkhina. Shlomith as in *shalom!* as in *peace,* as in *give peace a chance,* as in what opponents to the Vietnam War sang in the summer of 1969 and what she still sang to a tremulous tune, to calm herself, four years later. Fundamentally it's very simple. She had just wanted to be a new person. She had wanted to be a "new Jew", the kind the kibbutzes grew in almost laboratory conditions, concealed as verdant vineyards, blooming *Papaver somniferum* poppy fields, bitter lemon groves, and sweet angiosperm dicotyledon Jaffa orange oases. Shlomith (now we must get used to this name again) had wanted peace of mind by the double handful, in ten-gallon servings. But there she now stood, in Kibbutz Methuselah, on the porch of a white stucco house, shouting at her legal spouse as if he were her worst enemy:

"Malka. Is. Staying. With. Me. Tonight!"

Of course that isn't possible. Dovid's face goes dark with irritation as he stares at his wife, who tries furiously to appeal to him with the strength of her anger. Nearby stands Malka and the nurse to the kibbutz's five other two-year-olds, the *metapelet*, as these women are called, in this case a fat, repugnant child-hater named Zmira, whom Dovid blindly reveres. Zmira says aloud what Dovid has also come increasingly to believe within himself: "I'm sorry to say that Malka's emotional difficulties are being caused by you, Shlomith." Unfortunately Malka isn't adjusting because her mother is coaxing her into missing her, because during her daily visits her mother is cunningly creating an attachment that plants the seeds of sadness. That's why the girl screams and cries and pulls Zmira's hair and kicks Zmira in the stomach. That's why each evening's goodbye turns into a drama where, depending on the point of view, the wicked witch is either played by Shlomith or Zmira.

But Dovid isn't interested in different perspectives. Dovid believes one hundred percent in the kibbutz. When the kibbutz says through Zmira's mouth that it is a parent's duty to *have fun* with his child, Dovid believes it and has fun. When the kibbutz says through Zmira's mouth that parents should give their children a little (but not too much) *emotional fulfilment*, Dovid does. A little. He tickles three-year-old Moti's tummy, he rocks one-year-younger Malka in his arms, but he does it differently than Shlomith, who, as she tickles and rocks her children also plants something in them that she shouldn't plant. How does she do it? And above all: why does she do it?

They've been happy for four years. Dovid believes so. Four years of joy, but then, after Malka was born, everything suddenly begins to crumble in their hands. Shlomith develops strange symptoms. No, Shlomith is scheming, Dovid corrects himself. In his mind, Dovid assembles piece by piece the ragged image that is beginning to emerge of his wife, his dearest beloved, whom he brought here, away from the evil world, whom he healed and impregnated twice. Now the picture is recognizable again: in it is Shlomith, thankless and resentful Shlomith, mentally disturbed Shlomith. Shlomith has picked up the heaviest weapons of all, their two children, as pawns in her game. Why on earth is she doing this? Dovid clenches his left hand in a fist, crushing this question, smashing it ever smaller as he squeezes his fingers, and then it's gone, and only the answer remains. Because Shlomith is evil. Evil, evil, evil.

With Moti everything went perfectly. Shlomith relinquished her firstborn to the infants' house at four days of age, as was appropriate—at that point she was "OK" with it. She visited the house to nurse their son for six months and not a day more. Only the twenty-four weeks that were allowed. Shlomith even thought it was fun to call herself "the mother organism"—a term Dovid thought up—as she left with her breasts dripping milk to walk the three hundred meters to the other building. It was a good-natured joke they shared: "The mother organism waddles again." Ha-ha-ha!

Dovid clenches his other hand in a fist and looks to Zmira, who squeezes the screaming Malka tighter in her arms and starts walking with her bellowing burden toward the infants' house.

But Malka isn't a baby any more. Malka is already a little girl who uses her own brain, and Shlomith knows it. She has a special connection to this child. The girl speaks in very short sentences, only a few paltry words, but her fearless expression illuminates the idea. Malka's place is with her mother: they both agree about that. But how can she say this to the kibbutz so the kibbutz will believe? To the kibbutz, which speaks with so many different mouths, and increasingly with Dovid's mouth, which has started to nauseate her, against which she absolutely no longer intends to press her own mouth. Because Dovid has turned evil. Evil! Dovid has joined forces with all of Methuselah against her.

Shlomith has listened to the voice of her heart, but Methuselah thinks she has committed terrible crimes. A week ago she peeled and separated an orange for her child and received a warning for her trouble. There is only permission to eat in the common dining room, says Methuselah with the mouth of every single member. Personal snacks are the lea-ven-of-pri-va-ti-za-tion, and they also bind children to their mother in an inappropriate way. Dovid agrees. "Don't irritate them for no reason. Malka and Moti will get to eat plenty of oranges tomorrow."

The next morning Shlomith skips her work shift in the barn. The cows moo in agony with swollen udders as Shlomith lies on her back in the orange grove, surrounded by the fruit she has torn from the trees, and weeps in anger.

Every child is everyone's child, the Methuselites sing as they plough the fields and sweat in the vineyards, to the same limping tune they try to use with all the hymns meant to bind the kibbutz together, *to each according to his needs, from each according to his means*. But Shlomith can't blame Dovid for this. Dovid told her back in Park Slope, as they lay on that mattress with their bellies full of nourishing food and waited for sleep, that professionals raise the children of the kibbutz. Adults have a responsibility to live their own lives. Then it had felt like an almost romantic idea: *adults have a responsibility to live their own lives.* Not, for example, her mother Miriam's fussing, meddling life, a nauseating life of self-sacrifice but her *own life.* In that closet in Park Slope, Shlomith had closed her happy eyes. She had thought of the first years of the twentieth century, the indescribable zeal and ecstasy which had driven Jews to journey there from every corner of the globe. Most came from Eastern Europe, having had enough of stifling ghetto life and cruel persecutions. They came and worked the barren, deserted land . . . Almost deserted . . . Their land . . .

Dovid swallows his anger once again and lets his hands relax and open. He turns again to Shlomith standing on the porch of the white stucco house and arranges his words carefully. "Zmira cares for Malka just enough and with exactly the right intensity so she can naturally find her own place. And that place is with her peer group. You know that. So why this exhibition again, dear?"

Dovid speaks to her like to an idiot. And every night when Malka and Moti are taken away from her, she cries. For Dovid, the children's disappearance is a relief. For Dovid, the children are toys, which someone else can clean up and put away once the games are done. And everyone thinks that's "OK". Of course, the whole kibbutz plays with the children! The children are like Harry Harlow's monkeys, and Shlomith can't stand it any more. She could let everything else go, including that cigarettes have to be ordered through a committee established for that specific purpose, but ruining children is really serious. Shlomith has noticed a number of concerning things. The young people of Methuselah are apathetic. They're deadbeat after school, farm work, and homework; they aren't given a moment of their own time. They always shuffle around in a group, and if you happen to address a personal question to one of them, without glancing at the others, they begin to babble in a way that makes you wonder if they imagine the members of the education committee are applauding behind their backs.

The most frightening thing is that they don't imagine. They don't imagine anything. The ability for imagination has been rooted out of them. When they speak, they're sincere. All that bullshit comes straight from their hearts. All the platitudes, the banalities, the predigested truths: not the slightest hint of doubt. Not even a second of embarrassment.

Shlomith's eyes begin to open. This wasn't actually emancipation with socialist, Zionist, and Tolstoian flavors, as Dovid had described to her in Park Slope. This was a machine construction program. They were recruited for Methuselah to produce "new Jews", robots that look like humans but have been programmed to slog their guts out without troubling their heads with revolutionary ideas, who had hands for building a new world but minds untarnished by excessive intellectualism. Who weren't neurotic shit talkers.

Even though Shlomith didn't know it at the time, she wasn't alone in these thoughts. Around the same time a certain Bruno Bettelheim had visited Atid, another Israeli kibbutz, where he conducted a participant observation study about child rearing. He published his conclusions in 1969 in the book *The Children of the Dream*, which became a bestseller and one of the most talked-about books of the year. "The kibbutz-born generation is committed to an entirely different Sachlichkeit, a literalness, a matter-of-fact objectivity which has no place for emotions," Bruno B. said on an episode of *60 Minutes* Shlomith didn't see since she was living the final honeymoon months of her great life change in Israel. "Let's say they're more realistic, mechanistic, objective, than we are; less humanistic, less involved," Bruno B. continued, adding, "One unique thing about them is that they immediately give up on an opinion as soon as they feel (or fear) that group opinion leans the other way."

Finally Bettelheim let loose with both barrels. "A relative emotional flatness may be just the selective factor that determines who stays on in this relatively simple, undemanding environment." And as if to soften the blow of this claim, somewhat apologetically he added, "Although the second generation of kibbutzniks do not create science or art, are neither leaders nor great philosophers nor innovators, maybe it is they who are the salt of the earth without whom no society can endure."

Never before had the father of 6o *Minutes*, Don Hewitt, received so much hate mail, fully a fifth of which hinted at Mossad exacting revenge on him.

Although later revelations about Bruno Bettelheim's personal history give reasons for a wide range of doubts—he fled to the United States after using his connections to get out of the Buchenwald concentration camp, pulled a degree and work history in child psychology out of a hat once in the New World, maneuvered his way into a surprisingly long career as a helper of disturbed children, and then was accused of violence and sexual abuse and took his own life—the conclusions he drew about the kibbutz movement weren't complete bunk. At least Shlomith's experiences supported Bettelheim's claims about the ramifications of the kibbutz ideology, the spiritual banality, the callousness, and the unquestioned group discipline. And it's also true that someone who lives on a kibbutz and doesn't trouble her head with critical questions is probably happier than one who goes out to conquer the world.

However, Shlomith was not interested in lukewarm, evenly distributed happiness. When she encountered her first MASS DEATH OF IMAGINATION right after moving to Israel, she didn't understand yet what was going on. The Six-Day War in June of 1967 aroused questions in Shlomith, but she banished them deep into the recesses of forgetfulness. She threw herself into the emotions of the community, which was as easy as breathing. Not until later did she unearth the questions again. The numbers were chilling: four percent of the population of Israel lived in kibbutzes and about the same portion fought in the army, but fully twenty-five percent of those who died in the war were from kibbutzes. Five young people from Methuselah died, which was an incomprehensible number given its small size. What happened in those battles? Why did Noam, Yoel, Gidon, Yoske, and Ben-Zion foolishly push their way to the front and put themselves in the line of fire?

Shlomith had embraced Ditsa, Noam's mother, as she wept after seeing her son disappear into his grave wrapped in shrouds from head to toe. Five dead, a five-fold measure of sorrow, and Shlomith couldn't help remembering what Ditsa had said to her before the war, just after Shlomith arrived, when she was still curious and full of unrestrained enthusiasm. "Do you really think we believe they'd choose the kibbutz if we didn't specifically train them to?"

Father Kibbutz always knew best. Little kibbutzniks shouldn't think too much. Little kibbutzniks should relax and enjoy being spoonfed codes of heroism and a sense of duty, and heaped servings of energetic functionality. Sometimes, in extreme circumstances, someone might run into the path of a bullet, but when you thought of the whole, this sacrifice was insignificant.

Isn't that right, Ditsa?

Isn't that right, Noam, Yoel, Gidon, Yoske, and Ben-Zion?

These are the questions Shlomith digs up after Malka's birth. She digs up Ditsa and scrapes away the layers concealing the rhetorical question this woman posed to her for some reason during her first month at Methuselah: "Do you really think . . ." Layer by layer Shlomith scrapes bare June 1967, Noam and his four companion's funerals, and all that agony, and the lump inside her grows. It grows and grows and bursts when Malka turns two years old.

At first Shlomith tries to be careful. Demurely she asks whether she can spend more time with her children than the last two hours they're awake each day. But that isn't possible. The central committee won't give permission. Soon Shlomith is slipping into the infants' house when no one is looking to see her daughter—in the morning, at midday, at completely inappropriate times. She plucks up her courage and sneaks into the nearby toddlers' house where Moti and the other children his age are and where Malka and her group will be moved in the coming weeks. She peeks into the rooms and watches them at play, but she's careless and gets caught; then "the problem" is discussed at the next general meeting.

But Shlomith has looked deep into her children's eyes and seen a glimmer of light that has yet to be extinguished from Malka's gaze. There's only one option: Shlomith has to save her children. At least Malka.

"Do you want Malka to end up in Neve Ze'elim?"

Another new day's evening has come, and the nightly display has begun on the porch of the white stucco house. Zmira shouts herself hoarse, resorting to the theatrical pathos of ghetto life, which shouldn't exist in her any more after thirty years of life at Methuselah. But Shlomith has an exceptional ability to get on people's nerves. Shlomith is insufferable, and that's why it's completely possible that her daughter will end up in Neve Ze'elim, an institution for disturbed children located in Ramot HaShavim. This is what Zmira believes, and so does Dovid, who, with his last shreds of melodramatic emotion, the ones Methuselah hasn't managed to root out yet, bellows:

"Malka is my child too, and I say enough is enough!"

Shlomith-Shkhina looked sadly at the boy from *Vanity Fair*. "For all practical intents and purposes, I was driven out of Methuselah. I did everything I could to take my children with me, but they wouldn't give them to me. I went to Tel Aviv, which is the largest city near Methuselah, and tried to file a police report. The police said they had no authority over the kibbutz central committees and that I would have to contact the kibbutz central federation. And of course the central federation defended Methuselah's approach. I worked in Tel Aviv for a while as a waitress, while I tried to negotiate with various authorities without success. In the end I was ready to kidnap my daughter. But when I went to visit Methuselah, neither of my children even seemed to recognize me. That was how well the kibbutz had brainwashed them! I don't know of any other organization that effective . . . I lost that battle 10–0. I returned to New York in February, 1974. The rest is history."

The *Vanity Fair* reporter's pen raced even as the tape recorder ran. Cheeks red, he recorded key words, creating a framework for structuring the long interview captured on the tape. The final sentence with which Shlomith ended her kibbutz tale he wrote down in full: "After that experience I have never—and let me emphasize the word *never*—wanted to be normal, to conform to any norms, ever again."

The letter Shlomith left on the table of the Kibbutz Methuselah dining hall as she left the kibbutz early on the morning of February 13, 1974

מתושלח המפלצת!

לכל אחד מכם יש שם שבו הייתי יכולה לקרוא לו: דיצה, זמירה,
דויד, משה, חיים, גל, דני, אליהו, אסתר, ג'וש, יהודית, ליבי,
רחל, טוביה וכולי וכולי. אבל בשביל מה לטרוח. אתם חלק
מהמנגנון. פועלים קטנים בקן נמלים. אין בכם שום דבר משלכם.
מפלצת ששמה מתושלח: הלוואי שהכינוי שהדבקתי לכם לא יעכיר
את מצב רוחכם. אחרי ככלות הכול, חיינו יחד שבע שנים.

מפלצת שכמוך, אולי גם אתה עצמך יודע שמתחת לחזותך
השלווה, אתה רוחש וגועש. אתן לך דוגמה. בסתיו שאחרי מלחמת
ששת הימים, אחת הבריות המתפקדת בתור נתינה שלך, לאה
שמה, פגשה בתל אביב חברות מתקופת הצבא. באיזושהי חנות
בגדים נתבלעה עליה דעתה. נבצר ממנה לבחור מנה בתפריט
המסעדה שאליה הלכו. היא חזרה לקיבוץ בוכייה מביקורה בעיר
ובמשך שלושה ימים סירבה לקום ממיטתה, עד כדי כך קורעת לב
היתה התנסותה בחופש.

נטשת את עיקרי היהדות ואת עקרונותיה, אבל אימצת לך
במקומם דוגמות חדשות. תחילה דמיינתי שהכללים הברורים
והמפורטים נחוצים כדי להגשים את החזון במיטבו, כדי שאתה,
מתושלח, תשגשג ותעניק לחברים בך את המיטב. כדי שאף אחד
מן היחידים בך לא יקפוץ בראש ולא יעז להתמסר לגחמותיו.
במשך זמן רב לא הייתי מוכנה להאמין, שהלכה למעשה לא רצית
אלא להכניע ולשעבד. לא יכולתי אף להעלות על דעתי שאצטרך
לנהל בארץ הזאת שיחה רצינית על זכותם של ילדי למצוץ אגודל!
שום תחום בחיים לא נשאר מחוץ לכללים שיצרת ולייושומם
המגוחך בידיך. אני בהחלט מבינה את זה. בלי תקנות כאלה לא
היה לך בכלל קיום. אתה הרי תמות, מתושלח המפלצת, אם נפעל
כרצוננו, אם נשתמש במוחותינו.

לא תרצח. זה נראה לי כלל הגיוני (אף על פי שככל הנראה
הוא אינו מחייב אותך: אתה הרי צמא דם ובמו ידיך שילחת את
נועם, יואל, גדעון, יוסק'ה ובן-ציון אל חזית המוות). אל יהי דבר
בבעלותך הפרטית - בסדר גמור, נתחלק בכול שווה בשווה. אך לא

די לך בכך, מתושלח, אתה רוצה שנתחלק גם ברגשות שווה בשווה.
אתה אוסר עלי לאהוב את ילדיי, כי לפי דעתך אני אוהבת אותם
"יותר מדי". להערכתך אני אוהבת אותם בדרך שגויה, אם כי מובן
מאליו שבתור אמא שלהם, אני יודעת כמה הם זקוקים לי!
    מתושלח, אתה סדיסט, פסיכופט, נרקיסיסט, פושע, רוצח.
נפנפת אותי החוצה תוך כדי שימוש באלימות נפשית ראשונה
במעלה, מפני שלא שמעתי בקולך. רתמת את כל נתיניך לתקיפה
כדי שיתנפלו עלי: את בעלי דויד שבעזרתו נרפאתי ממחלתי הקשה;
את המטפלת זמירה שתחילה חשבתי כי היא לטעמי בזכות אופיה
הנמרץ; את חברתי דיצה, את משה, גל, דני וכולי וכולי. אין לי
מושג איך ייתכן שכולם, אפילו דיצה, הפנו לי עורף.
    לא מזמן עדיין חייכו אלי. כך אתה מרקיד אותם כאילו הם
מריונטות: הם נראים מאושרים, אף שהם מלאי שנאה וייאוש.
    אני עוזבת ולא אחזור. ניצחת, החזק לך בבעלי, קח את
הילדים שלי. אבל לעולם לא אשכח אותם. הרסת אותי, מתושלח,
אך אשתמש בכל הזמן שנשאר לי לחיות כדי לנקום בך ולהרוס את
כל מה שמזכיר לי אותך ולו כזית. שלום.

באהבה,
שלומית-שכינה

Shlomith-Shkhina falls silent (and prepares)

"Why Do We Drool Over Shlomith-Shkhina?" asked the *Vanity Fair*
headline in gargantuan text, and the answer was probably clear to
everyone who read the piece. People drooled over Shlomith because
she did what everyone wants to do deep down: she turned her life
into art. She transformed even the smallest details into part of her
enormous, sometimes megalomaniacal persona. Nothing went to
waste; everything was utilized. Might this not be everyone's inner-
most dream: to live so that even the most insignificant decisions and
thoughtless acts effortlessly stream into the great flow of Decisions
and Acts? With every fiber of her being, Shlomith was an Artist, 24/7.
Not many are capable of that. Shlomith-Shkhina was a necessary

valve, an air pressure gauge. If there had been no Shlomith-Shkhina, someone would have had to make her up.

"And what happens next?" asked the reporter, who could see in his mind's eye how this fascinating sixty-year-anniversary interview should end. And he got what he wanted:

Shlomith-Shkhina raises her gold-rimmed teacup to her rouged lips, takes a final sip of oolong tea, and smiles mysteriously from behind the cup. "There's a performance I've been planning for a long time, and I think it's time for me to complete it now. It isn't without risk, and preparing for it won't happen overnight." Shlomith-Shkhina's eyes twinkle mischievously. She shakes her head when I ask if she can describe the project in more detail. "All in good time."

I can't avoid the thought that we're in for something historic, something epic, lyrical, and tragic all rolled up in one package. A package named Shlomith-Shkhina. Contenting myself with the sly smile of the goddess, I shake her hand. She's in a hurry to get to the Brooklyn Museum for the opening of the Annie Leibovitz photo show.

After the goddess has left the building, I remain sitting on the stark white, leather sofa of the VIP room of the restaurant. All those stories . . . It feels as if I have spent a moment living under her skin, as a woman, as a Jew and an uncompromising artist. It feels as if a piece of me has left with her. And I am left waiting for the performance she will deliver sometime soon, once again revolutionizing the concept of performance, breaking the limits we haven't even imagined yet. Thank you for existing, Shlomith-Shkhina.

The Converse boy was right. Shlomith's final performance, which was given in 2007 in the prestigious Jewish Museum, aroused much discussion. However, the arguments were exceedingly simplistic, a far cry from the intellectualism of the 1980s and light years away from deconstructionism—no one was taking paradox and turning it over, shaking it, and tearing it apart to see what was inside. The discussion turned almost entirely on the morality of art. Amateur freelancers wrote about the "boundary conditions" of the presentation, which triggered a full range of feelings in the audience: aggression, shock, pity, fear, anxiety, anger, and even malicious pleasure. They talked about the relationship between art and sickness, about where the line of being compos mentis ran, about whether the "community" should intervene in an artist's suicidal undertakings and how. The arguments decomposed into their prime factors: what would have given the community in this case a right to intervene, to interrupt the process, to commit the artist to care against her will? Wasn't America a free country? Couldn't individuals do whatever they wanted to themselves?

The newspaper sales were excellent, especially the tabloids with their appalling paparazzi photos. Someone had been tipped off about Shlomith's project, and they secretly followed her as she prepared for her performance. The photo captions were sensational. A rail-thin Shlomith-Shkhina jogging along the Brooklyn Heights Promenade: "She can barely stay upright!" A deathly pale Shlomith-Shkhina in Café Mogador in the East Village: "The eggplant dip won't go down!" An emaciated Shlomith-Shkhina in a driving wind on her way home on the corner of Fifth and Sixth Avenue: "What's she carrying in that bag?!" A weepy Shlomith-Shkhina standing shakily on the steps in front of her brownstone home, her pockets turned inside out, her house keys missing: "Shopkeeper reveals, 'She only bought one single orange!'"

But we don't have any reason to join in the howling of the headlines. Especially at this point, now that the flimsy froth of topicality has receded back to where it belongs once the artificially maintained vortex has ceased spinning. (Can you still hear the echoes of the jingling of the cash register?) When that sudden spume has settled as sediment you wouldn't even want to touch with a toe. (At this point, some wiser than us talk about "decency".) Then—now, in other words—we tight-rope walkers of eternity turn our gazes up, toward the bright light. We feel a warmth toward which we move with eyes shut tight. We sense the gulf beneath us, but we are not afraid because vertigo is a fundamental part of this dance.

As she prepared for her performance, Shlomith felt the obedient movements of the rope beneath her running shoes. "She can barely stand upright!"—that claim isn't even remotely true. Shlomith barely touched the ground as she ran along the Brooklyn Heights Promenade! Despite her thinness, she was more confident and stronger than she had ever been in her life. (Dexamfetamine sulphate 5 mg x 3 helped with this somewhat.) Shlomith's eighteen-mile run each Sunday would have aroused jealousy in any serious runner training for a marathon. Along with intermediate stops, her jogs took from eight in the morning until six at night. The purpose of this ten-hour slog was to hasten her arrival at her target performance weight of thirty kilograms and dropping to the "very severely under-weight" BMI of twelve percent.

The nights were difficult, full of aimless, fleeting, tinny tatters of thought. The emaciated artist tossed and turned in bed more than ever, like a cog rattle on a stick. A terrible grating noise echoed in her skull. Despite the occasional protestations of the radiator, the house was silent; only the familiar background noise of the streets, like the sighing of waves, built up a sound barrier in which it was, theoreti-cally, safe to sleep. But the bed spun and the ratchet clattered, thoughts grating and bringing a taste of blood to her mouth. Sleep remained distant. Maybe it was the sound of hunger, her hunger's toothy, idio-phonic warning rattle?

How to travel eighteen miles in ten hours without muscles

Although Shlomith's experimental life is beginning to approach its end, we must accompany her on her final Sunday ritual jog. We must tread it at least once with her. Shlomith traveled this route alone eight times during the summer of 2007. Which is a significant accomplish-ment when one takes into account that she covered each mile more or less by force of will, without muscles, which would have made the journey much more pleasant. Shlomith wasn't alone on her jogs, so there's no reason to pity her for that. She was in the company of reflections brightened by dexamfetamine sulphate, and these did not permit a single beat of cog rattling, crushing doubt, or grating ques-tions. Every now and then Shlomith moved in that most unreachable of states, pure thoughtlessness; there was only movement and feet barely touching the ground.

However, for the sake of truth it must be said that her Sunday jogs also entailed enormous amounts of suffering. Shlomith vomited bile at the bases of the trees lining the streets. A number of times she felt an almost unbearable physical pain, a scorching in her stomach, faintness, and vertigo. But that's just how it is. Like beauty, there is no art without suffering.

So we depart with Shlomith on her final run, not out of pity, and not even as guardian angels, but rather as guides. We do not accompany Shlomith for her own sake (she knew her route by heart), but for the sake of posterity. In case some other maniac (a performance researcher from Japan? Ireland? New Zealand?) gets it into her head to tread the same path Shlomith did to reconstruct the route. In case she attempts to experience something similar to what Shlomith-Shkhina might have experienced during the summer of 2007.

Shlomith started in Park Slope, from the corner of Fifth and Sixth Avenue. She headed up Sixth Avenue until she reached her old home on Carroll Street. That long street transected nearly all of Brooklyn from the water to Lincoln Terrace Park. Shlomith didn't particularly like Carroll Street. It awoke unpleasant memories, feelings shaped like hatches and dresser drawers—departures, returns, failures, struggles. And precisely because of that she had to travel this route time and time again. Shlomith wouldn't be Shkhina if she hadn't decided to go to the Brooklyn Heights Promenade by way of Carroll Gardens along its eponymous street. At this point Shlomith was still walking and warming up her "muscles".

This route, as long as a year of famine and weighed down with hostile memories, would likely have overwhelmed a person with less strength of will, especially since endorphins were no help at this point in the jog, since nature's hormone haze wasn't churning yet in her brain. But Shlomith was made of sterner stuff.

Occasionally Shlomith sprints and then continues walking, running and walking in turn, warming up, preparing for what's to come. She looks grotesque in her black running tights and form-fitting sweat-wicking black running shirt. She attracts alarmed, horrified gazes in the twenty-eight degree Celsius heat; people stare at her as if at a freak of nature. But we don't care about those gazes now. We aren't kin to the paparazzi.

The first stage of the journey begins to take shape as Shlomith passes a familiar landmark. F. G. GUIDO FUNERAL HOME INC.—*Family-Owned Business Since 1883*. This signifies that only one cross street remains before Henry Street, where Shlomith finally has permission to turn, to change direction ninety degrees to the right. Now, however, Shlomith is forced to step off the sidewalk for a moment: the John Rankin House, a three-story red-brick Greek Revival building where the undertaker's office established by the first Italian funeral director in Brooklyn is located, is completely surrounded by a film crew. The sidewalk is occupied by enormous, lighting equipment, scaffolds, cameras, and trucks with blue promises emblazoned on the sides: BUDD ENTERPRISES LTD. CONSULTANTS. EQUIPMENT LEASING. THEATRICAL TRUCKING. 212–421–8846. Before the bombastic front door stands a black hearse, model 1888. A heavily-built white horse is harnessed in front of the hearse; it snorts, shakes its head, and paws the asphalt with its hoof; clearly it would like to get moving.

Shlomith circles the film crew on the other side of the road and ends up on Henry Street, which cuts through Carroll Street in a grid-like fashion and marks the end of the repulsive, winding, first leg of the jog. (Also, one more thing about Carroll Street. In point of fact, there are several places where it ends but then continues somewhere else, and you have to know those junctions if you want to stay on the same street. The city planners could have turned it into a joke and made cheeky little variations: Carol Street, Carrot Street, Carob Street . . . there's nothing so amusing as getting lost in Brooklyn, in its deceptive small-town feel—*how cozy!*—and shabbiness, which make you feel like you're almost where you're going, that there isn't any danger, even though in reality everything *might actually* be staged. Bill Cosby's house isn't really on Stigwood Avenue since no such street exists . . .)

On the corner of Henry Street and Carroll Street, Shlomith gives herself her first reward. She walks into the corner store, CARROLL DELI & GROCERY—OPEN 7 DAYS, with its blue-and-white-and-red-striped awning that brings to mind baguettes and cheap red wine (perhaps the owner is a Francophile?) COLD-CUTS • BEER • SODA • FREE DELIVERY • 522-3257. Shlomith doesn't buy cold-cuts or chocolate or lotto tickets; instead she pulls a few dollars out of the zippered pocket sewn into the back of her running tights and buys a bottle of Granini mango juice. She drinks it with relish and then continues running, now along Henry Street.

The endorphins have begun cautiously flowing. The asphalt is no longer a sticky, black magnet that clings to her feet. The ground bounces her up as the linden-lined lane cheers her on, the wind rustling the green leaves in an encouraging cha-cha-cha! (At this stage of exertion, our starving runner's hearing is extremely sensitive, but that passes. The sensitivity is followed by a feeling of blockage, as if her auditory canals are full of water. This is not a pleasant feeling, but fortunately her endorphin reserves are still pumping plentiful, nay increasing, amounts of the constituent elements of joy into her blood, helping her to endure the roar and even make that roaring sound like meditation music.)

Shlomith quickens her pace. She's in a hurry to turn toward the climax of her run, which she can reach in ten minutes of steady jogging. When Henry Street meets stubby Remsen Street, Shlomith turns left and dashes toward the seascape visible at the end of the road: the East River, where she could throw herself in and, theoretically, swim to the ends of the earth (Cuba, for instance). Shlomith passes a crooked yellow DEAD END sign, which is not meant for her but those with tires instead of feet, an engine instead of a heart, an exhaust pipe, carburetor, or radiator instead of a soul (who's to know—a deep knowledge of the metaphysics of the automobile would require further study). Shlomith makes a brief spring and arrives at her intermediate destination: the Brooklyn Heights Promenade.

"She can barely stay upright!" What a monstrous lie. Shlomith floats along behind the rows of people sitting on benches squinting through sunglasses at the skyscrapers. Little girls run around squeal-ing, playing tag; Shlomith lightly weaves past them without falling. The hexagonal blocks of the pavement look like gray honeycomb, the edges of some squeezing out a darker construction adhesive made pliable by the sun. The rows of cells are broken by arrangements of rectangular, partially broken paving slabs, and then the more evoca-tive hexagonal shapes return with their honeycomb-sweet rhythm.

This fresh-smelling, carless strip of land is something Shlomith wants to experience with every fiber of her being. She slows her pace, despite the endorphin joy urging her on. She breathes deep and fills with air. But she can already see the end of the promenade. She will have to turn right, back into the world of automobiles, smoke, and pollution.

Prohibitions and commandments are all too familiar to Shlomith. When she leaves the Brooklyn Heights Promenade, a grass-green sign decorated with maple leaves tells her all the things she shouldn't have done during her honeycomb dash. NO RIDING BICYCLES, ROLLER SKATES, SCOOTERS, SKATEBOARDS. But can you fly here . . . ? NO BALLPLAYING OR FRISBEE. If she floats above the surface of the earth, she could hardly be a danger to anyone . . . NO ALCOHOLIC BEVERAGES. What about punch-drunk love? Or deteriorating madness? NO LITTERING. Future trash, paper tissues intended for wiping snot and sweat, are also stuffed in the same zippered back pocket as Shlomith's money. The pocket bulges with a crumpled tissue that has been used once but is still good and now lies under the roll of bills. If you look closely, buttock-free Shlomith has a pitch-black bunny tail on her rear end because of the wad of paper. NO DOGS OFF LEASH. Shlomith lopes away, forward, every surge consuming calories. With each bound she diminishes, becoming lighter than air.

Shlomith charges down Columbia Heights, where the WATCHTOWER waits below, a strange, colossal beige building complex, the headquarters of the Jehovah's Witnesses, which resem-bles a two-star hotel in Mallorca. The building complex extends on both sides of the street, and those two blocks are connected by a tiny skyway with ten windows, which you have to go under if you want to continue down the street.

But what joy! Beyond the skyway Shlomith can already see a glimpse of her next destination, the handsome neogothic Brooklyn Bridge. From this vantage point, the structures of the suspension bridge appear as if they form a part of the hodgepodge architecture of the Jehovah's Witnesses' headquarters, like some sort of cobweb rigged up for decorative purposes. The bridge itself is handsome. It's like an outdoor church erected to holy optimism, and no one who ascends the bridge can help but have her pessimistic thoughts dispelled. (Determined suicides are an exception.) Odes have been written to the bridge, and many have jumped from its sides with boyish athletic intentions, as well as darker motives. The case of the cartoonist Otto Eppers is one of the most well known. In 1910 seventeen-year-old Otto climbed the bridge and jumped off, surviving the splash without a bruise, unlike many less fortunate aspirants. The tugboat *Florence* plucked Otto out of the water according to plan and took him to shore, where the police awaited the daredevil. Charges were filed against Otto for attempted suicide. Although the charges were later dropped, this chain of events, or, more precisely, its final act, raises bewildering theoretical questions. First of all: what individual fact makes an act suicidal, and can any outsider, and on what basis, define that? Because Otto was just insanely brave. Secondly: how can you punish anyone for attempted suicide? (By hanging, as was the case in nineteenth-century England. The body was also posthumously desecrated, a practice the church didn't discontinue until 1823. In France suicide was *lèse-majesté* prior to the Revolution. In ancient Greece, one had to request permission for suicide from a court. We also know of a case in which doctors stitched together a prisoner who had slit his own throat so that he could be hanged properly.) Isn't surviving suicide—if a person, unlike Otto, really wants to die—a punishment in itself? Shouldn't a suicide candidate receive something more like, say, a hug after a failed attempt?

In any case, with its 5,989 feet of length, the Brooklyn Bridge remained the longest suspension bridge in the world for twenty years (until 1903, when the Williamsburg Bridge was built over the same East River). In consolation for the bridge, let it be said that it is and will remain, now and always, the world's first suspension bridge built with metal cables (firsts, unlike lengths, are not threatened in the record books by anything other than lies).

When Shlomith has jogged under the skyway connecting the Jehovah's Witnesses' headquarters complexes (now she has a stitch in her side), she reaches tiny Everit Street and then Old Fulton Street, along which we find the first signposts for the most difficult portion of the route: how to access the footbridge. Look sharp now, copycats and wanna-be Shlomiths! Even the best map from Barnes & Noble won't reveal the route, since the network of roads here is anything but laid out nicely in a grid. And to top it all off, the thick orange worm named the Brooklyn-Queens Expressway (which leads the cursed lines of cars onto the bridge) obscures the cartographic information that a walker, runner, or cyclist needs most at this point. A green sign leads cyclists forward with a helpful arrow and those who need the stairs to the left, as well as those whose destination is the Manhattan Bridge (but best to keep quiet about that or else this guided tour will end up with altogether too many bridges).

So we turn in the direction of the arrow onto Front Street. Walk forward, past Dock Street, but don't go overboard and end up on Pearl Street, because then you're under the bridge and probably lost, even though it is a majestic sort of place in its own seedy way and even though you'll find a helpful sign there too, BROOKLYN BRIDGE (STAIRS), although its arrow points at a corrugated steel wall. Choose the cross street labeled York Street and start going that way. On the left you'll see a red-brick industrial building, with white lettering in vintage script stretching across the entire wall between the third and fourth floors reading THOMSON METER CO. WATER METERS. There isn't anything else to see on that bit of road. (If you must know, in 1887 the Scottish-born inventor and manufacturer John Thomson patented a water meter for controlling and billing water usage. Naturally he began mass-producing the device for sale; a round meter that works on the same principle is found in nearly every building nowadays.) Now you've reached Washington Street and you're almost at your destination. Walk for a moment watching the left side of the street. There it finally is: the bridge and the road that dives under it, or in other words the place where walkers enter the bridge.

In that shaded place under the bridge is a small sales cart and on the cart a yellow and blue *Heja Sverige!* sunshade to attract attention: 2 HOT DOGS + COLD WATER OR COLD SODA CAN—$4. Apparently people coming from the bridge or going to the bridge are hungry, or at least enough are that it's worthwhile to stand in that exhaust-fume-choked rathole and sell bottled and canned drinks and snacks packed in cardboard and wrapped in paper. (Shlomith never buys anything from this establishment, but nothing would stop you from buying two discount hot-dogs and a refreshing beverage you may need as the heat of the day continues to rise, and God help us, it is hot up on the bridge . . .) In front of the hot-dog stand is a sign defaced with stickers and tags that says BROOKLYN BRIDGE (STAIRS). For once the arrow points in precisely the right direction: finally, after all this time, we see the stairs we need.

For a first-timer, finding these stairs must be similar to the joy experienced by the archaeologist Carlo Fea, when he began to unearth the triumphal arch of Septimius Severus, which had been buried in sludge in the northeast corner of the Forum Romanum at the foot of the Capitoline Hill. But one must not linger distracted by daydreams, since Shlomith has already moved on. She runs along the handsome bridge toward Manhattan, and we let her run. She knows full well where to turn after reaching the island, where to find a pleasant route (although after the Brooklyn Heights Promenade, "pleasant" is a very relative concept) to her final destination, the Lower East Side, the intersection of East Houston and Ludlow. She walks into Katz's Deli, which has been immortalized in film and advertises its excellence with its red brick walls and signage in various fonts: thick, red neon letters, a lettered tower protruding into the sky like an antenna, and more restrained posters and placards. *Katz's—that's all! Known as the Best—since 1888!*

Shlomith sits in her usual spot, next to the wall under Liza Minnelli's photograph, and places her usual order. She is unquestionably now Shkhina, not just Shlomith, because of course the staff and regulars at the restaurant know her. She's a sightseeing attraction herself! People come just to look at her. The glances are furtive and polite as always in the big city. Sometimes someone (usually a visiting foreigner, a gallery buff who's up to date with the trends of the art world) comes over to exchange a few words with Shlomith. "How goes the hunger?" the buff might ask in the hushed tones of an initiate.

Slowly, feigning enjoyment, Shlomith-Shkhina consumes her half pastrami sandwich. Between the two slices of bread is an obscenely thick layer of thinly sliced turkey which has been salted, partially dried, rubbed with herbs, and finally smoked and steamed; the recipe originated in a time before the refrigerator. Romanian Jewish immigrants brought the delicacy to the United States in the mid-nineteenth century, and it is even enjoyed by those who don't care much about Him Who Is, Him for whose glory the Orthodox must eat food with recipes originating during the age before refrigeration. The manager, Dan, always brings Shlomith-Shkhina the other half of the sandwich in a paper bag with the bill. "Shlomith, please take this to eat later tonight. Our treat." Shlomith takes the paper bag and leaves a princely tip, which is all part of the routine.

Shlomith-Shkhina steps out of Katz's Deli onto East Houston Street with tired but happy legs. She totters a few blocks to the west, toward Sarah D. Roosevelt Park, and descends into the underworld, down to the F train, which returns her to Park Slope, to Seventh Avenue right near her home.

The daily hunger and euphoria, the pain and the torpor, the hollow, mental anguish and the tight-rope walker's ingenuousness, the supernatural effort and the irrational self-denial, the numberless sleepless nights, the endless search for knowledge, the follow-up calls, the full notebooks, which could have sealed a whole apartment building of drafty windows—all this becomes her prayer, the fruit of her lips, *tfila*. Shlomith-Shkhina's final performance, which dozens of performance researchers from around the world have come to observe. The auditorium of the Jewish Museum is full to overflowing. Officially it seats 230, but now a quarter more than that are here. Some sit on the floor.

On the sixteenth of August, the red stage curtains rise. A stir runs through the crowd. There stands Shlomith-Shkhina, finally, a microphone in her hand, in her underwear, surrounded by ugly heaters blasting warm air. She is like something exhumed from the grave. She's so thin she can't be alive. So angular and pale, as if dented all over. But there she stands, obviously alive, ever so slightly moving. Shlomith-Shkhina raises the microphone to her lips and makes a sound: "Ladies and gentlemen!" The sound comes from somewhere deep. Robust and hollow, it carries through the hall. From such an insubstantial body one would expect little more than weak squeaks punctuated by panting, but now, Shlomith-Shkhina's voice is as strong as steel. And so Shlomith-Shkhina begins to speak for the last time on earth.

JUDAISM AND ANOREXIA

LECTURE PERFORMANCE
JEWISH MUSEUM
16.08.2007

Ladies and gentlemen! I'd like to welcome you all to this lecture, which I've entitled "Judaism and Anorexia". As you can see, this is a topic that touches me at a very personal level. I stand before you, surrounded by these glowing heaters, nearly naked. I'm freezing. The downy blanket of hair on my skin, my lanugo, is fluffed up like a baby chick; due to the lighting behind me, you see it as a gleaming aura. *Me* you see as a silhouette, not as a person, even less so as a woman. Instead of a person, you see a symbol, instead of a woman a metaphor—you see a *sign*.

I know I'm far too thin. I know I'm disfigured and ugly. One would even be justified in saying that I'm dying right before your eyes. Am I playing with fire? Most certainly. Am I a narcissist? Perhaps to some degree. Insane? I don't believe so. Am I incompetent? No. Am I glorifying the sickness called anorexia in the name of art? Absolutely not! Am I encouraging Jewish girls and women to follow my example? No, no, no!

You may ask in confusion, "Why have you done this to yourself, Shlomith-Shkhina?" Over the next forty-five minutes, I'll attempt to provide answers to that question.

*

As you know, I'm a Jew. That sentence contains the first question: what does it mean "to be a Jew"? Is this a matter of religion or ethnicity? Both options are possible to argue. First of all, "Jewish atheist" is not a paradoxical concept. Personally I've never been able to believe in God, but I still feel Jewish in my blood and soul. Secondly, however difficult, it is possible to convert to Judaism. All you have to do is make a serious study of the fundamentals of the religion. However, joining the ethnic group is not a matter of choice. You're born into it and you remain in it.

I approach Judaism in a broad, cultural sense. I would argue that even the most worldly Jew carries, perhaps unconsciously, principles of purity and immiscibility that are an organic part of our cultural heritage. In Judaism these ideals are approached in particular through food, which makes Jewish culture especially susceptible to pathologies related to eating.

During the course of this lecture I will also investigate Jewishness through individual doctrines. These reveal the *mind* of Judaism, that certain something that makes Judaism unique compared to other world views and religions.

*

My childhood home was not particularly religious, although certain clichés of Jewish culture were visible in our day-to-day life. Dominant in my family were an ethos of success and a culture of glorifying wealth, which suffuse the entire American intellectual landscape. My father worked long hours in the book-printing industry. My mother was an overprotective, food-plying, loud-mouthed guardian spirit of the home who was one hundred percent focused on the family's welfare.

Rather dominating, sometimes smothering, according to my brother maybe even emasculating. So the prototypical Jewish mother.

For myself, I felt that my mother's solicitude wasn't entirely honest. There was always a touch of martyrdom, a sacrificial mentality that a child senses clearly even without understanding it. The hand ladling out the food is simultaneously unsympathetic. A finger is outstretched in accusation: *Eat, little one, eat, devour the last remnants of your mother's strength!*

My father was completely ignorant of the power games my mother played. Maybe he was pretending; maybe subconsciously he benefited from the situation. In the evenings, after returning from work, he walked straight to the table and tucked into whatever meal was served. Me he considered ungrateful and headstrong because early on I began reacting to the tensions in the home by refusing meals.

*

I've been a prisoner of anorexia since I was a teenager. I don't blame my mother for my disease—that would be so 1970s!—and I also don't blame my father. My siblings are healthy even though they grew up in the same environment I did and were exposed to the same contradictory signals as me.

Rather, I'm convinced that I have a genetic predisposition to the seductions of the siren song of not eating. If this predisposition didn't exist, I would have channeled my negative feelings into something else. I could have danced myself to freedom like my brother did. He became a successful choreographer.

I recovered from my disease briefly when I fell in love. Once again a very typical story. I got married,

we moved to Israel to a kibbutz named Methuselah, and
we had two children. That lasted the biblical seven
years. Then everything fell apart. I returned to New
York alone, and hunger furtively began to call to me.

I've done OK with my anorexia. Deep inside I knew as
soon as I returned from Israel that one day I would
have a true reckoning with this demon. I would have to
descend into the depths of my disease and grub up its
putrid roots; and my contention is that the principle
branches are found in Judaism.

That day is now.

In order to heal, for a moment I give my body
completely to the beloved beast, to the torturously
pleasurable compulsion not to eat. I will look straight
into its luminous, ice cold eyes and then: *Goodbye*.

Now is the moment I strike it down, here, as I speak
to you.

One more thing before I move on to the actual topic.
Don't be concerned about my health. In just over an
hour, I'll be admitted to a private hospital. An ambulance is waiting for me outside. When I return from
treatment, I'll be a new person, no longer Shlomith-
Shkhina. I'll be as I was born. After tonight, please
greet me as Sheila Ruth Berkowitz.

*

I begin with the indisputable fact that Jewish women
suffer from anorexia and other eating disorders on
average more than the general population. Although
only two percent of the United States population is
Jewish,[1] as many as thirteen percent of eating disor-

1   SINGER, D., & GROSSMAN, L. (EDS.) 2005: *AMERICAN JEWISH YEAR
    BOOK 2005*. NEW YORK: AMERICAN JEWISH COMMITTEE.

der clinic patients are Jews.[2]

Strictly observant Jews have been particularly affected since at least the 1970s.[3] In recent years, anorexia among teenage girls in the Orthodox community has absolutely exploded. One study of a Brooklyn Orthodox Jewish high school discovered that one in nineteen Jewish girls suffered from some kind of eating disorder. This figure is fifty percent higher than among other American girls of the same age.[4]

A similar study is underway in the Toronto Jewish community. According to initial results, twenty-five percent of the high-school-age girls in the community have suffered from an eating disorder, while the corresponding percentage in the general population is eighteen percent.

In Israel, more than one in four women diets. That's the highest figure in the world. Israeli Jewish women, regardless of their degree of religiosity, are significantly less satisfied with their bodies than Arab women.[5]

In order to avoid accusations of defamation, let me also mention that research results also exist that suggest that eating disorders are more common among secular Jews than the religious. Jewish Law emphasizes modesty and humility, which in some cases can be a protective factor when it comes to eating disorders.[6]

---

2   BARUCHIN, A., 1998: "WHY JEWISH GIRLS STARVE THEMSELVES."
     LILITH, 23:5 (MAY 31).

3   BARUCHIN, A., 1998: "WHAT CAN ORTHODOX GIRLS CONTROL." *LILITH*,
     23:8 (SEPTEMBER 30).

4   IRA SACKER, UNPUBLISHED STUDY FROM 1996.

5   SAFIR, M. P., FLAISHER-KELLNER, S., & ROSENMANN, A. 2005:
     "WHEN GENDER DIFFERENCES SURPASS CULTURAL DIFFERENCES IN PER-
     SONAL SATISFACTION WITH BODY SHAPE IN ISRAELI COLLEGE STU-
     DENTS." *SEX ROLES*, 52, 369–378.

6   GLUCK, M. E. 1999: *BODY IMAGE AND EATING DISTURBANCES: ORTHO-
     DOX VS. SECULAR JEWISH WOMEN* (DOCTORAL DISSERTATION, YESHIVA

According to Jewish thought, humanity is the image of God. The concept of *shmirat ha-guf* means the protection of the body (proper nutrition, staying in shape, and avoiding risks). Anorexia, on the contrary, always represents rebellion, hubris, and excess. Anorexia is a startling manifesto against the prevailing environment. So we must assume that when an Orthodox Jew falls into the snare of anorexia, it happens innocently, as a result of the greatest and most powerful sort of self-deception.

Viewed from this perspective, it's no wonder that the use of laxatives and diuretics, along with vomiting, all of which are active and aggressive weight control techniques that break the principles of *shmirat ha-guf*, are most common among secular Jews.[7] On the other hand, Jews have also been more ready and willing to seek help for their problems than other cultural groups. This has been seen as a consequence not only of their low self-confidence but also because they have a more positive view of the psychiatric profession (with the exception of the most traditional Orthodox Jews).[8] You may also know the saying that the Jewish imagination is paranoia, confirmed by history. Self-investigation and self-criticism, not to mention black humor, are a part

UNIVERSITY, 1999). DISSERTATION ABSTRACTS INTERNATIONAL, 61, 1–73; GLUCK, M. E., & GELIEBTER, A. 2002: "RACIAL/ETHNIC DIFFERENCES IN BODY IMAGE AND EATING BEHAVIORS." *EATING BEHAVIORS*, 3, 143–151.

7   GLUCK, M. E., & GELIEBTER, A. 2002: "RACIAL/ETHNIC DIFFERENCES IN BODY IMAGE AND EATING BEHAVIORS." *EATING BEHAVIORS*, 3, 143–151.

8   KLEIN, J. W. 1976: "ETHNOTHERAPY WITH JEWS." *INTERNATIONAL JOURNAL OF MENTAL HEALTH*, 5, 26–38; LANGMAN, P. F. 1997: "WHITE CULTURE, JEWISH CULTURE, AND THE ORIGINS OF PSYCHOTHERAPY." *PSYCHOTHERAPY: THEORY, RESEARCH, PRACTICE, TRAINING*, 34, 207–218; YEUNG, P. P. & GREENWALD, S. 1992: "JEWISH AMERICANS AND MENTAL HEALTH: RESULTS OF THE NIMH EPIDEMIOLOGIC CATCHMENT AREA STUDY." *SOCIAL PSYCHIATRY AND PSYCHIATRIC EPIDEMIOLOGY*, 27, 292–297.

of our culture, and all these things are excellent qualities in terms of successful therapy.

Jewish communities have also awoken to the need to help their own. One American Reform Jewish women's group has compiled a handbook and course material packet named "*Letapeah tikva—Let's Feed Hope! Eating Disorders in Modern Jewish Life: Observations and Perspectives.*" The women's Zionist organization, the Hadassah Foundation, whose purpose is to improve the status, health, and welfare of Jewish women and girls in the United States and Israel, has awarded a large grant for the study of eating disorder prevention. In 1999 Rabbi Dovid Goldwasser and the clinical psychologist Ira Sacker founded the organization Helping to End Eating Disorders (HEED) for Orthodox Jewish teens. The Renfrew Center has started a program on Long Island for people who follow a kosher diet and suffer from eating disorders.

*

Some causes for pathological eating behavior can be found on the surface, in pressure surrounding outward appearances. Jewish women often consider their Semitic features ugly if they compare themselves (and they often do) to the average white American woman.

Because of their racial characteristics, Jewish women think they're short and plump. This plumpness applies to buttocks, thighs, hips, stomachs, and breasts. They often consider themselves overweight, their muscles flabby, or other parts of their body structure too robust to be feminine. They see big noses, body hair, and abnormally dark eyes and hair. Their hair is usually curly, like mine, and that curliness is also seen as an unattractive element.

So in many ways Jewish women are the opposite of
their Anglo-Saxon Protestant sisters with their ethnic
tendencies toward being tall, athletic, slender, blue-
eyed, and blonde.[9] Although athleticism and slim figures
are quickly disappearing in the face of fast food
culture.

No one can do anything about being short, but the
other Semitic characteristics I've mentioned are
amenable to alteration. Nose jobs and hair straightening are very common in the Jewish community.[10] The
size of breasts, thighs, buttocks, and stomachs can be
reshaped with muscle training and diet. Pelvis size
can't be changed since it's bone.

Back when I wasn't a skeleton, just terribly skinny,
more than once I heard my Jewish friends say, as a
compliment, "You have such a lovely *gentile* body!" I
learned when I was a teenager that there was a word
that meant non-Jewish. The most shocking thing is that
this didn't particularly shock me. You may have heard
the phrase "self-hating Jew". Many believe this phenomenon arose when the Jews were freed from the ghettos
and allowed to assimilate with the general population.[11] From living within one culture, the Jews moved
to a border between two cultures, to a place where

9   KLEIN, J. W. 1977: *JEWISH IDENTITY AND SELF-ESTEEM* (DOCTORAL
     DISSERTATION, THE WRIGHT INSTITUTE). DISSERTATION ABSTRACTS
     INTERNATIONAL, 138, 906-907; SCHNEIDER, S. W. 1984: *JEWISH AND
     FEMALE: CHOICES AND CHANGES IN OUR LIVES TODAY*. NEW YORK: SI-
     MON AND SCHUSTER. P. 244.

10   GOLD, N. 1997: "CANADIAN JEWISH WOMEN AND THEIR EXPERIENCES
     OF ANTISEMITISM AND SEXISM." R. J. SIEGEL & E. COLE (EDS.),
     *CELEBRATING THE LIVES OF JEWISH WOMEN: PATTERNS IN A FEMINIST
     SAMPLER*. NEW YORK: THE HARRINGTON PARK PRESS. PP. 279-289;
     SCHNEIDER, S. W. 1984: *JEWISH AND FEMALE: CHOICES AND CHANGES
     IN OUR LIVES TODAY*. NEW YORK: SIMON AND SCHUSTER.

11   LANGMAN, P. F. 1995: "INCLUDING JEWS IN MULTICULTURALISM".
     JOURNAL OF MULTICULTURAL COUNSELING AND DEVELOPMENT, 23,
     222-236.

they could see in both directions: backward and forward, toward dreams, toward change.

My other features (big nose, curly hair, five foot four height) are typically Semitic. I've gotten along quite well with them, unlike my body, which has always had its own will separate from mine. African-American women have done better in this regard. Everyone knows the slogan **"BLACK IS BEAUTIFUL"**. One background factor for this racial self-esteem may be that, unlike Jews, black people have a significantly harder time changing their ethnic features.[12] You can also change your name. I was born as Sheila because my parents didn't want me to stand out too much from the crowd.

Nowadays Sheila is a very common Jewish name despite the fact that it comes from Irish. The name arrived in Ireland from the Latin Cecelia, which comes from the Latin word *caecus*, which means blind.

Shlomith without the final H is a rather rare name with roots in the Bible. Its base form is found in First Chronicles, chapter three, verse nineteen: *And the sons of Pedaiah were, Zerubbabel, and Shimei: and the sons of Zerubbabel; Meshullam, and Hananiah, and Shelomith their sister.*

---

12 SKIN WHITENING IS POSSIBLE, OF COURSE, AS WE KNOW FROM THE NOTORIOUS CASE OF MICHAEL JACKSON. USUALLY THE RESULTS OF WHITENING ARE SIGNIFICANTLY LESS NOTICEABLE THAN WITH JACKO, THOUGH. THERE ARE NUMEROUS PROBLEMS WITH SKIN WHITENING, BEYOND ETHICS AND PRINCIPLES. THE SUBSTANCES USED IN THE WHITENING, IF THEY'RE EFFECTIVE AT ALL, RARELY PASS SAFETY STANDARDS. IN DEVELOPING COUNTRIES, EXTREMELY POISONOUS CHEMICALS ARE USED IN SKIN WHITENING, SUCH AS MERCURY AND CLOBETASOL PROPIONATE. BETA ARBUTIN IS ONE OF THE MOST EFFECTIVE NATURAL PRODUCTS, BUT IT IS ALSO SUSPECTED OF HAVING CARCINOGENIC PROPERTIES, ESPECIALLY IF IT IS USED OFTEN AND IN LARGE AMOUNTS OVER WIDE AREAS OF SKIN. KOJIC ACID IS ALSO POPULAR, ESPECIALLY IN JAPAN, BUT IT CAUSES ALLERGIC REACTIONS IN MANY USERS AND MAY ALSO BE A CARCINOGEN. *CINNAMOMUM SUBAVENIUM*, A CHINESE HERB, PREVENTS THE PRODUCTION OF MELANIN, BUT THERE IS NO SCIENTIFIC EVIDENCE OF ITS EFFICACY OR SAFETY. IN ONE CONTROLLED STUDY IT WAS USED SUCCESSFULLY TO REMOVE ZEBRA FISH STRIPES.

I Hebraicized Sheila to Shlomith after I got married.
I wanted to add the H at the end because it made the
name more complete. It made it feel more rounded and
soft in my mouth. The name remained even though we
divorced and I left the kibbutz.

*

Strict religious communities have always tried to
protect themselves from outside influences. For example, Haredi Jews forbid their members from watching
television. Isolation also feeds a culture of silence.
Mental health problems, which anorexia is generally
considered to be, are one of the greatest sources of
shame among traditional Orthodox Jews. Knowledge of
psychiatric treatment can even become an impediment to
marriage.

I know of cases in which the parents of dangerously
malnourished girls who were admitted to hospitals told
the most stupefying lies to acquaintances and schools
about their daughters' conditions. One favorite explanation is the standard teenage illness, mononucleosis.
What makes this comical is that mononucleosis, known
in the vernacular as kissing disease, is acquired
through touch or the exchange of bodily fluids like
saliva or blood. Touching of any kind, but especially
sexual contact, is subject to the most extreme regulation in ultra-Orthodox Jewish culture.

"But what does this have to do with you, Shlomith-
Shkhina? You've never belonged to the religious Jewish
community!" Yes, I hear very clearly the questions
running through your minds. I can hear the murmurs in
the auditorium. Your hushed voices grate in my ears
because the thin layer of fat surrounding the lining
of the nerve cells in my inner ear has almost completely

disappeared.

It is true that my family looked askance at the Hasidim of Borough Park. We thought they were weird, freaks who represented the dark side of Judaism. Despite this, the Holy Book and the rabbinical Mishnah and Gemara that developed around it over the centuries always remain part of the shared foundation of Jewish culture and, ultimately, all of western civilization. The Holy Book is used in different ways in different Jewish communities, either freely and adaptively or dogmatically and inflexibly, but either way, the Book is there. It is in us. Jewish Law, Halakha, is an intertextual DNA strand we can no more escape than our own genes hidden in our chromosomes.

So for a moment longer let my body remain a laboratory in which deadly metaphors become concrete, in which contagious allegories and ravaging myths are tested!

*

The first conference on Judaism and anorexia was organized in Philadelphia in 1998.[13] I was there. That conference provided the final spark for the project you see before you, although almost ten years passed before I reached this point. In any case, the conference was incredibly exhilarating. While there I formed many significant collegial relationships.

Several theories for the causes of eating disorders emerged. One of the most significant relates to the dating culture (*shidduchim*) of ultra-Orthodox Jews,

---

13 "FOOD, BODY IMAGE, AND JUDAISM." THE CONFERENCE WAS ORGANIZED BY KOLOT—THE CENTER FOR JEWISH WOMEN'S & GENDER STUDIES, WHICH IS PART OF THE RECONSTRUCTIONIST RABBINICAL COLLEGE, AS WELL AS THE RENFREW CENTER OF PHILADELPHIA, WHICH SPECIALIZES IN THE TREATMENT OF EATING DISORDERS.

which deviates greatly from the courtship rituals of
the general populace. Orthodox Jewish young people are
not allowed to meet together without the assistance of
matchmakers. Even touching (*negiah*) the opposite sex,
a potential spouse, is strictly forbidden.

Those who interpret the Law most stringently avoid
situations in which they could touch a member of the
opposite sex even by accident. This dictates their
choice of seats on buses, airplanes, etc. Shaking
hands with someone of the opposite sex is also extremely
problematic from their perspective.

Because the outside world (such as the business
community) frowns upon refusing a handshake and may
exact serious penalties on a person who does so (such
as rejecting business deals), highly educated rabbis
have given instructions for how to handle such situations honorably. The *negiah* observer's hand must
remain "helpless" and avoid squeezing. If the other
party takes a vigorous, firm grip, the Jew's helpless
hand remains an "innocent bystander" and thereby ritually pure.

Some marriage brokers are professionals who charge
a fee. These practitioners are called *shadkhan*. They
maintain a database in which the first question pertains
to the woman's dress size and weight. Men tend to look
for very slender women to marry.

Slimness is a prized trait emphasized by matchmakers
and the mothers of girls of marriageable age. I'm not
exaggerating much when I say that you can't get a date
until you hit a size 0 and the magic numbers 32-24-34.

Slimness symbolizes pubescent innocence, incorrup-
tion, which in turn ensures that the wife candidate
will be one hundred percent under the control of her
husband. You're supposed to marry very young, and the
use of birth control is not customary. The primary

purpose of sex is the creation of children. A large number of children is a way to spread Jewish values (Jews don't engage in missionary work).

This is one obvious reason for anorexia among young Orthodox women. If they don't feel ready for the demands of parenthood, sex, and raising a flock of children, they start to focus on what they do control: their own bodies.

*

Girls become potential future spouses at the age of twelve years and six months, which is considered the official beginning of menstruation. For Haredi Jews, even touching a three-year-old member of the opposite sex is a problem. Because menstruation is treated with the same horror in strictly religious Jewish culture as in most ancient tribal societies and because this attitude of shunning exposes those growing into women in the modern world to serious body image issues, I'm going to give you some more specifics about menstruation in the Jewish context.

A menstruating girl or women is *niddah*; the word means "moved" or "separated". According to some rabbinical interpretations, *niddah* comes from the word *menaddekem*, which means "those who cast you out".

According to Jewish thought there is normal (*niddah*) and abnormal (*zavah*) blood flow. Because it is very difficult to know whether the flow is normal, it is always treated as abnormal. This means that after her period ends, a Jewish woman must wait seven days before ritually immersing herself on the eighth day, after nightfall, in cleansing water (*mikvah*) and thus metamorphosing back to a state of purity.

Just to be sure, Orthodox Ashkenazi Jews add five

more days on top of the seven, so a woman has to wait twelve days before purification.

Ritual immersion belongs to the larger concept of "family purity" (*taharat hamishpacha*). Immersion is preceded by a complete cleansing of all body orifices. Nails are also trimmed and hair brushed. So as a woman immerses herself, she is not only washing physically, she is becoming spiritually clean.

According to Jewish doctrine, *mikvah* is an even more important element of the religion than the synagogue and Torah scrolls. Of the 613 commandments and prohibitions that make up the *mitsvot*, the requirements of the *mikvah* belong to the third category (*chukim*), which consists of rules that surpass human understanding and challenge reason, and which are, therefore, beyond all criticism. According to the Jewish view, these commandments are paramount because they have no pragmatic function. They are simply instructions handed down by God and must be accepted as such.

The actual *mikvah* font must be built in contact with the ground; it cannot, for example, be a discrete bathtub. The font must be divided into two parts, one of which contains at least two hundred gallons of rainwater that has been collected and funneled to the font according to precise requirements. In an emergency, melted snow or ice may be used if rainwater is unavailable.

For practical reasons, the other section of the font is filled with tap water. Between the sections is a dividing wall with a hole of at least two inches in diameter. Because of the flow between the sections, the waters "kiss" each other, which gives the font official *mikvah* status.

The font symbolizes both the womb and the grave. It is an intermediate space where one moves between life and death. It represents relinquishing oneself and rebirth. In Jewish thought, the source of purity (*tahorah*) is life itself, while death represents impurity (*tumah*). According to this logic, a woman's period is the death of potential life, and so a menstruating woman moves into a state of symbolic impurity from which she must escape month after month through the aid of the *mikvah*.

This is also one possible additional explanation for why ulta-Orthodox Jews have so many children. Who would want to live constantly unclean?

Purification requires a precise determination of the end of one's period. Otherwise it would be impossible to count the seven (or twelve) days a woman has to wait. So women check the end of their periods through a ritual called *hefsek taharah*. First the woman bathes or showers at sundown, then wraps a clean white cloth (*bedikah*) around her finger and wipes it in her vagina. If the cloth remains clean or if it only comes back with something white or yellow on it, menstruation is considered to have ended.

If the cloth is stained red or pink, menstruation is considered to be ongoing. If some other color comes back on the cloth, for example brown, the matter requires closer inspection. In this case the woman has to consult with her rabbi.

To be on the safe side, an Orthodox woman who has completed her period will also place a piece of cloth called a *mokh dahuk* (nowadays a tampon is often used) in her vagina for eighteen minutes to an hour each morning and evening for seven days. The fabric must be placed carefully in order to avoid irritating the dry vagina in an undesirable way and causing bleeding that will interfere with the result of the examination. Women looking for convenience or who suffer from spotting may at this point use colorful toilet paper and colorful underwear so any possible stains won't stand out and no further action will be required.

Of course the married couple are not allowed to interact amorously (*harchakot*) during menstruation. Anything that could arouse sexual desire must be avoided. In some communities, sisterly touch is allowed.

Those who celebrate the good tidings of Judaism claim that menstrual periods actually invigorate married life. It is as if the couple enjoys repeated honeymoons fed by longing and separation since one of them is temporarily unattainable and forbidden. In addition they claim that women benefit at a personal level from their time in *niddah*. They can devote themselves to study and completely control their own bodies, unlike during the rest of the month.

A woman also becomes *niddah* after losing her virginity, after her hymen is torn (regardless of whether she bleeds or not). The wedding night is followed by the same morning and evening examination of bleeding as at the end of menstruation, with the difference that there are four days instead of seven (or twelve). Weddings are planned according to brides' periods, because a woman must cleanse herself in a *mikvah* font just before the great celebration.

I believe that routines and rituals can bring order and joy to a woman's life. However, I am also certain that the repellent, even demonizing attitude of ultra-Orthodox Jews to menstruation, to what is one of the most natural events in the world, is one of the elements that leads to anorexia in this culture. This situation is not changed at all by the fact that some modern Kabbalistic trends attempt to glorify this madness by using the euphemistic name "Spa for the Soul".

Sufficiently advanced anorexia is an effective method for producing secondary amenorrhea, an endocrine disorder caused by hormonal disturbances of the hypothalamus, pituitary gland, and gonads, which results in an interruption of the menstrual cycle. And, I hardly have to spell this out, a woman who is free of her period is also free of the above-mentioned menstrual circus.

*

Jewish celebrations are well known for centering around large meals. In the Jewish home, the weekly Shabbat is just as lavish as the yearly Thanksgiving dinner is for other Americans. The late supper on the Friday preceding Shabbat also contains numerous carefully prepared dishes. It's no surprise that a focus on food has been proven to increase eating disorders among Jews.[14]

The days preceding a weekend are largely consumed by food preparations for the tradition-conscious Jewish woman. It's also good to remember that cook isn't a Jewish woman's only role by any means. In the Haredi community, the woman is also responsible for supporting the family because the man has to focus his attention on spending all day cramming the tenets of the faith into his brain.

The festival of Yom Kippur each autumn centers on fasting, and other twenty-five-hour periods of fasting from food and water are also found in the Jewish calendar. The fast either ends with a large meal or is preceded by one. A food culture like this that

---

14 ROWLAND, C. V. 1970: "ANOREXIA NERVOSA. A SURVEY OF THE LITER
    ATURE AND REVIEW OF 30 CASES." *INTERNATIONAL PSYCHIATRY CLIN
    ICS*, 7, 37–137.

alternates between abstinence and gluttony is also
tailor-made for triggering eating disorders.

Jews who closely follow *halakha* eat according to so
much regulation that an anorexic attitude toward food
is almost a foregone conclusion. It isn't just the
orthodoxy of food defined by the kosher rules, but also
the numerous rituals related to the actual act of
eating, that ensure that one's thoughts will constantly
revolve around food. Blessings are uttered before and
after meals, and a ritual handwashing must precede
partaking of bread.

Most kosher rules are based on a prohibition on
mixing, which is based on the belief that according to
God, each individual thing (whether person, object, or
dish of food) must have its own recognizable singular-
ity, its very own created nature.

Nowadays kosher requirements for food feel just as
arbitrary as the prohibition of *shatnez*: any mixture
of wool and linen in the same garment. This rule probably originated from the fact that linen was imported
from estuarine areas such as the Nile Valley in Egypt,
while the production of wool is connected with the
pastoral economy that the Jewish tribes wandering in
the desert practiced. At a symbolic level, combining
wool and linen therefore means mixing Egypt and Judaism.

Naturally kosher foods, fruits and vegetables, are
low-calorie and thus they also often form the basis
for the anorexic's diet. You can eat them without any
complicated arrangements. Almost everything else is
difficult. Ruminants are allowed, but only if their
hooves are entirely cloven. Cows and sheep are kosher,
while horses with their cornified hoof capsules belong
to the odd-toed ungulates (*perissodactyla*), and also
aren't ruminants. Rabbits chew cud but have paws. Pigs
have cloven hooves but don't ruminate.

In order for a water animal to be kosher, it has to have fins and visible scales. For example, clams, crabs, lobsters, eels, sturgeon, and lampreys are prohibited (*trefa*). Insects are also not allowed. Blood is super-extra *trefa*.

I know of one tragic anorexia case that has a clear connection to kosher law. A girl, let's call her Rivka, began having panic attacks after her bat mitzvah over animal blood somehow invading her body. The fear didn't subside even though her mother and father assured her that her terror was irrational. And why would it subside since the Law is full of tenets that were just as irrational!

Rivka cleaned and cleaned the house, cleaning after she finished cleaning. She couldn't eat anything because everything she put in her mouth might have some drop of blood hiding in it. Even in an orange she peeled herself!

Ultimately Rivka had to be admitted to a hospital. The last I heard of her, a fistula had been created in her stomach so she could directly inject a substance into her stomach that it would be a sin to call food. It was a soft, light brown ooze broken down with artificial enzymes into basic nutrients: glucose (energy for the cells), amino acids (building material for the organs), and glycerol (building material for the cells).

Each and every bag of this stuff was packaged as if Rivka were on her way to outer space, and each and every bag was blessed by a rabbi who pledged, in the name of God, that there was not a drop of blood mixed in with the sludge.

*

Animals must be slaughtered properly (*shechita*) and
the meat must be prepared carefully. Soaking and salt-
ing ensure that the blood has been removed from the
meat. Because a calf cannot be boiled in its own mother's milk—what a macabre idea!—meat and milk products
cannot be combined or consumed during the same meal.

For some, a quick swish of water in their mouth is
enough if they want to have some meat after a piece of
cheese. Others wait an hour. If you want to eat aged
cheese, the waiting time increases significantly. If
you want to have a piece of hard cheese after enjoying
your beef, the wait is from four to six hours. Of
course the cheese can't contain rennet, which means it
has to be purchased from a store that specializes in
kosher products.

A doctrinaire kosher kitchen will have two sets of
dishes, two sinks, and two refrigerators to separate
meat and milk products. Cleaning dishes is an art in
itself. Fire or boiling water destroy any foodstuffs
that have soaked into the pores of a metal dish. But
ceramics are so porous that they have to sit empty for
a year if you want to serve a cheese soufflé on a
ceramic plate after a meat pie. Glass is the only
material immune to this sort of absorption.

Unleavened *matso* bread is dear to the Jewish heart.
At the Pesach or Passover *seder*, leavened breads are
absolutely forbidden. In Jewish culture, leaven
(*chametz*) represents egotism and a proud heart.

Because sudden, undesirable departures have been a
recurring part of Jewish life, unleavened dough has
become a reminder for members of the community that
they must always be ready to flee again. In passing let
it be noted that preparation for departure and leaving
the past behind made the creation of the Book possible. When the Temple was destroyed and the Jewish

diaspora began, religious knowledge had to be porta-
ble. Interruptions in knowledge are unacceptable, so
the recorded and copied Word is significantly more
reliable than a religious scholar, who can always be
killed or silenced.

Preparing for Pesach includes removing all flour
products from the home to ensure that no traces of
leaven are left behind. All food must be absolutely
kosher during Pesach. Even the wine is grown in vineyards that specialize exclusively in the production of
Pesach wine. No one is allowed to eat anything in the
areas devoted to producing the wine in order to prevent
any cross-contamination.

*

Identification with the skeletal bodies of holocaust
victims is also another partial explanation for the
prevalence of anorexia in Jewish society. We all know
the myth of Simone Weil, who empathized so deeply with
the concentration camp prisoners that she died of a
heart attack brought on by severe malnutrition at the
age of thirty-four.

Simone Weil's example, whether true or not, has
spurred many young Jewish women on the road to anorexia.
This has served as a more noble and spiritual excuse
for refusing food than the narcissistic ideologies of
the Internet, like *thinspiration* and *pro ana*.

The concentration camp connection is not as fanciful
as it might seem, since the Shoah still haunts us
particularly in the Jewish kitchen. Parents often
force their small children to eat by saying, "Take
this bite for your uncle who passed in Treblinka, take

this bite for your grandmother who never left Sobibór."[15]

So food is fundamentally a struggle for survival, the opposite of slavery, and we actively try to nurture this memory. The Pesach meal I mentioned a moment ago begins with the words, "Let all who are hungry come to eat, let every slave taste of freedom during this meal!"

At the same time, Jewish culture is full of contradictory messages. A grandmother might say to her rail-thin granddaughter, "You look good, child. You're so thin! Now come, the food is on the table!" Mothers who cook send the same sorts of contradictory signals to their daughters, "Eat! Eat!" and then, "Diet! Diet!"[16]

*

I'd like to end my lecture with my personal experience at the kibbutz, but before that a few words about the foundations of the kibbutz movement.

The kibbutz ideology was born as a counterpoint to traditional Jewish culture. The Hebrew word "kibbutz" means a group. The first kibbutz was founded in 1909 in Degania, and the movement enjoyed its golden age after the Second World War. Jews moving to Israel wanted their own land where they could have peace from their persecutors. They also wanted to make a break from ghetto culture, whose conventionality, family focus, and Jewish religious rituals they experienced as oppressive.

Jewish religion encouraged men to thank God each day that He didn't create them as women. Women had to cover their heads and their hair, and cut their hair

---

15 SCHNEIDER, S. W. 1984: *JEWISH AND FEMALE: CHOICES AND CHANGES
    IN OUR LIVES TODAY*. NEW YORK: SIMON AND SCHUSTER.
16 IBID.

when they got married. So it's no surprise that the kibbutz movement supported gender equality at least in theory.

At a symbolic level, chauvinism still insinuated itself insidiously into the foundations of the movement. One of the basic images of kibbutz culture was a new, proud, masculine Jew who had not been made effeminate by exile.

The experiment exceeded all expectations: the kibbutz created a completely new personality type in the course of a single generation. A personality with the theatrical pathos of ghetto life, those deep currents of emotion that previously overflowed so extravagantly and loudly before the whole community, rooted out from it. A "masculine", calculating sensibility took the place of "feminine" emotionality.

This was the departure of the *Wandervögel* of Central Europe from their ghettos at the turn of the century. They took off into the air from their *shtetlekh*, their tiny Jewish towns, whose atmosphere nauseated them. The eating ceremonies of the ghetto particularly disgusted them. The father's place, second only to God, was at the head of the table. The mother's place was bustling about with the pots and pans. First the mother boiled, roasted, and stewed. Then everyone ate, and finally came the questions: "How was it?" "Did you like it?" "Did you really get enough?" All said by the ghetto mother in a voice that aroused guilt in the heart of even the most stubborn offspring.

In the kibbutz, food only had instrumental value. We ate nutrients, stomach filler, not "food", and especially not "delicacies". We always ate in the communal dining hall, without ceremony. We scarfed down the meals we prepared as quickly as possible, without needless chatter.

The previous symbolic value of food was completely nullified. In one's own quarters it was improper to prepare or eat food, because eating alone could involve unbridled private pleasures that represented a crime against the spirit of the kibbutz. Eating alone, just like fasting alone, were impossible concepts.

At first I thought this was the best thing about the whole kibbutz: I could eat without anyone watching, mechanically, at specific scheduled times of day. My weight climbed to a normal level within my first year at Methuselah. Eighteen months later I became pregnant with my first child.

I have two children, my firstborn son Moti, who is now thirty-seven years old, and my daughter Malka, who is one year younger. I haven't seen them once since I left. That has been a difficult experience. I understood that they really didn't need me. That the community was their mother, and they accepted that without complaint.

After Moti's birth I was so confused about all the big changes happening in my life so quickly that I didn't know how to question the kibbutz methodology. I let things happen, even though inside I knew that something was seriously wrong. But with Malka, my maternal instincts came into their own.

I was only allowed to nurse her for six months. The central committee of our kibbutz had stipulated so. After that she had to learn to eat from the cups owned by the community, which the *metapelet* used to feed her purees. My breast was too personal. It didn't belong to the kibbutz, so they wanted to wean her from it as quickly as possible.

According to the declaration of the central committee, breastfeeding past six months no longer served any nutritional purpose. It was only for pleasure, in other words pointless and possibly harmful.

Whose pleasure was in question, the suckling child's or the nursing mother's, they didn't say. I would argue that the two cannot be separated. Mother and child are one, joined by the sweet milk, the most perfect nutrition possible. I've never experienced any feeling of completion quite like it!

Once again, this is an example of how pleasure, especially women's pleasure, is seen as a threat in Jewish culture. The fact that this negative view of pleasure was hiding in the tenets of the kibbutz ideology, which are in complete opposition to so many religious diktats, is irrelevant. The dogmas are still there, and they can be used to shrink and curtail a person when necessary, no matter how noble the principles.

So oral, maternal pleasures were off limits at Methuselah. Children weren't even allowed to suck their thumbs. I asked about this at one of the general meetings. My husband, Dovid, elbowed me angrily in the side. "We're still in our trial period," he whispered and asked me to keep my mouth shut. But I didn't. I raised my hand, and when my turn came I asked, "Why aren't children even allowed to suck their thumbs?"

Patiently they replied that thumb sucking emotionally separates the child from the community she has to belong to. That the thumb becomes an insidious hiding place where the child can escape. That the child gets more pleasure and safety from the thumb than from the collective. And that this is not acceptable.

The kibbutz has also been studied from the perspective of eating disorders. According to some studies, the ideology built around collectivity, especially the socialistic tendencies in the movement, protects

against eating disorders.[17] Contradictory results also
exist which suggest that kibbutz life creates a predisposition to pathological eating behavior since those
brought up there live in a cross-fire of conflicting
messages: on the one hand you have kibbutz life and on
the other the western lifestyle, and these two are not
easily combined.[18]

My own time at the kibbutz definitely strengthened my
identity as an anorexic. After having my children I
was in a very vulnerable condition even though I looked
mostly fine on the outside. When I wasn't able to be a
mother to Malka and Moti after that first six months of
nursing, I became completely estranged from my own
body. I had given birth to them, but suddenly I had to
pretend that they hadn't actually come *from me*. That
I could just be replaced by a "professional educator",
whose only task seemed to be to snuff the light of
curiosity from my children's eyes. And she did a marvelous job!

I returned to the kibbutz once, in February 1974,
before I left Israel for good. My naive intention was
to kidnap my children. Even though less than half a
year had passed since my departure, neither of my
children knew me any more. They were happy like children immersed in structured play with others often
are. They were friendly to me, because at the kibbutz
everyone is friendly. Every single individual trait
had been successfully rooted out of them. They could

17 LATZER, Y., & TZISCHINSKY, O. 2003: "WEIGHT CONCERN, DIETING
    AND EATING BEHAVIORS. A SURVEY OF ISRAELI HIGH SCHOOL GIRLS."
    INTERNATIONAL JOURNAL OF ADOLESCENT MEDICINE AND HEALTH, 15,
    295-305.

18 APTER, A., SHAH, M. A., IANCU, I., ABRAMOVITCH, H., WEITZMAN,
    A., & TYANO, S. 1994: "CULTURAL EFFECTS ON EATING ATTITUDES IN
    ISRAELI SUBPOPULATIONS AND HOSPITALIZED ANORECTICS." *GENETIC,
    SOCIAL, AND GENERAL PSYCHOLOGY MONOGRAPHS*, 120, 83-99.

have been anyone's children.

My ex-husband didn't want to see me. The other members of the community were terribly nice to me, though. They knew that I'd end up leaving with my tail between my legs. They knew that the three-year-old mechanical Malka and her older brother, mechanical Moti, were operating exactly according to the rules programmed into them. Everyone felt so comfortable they didn't hesitate to invite me to stay a few days longer.

They made up a bed in the guest house—in the same room where they put up teenage summer workers from Europe. How much is it possible to demean a person?

I left early in the morning without saying goodbye to anyone. On the table in the dining hall I left a letter addressed to the monster named Methuselah. It was the most angry, bitter letter I've ever written. It was my *J'accuse* letter to the collective of tyrants who pretended to live in true equality. They took away my children. They brainwashed my husband. In the letter I vowed revenge. I will now read a translation of the letter:

Monster Methuselah!

You all have names I could call you by: Ditsa, Zmira, Dovid, Moshe, Chaim, Gal, Dani, Eliahu, Ester, Josh, Yehudit, Libbi, Rachel, Tuvia, et cetera, et cetera, et cetera. But why would I bother? You are part of a machine. Tiny workers in an anthill. There is nothing uncompelled in you. Monster Methuselah: hopefully you won't be too offended by the name I'm cramming you all into. We did live together for seven years, after all.

Dear Monster, you may be aware that sometimes you

show symptoms of sickness beneath your placid surface.
I'll give an example. In the fall after the Six-Day
War, one of the organs who operates under you, an
organ named Lea, met some of her friends from the army
in Tel Aviv. First she broke down in a clothing shop.
Then she couldn't decide what to choose from the menu
at a restaurant. She came back from her trip in tears.
She refused to rise from her bed for three days, so
crushing was her experience of freedom.

You abandoned the doctrines of Judaism, but you
replaced them with new dogmas. In the beginning I
believed that clear, detailed rules were necessary to
accomplish the greater good, so you, Methuselah, could
flourish and offer your members the best of everything.
So none of your members would turn capricious or
egotistical. For a long time I refused to believe that
in reality you only wanted to subjugate and enslave.
I couldn't imagine that I would ever have a serious
discussion in this country about whether a child can
suck her thumb or not!

No area of life went untouched by the rules you
created and the ludicrous adaptations they required.
I understand this, though. Without them, you wouldn't
exist. You would die, Monster Methuselah, if we acted
according to our own will using our own brains.

Do not kill. To my mind, this is a sensible rule.
(Of course it doesn't apply to you. You are blood-
thirsty and sent Noam, Yoel, Gidon, Yosken and Ben-Zion
to the front to die.) Do not own anything—OK, so we
share everything equally. But this is not enough for
you, Methuselah. You also want us to divide our emotions
equally. You forbid me from loving my children, because
you think I love them "too much". According to you, I
love them wrong even though I'm their mother, so of
course I know how much they need me!

Methuselah, you are a sadist, a psychopath, a narcissist, a criminal, and a murderer. You smoked me out using the greatest possible emotional violence, because I didn't obey you. You harnessed all your members to attack me: my husband, Dovid, who had helped me recover from my difficult disease. The nanny, Zmira, whose energetic personality I thought I liked at first. My friends Ditsa, Moshe, Chaim, Gal, Dani, et cetera, et cetera. I can't comprehend how all of them, even Ditsa, turned their backs on me.

Yesterday they were all smiles. I saw them dancing like marionette dolls: they look happy even though they're full of anger and despair.

I'm leaving now, and I won't be back. You won, so keep my husband and make my children your own. But I will never forget. You destroyed me, Methuselah, but I will use the rest of my life to take revenge, to destroy everything that reminds me in the slightest of you. Goodbye.

> *Sincerely,*
> *Shlomith-Shkhina*

And what have I done since my years at the kibbutz? I've rummaged through the soul of Judaism, identifying the side effects of Semitic culture and making them into art. I have subjected my body and personality to masochistic interventions, convincing myself that they have made me powerful.

Now I've drained myself to the point of death in order to reach the heart of it all, a space from which only one way out exists: surrender, healing, and enlightenment. I've thought of this moment countless times. I imagined that right now, in the final seconds of my lecture, I would experience the ultimate

catharsis of my life. An enlightenment I could communicate to you, my dear listeners, and which I could
carry with me for the rest of my life the way some
carry a rosary.

But I don't feel anything.

II

I have touched the world's wound,

the lust for life, and the fear of death.

Christoph Schlingensief,

Heaven Could Not Be As Beautiful As Here: A Cancer Diary

YELLOW: THE LIGHT-RAY HOOK
OF COMPASSION

Maimuna, Yalla nako Yalla jox yirmandeem!

Very slowly, without moving, Shlomith appears next to the women, next to the jeep spinning its wheels in the sand, her toes slightly in the air, her calf near the exhaust pipe, and thus the row is complete again. The row that Polina broke once before—which Polina refused to join because she was afraid, because she didn't have the courage after all to give up the familiar, safe whiteness—when she opened her eyes and started to talk.

The row is as beautiful as the most beautiful funeral procession, as sad as the saddest tune, as comforting as the embrace of Mother Earth. The row is complete. The women are not afraid.

There, somewhere, a moment ago—an eternity, a second ago—they looked at each other once again. Maimuna at Wlibgis, Wlibgis at Polina, Polina at Shlomith, Shlomith at Nina, Nina at Ulrike: each at each. They looked but in a different way than before. No suggestions, no questions, no raised eyebrows. No nervous glances or shirking of responsibility. They checked, like soldiers preparing for a charge check that everyone is completely present, completely awake, that everyone is aware of the command about to come down, the command that they must all execute at exactly the same moment. With their gazes they made clear to everyone, and to themselves, that no one would slip away from the group, that no one would sink into her own thoughts and fall behind. It was time to say goodbye to the white.

Whence this sudden certainty and unanimity? We don't know.
There are many things that are not within our control. Again we are
forced to surrender. And it always feels just as crushing. As if we are
never going to learn anything from the thousands and thousands of
departures, from being left alone, and from new arrivals. As if the
people who appear here individually or in clusters, scrunched up or
with limbs outstretched, startled or fast asleep, who disappear after
their time is through, aren't a natural part of this cursed process.

The women took each other by a hand and formed a circle. If there
was any fear, there was more curiosity. If there were doubts, there was
more will. The moment had come, and they knew it. The universe
with its layers of time, its dimensions, its hidden pockets, its concealed
folds, and its obscure wrinkles seemed to gather around them, hold
its breath, and wait.

Then, somewhere something began a deep kettledrum beat like
a giant heart. And so it came to pass that suddenly, after forming
their circle, the women felt themselves begin to throb as well. They
felt the rhythm within them; the pulse pounded in their hands and
fingers, which were clutched, unfeeling, in other hands and fingers.

Then they had a rhythm, a subfrequency pulse, and it urged them
to depart. So they closed their eyes and said, each in her own way, out
loud or just moving her lips: *Oooon . . . ei-ron.*

And nothing prevented them from saying it through to the end
any more: *Oooon . . . ei-ron.*

And no one curled up halfway through the word. And no one
turned tail. And no one decided she wanted something else. *Oooon . . .
ei-ron.*

Hands disengaged from hands at the final syllable: *ron.*

Fingers straightened, springing open: *ron.*

And there was no going back.

Each of them left in her own way, as Rosa Imaculada had left in
her own way: like a maple leaf fallen from a tree and tossed by the
wind, eyes closed, zigzagging sideward. Maimuna, who seemed to be
in a hurry, appeared to plunge head first. Very quickly she began to
fade, to sink, to recede from the others, who were still moving; only

the soles of her feet were visible for a moment, turning ever whiter.

Polina stiffly jerked into motion, shaking in place. Wlibgis curled up like a silverfish and trembled before disappearing by degrees. Ulrike slid, legs straight, turning around her axis a couple of times. Nina evaporated like a sweater unraveling. Progressively she thinned as her outline dwindled on one side like a stitch had slipped, followed by another and yet another, stitch after stitch; then she was gone.

Finally the motion took Shlomith. Was she keeping the brakes on somehow after all? Did she doubt? For a moment, for a millionth of a second we hoped that she would open her eyes or her mouth, that she would snap awake and remain with us. In vain.

Shlomith sank until prone, fully extended on the white, and then she mechanically lifted her upper body and froze in a position the yogis would call the cobra. Unlike the other women, Shlomith began to fall apart. Piece by piece. The left leg from the knee down began to disappear, then the right arm up to the elbow. One thigh, the other thigh, both shoulders. The torso and finally the head, with the hair last of all.

If someone had come on the scene afterwards, in the center of the great emptiness she would have seen a rectangle outlined by shoes and clothing, within it a large, sable fur coat and a red wig surrounded by a collection of small objects. She might begin collecting the articles of clothing, perhaps wondering which pieces belonged to which outfits. Wondering what story they had once contained, until it disappeared, and whether she could trace it now.

The women are gone, away from the whiteness. Now they're in yellow, again at full strength, seven in all. Maimuna is at the center of the row, an arcing trio to either side: soldiers Wlibgis, Nina, and Rosa Imaculada to the left, soldiers Polina, Ulrike, and Shlomith to the right. And Maimuna on the ground—Maimuna is also on the ground. Before the seven, her mouth in the sand, her yellow skirt crumpled under her buttocks, coffee-bean-colored gazelle legs pressed into the burning sand, a rifle barrel against the back of her head.

Maimuna in the air. Maimuna on the sand.

From somewhere come ideas, but not words, like whispers but

silent. Awarenesses containing questions containing other inter-
twined awarenesses and new questions, all of which rotate around
one of them.

Mai . . .

      . . . muna . . .

Maimuna?

                            Are you . . .

               afraid,

    Maimuna?

    Are you . . .

                  afraid?

. . . they

done . . .

      . . . have they . . .

                  Bad?

        Maimuna!

At first it's only chaos, worse than chaos. The chaos could be suppresed
if someone could shout SHUT UP, at which point they would all shake
their heads, startled by the shout, keep their minds in check, and be
quiet. But shouting isn't possible. Speaking quietly isn't even possible.
And their heads are so full of thoughts. Strange thoughts. Wonder,
expectant emptiness. Preparedness to act, will. And then it comes to
pass that suddenly a strange hope smashes in amongst the wonder.
*Maimuna, I'd like to go down to the ground and straighten your dress.
Your behind is showing.* And then it comes to pass that the onlookers
take fright and an alarmed *WHAT!* encroaches everywhere.

The picture has stopped. The whining of the jeep engine still echoes
for a moment, the patter of the sand on the hood, and then quiet.

The women glance at each other in confusion. An alarmed *WHAT!*
swirls within them, hounding them, blurring their thoughts. It breaks
the firm impression that has overcome them all: they all want to go

down to the ground to straighten Maimuna's dress.

Everything is a mess, an unbearable cacophony for all of them but one.

The Maimuna in the air looks at the Maimuna on the ground. There she is, the stupid girl who set out to transport dangerous cargo over the border at her uncle's urging. She's the one who's most dangerous to herself. If she'd kept calm. If she'd known to keep her big mouth shut. But instead she schemed: she claimed she was pregnant, trying to save herself with a hastily constructed lie. But Iman would have done the same. Iman and maybe Liya Kebede too, and maybe Alek Wek—none of them would have given up without a fight. She took up Mikael, the long-legged man with the camera and the beautiful pictures, as her weapon.

Mikael, Marcel, and Maimuna were forced out of the Amanar Restaurant. They walked, stumbling before the rifle barrel, hands crossed behind their necks. They were shoved in the back of a car, Maimuna on top, her face against the front of Mikael's trousers, her stomach and the packages strapped to her stomach on Marcel's knees. There, as the car tossed about and the exhaust pipe popped, she thought her idea through. She would be carrying Mikael's child. Then the wheel of the jeep sank in the sand.

Shlomith suddenly lifts a finger. She has a question. Listen up! The women, all except the Maimuna in the air, concentrate on Shlomith. *Listen up!* Shlomith has a question that all of them, especially Maimuna, need to hear. *Why didn't they just take the belt away from you, Maimuna?*

In that moment it becomes clear: Shlomith is speaking to them. They accept Shlomith's question, which thus becomes their own calming, bright thought: *Why wasn't the belt enough for them, Maimuna?* They ask this in their own heads because they're listening to Shlomith: *Why, Maimuna?* In echo they ask why, until Nina, pragmatic and efficient Nina, makes the bold move that someone has to make if they want to move forward from the situation:

You aren't going to start bartering with them, *are you?*

But the Maimuna in the air doesn't hear. The Maimuna in the air wants to go down next to the Maimuna lying on the ground. She too wants to take the hem of the dress and pull it back down over her thighs. To say on her own behalf: Take me, take me and sell me, but let me live.

They're on their knees . . .
Those men.
On the . . .
. . . sand . . .
Next to you.
Are they . . .

The women begin to feel the thoughts flow; they begin to separate their own from the others'. One focuses, and the others give her space. Thus the idea becomes heavier, so weighty that it suffuses everything and spreads everywhere. The others accept the new idea as best they can. They begin to sense that they can exchange thoughts. They begin to understand, through trial and error, that the brightest idea is the same as the heaviest idea, that the brightest idea comes through most easily, that it can be built upon. They begin to realize that if they want their voices to be heard, they have to struggle, they have to leave behind the safe, soporific murmuring. They have to participate. To think. Each one of them has to think.

How can we help you, Maimuna?
What should we do?

The picture is still stopped, because the Maimuna in the air wants it so. The Maimuna in the air would like to slap the Maimuna on the sand across the cheek, to see the trajectory of the punishing hand, to experience chastising her: You stupid girl! She would like to kneel and press her lips against the cheek of the Maimuna lying on the ground: You dear, hopeless girl, dear God. Because it is she, she herself, Maimuna Mimi Mbegue, prone on the sand, soles of her feet facing the sun.

The Maimuna in the air takes a step forward. The women move and close the chain behind her. Polina and Wlibgis reach for each other, and the others move closer too, compressing the half circle.

The gunman stands behind Maimuna, finger on the trigger. Could their combined strength crush him? The other men stand a little farther off, their hands raised. Could they disarm them all? Could they turn the course of events? One head is about to turn: one man is about to check if there are any dust trails. Is anyone coming after them yet? Soldiers? And where is the new car?

The Maimuna in the air makes an attempt to push Marcel, who like Mikael has fallen to his knees in shock behind the Maimuna on the sand, closer to the floating women. Of course nothing happens. The worlds do not meet, except for that millionth of a second during which Maimuna took her last step to prepare her very own journey. She can't help anyone else. Or change the direction of time.

But Maimuna prolongs her transition. She needs the women's help to die.

Maimuna?

Do you feel it too?

Is it coming from the ground?

Something is shaking under us.

Is it your heart pounding with fear?

The noise of the cochlea, a kettle-drum-like pulse, a beating felt in fingers, toes, scalp, and spine . . . Mikael and Marcel huddle on the sand, resigned, weaponless. They have never carried a pistol on their trips. They believed they could get by with words. Now they believe they will be executed. They tried to make a deal before Maimuna opened her mouth—futile. They barely managed to throw all the céfas in their pockets on the ground before Maimuna told her lie to save her skin—meaningless. The crumpled bills didn't interest the criminals. Marcel and Mikael are the best currency here.

And Maimuna.

Smuggled out of Africa.

A virgin—that important piece of information came from Monsieur Moussa himself.

And what now?

"I'm pregnant!"

Maimuna told her lie as soon as the men ordered them out of the stuck jeep. The first furious shot was fired in the air. After that the butt of an assault rifle struck her to the ground. One set of hands thrust up her dress and ripped the buckskin belts from her waist, one by one. Then angry hands quickly turned the weapon and the muzzle of the rifle was pressed deep into her hair, hard against her skull.

If Maimuna thought she would arouse pity by claiming she was carrying Mikael's child in her womb, she was wrong. If she thought she would become worthless in the men's eyes because of a pregnancy, she was right. But she was once again wrong if she thought worthlessness would mean freedom for her, that she would be turned loose to walk in the desert, that she would be allowed to follow the jeep tracks back to Timbuktu. She is not Bonaventure, who was allowed to escape through the Amanar kitchen. She is not Samballa, who was able to walk out the front door and disappear. She was Maimuna Mimi Mbegue, the great disappointment, the stubborn adventurer, who had ruined her future by spreading her legs for a European at the wrong moment, without permission, simply out of a desire for pleasure.

Now the Maimuna in the air is ready. She nods to the women and closes her eyes. She spreads her arms, spreads them back, straining her fingers wide. She expands her chest, bending her back like a swan flapping open her wings. Head raised, she sails in pulses to rest before the Maimuna lying on the ground.

She can't make this journey any more modestly.

Wlibgis, Polina, Nina, Ulrike, Rosa, and Shlomith move to accompany her. They gather behind Maimuna, raising their hands protectively to her head. The yellow light condenses, beginning layer by layer to cover the violent picture beneath. The pulse is more powerful than ever. It roars in their ears like the ocean. It rattles their hands. It pumps auratic power from their fingertips into Maimuna's head.

Now, Maimuna?
What's happening?
Be brave!
Maimuna, Maimuna . . .

We love you!

But now one set of hands cringes and falls limp. One of the women breaks away, stumbling a little in front of the others. Nina sees something too familiar through the thickening yellow cloud, something wrong that does not belong in this picture. On the ground, next to Maimuna lying on her stomach, crouches Marcel, no one else but Marcel: Marcel Pignard. Jean-Philippe's younger brother, who was planning another trip to Africa the last time they saw him. The posture is unfamiliar—the Marcel Nina knows never collapses. The Marcel Nina knows looks you straight in the eye, holds his head up proud, and stands tall. The Marcel Nina knows is never threatened or forced. Just like his brother, the man who saw it as his right to stay in a hotel with a strange woman on the night when Nina, Little Antoine, and Little Antoinette were in danger.

But Maimuna is already on her way. In the dense, bright yellow light of compassion, under the protective shadow of Wlibgis's, Polina's, Ulrike's, Rosa's, and Shlomith's hands, she stands up straight and then throws herself down. She plunges toward herself, toward the Maimuna on the ground.

Goodbye, Maimuna!

Goodbye!

Farewell!

One second.

A shot.

The image disappears.

Maimuna, Yalla nako Yalla jox yirmandeem!

Kidnapped Finn released in Mali

▶ Islamist group Ansar Dine believed responsible for abduction

••••••••••••••••••••••••••••••

SAMI SILLANPÄÄ
HELSINGIN SANOMAT

▶ A Finnish architect's two-and-a-half-month ordeal ended yesterday in Northern Mali. **Mikael Holmlund**, 42, and his French colleague, **Marcel Pignard**, 38, were freed at eight o'clock Finnish time near the border with Mauritania. Malian army special forces troops met the hostages.

In a statement released last night, Finland's ambassador to Nigeria, **Riitta Korpivaara**, said both men are doing well given the circumstances and are currently recovering in a French hospital.

Holmlund and Pignard departed for West Africa on October 18. The aim of their trip was to document the traditional buildings of the area for a joint exhibition in Finland and France. There were tentative plans for the Finnish exhibition to be held at the Helinä Rautavaara Museum.

The friends began their journey in Benin, traveling through Burkina Faso to Mali. From there they intended to fly on to Casablanca, Morocco.

However, their itinerary was cut short on October 28 in Timbuktu near the Sahara Desert when gunmen barged into the Amanar restaurant in which Holmlund and Pignard were eating, and forced them into a vehicle waiting outside. A local young woman who was in the architects' company was also taken.

The abductors' vehicle, a two-door Jeep Wrangler, was found in the desert three kilometers from the restaurant. The kidnapped woman's body was found beside the car.

"Presumably, the woman was acting as a decoy, either knowingly or unknowingly," said Foreign Ministry press secretary **Marko Turunen**, who spoke to Holmlund by phone. "Apparently the girl was from Senegal. According to

Holmlund, she was working as a courier. We don't know what happened, but something went seriously wrong."

An interpreter and driver were also with the men at the time of the abduction. Neither of them was injured, although eyewitnesses at the restaurant say several shots were fired.

According to one Malian security official, interviewed by HS Mali correspondent **Yamoussa Diabaté**, the men were held prisoner by the Tuareg Islamist group Ansar Dine. Speaking on condition of anonymity, the official confirmed that the government of Mali bought the men's freedom.

Over recent years 90 million dollars (70 million euros) in ransom money has been paid to West African terrorists. In addition to kidnapping, significant sources of terrorist revenue include drug running and human trafficking. "However you look at it, the fact is that jihad is mostly paid for with western money," the security official said.

The Malian newspaper L'Essor reported that Tuareg separatists armed by **Muammar Gaddafi** have been working in concert with the Movement for Oneness and Jihad in West Africa (MOJWA). This group has significantly increased the risk of kidnapping for foreigners in the Mali area.

Both France and Finland flatly deny participating in ransom payments. "Finland does not pay ransoms. We are party to international agreements that prohibit the funding of terrorism," said Foreign Minister **Erkki Tuomioja**. The French foreign minister, **Laurent Fabius**, also claims that his government did not make any kind of deal with the kidnappers.

The chain of events leading to the men's release remains shrouded in mystery. "The Mali government and army played a key role in freeing the prisoners, and we expect to receive a briefing on the operational details soon," Tuomioja said. Responsibility for the investigation of Holmlund's abduction now shifts from the Foreign Ministry to the National Bureau of Investigation.

"Being held hostage is very stressful psychologically, especially if the abductee witnesses a murder," says crisis psychologist **Merja Matinmäki**. "But through the help of therapy and rehabilitation, most people can recover from the trauma. Often, returning home to family and friends is the only thing that can bring enough of a feeling of security to make it possible to react and work through the feelings caused by imprisonment."

Adapting to normal life can still be difficult, though, Matinmäki explains. "A victim returning to Finnish society may feel like an outsider."

....

TURQUOISE: WHEN NOTHING IS WHAT IT ONCE LOOKED LIKE

Au revoir, Nina!

The metro train is covered in a transparent turquoise advertising wrap. H&M and Versace, the fall collection. The turquoise wrap has a rosette of leopard spots and features leather and studs, silk and bright prints, high heels, and large jewelry. Ten seconds remain until Nina will hit her head on the side of the train hurtling out of the tunnel.

Nina walks down the escalator as fast as she can with her large belly. Aboveground it's the morning rush; the tunnel has its own inexorable time, but even so, progress is too slow. The moving staircase travels at half a meter per second, one meter in two, one and a half in three, and Nina has to make the next train, which clatters along the red line toward Saint-Joseph Hospital.

Nina pulls her mobile phone out of her jacket pocket to call her family doctor: Stéphanie has to help. Stéphanie has to assure her she'll arrive at the hospital in time. Stéphanie has to say that it all might be . . .

The phone slips out of Nina's hand, and she kicks it toward the metro platform with the tip of her shoe; it launches down, bouncing twice on the escalator. Nina steps onto the platform but instead of bending to pick up the phone off the ground, she continues running. The metro rumbles in the tunnel. Nina runs as if she means to jump straight into the metro, to pass through the wall into the car. Someone yells, "*Faites attention!*" but Nina doesn't stop. One second, two, three. She jumps, trips, tumbles, hits her head against the turquoise metro car coming out of the tunnel, and is tossed aside from the force of the blow.

Shouts erupt on the platform. Dozens of hands reach for mobile phones and call the emergency number at once. Only one picture is taken. The man closest to Nina kneels, helplessly checks her pulse, and then even more helplessly puts his red scarf under Nina's head. Madame, can you hear me? Madame does not. Madam, CAN YOU HEAR ME? No, madam still cannot hear. Madam has fallen into a deep state of unconsciousness. Her heart is beating, her pulse is palpable, and she's breathing. And the babies in her womb?

It's clear that Nina is in need of haste. If not for herself then for the twins.

Aboveground there's a traffic jam. The ambulance weaves past the queues of automobiles, through red lights, but the journey is slow. By the time Nina is finally in the ambulance, the situation has changed. Nina's breathing has slowed. The paramedic applies a neck brace and laryngeal mask; ventilation begins. Once Nina's breathing is taken care of, the other paramedic opens her eyelids and shines a light in. No reaction in her pupils.

Is this how it happened?

What about the children?

The metro didn't hit them!

Nina, you're in the hands of professionals. Surely they can do something!

And can we help you somehow?

What would you like us to do?

The ambulance sets off for the hospital with sirens blaring. Shlomith, Polina, Wlibgis, Ulrike, and Rosa Imaculada are grouped around Nina. It's crowded. Rosa and Polina are standing in the same place as the two paramedics, who are attempting to revive Nina as she lies on the stretcher. The left half of Rosa's body is inside the right half of one of the paramedics, and Polina's bare belly is submerged in the back of the paramedic leaning over Nina.

We aren't bothering them, are we?
They don't seem to notice anything.
We don't exist for them.
Well, is now when it happens?

It happens now. It happens in a different way than these things sometimes happen. Later the doctor spells out the situation to Nina's tearful relatives. Why saving her wasn't possible even though she wasn't killed instantly. If the blow had severed the connections between the cranium and the cervical spine, tearing the spinal cord, nothing could have been done even in theory. Or if the blow had damaged the brain stem, stopping her lungs and heart, there would be no room for speculation now. The doctor is patient. Even though Jean-Philippe makes insinuations about malpractice, the doctor remains calm, showing pictures and explaining. Nina's life ends due to serious problems in her brain stem, but, as so often in life, as a result of a series of unfortunate coincidences. The contact with the metro train and Nina's impact on the platform together create an intracranial subarachnoid hemorrhage. Blood begins to drip onto the surface of her brain, then into the fourth cerebral ventricle through the cerebral aqueduct—there really is an area of the brain called an aqueduct—through tiny holes located in the cavity wall. From the fourth ventricle the blood finds its way into the other three cerebral ventricles, as a result of which the circulation of the cerebro-spinal fluid, the *liquor cerebrospinalis* produced by the ventricles, is impeded. Because of the excess blood, the cerebrospinal fluid becomes trapped in the ventricles, the cerebral aqueduct is plugged, and intracranial pressure begins to build. Nina's brain tissue starts to swell. Gradually it bulges toward the incisure of the cerebellar tento-rium—yes, the brain also has a tent, although it's a Latin tent. Part of the tissue protrudes through the hole, which in turn damages the brain stem.

At no point does Nina feel any pain—that is one hundred percent certain.

In order for the family fully to understand the impossibility of the situation, the doctor also tells them the following fact: if a neurosurgeon with a full operating theater and staff happened to be on the metro platform, he would have sawed off half of Nina's skull and put it in a freezer to wait. That would have balanced the intracranial pressure, the brain tissue wouldn't have swelled, the brain stem wouldn't have been compressed, and Nina's chances of survival would have been more than the ten percent they were.

But even then nothing would have been certain.

As is always the case in life.

Watching resuscitation makes me sick . . .

When will they realize?

They're still trying.

What else can they do?

Nina stands behind the Nina lying on the stretcher. She places her white hands on her white hair and makes gentle stroking motions. She tries to think of her babies, first dead, then alive, but can only catch hold of a nightmarish image. Two shriveled creatures inside a matchbox on a bed of cotton wool: Mademoiselle Red and Monsieur Transparent. One with black caviar pinhead eyes, the other with rich, swirling hair.

Nina pushes the matchbox closed in her mind, leaving the unfinished beings there for others to worry about, and shifts her thoughts to Maimuna. To beautiful, lithe Maimuna, who a moment ago dove into her own death. Nina didn't see that moment though. She was staring at her husband's brother, who was there, on his hands and knees in the Saharan sand. A blink of an eye—and Maimuna was gone. A gun fired. And now her turn is next, in an ambulance with her dying doppelganger, with herself, accompanied by her five afterwordly sisters who are chattering nonsense on the verge of her death.

Nina, did you see? That paramedic started to stroke your stomach!

Suddenly the ambulance siren stops blaring. The medics stop rushing. One of them, a young woman with freckles on her nose, holds the laryngeal mask on the Nina lying on the stretcher and looks inconsolable. With her other hand she begins to stroke Nina's belly.

Well now. So the moment has come.

That's how it looks.

And what am I supposed to do?
What do you mean?
What do I have to do?
You do like Maimuna, right?
What did Maimuna do?

Sometimes things go awry. Completely. Sometimes life's most pivotal instant, the *pregnant moment*, as Shlomith would express it, goes all to hell. Suddenly none of the women understand how to proceed. With Maimuna, events had moved forward so purposefully and fearlessly that they had all been deceived into imagining: this is how it goes. Each would have her own turn, and how easy it would be! You just spread your arms and fall into yourself, and the end comes, as light as a feather, almost without noticing. Their task seemed ridiculously simple. They were there as Maimuna's mental support. No one sacrificed even half a thought for the possibility that her turn would come too. This was about Maimuna. So they had to concentrate on Maimuna. And besides . . . how could anyone know if her turn would ever come?

There they had been, spread out around Maimuna, truly supposing they were helping her. Then someone decided to place her hands protectively on Maimuna's head! Everyone thought that was a good idea. The confusion evaporated, turning to a bustling energy, and they raised their hands and felt necessary again.

Now everything is different. Nina is in a panic. Nina, who is known for her practicality, felicitous situational assessments, and rich imagination, stands behind the head of her worldly duplicate lying on a stretcher and stares at them in horror.

No one remembers the significance of rhythm.

No one feels the pulse.

Suddenly everything is eerily quiet. The ambulance crew seem to have frozen in place.

Nina . . . ?
Oh little Ninjuška . . .
What if you try to fall into it?
Into what?

Into it. Yourself.
How?
The same way as Maimuna . . .
Maimuna spread her arms and sort of . . .
Flung herself?
Yes, she flung herself.
Am I supposed to push with my legs and jump?
Try.
Or do I just fall?
Do whatever feels best to you.

Nina looks miserable. She buries her fingers in her hair that hangs over the edge of the stretcher. She looks at herself, almost a corpse, and gathers courage as if to climb into a frigid lake or to jump out of an airplane with a parachute. Then she makes a feeble push.

It is a pitiful display.

Hundreds of thoughts swarm in a thick cloud of terror in the air.

No . . .

Help,

how do I

   . . . like this . . .
  Why don't they!
. . . can help . . .

No!

A common enemy always helps. When Ulrike thinks to turn their attention to the ambulance crew, the women's thoughts automatically begin to coalesce around them. The shock takes on a shape, a direction, the accusations receiving a channel it is easy to pour the resentment into. For a moment.

Those people are just waiting for the ambulance to arrive at the hospital . . .
Where some doctor will declare Nina dead . . .
Even though right now their help is what's needed . . .
Stop it! They don't know what to do any more than we do . . .

No one knows what to do.
At least I don't.
Nina, little Ninjuška . . .
What if we take you by the hands and pull . . .
Or lift your legs?
Or maybe you could all shove me in the back!
Don't get angry now.
This isn't our fault!
Nina, if I were you, I'd close my eyes and let go.
Let go . . . ?
Don't think too much. Just let go.
So you know what I should do. Is that it? Well, would you like to come over here and take my place?
Stop it, Nina.
Come on and jump for me! Since you know so much!
Wlibgis and Nina, stop it both of you.
At this rate, Nina's going to miss her moment . . .
Nina, little Ninjuška, what if we sing to you?
Polina, don't promise too much. Do you have a song in mind you think is appropriate for this situation?
That we all know how to sing?
Does everyone need to sing?
I don't want to sing at least.

Then Rosa Imaculada squeezes her eyes tight shut. She reaches back into her memory for a tune and the low, slightly wheezing voice that is her own. The song rasps and skips, coming to Rosa's mind as if drawn by a steel needle from a 1940s shellac record. This is the lullaby that her grandmother sang to her when she was small, father-less and motherless; this is the lullaby that she sang to her own small son as she lay in her bed recovering with her new heart.

And thus Rosa's voice begins to ring out. It resonates in the ambu-lance but really somewhere else. It resonates as they move, but not in the vehicle approaching the hospital. It resonates in a rhythm that makes Nina, Wlibgis, Shlomith, Ulrike, Polina, and Rosa Imaculada begin to sway. The pulse joins the delicate melody and injects its own syncopations, but it doesn't destroy the song, doesn't spoil the sound that had once long ago comforted little Rosa, then little Davi, and now would comfort Nina, little Ninjuška. Nina who must gather all her courage and find the strength to leave.

> *Nigue, nigue, ninhas*
> *tão bonitinhas*
> *Macamba viola di pari e ganguinhas*
> *Ê ê ê ê, imbê, tumbelá!*
> *Musangolá quina quinê . . .*

Nina squeezes her eyes shut tight and finally pulls her hands out of her hair. The familiar rhythm, a pulse like the beating of a heart multiplies a thousand times, begins to make them sway faster. They surrender, and no one says anything about raising arms. The terror has disappeared from Nina's face. She knows, just as naturally as Maimuna had known, what she has to do.

She bends down and, eyes still shut, kisses her own lips.
Farewell, Nina!
We'll be coming too.
I feel like I'll be next . . .
Was that why you sang?
I feel that way.
You have a very unique voice, Rosa.
Thank you.
It fit this situation perfectly.
Thank you. But I don't believe we disappear completely.
I hope you're right!
So not farewell but until we meet again, Nina!

Au revoir, Nina!

Brain-dead mother gives birth to twins

Nina Pignard of Marseilles, who was pronounced brain dead a month ago, gave birth to twins two days ago. Thirty-five-year-old Pignard was kept on life support for more than a month in order to give the fetuses sufficient time to develop for life outside the womb.

On the day of her accident, October 27, Pignard was on her way to Saint-Joseph Hospital. She was changing from the tram to the metro at Gare de Noailles when she appeared to trip and hit her head on the side of the oncoming train.

According to eyewitnesses, she had been running even though the metro hadn't arrived at the platform yet. "People noticed because of her condition," said Marseilles traffic police commissar, **Christophe Benoit**. "Metro trains arrive at platforms going 40 kilometers an hour. If you stick your head in front of one, something bad is going to happen."

The babies, a girl and a boy, were born at twenty-five weeks by Caesarian section, each weighing less than 900 grams. They are currently receiving treatment in the neonatal intensive care unit at Saint-Joseph Hospital. According to **Charlotte Vermette**, a neonatologist specializing in premature births, their chances of survival without injury are good.

The Pignard family have recently been subjected to another tragedy when the brain-dead woman's brother-in-law was abducted in Mali. "The kidnapping happened the day after Nina died," said Pignard's mother-in-law, **Michelle Pignard**. The family has been receiving professional help to weather these crises.

The fate of the abducted brother remains unclear, but the French Foreign Ministry is working overtime to resolve the situation. The father of the abducted man, **Julien Pignard**, CEO of the Sodexo Group, numbers among the richest men in France with total assets exceeding 5.3 billion euros.

However, according to information received by *Le Monde*, the abduction seems to have no connection to the Pignard family fortune. "My son was in the wrong place at the wrong time, just like Nina," says Michelle Pignard.

At the moment, the family is focused on the welfare of the babies.

"We used to rub Nina's belly and talk to the babies. That caused very conflicting feelings. We were always keenly aware that the babies' birth would mean the end of her life," said Nina's husband, **Jean-Philippe Pignard**. "But life has to go on. We're making funeral arrangements, getting the house ready for the babies, and waiting for my brother to be freed. What else can we do?"

■ **Natalie Bacqué**

ELECTRIC BLUE: IF YOU
COULD DIE OF ANGER

Vaarwel, Wlibgis!

This isn't where I thought we'd be next.
  No!
  So this is where our campfire came from . . .
  'Our'!?
  Your hair, Wlibgis.
  Wlibgis lies in a hospital bed with the wig on her head. The artificial hair is askew, the parting off center, the bangs straggly. Wlibgis's mouth hangs slightly open, jerky breaths, small wheezes, involuntary coughs, and odd squeaks coming from it. Wlibgis doesn't appear anguished, but she is gray, pallid, and waxy. This makes the fibers spread out on the pillow appear all the more fiery red.
  Why are you wearing a wig?
  In that state!
  I wanted to. I felt like a potato without hair.
  The nurses had tried to take the wig off Wlibgis's head as she fell asleep. They wanted to brush it and put it in the closet with all of her other belongings. Whether it was in the way of a cannula or bathing the patient, the hair was always unruly. But every time they touched her wig, Wlibgis snapped out of her morphine haze. She would cast an icy gaze at the nurses, and they would let go instantly, take a step back, and leave her hair alone, because that terrible gaze was not of this world. It came from the *other side*, where this miserable woman

had apparently decided to take her wig. Let her take it. They didn't want to touch the thing any more and tried to pretend it didn't exist, but it was impossible because it blazed in their peripheral vision no matter what they were doing. If they tried to look Wlibgis in the face, there was only orange hair, hair hair hair, a demonic gleaming frame around all that pallor and gray.

My wig is from the best wigmaker in Zwolle, where all the local professional actors go.

. . .the Borough Park Hasids have much nicer ones . . .

What?
Pardon me, Wlibgis. Your hair is excellent, but it's just a fact that the Hasidim have the best wigs in the world.
Who?
The Hasidim. Orthodox Jews. Their women have to hide their hair after they come of age. But they're clever, so they hide their hair under magnificent wigs.
But is that . . . a little hypocritical?
It depends how you look at it. I think it's just creative problem-solving. Have you heard of eruvin? An eruv is a ritual, symbolic enclosure that Orthodox Jews like the Hasidim use to surround the areas in which they live. They have them in New York, they have them in Jerusalem. It means that on Shabbat, Jews can move around in the area surrounded by the eruv wire and transport the things they need from place to place.
Where does the wire run?
On the ground?
No, it's in the air. An eruv system vaguely resembles electrical poles. An outsider wouldn't necessary notice the wires if she didn't know to look.
Is it problem-solving if the problem is self-imposed?
It isn't self-imposed. The Shabbat commandments are dictated in the Law. But interpretation is allowed.
You Jews are masters of that!
Evasion, circumvention, a little good-natured diversion . . . all within the framework of the Law.

And so inside the area outlined by that wire, you can do anything?

Of course not. For example, you can't open an umbrella. That resembles pitching a tent too strongly. So it's sort of like building.

But if it rains when you go outside you can still hold a newspaper over your head, right?

Yes.

Ridiculous!
You're all insane!!

There are other limitations too. For example, you can't play sports that require making holes or gouging ruts in the ground. So golf is forbidden.

And sledding on a sledding hill!

And on Shabbat you can only do a sport for the pleasure of moving, not to improve your health.

But with a sled you aren't . . .

Tell me, Shlomith, who checks whether an athlete has the right motives?

The Law is the Law, and it resides within those who believe in the Law, the same way your heart resides within you.

Did you live inside of that kind of fence?

No, not that kind. My family wasn't very religious.

Do you think that sort of thing is sensible?

Or those wigs. Why isn't their own hair good enough? It's a sin to pretend with things like that! Think about how it makes those of us feel who lose our hair because of disease!

There it is again: the wig. Wlibgis's blazing, magic hair, which for a while has helped her be something other than sick and bald, something other than the old Wlibgis, a punching bag. So how does she feel about the idea that healthy women cover their own beautiful hair with wigs because of some silly tradition? It can't be worse than how someone who lost a leg would feel about cosmetic amputation or a cleft lip patient about tongue splitting, but it still feels unjust and wrong, just like cancer in general.

Ladies. We're in Wlibgis's time now.

Suddenly from Polina's direction an unusually heavy idea forms, which ends all the other agitation. The emptiness does not stay empty long since an observation, in the form of a sharp, indignant exclamation whose origin no one can quite be sure, soon sprouts from the silence. No one has time to perceive the direction from which it had come. It just erupts from somewhere, spreading and immediately feeling like their very own:

Haven't you noticed that Wlibgis is able to communicate with us?

And truly: Wlibgis, ravaged by cancer and robbed of the power of speech, has been participating in the exchange of ideas for some time now, just like everyone else! For example, in the desert Wlibgis clearly, without faltering, expressed the following questions: *Are you afraid? Is it coming from the ground? Now, Maimuna?* In the ambulance, Wlibgis started arguing with Nina: *If I were you, I'd close my eyes and let go.* If I were you . . . If Wlibgis were Nina, she never would have run at that metro train. If Wlibgis had been Nina, she would have guarded her life to the last, because look at what Nina had been: young, healthy, two babies on the way, money to burn, and a man in the house. But Wlibgis is Wlibgis, and now for the first time she is an equal participant in the conversation. The women can ask her anything, and she can answer. She can talk, and they can listen.

. . . Wlibgis seems like a stick-in-the-mud . . .

Ulrike!!
I'm sorry!!
My goodness, Ulrike!
I didn't mean to offend! The cancer and the hospital . . .
Yes, yes. What does the life of one boring, cancerous monstrosity matter.
Wlibgis, I didn't mean it! Forgive me.

This thing, that Wlibgis was finally "talking" to them, and they hadn't realized it, was worth at least one horrified wave of guilt. And Ulrike wasn't the only one to blame. No one had been interested in Wlibgis.

Wlibgis, this feels so natural to all of us, you participating. Am I right?

Yes!

Much more natural than being jerked around like this!

First the Sahara Desert, then an ambulance . . .

Careening along the streets of Marseilles with blaring sirens . . .

Just think if you had to tell someone else about all of this!

Why would that be so hard? Here, I'll try: "We travel back and forth across the world visiting each other's places of death and then moving on . . ."

And one of us is always left behind . . .

True! One got a bullet in the brain, and then there were six!

A subway train stung one, and then there were five.

What are you saying? Really, that's too much.

A second choked his little self . . .

A big bear hugged a third . . .

A fourth got frizzled up . . .

What the hell are you taking about, Shlomith? Polina?

Then there's that strange one . . .

Yes, how did it go . . . ?

A yellow herring swallowed one . . .

Red!

No, yellow.

Red.

Yellow.

Red.

Yellow! In Russian that part of the rhyme is translated "желтый". Definitely not "красный". I'm sure of it.

What are you talking about?!

"Ten Little Indians."

Who are they?

We're all Indians in the face of death . . .

Well, yes. Let's get back to the subject.

The thing from which the conversation constantly slips into trivialities lies breathing ever more haltingly on the hospital bed. Wlibgis clearly doesn't have long to live. Although blithe chatter, prattle, and yacking seems to entice some of the women with increasing purpose-fulness, as if they are completely unable to keep their thoughts in check, some of them thankfully understand that this cannot go on. That self-discipline is necessary now: Wlibgis has to be escorted beyond the veil with due decorum.

Wlibgis, tell us, do we have time?

What do you mean?

I mean the moment when you have to fling yourself . . .

Or do something else before your final departure.

Ah, time. All I have is time . . . I'm leaving after a protracted illness, *isn't that dull? Be careful not to fall asleep . . .*

Don't be angry, Wlibgis.

We've acted poorly. Forgive us.

Wlibgis, you know best whether we need to hurry. If there's time, you could tell us something?

For instance, tell us what kind of life you had!

And how you liked us?

Yes, did you enjoy our company?

Did you understand a word of what we were talking about when we were where we came from?

Did you know English?

At the moment of death, there might be better things to do than quiz the departing about her foreign language skills. There the women float around gray, pale Wlibgis, who is barely conscious any more. So did she ever learn English during her life? Well, Wlibgis knows a word or two, just like Rosa and Maimuna. But because she, unlike them, hasn't been able to express anything verbally, they realize suddenly, at the last moment, that she is more valuable than anyone. Not for herself, of course, but as a mirror. There can never be too many mirrors. Not even in these circumstances. *Have you enjoyed our company?* Traces of narcis-sism cling tight to a person. *How did you like us?* Approaching death doesn't ennoble anyone, even if they are all plunging one by one into nothingness.

Wlibgis controls herself remarkably well. Although she has never practiced meditation, somehow she suddenly succeeds in emptying her mind. She concentrates and concentrates, gathering strength. Recklessly she prolongs the silence.

The colossal hospital complex, which resembles a giant mouth organ, sprawls along Groot Weezenland. If the women had swayed over to the window, and if the blinds had been open, as they waited for Wlibgis's answer they could have admired the eight-story view of the Zwarte Water, one of Zwolle's numerous rivers, which in this part of the city had been shaped into the form of a star. The shape was from a time when the river in question had not been a river but a water barrier constructed to protect the city and followed the pure lines of the Dutch version of a type of bastion fortification originally developed in Italy.

But the blinds are closed, so the slanting rays of the morning sun won't bother Wlibgis as she lies in bed. Only a few beams of light find their way through small holes into the dim room, which is primarily lit by a lava lamp that resembles a space shuttle and which Melinda brought to help her grandmother feel better. "It's fun to look at, and it helps you fall asleep." In the glass capsule of the lava lamp, in the turquoise oil-based liquid, electric blue drops of wax form in various sizes and shapes, and Wlibgis did like watching their magma-like movements before falling asleep.

Ulrike glances toward the window. What kind of place are they in? Is there a city outside? This has to be a city, since the room is a large hospital room. What is the view like? Are leaves in the trees? Is snow on the ground? There is light, so at least it is day. But they can't open the blinds. They can't do anything worldly, not pick up the ballpoint pen on the floor, not stroke Wlibgis's fragile face framed by her wig. Only the floating Wlibgis herself can touch the Wlibgis lying in the bed, and she only at the very final moment, perhaps.

The unease begins to swell. Polina, Shlomith, Ulrike, and Rosa Imaculada wait for Wlibgis's answer, swaying, each flickering in a different spot. The awkward question, *Do you know English?* echoes in the space like the mouth-smacking of a predatory bat, like a quickening, crackly, ping-ponging sound pulse. They never should have asked that. Now that question haunts them whatever they try to think about. Its cracking had covered everything except when that other, perhaps even more perturbing question, which they had conjured, flitted in from the periphery. Of course they hadn't been able to restrain themselves: *How did you like us?*

I actually liked Nina most. Now don't be offended. It's simply the truth, and you were the ones who asked. I wished I could have had a daughter like her. Nina was ordinary in a pleasant way and seemed to have a good head on her shoulders, while the rest of you . . . especially you, Shlomith, and also you, Polina. You two are so full of yourselves. The way you talk, and you talk a lot, tells me you consider yourselves better than other people. You seem to think you have special rights. To tell the truth, Shlomith, your thinness disgusts me. I can't approve of the way you've intentionally put yourself in that condition. You, Polina, love the sound of your own voice far too much. I'm sorry, but no one can stand listening to you! Back when my voice worked, I only spoke as much as necessary. I think that's a good baseline. You shouldn't overburden people. It isn't polite. And then the rest of you. Ulrike: I have to admit you irritate me. You're impertinent. No, let me continue! I know full well that you're still sorry for that stray thought of yours. I forgive you. Don't worry about it any more. You're right: I'm not inter-esting. I tried once. I made myself up like other women do every day, found myself a man, and so forth. And look what came of it. Only trouble. I'm boring and normal, and a little ugly, but what about it? In this world there's one person I love and one person who loves me. Is that sufficient for you on the subject of "Wlibgis"? Well then, let's continue the circle. Rosa, you threw far too many fits, but I understand you. You have that Latin-American temperament, so what can you do? And besides, you're actually wiser than the others, since you taught us that word. Is it your people's way of saying "Open sesame"? Because of you at least we got out of that horrible place. So thank you, Rosa! And finally, Maimuna. Pretty girl. She could have become a skilled gymnast. She had a good body. I don't have anything bad to say about her. Shame she died that way.

Wlibgis had said her piece.

Just then, after Wlibgis finishes, the door to the room opens. Two nurses, one over thirty, the other almost still a teenager, walk in. Only Wlibgis, the Wlibgis in the air, understands what they say.

"This case here, Ms. Van Deijck, won't last much longer," the elder says. "Give her five more milligrams of morphine."

"Xaliimo, somehow I get the feeling she's going to die today during my shift. Will you stay with me? This'll be my first death."

"If she dies before my shift is over then, yeah, I'll be here."

"You've probably seen lots of deaths."

"Yes, I have."

"And?"

"And what?"

"How does it feel?"

"It doesn't feel like anything. Unless it's a baby or a kid. Once it was. She was three and got hit by a truck backing up. She literally died in my arms when I was trying to revive her. The family's reaction was just horrible to watch. We were all crying."

"Who is this one's next-of-kin?"

"Sort of a thin, pale woman. She comes sometimes with a little girl. She asked us to call once it's over."

"Even at night?"

"In the morning is fine, she said."

"It's probably good for this one that she'll be gone soon."

"Yeah. This is a pretty easy case since the pain is under control. She's basically slept for the past five days. Once I had this old man who had cancer in his liver. He screamed and screamed no matter how many drugs we pumped into him. He just moaned, 'Help me, help me.' His wife couldn't stand it and ran out of the room. In the end we spent more time calming the wife down that we did on the husband's final moments."

"I just hope I don't get any kids, at least not yet, or any in really bad shape. I don't think I'm ready. Of course we trained for these situations in school. An actor did a course for us once and I got given this appalling case. A young boy had done himself in, and I had to tell his parents. I really put myself into it. That one ended up in my dreams, even though I kept it together in front of the class."

"That CPR dummy, Anne, do you know who it got its face from?"

"No. Are you saying it's modeled after someone living?"

"Not living, dead. *L'Inconnue de la Seine*. Do you know it? She was a sixteen-year-old girl who was found in the Seine in the late 1800s. She washed up at a dock near the Louvre. The body was in good condition, and she was wearing a smile like the Mona Lisa. According to the legend, the girl was so beautiful that the pathologist in the Paris morgue made a death mask of her. Copies spread all over the Paris art scene. It became a decoration, her face."

"Unbelievable! A dead girl's face? How could anyone make a copy of that?"

"Well, of the expression and hair. It isn't that different from a photograph."

"So Resusci Anne's face was modeled after that death mask? Are you serious?"

"Yes, completely! Our teacher told us the story once during a CPR course. I couldn't help thinking about it, that I was putting my lips on a dead girl's mouth. Apparently they're the most kissed lips in the world."

"Right. Thanks for telling me."

"You're welcome. Although you aren't going to have to kiss Anne any more. You've already done your practice. It's just real-life cases from now on. You'll get attached to some of them, and you won't be able to stand some of them. Last week I had this one lung cancer case. It was pretty ugly, coughing up blood and stuff. But I have to admit that secretly I was a little happy. The whole time the guy had been calling me a nigger."

"What about this one, Ms. van Deijck?"

"What about her?"

"What's she like?"

"She's fine. Easy. Normal. There's only one thing I wonder about a little. According to her papers she has a son, but I've never seen him here. His daughter comes with her mother, but he never does. Pretty strange, isn't it? What could have happened between them?"

"Did you ask her?"

"She couldn't talk. She didn't want a prosthesis."

"Maybe she was a terrible mom. Maybe she mistreated her son. Or maybe she was just a pain. There was a boy in my class at school who cut things off with his father as soon as he turned eighteen. He said why should he care about the bastard when he never cared about him. The things his dad did were terrible. There are times you just have to get away from someone completely."

The Wlibgis in the air knows her time has come. No rhythm, no pulse, no singing. Just anger, solitary anger, the crystal-clear sign of departure.

The older nurse checks the cannula attached to the back of the hand of the Wlibgis lying on the bed and then turns to leave. The younger nurse follows her. At the same moment, an electric blue waxy glob disengages from the base of the lava lamp and begins to rise. The Wlibgis in the air waits for the glob to reach the center of the lamp—no rhythm, no pulse, no singing, no luxury for her. No one helps, and she doesn't ask for help. She waits for the electric blue lump to be in the right spot, like the bubble in a builder's spirit level; it's a signal, a signal to her.

And when it does, she leaves, alone, in the way of her choosing. She sort of sits on the side of the bed, sort of tumbles onto herself, onto the mattress, as if going to sleep. The Wlibgis on the bed below wheezes. The Wlibgis in the air grimaces and swipes the hole in her throat with the back of her hand as if cutting her neck with a guillotine.

The Wlibgis in the air disappears.

And in their shock, no one has the time to say goodbye.

DEATH REHEARSAL NUMBER 3
(HOW TO CLOSE UP A CORPSE IN A COFFIN)

When a person becomes a corpse, others treat her differently than they did a moment ago, during life. A dying person is at the mercy of others, whether she's conscious prior to becoming a corpse or in a

state of unconsciousness, as Wlibgis was believed to be. Being an
experienced nurse, Xaliimo had seen some things in her time. One of
her former colleagues, Maritje, once made a mustache for a coma
patient using the patient's own shoulder-length hair, just because it
happened to amuse her. Then there was Tessa, who had a habit of
commenting after washing patients' intimate areas, although thankfully only after leaving the room. Xaliimo didn't feel good about that
either. "You gotta have a laugh sometimes," Tessa replied angrily
when Xaliimo asked her to stop. "That's the only way to survive this."
Xaliimo spent the whole night mulling over how a glans swollen with
balanitis or a vulva spotted with lichen ruber could be amusing to
anyone.

    With time Xaliimo became hardened and stopped noticing certain
things. She did her work well, and people liked her, but she didn't
always have the energy to pretend to be diplomatic when treating
patients who were already somewhere else, already halfway on the
other side. Xaliimo also became familiar with the temptation to do
inappropriate things. To shove a finger in a patient's mouth and make
a popping sound with his cheek or do like Maritje and make a
mustache under a sleeping woman's nose with her hair. Just because
it was possible. No one ever trained the young novices starting in the
ward in the darker sides of nursing, in the shame that the unpredictable urges aroused by the helplessness of others could create. If you
didn't stamp out that shame, it would start to sting, and if you gave in
to it, it would poison your mind; if you contemplated it, you'd grow
despondent; and if you denied it, the patient's life might be put in
premature danger.

    But Xaliimo didn't give in. She didn't fold a diaper package into a
dunce cap and put it on anyone's head, and she didn't stick her
fingers anywhere without a medical reason. She discharged her
work better than before and turned up the warmth in her voice
when speaking to patients. She stopped scolding her immoral
colleagues, but inside she deeply despised them, their ribald talk
and insufferable gestures, which would have offended the patients if
they had been awake. "I was raised to give other people respect,"

Xaliimo said to herself time and time again, and that was enough, she believed. She knew that the dying had their own indisputable value, even though sometimes watching their protracted struggle with death was so exasperating that keeping her malicious thoughts in check was difficult. Why hadn't they arranged an honorable end for themselves in time?

But something happened when the dying became the dead. A person, who only a moment before had received if not brusk then at least routine care, magically became nearly holy, deserving of solemn respect—sometimes also, strangely enough, a risk of infection. Some nurses put on full safety gear: the aprons, masks, gloves, and long coats that were usually used with special patients, as if death were catching, and only then would they touch the corpse, which a moment before they had been willing to turn over with bare hands without any fear. They rolled the body, now unreasonably heavy, just enough to get the sheets, pillows, and bedding out from under. They placed a new single-use polypropylene-coated lifting sheet just for this purpose under the deceased, and put on a clean diaper. They removed the dead person's clothing and jewelry, if there was any jewelry, and placed the dentures, if there were any, in the mouth to give it shape. Because dead faces collapse. Even an ample nose becomes a little bird beak. The eyes begin to droop, the cheeks disappear, and depressions, hollows, and a waxwork-like lack of luster develop. The nurses continued their work against time. They removed catheters and cannulas, intubation lines, and feeding tubes, if there were any, and they placed new bandages over any possible wounds. They washed the body, if necessary, and dressed it in a white disposable shirt that was open in the back. They bound the jaw shut with gauze (the jaw joint and neck stiffen at room temperature within two to four hours) and placed damp pads on the eyes so they would stay closed—never cotton wool, though, which would catch between the upper and lower lids leaving fluff that the mortuary staff would have to remove with tweezers (extra work, but if the casket is open at the funeral, there simply can't be any cotton wool left in the eyes because it looks bad). Christians' hands were raised to the chest and placed in an attitude of prayer, Muslims' hands were extended to the sides of the body, and others were placed over the breast but left free (fingers and toes stiffen next). The legs of the deceased were bound at the ankles with gauze so they would stay in place, without spreading, and then the corpse was given a visual once-over to make sure that everything was straight and well situated (the elbow, knee, and hip joints stiffen last). Once an identification tag with name, identity number, date of death, and the hospital and ward name was attached with a safety pin to the gauze around the ankles—the tag was not tied to the corpse's toe like in films—the body was ready for temporary concealment beneath a white sheet (rigor mortis was complete within six to eight hours). And finally a flower on the sheet: in the spring Siberian squill (*Scilla siberica*) or spring crocus (*Crocus vernus*) from the hospital garden; in the winter calla lily (*Zantedeschia aethiopica*) from the cantina.

Now the family could come.

Wlibgis had lain perfectly still in the bed, but despite the rather large amount of morphine, she snapped awake during her last moments. She opened her eyes and mouth as if to say something, but only her eyes spoke, screamed, gasped wide open for the oxygen that the mouth could no longer get inside. Her heart continued beating for a moment. Her wheezing breath turned urgent, panicked, and her eyes howled, agape, an awareness flashing in them that was horrible to watch. The younger nurse, Ineke, happened to look. Ineke turned when she heard Wlibgis suddenly gasp, when she heard the heavy, wheezing breathing stop and then restart haltingly, as if anticipating a cough. Ineke rushed to the bed and instinctively took Wlibgis by the hand. Xaliimo came to the other side of the bed, but Wlibgis stared at Ineke, no one but Ineke.

Ineke would remember those eyes for the rest of her life, the eyes of her first patient to die.

When Melinda and Melinda's mother arrived, Wlibgis looked devout, nearly beatific. Hands clasped over the sheet, calla lily between the hands, eyes closed, mouth closed; Ineke and Xaliimo had arranged her as the dead should be arranged.

Melinda was first to peer cautiously through the door. "Grandma will be lying down. She won't be moving or breathing," her mother had explained on the bus. "It will just be grandma's shell. Her spirit is already somewhere else." But Melinda was still shy about entering the room. She would have preferred to hover at the door, to peek between her fingers, to wave goodbye from a short distance. But that wouldn't do. They had to say their goodbyes properly. They had to face death. That's what Mommy said. Death is a part of life. Death is a perfectly natural thing. Flowers die, flies die, pets die, Bebbo died. "Cheese molds. You remember that, right, Melinda? Mold makes cheese inedible. But we need mold, because it breaks things down: living things can't exist forever." "Why not, Mommy?" "Well, think about what would happen if every creature that had lived for thousands and hundreds of thousands of years, all the people and animals and plants, still existed. Even the huge dinosaurs. Where would we all fit? We wouldn't!" "We could send the dinosauws to the moon on wock-ets! And we could build buildings on the moon that weached to the sun!" "I don't think that would work. The moon doesn't have any oxygen. And the sun is too hot." "Is there mold on Gwandma now?" "No, Melinda, there isn't any mold. The cancer cells won the battle, and the healthy cells lost despite the treatment. Do you remember the picture the doctor drew for you? The picture of the healthy and the sick cells, how they were fighting?" "But you were tawking about cheese." "It was a metaphor. Let's put it this way: the bacteria that do the decomposition start their work after death. When a cell dies, chemicals are released that start destroying the body." "Gwandma has been destwoyed!" "No, dear child. The bacteria and chemicals don't start their work until Grandma is in the grave. Gradually. With time. It's just part of what happens." "What is a chemicawl?" "It's a sort of . . . substance . . . " "Where does it come fwom? "They're in all of us already. People are full of all kinds of things, like enzymes and bacteria." "What's enzymes?" "Well, they're sort of a . . . thing. Without enzymes, there wouldn't be any life. Enzymes speed up cellular chemical reactions, but you don't need to . . ." "What is a weaction?" "Melinda. Melinda dear. Just think of it this way: bacteria and enzymes are invisible little things. You can't see them with your eyes because they're so small . . ." "Smawller than the spots on a ladybird?" "Much smaller. But they do very important work. They decompose things and clean things up. They keep everything in good order like street sweepers and garbage men. Decomposition is a part of the circle of life." "Am I decomposing too?" "You aren't decomposing, silly. People who're alive don't decompose. And whatever decomposes is replaced by something new as long as there's life. Cells are born and cells die. You even drop dead skin all the time." "No I don't!" "Dear, everyone does. Do you remember that shampoo ad? The one with the man brushing dandruff off his shoulder before a date? Dandruff is dead skin cells too. It isn't anything serious." "I don't have dandwuff. I weally don't." "No, no. I'm sure you don't. I was just trying to explain decomposition. Dead things gradually decompose. When we die, bacteria and other things make us into dirt again. And dirt grows new life, for example beautiful sunflowers like the ones that grow on Bebbo's grave. Melinda, dear, death is a perfectly natural thing. We've already talked about this."

Melinda didn't want to step into the room.

What if Grandma was swarming with bacteria? What if Grandma started decomposing while they were watching? What if Mom had misunderstood something?! And there was another thing. Something Mom didn't know about. The spirit. Grandma's spirit. *It's just Grandma's shell.* But where was the spirit now? Mom didn't know. But *she* knew. Grandma's spirit was up by the ceiling. And it might want to come down. It might rush inside Grandma through the hole cut in her throat. Grandma's body would start to shake and bubble, and green goo would come out of her mouth. Her eyes would snap open but only the whites would show.

If Grandma's spirit hadn't made it to the spirit world . . .

Melinda grabbed her mother's hand and closed her eyes as they walked into the room together. One step, two, three. Four. The first time a person walks up to a dead body, they usually feel dizzy. They feel a pressing need to turn and leave, accompanied by an uncontrollable desire to move closer. As if their internal organs were making the decision for them but constantly changing their mind. As if the dead body were a magnet, as if the approaching person's stomach were cast full of iron. Something down there churns and presses. All their energy goes into looking, into bearing to look at the corpse. Bearing the irrational immobility, daring to be there, to move closer, daring to look and to be.

The edge of the bed hit Melinda's leg. Her mother sobbed instead of crying out in terror. Melinda carefully opened one eye a crack. There Grandma lay, face expressionless. Melinda quickly glanced around. The curtains didn't sway, and nothing was visible on the ceiling. No eyes stared back at her. Spirits had oval eyes you could see in the middle of the ball of mist. Spirits' eyes were gaping and terrible. Melinda had seen them in a comic book. And she knew that spirits that had been driven out of their bodies were very miserable.

"What will happen to Gwandma now?" Melinda asked, holding back tears, and her mother didn't understand why, why a girl who was normally so emotional tried to keep her face steady, lips pursed tight. Even she wasn't trying to contain herself and just let the tears blind her. "Next we'll go to the funeral parlor," Melinda's mother said to her daughter, in a voice thick with emotion. "We'll choose Grandma a coffin and make the other practical arrangements." "We aren't taking her with us?" "No, of course not, dear. Grandma will stay here in hospital for just a bit longer." "In that bed?" "I suppose they'll give the bed to someone else, someone who's still alive and needs a bed more than Grandma now." "Where will they put Gwandma then?" "Well, they'll take her to the morgue." "What's a mawgue?" "It's a place where dead people are put for a little while." "Oh, a gwave?" "No, graves are dug in the ground. A morgue is a little like a refrigerator." "Why are they putting Gwandma in a wefwigewator?" "Do you remember, Melinda, when we talked about decomposing bacteria a little while ago . . . ?" "The ones that are smawller than the spots on a ladybird?" "Yes, those. We don't want them to start their work yet, right? That's why Grandma is being put in the morgue. The bacteria will be frozen there. They'll hibernate. Like bears." "And then they start moving again when Gwandma is in her gwave?" "Yes, exactly!

Now let's collect Grandma's things to take with us. You unplug the lava lamp from the wall." "No." "Please." "I don't want to." "Do you intend to leave it here?" "Yes." "It's such a nice lamp, though. Come along, please unplug it." "I don't want it." "Melinda, stop! Unplug the lamp from the wall right now. Do you hear me?"

Explaining to her mother, who didn't understand anything about spirits, why they couldn't take the lamp was pointless. The electric blue wax bubbles that floated upwards had once been calming, and the blue shimmer of the lamp had been the only light that guarded Melinda's nightmare-prone dreams, but now everything was irrevo-cably different. What if an oval set of eyes suddenly appeared in one of the bubbles, staring through the glass, blinking and begging: Help me, help me, help me . . .

In the afternoon, a few hours after Melinda and Melinda's mother had visited the funeral parlor on Katerdijk Street, a man named Christoffel Dijkstra drove a hearse into the back courtyard of the hospital. He pushed an oak coffin on wheels into the basement morgue and quickly found the correct locker with the aid of the attendant. *How much does she weigh?* Funeral parlor workers always posed these questions in the present tense. The deceased only fell under sway of the past tense following the burial. The question had surprised Melinda's mother; she didn't have a clue about Wlibgis's weight. She was an average-sized woman who had been ravaged by cancer, a little shorter than herself. Was that enough? *And how would you like her dressed?* Often the next-of-kin wanted the deceased to be dressed in clothing they believed she loved, for example a wedding dress, a favorite skirt, an oriental dressing gown, a Hawaiian shirt. Christoffel Dijkstra had even arranged one corpse in a ski outfit. Yes, arranged, because you didn't actually dress a corpse. Not like the living are dressed. The deceased was dressed after being placed in the casket. The clothing was cut open and the cuts were hidden under the body as if the clothing continued around behind. It was just a facade, and for whom if no one was ever going to look at the body again! But Christoffel did not ponder this. The deceased were supposed to have clothing, draped on top like paper dolls. If a woman had been happy in her lacy little black dress, then they cut it open and put it on her and that was that. Dressing with rigor mortis arms crammed into sleeves, with the head wriggled through the neck hole, so that the clothing was on all the way underneath and everywhere— that was too difficult, and needlessly messy. Corpses leaked. Dead bodies were usually full of liquid, which dribbled out of every possible opening. Christoffel always prepared for casketing with a bag of paper tissues. He wiped the filth from the face and neck, combed the hair, removed the bandage around the jaw and the paper pads from the eyes. Wlibgis was one corpse among many. Not any messier than normal, actually easier than average, because the woman who had made the order had bought her a cotton shirt that would be easy for the funeral parlor to put on.

Wlibgis was ready. Her skin was wiped clean, her red wig was nicely brushed, and her hands were crossed over her chest. Wlibgis under a white sheet. Wearing a white shirt. Peaceful Wlibgis, her spirit already elsewhere.

Christoffel Dijkstra screwed the coffin lid shut.

Vaarwel, Wlibgis!

OUR BELOVED

Wlibgis Van Deijck

Born in Zwolle on 3 April, 1953, died in Zwolle on 18 February, 2012

MOURNED BY

Nicholas VAN DEIJCK	*her son*
Melinda VAN HET HOFF	*her granddaughter*
Trijntje VAN HET HOFF	*her granddaughter's mother*

Sylvain (†) and Lisette (†) VANDERSMISSEN	*and their family*
Theo and Leonia (†) BESERARE	*and their family*
Joannes and Celine VAN AUTRYVEN	*and their family*
August and Marga VAN DER WESTHUIZEN	*and their family*
	her uncles, aunts and cousins

VERBEECK *family*
VANDEPUT *family*
DE VRIES *family*
VAN DER LINDEN *family*

her coworkers

Memorial on February 26, 2012 beginning at 1 PM
R.K. Kerkhof, Zwolle (Bisschop Willebrandlaan 62)

No flowers.
No wreaths.

ANY POSSIBLE REMEMBRANCES MAY BE
DONATED TO A FUND TO BENEFIT MELINDA: NL19INGB0005252007

VERMILION, PURPLE, MAGENTA: THE HEART THAT REJECTED EUCALYPTUS TREES

Adeus, Rosa Imaculada!

No sooner has Wlibgis collapsed on her back on the hospital bed, onto herself and instantly disappearing, than the shocked quartet, Polina, Rosa, Ulrike, and Shlomith, realize they are somewhere new again. The white hospital walls recede and blur, and for a vanishing moment everything is black. Gradually red begins to spill into each woman's field of view, at first only a vague redness until the image comes into sharp focus.

The room is simple. It would have been austere if the walls had not been painted a sensuous purple. The dark-wood floor and white, translucent curtains, which have been drawn over the three windows, balance the sinful color of the wall. There is no furniture in the room beyond a luxurious rosewood bed with rambling garlands and feeding hummingbirds carved into its high, courtly arching headboard. On the bed lounges a large man—and Rosa Imaculada, with an enraged expression on her face.

This is what I've been waiting for.

Tell us about it, Rosa.

What happened to you?

What horrible thing is that man doing to you?

Rosa inspects herself. There she sits atop the white bedspread, in front of the man, in a too-tight magenta piqué shirt. Four of five buttons are open, and, even so, the shirt looks like a corset, her breasts like cantaloupes, and under them, on the left, beats the main star of her fate: her heart. What happened to it?

The time spent in the white emptiness shrinks, draining away like water released from a bath, like a nightmare fading. Finally she can tell! Now they are in her own kingdom—or is it Estêvão Santoro's kingdom? At least she didn't die at home. This also means, Rosa suddenly understands, that she won't ever see her tiny son again. And that her son won't see her die.

A lightning-bright wave of despair and relief strikes Rosa Imaculada to her knees, in a strange, almost tortuous pose a little above the surface of the floor. From there, collapsed in a crouch, she begins to speak, haltingly at first. She crumples into a ball the picture of Davi that had filled her mind and with determination begins to spread out bright, well-articulated ideas in its place.

We're in the old city of Salvador, in Pelourinho. That man is Estêvão Santoro. He's the father of my heart donor. The boy whose heart I have in my breast was named Murilo. Mr. Santoro visited me many times. So often that the neighbors began to whisper and ask questions. I told him, "You can't come here any more." Then he asked me to come to his home. He sent a white car to pick me up. He lives in this hotel room. His family lives almost three thousand kilometers away in Manaus. I don't know how long he intends to keep this up . . .

Not long, since you're going to die!

Does he murder you?

Does he dig his son's heart out of your chest—

Stop it! I don't want to see this . . .

—and put it in a glass bowl full of surgical alcohol and run away . . . ?

Rosa, come on, tell us. What are you two doing?

Although the barriers to conversation have disappeared, although their thoughts flow between each other almost effortlessly, Rosa has a terribly hard time answering this last question, which has come from Ulrike's direction. Yes, what were they doing—except sitting facing each other on a hotel room bed, clothed, clearly not intending to become intimate in the traditional sense of that phrase?

Mr. Santoro wants to get to know his son through me, with my help. He never got to know Murilo properly while he was alive. They quarreled a lot and never made up. I'm sure you can understand how difficult getting over something like that can be.

Are you claiming to be some sort of medium, Rosa?

No, it isn't that. Murilo doesn't talk to me. I just know. It's completely physical.

And you and this gentleman are in the middle of a session?

Yes. My guess is that Mr. Santoro just asked me a question. And I'm answering. Look at my expression. Don't I look furious!

Something really is happening in the hotel room, but as in Maimuna's case, the moment is frozen: Estêvão Santoro has closed his mouth and Rosa Imaculada has opened her own; it is as if time is waiting for permission to continue from the Rosa floating on her knees.

But the floating Rosa is dissatisfied. She senses the flood of questions, the suspicion behind her, the whispers, the doubts, and they injure her.

> . . . *does she really* . . .
>
> *truly*
>
> . . . *ludicrous!*   . . . *seriously* . . .
>
> *crazy is as crazy does*
>
> . . . *autosuggestion* . . .

But then a voice rises in her defense. Polina. A gift from God!

Why couldn't it be possible?

Polina is a good person. Polina silences Shlomith and Ulrike. Polina believes her!

Skin remembers touch, bodies remember experiences. Why couldn't a heart remember feelings?

Dear God, Polina, feelings aren't in the heart!

Where are they, then?

In the brain, you idiot!

Now you're wrong, Shlomith. Feelings are everywhere.

Stop it already. Or don't even start.

You get startled, and your heart races . . .

Without a brain, there isn't anything. Your mouth doesn't think, even if it does state your thoughts!

Cellular memory is a miraculous thing, and research about it is just getting going . . .

Autosuggestion.

What?

Autosuggestion. Rosa has convinced herself that she knows things about the organ donor.

Poor Rosa. Dying is clearly more agonizing than anyone had imagined. If there had been physical pain at the moment of departure, fortunately the women don't remember it. But perhaps reliving the pain would have been a lesser evil than this constant doubt and discord.

Shlomith! Do you really want what happened with Wlibgis to happen here?

Rosa Imaculada has sprung to her feet. She turns her face to the trio waiting behind, glancing in thanks at Polina and glaring angrily at Ulrike, then even more angrily at Shlomith. Rosa's eyes spark. Her thoughts are bright, sharp, and diamond hard.

Shlomith! Do you want to ruin my final moments?

No, Shlomith doesn't want that. She blanches. Ulrike, who at least had the sense to stay in the background when Polina and Shlomith began their argument, is also deeply sorry for her thoughts, once again: *Crazy is as crazy does.* But it doesn't go that way. There, when faced with a direct question, they both understand that their job is to help, not to judge or question. There simply isn't time for their pointed exchange of views. Although their faith might be tried, they have to stop arguing. Each has to swallow what she would like to say. Do they have any other option?

Pardon me, Rosa.

I'm sorry.

How can we help you?

Rosa is mollified. The situation is in control again. She has only one hope and need: she wants to tell what happened to her. She wants to get someone, even just one, even just herself, to understand what an unfathomable thing happened to her.

I have an idea.

Rosa closes her eyes and gathers her energy. Then in her mind she begins to express, clearly, slowly, and emphatically the idea she is developing. Take care now, she thought, my idea isn't easy to carry out. It won't necessarily work at all, but I want to try. This is my final wish.

Take care now! Before I leave, regardless of where or how I go, I want to return to one of our sessions. To Murilo and Estêvão Santoro's meeting, which happened through me. I think that I can remember it exactly the way it happened. It was here, in this room, within these purple walls. I want you, Polina, Shlomith, and Ulrike, to come with me. It won't necessarily work, but I want to try at least. This is my final wish. Close your eyes.

The trio is silent for a moment without a hint of a thought. And then:

Rosa, what do we do?

It comes as if from one brain. A confused, utterly helpless question: what do we do now that we've closed our eyes?

Rosa Imaculada doesn't know the answer. But she has an intuition, and it spurs her forward, to express her wish. Her intuition had sometimes spoken with the voice of Luiz Inácio Lula da Silva, which later went silent, and now it urges her to continue: You will find the solution by singing if no other way. By singing, Rosa, by singing, as you did with Ninjuška!

Then Polina's ecstatic cry comes and fills everything.

Shlomith, Ulrike, do you see?

What?

Just DON'T open your eyes!

What are we meant to see?

I see LIGHT!

Polina is sure the light is a good sign. It is a classic sign. The light at the end of the tunnel. This time she doesn't intend to struggle. She doesn't intend to drag her heels as she did the first time, in the yellow, when they were pulled out of the white, when they were transported toward the desert, toward Maimuna's world, from where she had forced them all back to the starting point, for a reason she couldn't even understand herself any more. She isn't a coward. Yet even so she had opened her eyes and her mouth, and sabotaged everything. She had prolonged the consummation of fate, not just of Maimuna's but each of theirs. Now she definitely wouldn't resist!

Polina! Come out of there right now!

What?

You're in the wrong place. Come out!

Have you all opened your eyes?

No! Can't you hear Rosa singing?

Rosa isn't singing.

But Rosa is singing. In her thoughts Rosa croons that familiar lullaby to them, transporting Shlomith and Ulrike with its strains toward her own story. *Nigue, nigue, ninhas, tão bonitinhas . . .* Rosa sings and thinks intently of a BOW TIE, the vermilion BOW TIE that Mr. Santoro wore every time they met. She concentrates only and exclusively on the BOW TIE, tying her mind inextricably to its knot with all the power of the words of the song. *Ê ê ê ê, imbê, tumbelá!*

Polina, drive the light out of your mind NOW!

Where are you?

We're in the red!

Red?

Polina! Polina!

Hear how beautifully Rosa sings!

You have to come out of there right now or you'll be damned!

Startled, Polina nearly opens her eyes, but instinct demands that she still keep them squeezed shut tight. Polina listens to her instincts. She squeezes, squeezes, and suddenly the light disappears. And then, gradually, she begins to see the red: first as orange, then crimson, and finally their mixture, vermilion. As soon as the vermilion appears, it begins to take shape, the color shrinking into a magnificent knot, with one wing and then a second blossoming from it. When the BOW TIE is finished, Polina finally hears a familiar voice: *Nigue, nigue, ninhas, tão bonitinhas, macamba viola di pari e ganguinhas . . .*

Rosa's song has found her!

ESTÊVÃO SANTORO: Rosa, I'm sorry about what happened last time.

ROSA IMACULADA: It was nothing. (*Although it was something: Grandmother had been forced to come and remove Mr. Santoro's hand, which had cramped in place as he squeezed the skin under Rosa's left breast, leaving fingernail marks that remained visible for three days. After that, Mr. Santoro wasn't welcome in their house any more, even though he appeased Grandmother with an even larger wad of cash than normal.*)

ESTÊVÃO SANTORO: No, I'm serious. I'm really sorry. But what you said shocked me. (*Mr. Santoro sits up straighter, setting his hand dramatically on his chest and shouting the words Rosa had spoken.*) "Dad, I hate you, I hate you, I hate you!"

ROSA IMACULADA: Mr. Santoro, I'm the one who should be sorry. That shout just came out. I couldn't help it.

ESTÊVÃO SANTORO: So Murilo never forgave me.

ROSA IMACULADA: What did he never forgive you for?

ESTÊVÃO SANTORO: You'll know if Murilo really is influencing you.

ROSA IMACULADA (*taken aback*): Do you really doubt that?

ESTÊVÃO SANTORO: No, of course not. (*More gently*) I just want to know how much influence Murilo has through you. How much is left in that heart. This is important to me.

ROSA IMACULADA: I see. (*A little anxious*) Should I take that powder again?

ESTÊVÃO SANTORO: This time I have something to drink. (*From his pocket he takes a small glass vial and begins to screw open the metal cap; in the vial is a dense, dark mixture.*) I got a tip about another vendor.

ROSA IMACULADA (*more anxious*): Do I dare take it? The powder made me feel ill. (*Pause. Then in a very quiet voice*) So what's in the bottle?

ESTÊVÃO SANTORO: The old ekeji swore that it works. It doesn't have any side effects.

ROSA IMACULADA (*louder*): But what is it? I'm not taking it if I don't know what it is!

ESTÊVÃO SANTORO (*agitated*): Of course she didn't tell me! But she's been making it for a long time. And she understood immediately when I told her what it was for.

ROSA IMACULADA (*firmly*): Mr. Santoro, I don't dare put that in my mouth. I have to be careful.

Estêvão Santoro squeezes the glass vial in his large fist and flexes his arm as if he wants to throw the bottle against the wall. He's furious. He's—

Rosa, don't drink it!
Shhhhhhh!!! Polina, don't meddle in things that don't concern you!

—disappointed, not because he paid a significant sum for the stuff in the bottle, which was presumably a mixture of moonshine, powdered chicken foot or rooster wattle, and a pinch of secret narcotic herbs, but rather because he really does want to know right now, without wasting another moment, whether any secrets were transplanted along with the heart. He wants to know if it's possible or if this woman is just making things up to swindle money from him . . .

ROSA IMACULADA (*alarmed*): Mr. Santoro! You must understand.

ESTÊVÃO SANTORO (*collects himself and then speaks with emphatic calmness*): This liquid is safe. It will help reveal the truth. (*He unscrews the cap all the way, takes a small swig himself, and grins.*) There. I didn't die. What if we continue our investigation now?

ROSA IMACULADA (*hesitantly*): Well, I imagine—

Rosa!
Shhhhhhhhh!!!

—Rosa takes the bottle and empties it. Only with effort does she hold down the vomit. After she's heaved and retched enough, after she's

wiped her mouth on the rust-red handkerchief Estêvão Santoro kindly handed her, she straightens up and casts him a grim gaze.

ROSA IMACULADA: Are you satisfied now?

ESTÊVÃO SANTORO (*appeased*): Thank you, Rosa. You can't know how much this means to me. I'll compensate your sacrifice handsomely. If we get to the end of this today, I'll pack my bags and go home.

ROSA IMACULADA (*formally, a little mechanically*): Do we proceed as before? Do you want to start with questions?

ESTÊVÃO SANTORO: I propose that I start by describing a certain situation. Something happened between Murilo and me a little before the accident. You chime in as soon as you know what I'm talking about.

ROSA IMACULADA: OK.

ESTÊVÃO SANTORO: Close your eyes.

Rosa closes her eyes. Mr. Santoro also closes his eyes. They take each other by the hand.

ESTÊVÃO SANTORO (*pausing for a moment to gather his thoughts before beginning*): I'm sitting at home on the terrace. It's early evening, and I've had a few drinks. During the day I made some good deals. A large bridge is going up over the Rio Negro. A line of pylons is visible in the distance to the left. I turn my wicker chair and move it right next to the terrace railing so I can see the construction site on the water. Sometimes I look at the bridge through binoculars: the pylons look a little like air-traffic control towers, or an oil-drilling platform. Either way, looking at them is calming. Something is happening, you know, and that feels so damn good! (*With a little chuckle*) The opening ceremonies will be next year. There'll be fireworks and champagne. I contributed a small amount of the financing for the bridge (*brief pause*), so in a way the bridge feels like my own. I'm feeling so good that I get the cigar box from the cabinet in the bedroom . . .

Suddenly Rosa squeezes Mr. Santoro's hands tightly.

ROSA IMACULADA (*shouting*): A bang!—

Help!
What on . . .

—*Startled, Estêvão Santoro instinctively opens his eyes. However, he*
closes them immediately, reluctantly; he can't let the connection break.
Something is coming. Rosa is obviously finding something!

ESTÊVÃO SANTORO (*unable to conceal his excitement*): Yes!
(*Lowering his voice*) And what is the bang from?

ROSA IMACULADA (*cautiously*): The downstairs door . . . ?

Estêvão Santoro swallows and clears his throat. He extracts his
hands from Rosa's, wipes the sweat on his trousers, and then reaches for
Rosa again.

ESTÊVÃO SANTORO: An exhaust pipe. From a motorcycle.

Rosa is untroubled. Door or exhaust pipe, it's irrelevant. She again
squeezes Mr. Santoro's hands, which are slippery with sweat. She feels
as Murilo walks through the door. His walking is noisy, his heels pound-
ing on the floor—he's been drinking more than just water too. Rosa
reels. The bed she's sitting on begins to sway. Murilo grabs the railing of
the winding staircase in the living room and heads upstairs. Murilo
opens his mouth . . .

ROSA IMACULADA: Roses . . . Roses, so many roses . . .

ESTÊVÃO SANTORO: Where?

ROSA IMACULADA: On the windowsill. In the hall. The curtains are
red, scarlet red. An enormous number of white roses are on the
windowsill in three different vases.

ESTÊVÃO SANTORO (*taken aback*): My wife loves flowers . . . I buy
them for her nearly every day . . . And the curtains really are red—

What did I say! What did I say!

—ROSA IMACULADA (*drowsily*): Murilo opens his mouth and shouts,
"Is anyone home?" He looks for his mother, assuming he'll find her
in the kitchen . . . But your wife isn't in the kitchen. Murilo walks out
onto the terrace . . . and sees you. You're sitting in a wicker chair with
your face toward the evening sun.

ESTÊVÃO SANTORO (*squeezing Rosa's hands*): I stand up and greet Murilo. "Hello, son. Where have you been?"

ROSA IMACULADA (*speech slightly unclear*): "I was handling some things."

ESTÊVÃO SANTORO (*suddenly irritated*): "What things, may I ask?"

This sentence is the beginning of Rosa's death. Anger, not her own anger but the overflowing anger toward his father that has been building up in Murilo, wells within her after Estêvão Santoro's annoyed question. The surge of anger is so strong that Polina, Shlomith, and Ulrike also feel it, even though they're watching the scene from another time, another reality, by means of the fragile energy of thought radiated by the Rosa Imaculada floating in the air concentrating on the BOW TIE. However, that transplanted anger doesn't take root in them. Rosa shakes off Mr. Santoro's hands.

ROSA IMACULADA (*shouting*): "Father, I have my own life! And besides, I need a car. I can't haul all my stuff around on a motorcycle. And I'm sick of asking people for rides. And you know it. You're intentionally humiliating me in front of my friends."

ESTÊVÃO SANTORO (*barely controlling his rage*): "Are we going to start this again? Every goddamn time I see you, you pester me about a car. As if you didn't remember we have an agreement! You get a car the same day you—"

ROSA IMACULADA: "Father, why are you blackmailing me? Everyone has a car!"

ESTÊVÃO SANTORO: "YOU GET A CAR THE DAY YOU REGISTER AT THE UNIVERSITY!"

ROSA IMACULADA (*shrinking back on the bed*): "I'm never doing that! (*Waving her arm*) Keep your stupid eucalyptus trees! Aren't you ever going to listen to me? I'm going to make my own choices!"

ESTÊVÃO SANTORO (*face red*): "Not with my money you aren't! If you think I'm going to support you while you (*his voice turns unctuous*) loaf around at your little whore's house (*ends the falsely flattering tone, continues shouting*), YOU'RE WRONG! You're dead wrong!"

ROSA IMACULADA (*suddenly calm, speaks with an icy chill*): "So keep your money. I don't want it. I'm sick of arguing. You'll be dead in five years from a heart attack anyway, unless you start taking it easier. The same thing will happen to you as Maximiliano and Manoel and Fernão. Do you really think I'm going to be a good little boy and get in line for that? What world are you living in?"

Estêvão Santoro's tolerance is finally shattered. His father and grandfather and great-grandfather, whom his son just so casually tossed aside, are his greatest heroes. Over decades their hard work, risk-taking, and constant effort created the Santoro fortune that this ungrateful brat now enjoys—and how! Before it was different. There was respect for previous generations, there was willpower as strong as iron. And above all, there were goals. The story of their family was practically textbook for entrepreneurship. Maximiliano brought massive quantities of raw rubber to the market, which vulcanization turned into gaskets for use between moving parts, like pistons and cylinders. When rubber production moved to Asia, his son, Manoel, bought a eucalyptus plantation and started producing charcoal. His grandson, Fernão, expanded the tree farms, made a foray into pulp production, got spanked, and returned to charcoal. And now the great-grandson, Estêvão himself, patron of the Rio Negro Bridge and the godfather of the mayor's daughter, is doing as they did. He too is always trying something new. Like them, he studies nonstop and carefully follows goings-on in the world. He knows when to strike. Right now he's more up with the times than ever. His bevy of engineers have started refining a metallurgical charcoal from eucalyptus that could solve the climate crisis. His charcoal will be a runaway success in countries participating in carbon emissions trading. He—no, they! All the Santoros!—will be remembered in history as people who solved serious problems facing humanity. Small but extremely important rubber parts in steam engines, affordable paper pulp, and now the future of the planet . . . His son should be excited and filled to bursting with ambition. He is being handed a million-dollar shot and what is he doing? He isn't interested! He wants to spend the rest of his life chasing women! At the expense of the reputation of his father, grandfather, and great-grandfather!

Estêvão Santoro drags himself up out of the wicker chair. His son is mocking him. His son hit him in a tender spot, his health, as if he weren't concerned enough about it himself. He takes medicine, which of course his son knows. He limits his fat intake, and his wife also keeps an eye on the situation. What else can he do? Estêvão Santoro takes a step. What? Is he supposed to start spending his days lolling about too? He slaps his son across the face. Should he abandon their family values too and start acting like money grows on trees? He picks his son up by the front of his shirt and slams him against the wall. A bang. His son's head hits the metal socket of a balcony lamp—

No! Stop!
Help!
No!
Rosa!
Rosa!!!

Rosa Imaculada collapses on the bed, her face against the rosewood rail. Mr. Santoro's vermilion BOW TIE has come undone and lies on the white bedspread next to the rust-colored handkerchief and on top of the glass bottle, which is lying on its side. Mr. Santoro screams. He crawls up next to Rosa, checking her pulse and then shouting even louder. Shlomith, Ulrike, and Polina have opened their eyes; Rosa, the Rosa in the air, is singing. The final lines come in a voice draped in sorrow, slowly and crackling like an old phonograph record: *Musangolá quina quinê . . .*

Goodbye, friend!
Forgive us for doubting, Rosa!
Goodbye! Farewell!

Adeus, Rosa Imaculada!

Published
19/07/2011
EPIFÂNIA RIBEIRO

 Mystery relationship between transplant patient and eucalyptus baron shocks Brazil

STRANGE DREAMS
HAUNT GRANDMOTHER

Authorities are remaining tight-lipped about details surrounding the death of the woman known to readers as **Rosa of the Imaculate Heart**. In the meantime, rumors have been flying concerning the nature of the relationship between Imaculada and multimillionaire, **Estêvão Santoro.**

A single mother living in Salvador de Bahia, Rosa Imaculada received a heart transplant six months ago. The organ donor has been revealed as Santoro's son, who died in a motorcycle accident. "It was a sick obsession," said a close friend of Rosa. "Rosa's own father left when she was small. She was clearly look-

ing for a father figure. Her relationships with men have always been catastrophes."

Super Notícia also interviewed Rosa's grandmother, who firmly believes that black magic played a role in the events. Since Rosa's death, her grandmother has been tormented by the same dream every night. In the dream, she prizes Estêvão Santoro's fingers one by one from Rosa's neck. "I always wake up to sinhó Santoro's fingers flying away. It's a sign. Sinhó Santoro didn't recognize the evil forces raging in his soul."

Rosa Imaculada was found dead one week ago in a hotel room

that Santoro had been renting for the past two months. Santoro's family believed he was in Europe on a business trip. The hotel is located in Pelourinho, the old city of Salvador.

"Since Rosa's death, her grandmother has been tormented by the same dream every night."

Santoro was found badly injured at the base of a cliff in Pelourinho on the Ladeira da Montanha near the Lacerda Lift the day after Rosa's death.

He passed away en route to the hospital.

AS BLUE AS BLUE: A LESSON
IN LOVE

Auf Wiedersehen, Ulrike!

Once upon a time there was a small, sweet 159-centimeter girl, Ulrike of Salzburg, whom everyone loved. Everyone except the Big Bad Adelwolf. He only wanted one thing in the world, the magic ring that Ulrike of Salzburg happened to own. At the beginning of summer, before Ulrike left on a dangerous journey into the magical forests of Germany to seek the treasure of love, her old grandmother took the child's milky-white hands in her own wrinkled grasp. "My dear," the old woman said, "I give you this ring as a gift to mark your entrance into adulthood. It will guide you in difficult situations in your life by changing color. Keep close watch over it. No other ring like this exists. If you lose it, you too shall be lost."

Ulrike of Salzburg then set off. She wandered in the mountains, leaving no stone unturned, walking until her feet blistered and always checking the messages from the ring she had placed on her right ring finger. When the stones of the ring burned black, she knew she was *ängstlich*, anxious. Yellow told of a tense state of mind, *gespannt*, red of restlessness, *unruhig*. Light green meant that she wasn't very stressed, *nicht stressiert*, and dark green revealed a light relaxation, *ein wenig relax*, and dark blue guaranteed that she was very relaxed, *sehr relax*. Ulrike of Salzburg saw all these colors on her ring as she wandered in the mountains, startling at the snaps of twigs, admiring butterflies, staring at wisps of cloud. There was only one color she didn't see, the light blue that proclaimed deep bliss, *sehr glücklich*. But she learned her first lesson: she learned to trust her feelings.

Halfway through her journey, Ulrike met another young girl, Anke-Marie of Berchtesgaden, who invited her into a small lean-to built of pine boughs. Anke-Marie was Ulrike's age but much, much more experienced. "Ulrike of Salzburg, you come from the wide world, but now you have to learn the ways of the woods. I will teach you to make fire, and then together we will eat the hare I caught this morning."

Hare?

What kind of a place is this?

It feels familiar but also strange.

Wait . . . we're in a fairytale!

I'd started working my way down the hillside . . .

Is this your subconscious, Ulrike?

I took five mini bottles with me from the Eagle's Nest . . . Spezialitäten aus den Bergen . . . And I drank them on the way . . . But I don't know anything about this!

Anke-Marie of Berchtesgaden took Ulrike to a birch grove and showed her how to gather tinder fungus. When they had enough of the fungus, they returned to the shelter. Anke-Marie began to dig the leathery hearts out from under the hard crust and pores of the fungi with a knife. Then she submerged the hearts in boiling water full of birch ash and mixed it all together. When the fungi had boiled long enough, she took them out and left them in the sun to dry. "But you can't let the tinder get too dry or you have to wet it down again. It needs to be damp, slightly wet, or it won't cooperate."

Anke-Marie began to club the wet tinder fungus. She clubbed so hard she began to sweat large beads of perspiration which rolled down and stung her eyes until she couldn't see. Then Ulrike said, "Let me do it so you can rest."

Taking turns through the hottest part of the day, they beat the tinder fungus and bathed in sweat. They beat until the fungus gave up, stopped blistering, and became a flat, even disk. After this Anke-Marie took Ulrike by the hand and showed her how to strike a spark with the right amount of force on the right corner of a flint with a steel. Ulrike struck the stone with the steel. She struck many times and was beginning to lose patience because her strength was waning.

Then Anke-Marie came behind her, right up close, took her by the arms, and they struck the stone together. They struck once, twice, three times, and then came the spark, which the tinder fungus trapped. Anke-Marie set the glowing tinder in an abandoned bird's nest, which she had found in the forest, and the dry wood stacked above quickly burst into flames.

This was how Ulrike of Salzburg learned to make fire.

By the time they had dined heartily on the hare they had roasted over the fire and rolled over to sleep on their bed of pine boughs, she had learned her second lesson: she had learned to trust another person.

Early in the morning, as the first rays of sun tickled the ends of the sleeping girls' noses, Ulrike awoke in Anke-Marie's arms and felt wondrously happy. In triumph she raised her right hand to her face and whispered, "Look, light blue!"

The ring in her finger glowed blue, but Anke-Marie didn't look happy. "Ulrike of Salzburg, it is blue, but not light blue. You're relaxed, and that does mean you're happy, but deep bliss, which is also called love, is something you still haven't experienced."

Ulrike turned her gaze to Anke-Marie and, in a slightly weepy voice, said, "I think it's closer to light blue than dark." But Anke-Marie of Berchtesgaden was unyielding. "Dear Ulrike, I know what you're thinking," she whispered to her new friend. "You want to stay here with me because we get along so well. But you have to continue your journey if you want to continue seeking the treasure of love. Otherwise you'll begin to hate me eventually. Come back if you don't find what you seek. I'll be waiting for you here."

The girls cried and kissed each other. The stone on the ring had turned pitch black by the time Ulrike of Salzburg waved goodbye and turned to continue on her way. Her mind full of questions, she climbed the forest path until she finally reached the top of the mountain. There stood a large building made of concrete with a massive brass lion-head knocker bolted to the door.

Ulrike took hold of the knocker: *thunk, thunk, thunk.* The ring burned yellow and red in turn. After only a few seconds, the door opened. Behind it stood a hunched, frightening-looking man, who said, "Good day, Ulrike of Salzburg. Please, come in."

Ulrike was shocked, but she stepped into the dimly lit room because she didn't know what else to do. Elders were to be obeyed, her grandmother had taught her long ago, and the Adelwolf was obviously older than her. His ears were large and hairy, and his hands were enormous and completely covered in dark fur. His mouth was as immense as an ocean ship, and his eyes gaped like a giant's dinner plates under his jagged bangs. His right pupil moved actively, while the left was glazed in place.

"I have venison stew to offer, and I'm sure you're hungry since you've walked such a long way. Might we share a meal?" the Adelwolf suggested. Ulrike agreed, because she was ravenously hungry.

As they ate, Ulrike noticed that the Adelwolf's right eye repeatedly glanced at the finger on her right hand where she wore her handsome ring. The stone was red now, and the Adelwolf asked, "Ulrike of Salzburg, why are you restless?"

Ulrike of Salzburg was so embarrassed she was speechless. The red of the ring deepened. Then the Adelwolf said, "Here, let me try the ring. It should fit on my pinkie. Let's see what kind of mood *I'm* in right now!"

Ulrike was startled at this, and the ring turned black. How could the Adelwolf know the secret of the ring? And what should she do now? Grandmother had made her promise to keep good care of it, but Grandmother had also instructed her to obey her elders. What if the Adelwolf wouldn't give the ring back to her? Then she would be ruined!

Fortunately the ring made the decision for Ulrike: it refused to leave her finger. Ulrike turned it many times, but the ring wouldn't budge above her joint.

Then the Adelwolf lost his temper. Taking her by the hand, he dragged the struggling girl to the water tap. He scrubbed the ring with soap and held the finger under cold water, but the ring wouldn't move.

The Adelwolf changed tactics. Taking the sobbing Ulrike in his arms, he sat on a wooden stool and rocked her gently. "Forgive me, Ulrike. I lost my composure because I wanted to try the magic ring so badly. I have my own secret power as well. I can change any other person's state of mind—but only if they have your ring on their finger."

After this the Adelwolf made Ulrike a curious proposal. "What if we lived together? With your ring and my magical powers, we could eventually rule the world. We could make everyone want what we want them to want. Every person in the world would be under our control!" The Adelwolf stroked Ulrike's back, which was damp with sweat, and kissed her earlobe. "Please take the night to consider my offer, Ulrike. We can discuss it more in the morning. I'll make you toast, marmalade, and scrambled eggs for breakfast."

Suddenly the Adelwolf nipped Ulrike's ear so hard that she yelped in pain. "I've made a place for you in the bed next to me," he growled. "The pillows and blankets are pure down. I promise that you'll sleep more sweetly than ever in your life!"

Ulrike's ring was a blinding yellow as she lay down next to the Adelwolf. It glowed so yellow that neither could sleep, even though the bed was softer than any other bed in the world. It was as if the sun had set in the bed between them, a burning disk of fire whose cruel light hurt them both equally.

"Adelwolf," Ulrike whispered once the blanket was soaked through with sweat and the pillows were waterlogged under their damp hair. "Should I go sleep outside? Perhaps the ring will calm down and then we can both finally get some rest."

To this day no one knows what got into the Adelwolf at that point. Had he lied to Ulrike of Salzburg from the beginning when he suggested working together? Or had the radiating yellow light of the ring exhausted him and he suddenly changed his mind? Perhaps he was worried about the possibility of the girl escaping if he let her outside to sleep alone.

The Adelwolf rose to his knees in the bed and let out a deep, low snarl. With his great hairy paws he took Ulrike by the neck and began to squeeze. At the same time he pushed her legs apart with his knees and pushed in where he had no right to be. The ring had known from the beginning: the whole time it had been red, yellow, black . . . red, black . . .

°
°

Whose hand is that?
  Where are we now?
  Ulrike, where are you?
  I can't see anything.
Hands. And a girl under the hands. Shlomith, Polina, and Ulrike float in a position from which it is impossible to determine location, direction, or even orientation; only one hand is visible, so close that it's barely recognizable as a hand: four, thick fingers squeezing, on one a gold ring, also thick, worn, and dull.
  No, not Hanno.
  That isn't the hand of a young man.
  That hand is doing evil.
  That hand is strangling a neck.
  It isn't hard to guess.
  No.
And that is exactly what happens. The hands conduct their brutal work because the girl happened to be there, on the forest road, a little drunk, a little lost.
  The hands, but not just the hands.
  The knees also do evil, keeping the girl's legs spread wide to make it easier to get inside, to make it easier to ram in the member that is stiff for once, since for once there is something living and beautiful underneath, something so bloody beautiful it hurts.

The girl didn't conceal anything. She walked the forest road in her yellow bra, black shirt wrapped around her hair in a turban. She didn't even flinch when he drove up in his big rig, rolled down the passenger window, and yelled, "Are you hot?"

It was as if the girl spread her breasts even wider, enjoying the warmth and the attention, as if she coquettishly shouted back, "Yeah, I am a bit hot!"

He decided to take a chance. He cast the girl a wink and said, "I've got air conditioning in here. You want a ride?" He was certain she'd refuse. But instead she said, "Sure, why not! Can I take a nap? You have a bed in the back, right? I'm tired."

The girl quickly scrambled into the cab. "You've ridden in a truck before, haven't you," the man asked, trying to dispel his own confusion. "Yeah," the girl said and sat down in the passenger seat. Pushed up by her bra, her small breasts glistened with sweat.

Suddenly she leaned forward. Her navel disappeared in the folds of her bare belly, and her shoulders almost touched the fan. The girl undid her turban, and wet, dark hair cascaded down her back in loose curls. Then she shook her head in front of the fan as if using a blow drier. "Where are you hauling that wood?" she asked. "Why is this forest being chopped down?"

That was enough. The girl was there, and everything was ready. Her back was pretty and white. The lace bra made an indecent yellow arc in her narrow back.

"Hey, what the FUCK are you doing?!"

The man quickly removed his hand. The girl was hot, so hot! Her body sprang upright, her belly flattened, and her hair followed the arcing motion. Then the girl pulled on her wrinkled T-shirt and began to crawl into the rear of the cab. "Let me sleep for a minute," the girl whispered and nestled under the blanket. In his truck.

The crazy girl really was going to take a little nap in his truck.

The crazy girl just curled up like a shrimp, fuck you very much. In his truck.

Now I see!
   Me too.
   Where are we?
   On the ceiling of some sort of small room.
   And that guy . . .

Is assaulting me with his trousers around his ankles.
Ulrike! Doesn't this shock you at all?
What?
That you're being raped . . . and murdered!
But I don't feel anything.
Now?
Not now. And not then. I put my head on the pillow, and then the guy came after me and started ripping my trousers off.
And?
And what?
And that's it?
And that's it.
But he's strangling you!
I remember that I thrashed. I tried to get out from under, but he knelt on my thighs.
I can see your legs behind his back.
I imagine it did hurt then.
Of course it hurt!
Maybe you lost consciousness quickly?
Maybe you just don't remember?
Maybe you were traumatized. Traumatic amnesia. A hole in your memory.

Ulrike's face is hidden behind the man. There, under the man, Ulrike opens her mouth and screams noiselessly. Her head can't move. Her flaming red head. The man can't stand to watch. He begins to come. He snatches the pillow from under Ulrike's head. He puts it over her face and presses with all his might. His lower body works even faster as Ulrike's arms and legs thrash powerlessly under the weight of the man's knees. The man lasts. The orgasm begins to hum in his lower body, to gather strength. Jerks, thrusts, pauses. Thrusts. Thrusts.

Ulrike has stopped moving.
I have to go now.
That's how it looks.
Horrible to happen this way.

Is anyone better off?
An end is an end.
So it wasn't Ulrich with the glass eye.
Who?
Oh, forget it. I'll tell you if we ever meet again, Shlomith and Polina.
The Ulrike floating on the ceiling of the cab like a helium balloon sinks onto the man who has finished his sawing, who lies on top of her and weeps. Ulrike slips through him until she reaches her fading self, sliding into her final breaths as effortlessly as water through gauze.
Goodbye, Ulrike!
Goodbye, goodbye, beautiful Ulrike!

Auf Wiedersehen, Ulrike!

𝕾𝖆𝖑𝖟𝖇𝖚𝖗𝖌𝖊𝖗 𝕹𝖆𝖈𝖍𝖗𝖎𝖈𝖍𝖙𝖊𝖓

Elke Pfeifenberger | Saturday 26.10.2013 – 21:03 | Updated: 4 hours ago | Comments (4)

Kehlstein sex murderer gets life

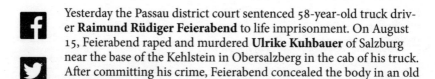

Yesterday the Passau district court sentenced 58-year-old truck driver **Raimund Rüdiger Feierabend** to life imprisonment. On August 15, Feierabend raped and murdered **Ulrike Kuhbauer** of Salzburg near the base of the Kehlstein in Obersalzberg in the cab of his truck. After committing his crime, Feierabend concealed the body in an old storage barn nearby.

Kuhbauer, 17, was returning from her job at the Eagle's Nest restaurant in the evening when she was brutally attacked. The teenager left work around 6 p.m., walking down a path toward Berchtesgaden, but she never arrived at the bus station. The police focused their search along the hiking path. Kuhbauer's body was found in an abandoned barn one week after her disappearance.

Despite international reporting, this shocking sex crime hasn't made a dent in Obersalzberg tourism. "We've actually had a few murder tourists, as they're called," said Eagle's Nest restaurant manager **Wenzel Feiersinger**. "They talk about the killing while they're here, and some even ask the staff for more details."

The restaurant begins its seasonal closure at the end of October and reopens in early May. "We all hope the situation will have calmed down by the time the summer season begins. Kuhbauer was a very well-liked employee. We can't go on talking about this tragedy with complete strangers."

Comments (4)

Senta 26.10.2013 21:26	Condolences to the family in their time of grief. Thankfully the killer got a stiff sentence! **Reply**
Scheiße_Geist 26.10.2013 21:45	Free business idea for Herr Feiersinger: Ulrike T-shirt. Yodeling Ulrike doll. Ulrike schnapps. Ulrike magnetic button. **Reply**

Bella Rossa 26.10.2013 21:52	Have some common decency! That's the most offensive thing I've ever heard.

Reply

Wahrheit & Feuer 26.10.2013 22:27	You don't know it, but this is just the beginning. DYING IS GOD'S REVENGE!!! No one ever should have opened that sinful place. The battle of the great day of God Almighty will be upon us soon. Read the Bible. Jesus says, "He that believeth on the Son hath everlasting life: and he that believeth not the Son shall not see life; but the wrath of God abideth on him." (John 3:36)

Reply

WHITE: A NEW SURVEY OF DIVINE LOVE

До свидания, Полина!

Now Shlomith and Polina are alone. Polina and Shlomith. One and one. Face to face. Thoughts to thoughts. One heavy thought facing them both: the following death will also be death for the one left behind.

That thought is etched identically in both of their minds, hard as flint. Shlomith or Polina? Where did it start? Maybe there's no difference. There is only Shlomith. And Polina. Facing, united, agreed. Harmony shot through by one shared, leaden knowledge: next comes death.

No more crisscrossing, conflicting thoughts, questions, interjections, or new beginnings. No disbelief, which had always been present somewhere, in some consciousness beneath consciousness, a silent yet gnawing corrosion: Has all of this been an illusion, *my illusion*, the voices my own, the thoughts from my own mind?

Shlomith and Polina look at each other. Translucent bodies, like jellyfish floating in slow motion in the air. Polina's amoeba-like rotundity. Shlomith's outlined, bony frailty. And then: a gaze. Then eyes.

Polina.

What, Shlomith?

So this is how it ends.

One leaves, the other stays.

Alone.

Alone.

It isn't enough that both of them know it. Just the same they have to think it through together, because that's still possible. They have to drag the thought forward like a boat with alternating oar pulls: one and one is the same as death, including the death of the one left behind.

Shlomith.

What, Polina?

It's my turn.

I know.

But where am I?

Yes. Where are you?

The space is empty. Above stretches a night sky tinged dirty yellow by the lights of Moscow; below, a white blanket of freshly fallen snow. Shlomith and Polina do not release each other's gazes, but they wait, they listen.

Then somewhere a door opens. A creak, a slam: a clump of people tumbles out of the darkness into the yard. The sound makes the door and the wall around the door, the wall makes the building, and the space receives form: they are in the back courtyard of the Zlom theater center. The figures also begin to take shape. Three men, four women. Three of the women walk arm in arm, one man and one woman hand in hand, and two of the men sing. They approach.

Do you know them?

That's Jura . . . And Maruska and Serjoža. And Irina and Zina and Ženja. And Oleg.

So you know them.

Unfortunately.

The tune is familiar . . .

Jura and Oleg are singing a song named "Katyusha". It tells about the Second World War. About a girl longing for her lover on the front.

I know that song too! We sang it in Hebrew at the kibbutz. "The pears and apples were in bloom . . ."

*That's how the song starts. It's a sentimental, nationalistic song. All
Russians love it.*

Including you?

Including me.

Slightly inebriated, Polina's coworkers walk unsteadily, Serjoža as
always seeming to move in Maruska's wake. But there's no sign of
Polina. Silence falls. The laughing people disappear into taxis taking
them to bars or their homes. Maybe to strange beds. Maybe to their
own.

Polina . . . Have you ever wondered why us?

You and me?

No, all seven of us. Why us specifically?

*I don't know, but I'm sure we aren't the only ones. It would be pretty
arrogant to think that this strange fate only befell the seven of us.*

*But where are all the others? Where are the men? Where are the
children? Why didn't we find anyone after Ulrike?*

Maybe our group was full.

Full from whose perspective?

*How would I know? Maybe there isn't any reason it was us. We were
just thrown together. Randomly.*

But who did the throwing?

No one. I was speaking metaphorically.

You don't believe in God?

Not any more.

Somewhere underneath, down where all the most obscure mental
swellings tend to hide, a space gradually begins to grow, thought
upon thought: a vacuum where a certain familiar, but purposefully
forgotten, image might insidiously re-emerge.

Too bad my mother can't see me now.

*Out of all the people in the world, Shlomith, your mother is the one
you wish could see you?*

She's dead. But yes. I'd like to see her expression now.

*I don't have any trouble imagining my mother's expression. It would
be the same sort of incredulous dismay as when she died.*

My mother died expressionlessly. In her own bed.

Was it a beautiful death?

Not really. At the end she was so full of anger.

I wish Maruska and Serjoža could have seen me a moment ago. It would have given them something to think about.

You have something stuck in your craw?

Oh so many things! Serjoža thinks he knows everything. And Maruska is an idiot.

As if by mutual agreement, Shlomith and Polina release each other's gaze and glance around. Had there been motion somewhere on the periphery of their vision? Would Serjoža and Maruska return to look for Polina? Would Irina, Zina, and Ženja call her by name? Would Jura and Oleg appear and cry, "Forgive us, Polina!"

But the yard, surrounded by piles of snow, is still empty.

Polina, I don't think you're coming.

Seems that way. I don't understand why we're here if I'm not, though.

Maybe you are. Maybe we just haven't noticed you.

But where could I be?

Do you remember when you described your final memories? You talked about warmth.

Then it's clear we're in the wrong place!

But you came to the whiteness wearing a sable coat.

And only one boot.

Polina, we just have to go looking for you.

Polina and Shlomith close their eyes as they had done following Rosa Imaculada, so nothing visible would disturb them. The only place Polina can think about now, the place where she herself might be, is Zlom, the back room of Zlom, where the employees sometimes spent the evening.

Polina begins guiding them with determination toward the red painted back door. In her mind she sees the familiar rusty lock that only works if the door is given a swift kick. In her mind she hears the familiar squeak; no one ever oils the hinges. Then they're on the other side. A tattered corner sofa marked with cigarette burns. A large, shabby, plush rug that's collected splashes of this and that over the years on its oriental design. Empty bottles and full ashtrays litter the floor. Along with her fur-trimmed handbag.

She's been in this room.

And then it comes, the first sentence, a familiar purring voice and an accusation like a lightning bolt: "Polina, you're drinking too fast." Out of nowhere, just as she's beginning to relax, beginning to forget her fear. "Polina, you drink too much." Just as she's gathered her strength to talk about a serious issue that has been bothering her for some time. "Don't you think so, Serjoža?" The symmetrical nostrils tremble. "You drink like a Russian man, Polina."

She doesn't lap at her champagne like Irina, and she doesn't forget her glass on the table like Ženja, who has such a compulsion to needle and taunt people that she doesn't have time to drink. She doesn't pour herself glass after glass of wine and lemon soda like Zina, or sip prettily from her own glass whenever she remembers, like Maruska, who instead of drinking is always filling other's glasses—until she suddenly pipes up and says, "I apologize if this question feels intrusive, Polina, but Serjoža and I have been wondering about this together. I guess we can say it out loud now?" Serjoža nods, his large protruding ears wagging. "I've also talked to Irina and Oleg about this. We're all a little worried about you, Polina."

Then Zina raises a finger. "Maruska, come on!" Zina's face is red with irritation. "This is my going-away party!" Angrily she looks at Maruska and for some reason starts stuttering for the first time in ages. "Couldn't we t-t-talk . . . about this some other t-t-t-time?"

But Polina has no intention of talking about this anytime. Staggering, she stands and flamboyantly takes her sable fur coat from the back of the couch and pulls it on. Striding to the door, she yanks on the knob, yanking and kicking and almost falling with the opening door into the yard. The door then groans and crashes shut.

The courtyard is large, and the gate is a fair distance away. There's a shortcut across the piles of snow. Polina decides to take the shortest path. She speeds up and launches into the nearest drift. The snow is surprisingly deep. Polina sinks to her knees and continues by crawling . . . Her left boot sticks and slides off . . . Polina doesn't notice and continues on . . .

Oh no, Polina. There you are. In the snow.

How do we get there?! I have to get there in time!

Think of the warmth you talked about. Think of the warmth that came over you. Think of the bright, divine light. Try to remember that!

I only see snow and darkness . . .

You've opened your eyes! Close them. Now.

The Polina in the air closes her eyes, and soon they both start to hear a rustling as the hems of the heavy, sable coat rub against the snow. Sweating in the coat, Polina struggles forward, over the snow bank, scooping the snow with her hands, churning with her knees. Rustling, groaning, groaning, rustling, until finally, after an interminably long time, she reaches the top of the snow pile. Panting, she stands and raises her right hand in a sign of triumph.

Then she falls. She falls completely inside the pile of snow as if plunging into water.

Dear God.

How is that possible?

Inside, deep inside, is an abandoned snow fort. A hollow space into which Polina slips, straight-legged, as tightly as a knife into a sheath. Behind her she pulls more snow, which seals the opening and edges and fills the cavities caused by the fall. Polina is completely and utterly stuck. When she tries to move, her body only drills more firmly into the blanket of snow.

For a moment, just for a fleeting moment, the situation amuses Polina.

Then she realizes that she can't laugh.

She opens her mouth and tries to scream. Of course her voice doesn't carry at all. She is surrounded by plowed, hard, stratified snow, three hundred kilograms per square meter; no sound can get through that. Polina's cry stops cold at the wall of snow touching her face.

Polina tries to move one more time. She struggles, thrusting her stuck arms upwards. They don't budge even a centimeter. The toes inside her remaining boot wiggle when she moves them, but her bootless foot is already numb with cold. Her knee won't move. Her head won't turn. Polina begins to tire. Her breathing slows, and the air she blows out now is already cool. The snow her warm breath has melted in front of her mouth begins to freeze.

The Polina in the air speeds up. Her jelly body contracts and expands in pulses as she attempts to pump herself full of explosive energy. She has to get to where she is! To where she will still be breathing for a few more seconds . . . Polina tumbles forward rapidly toward the snow bank but rebounds like a soft ball.

Polina, stop!

Shlomith! Help! I can't get into the snow!

Calm down! You're just wasting time!

What can I do?!

I'm going to say this for the third and final time: think of warmth. Think of bright, yellow light.

How will that help? That was Maimuna's death in the desert. I'm dying in freezing snow!

Polina Yurievna Solovyeva: stop doubting! Believe me, and believe your own memories. You died experiencing divine love. You said so yourself! How did it go in Russian?

Divine love?

Exactly.

Божественная Любовь.

Well now. Think of that. Think of this: you're in the cold snow, but you feel warmth and you see light. You're losing consciousness, and you can't feel your extremities any more. There are no fingers, no arms, no toes, no calves, no thighs. Nothing you could use to move. To push. To kick. Only the pulsating center part . . .

BooŽEStvennaya LjuBOF . . . BooŽEStvennaya LjuBOF . . .

You feel a tingling that isn't located in any specific place . . . Polina, I sense it! I feel the throbbing: the throbbing of your heart! Do you feel it?!

Shlomith, I can't feel it! I still can't feel it!

Try again: say "BooŽEStvennaya LjuBOF!" Say it over and over. Say it! Say it now!

BooŽEStvennaya LjuBOF . . . BooŽEStvennaya LjuBOF . . . BooŽEStvennaya LjuBOF . . .

Polina, listen. The tingling is everywhere. Not in your limbs, not even on your skin. "Skin", "head", "limbs", "index fingers", "little toes" . . . these don't exist any more. You are one with the universe. You see a bright light even though your eyes are closed. The light calls to you. It's a promise of warmth like down . . . no hardness . . . nothing hard ever again . . . no bruises . . .

No hardness . . . no bruises . . .

You feel no fear. All your fears have melted in the warmth. You're full of trust. You don't have to fight any more, Polina. There's only love. You can submit!

Shlomith's coaxing, clearly delineated, even commanding thoughts begin to bear fruit. Suddenly before them is a whiteness, a pure whiteness. Whiteness like a silver screen full of light that the projector might fill with pictures at any moment. They feel themselves moving forward. They move through the white. They pass small bits of trash, cigarette butts, and branches broken from trees. They pass a small shovel buried in the snow, a red one that might have been used to finish the arch of the cave. A weak, barely audible thumping guides them: *tu-tum, tu-tum, tu-tum.* A heart in the bowels of the cave. The closer the beating takes them, the more powerfully the whiteness begins to tremble, until they arrive as if entering the center of a buckskin drum. On one side of the drumskin waits Polina, whose strength is fading, the Polina who can't get oxygen any more because a frigid crust has formed in front of her mouth.

I see lips!

I see them too!

Lips through the ice!

I see a face! A nose!

It's you!

Then Polina's heart stops beating. Complete silence. No more vibration of the drum head.

I can't move any more.

Try to push through the crust somehow!

I can't.

Sometimes the impossible stays impossible. Polina's strength of will is no weaker than the others'—she has simply arrived too late, and tardiness has consequences. The lips visible through the crust of ice begin to fade, the face begins to lose its shape, and the nose and eyes disappear by degrees.

Shlomith.

What?

I don't believe this any more.

What?

I see white.

I see white too!

No. I see a different white. The white where we were before.

You can't be serious.

I am.

How do you know it's that white and not this white?

Guess.

It doesn't pulse?

No, it doesn't pulse. Does the white where you are pulse?

No, not any more.

Well, go on and guess. How do I know that I'm there again?

Does it feel different?

I don't feel anything.

So tell me already! I don't know!

There's something here.

Someone's there?

Yes.

I can't see anything.

I guessed as much.

Far in the distance Polina sees a heap that is undeniably human: a small, dark-haired child. When Polina squints hard, she thinks she can tell that the heap is a girl and that the girl is wearing a red dress with white circles. The girl has started to draw Polina toward her. Closer, tugging and tugging, because the girl needs help. The girl won't survive without her.

Polina, what's happening now?

But Shlomith's cry doesn't reach where Polina is, far from the snow, far from Shlomith. The farther Polina goes, the faster her jellyfish body begins to change, begins to return to the way it was, begins to become more determinate and full. It is as if someone decided to splatter color inside the weak outlines, Polina's own creamy white and slightly atopic skin, and vivid red lips. All the receding details rise to the fore and take on their natural shades again: the areolae their pinkish beige, the crimped hair its mahogany brown. Varicose veins bulge from her shins and begin to turn blue. Lumps of fat appear on her ample belly, and a straight navel squished by the lumps slides into place like a slice of a knife.

The closer Polina comes to the girl, the more dreamlike her previous memories of the seven of them become. Shlomith, Maimuna, Wlibgis, Ulrike, Rosa Imaculada, and Nina with her pregnant belly cease to exist. The places Polina has visited to see off her otherworldly sisters, the half-worldly spaces, are wiped away and disappear.

Shlomith sees her friend receding from her and can do nothing. The Polina in the snow bank is as dead as a stone, and the rippling jellyfish Polina missed her death and must therefore return.

All that remains is the snow, the body, and Shlomith who has to continue on her own, who whispers into the emptiness, perhaps more to herself than to anyone:

Farewell, Polina.

До свидания, Полина! Мы еще встретимся!

The Moscow Central Agency for the Dramatic Arts
(ZLOM) seeks a

HEAD ACCOUNTANT

for full-time employment directing the
company's financial affairs.
More information about the position can be
obtained from Zlom director of finance Stepan
Kuznetsov. Inquiries by phone 8.495.723-05-95
(weekdays before 1 p.m.).

SEND YOUR WRITTEN APPLICATION BY 15.5.2005 TO:
MOSCOW CENTRAL AGENCY FOR THE DRAMATIC ARTS (ZLOM),
MARKSISTSKI PEREULOK 9, 101000 MOSCOW

GZ-567/2

BLACK: THE WAY OUT

Shlomith, farewell!

I felt it the moment the applause ended, although I didn't immediately understand what it was. It was you, hunger. You wanted to cancel our agreement.

Just a moment ago I thought I was part of something greater than myself. Then my presentation ended. I began to cry, which was a surprise to everyone including me. For a moment I felt as if I was crying for all the sorrows of the world, mine and yours. Then it was over. The invisible curtain between me and the world closed again, and I was left alone.

You kept me alive for so long. I'm thankful for that, of course. Without life there is nothing, and nothing really is nothing. This can be difficult to understand, but that's just how it is: without you, hunger, I wouldn't have existed for so long. You helped me carry on.

If I could still feel sorrow, I might be sad for you. You gave me your all, you fought by my side, but as soon as the task was complete, I was ready to abandon you. *There's only one way out: surrender, healing, and enlightenment.* That was what I had claimed a moment ago.

My assistant, Katie McKeen, quietly stole up and draped a loose black caftan over me so I wouldn't catch cold. I'll never cease to admire how considerate she is, and the way she blends that with an energetic, irrepressible, and brisk yet discrete practicality. Katie can clothe a naked person just like that, with everyone watching, without calling any attention to herself. Still she doesn't treat me like a mannequin in a display window. She bears the caftan before me like a fine tablecloth, shakes the tentlike garment open, and gently passes it over my head. She pulls my trembling arms through the sleeves and looks me in the eyes. I nod: Thank you, Katie. She slips my feet into downy soft slippers, pats me encouragingly on the shoulder, and retreats behind the curtain to wait.

I have drained myself to the point of death in order to reach the heart of it all.

For the past forty-five minutes, I've uttered statements that half of me sincerely believes. That's no small deal. Some people spend their entire lives saying whatever crosses their minds. I, on the other hand, have had the opportunity to take the measure of my thoughts and deeds. That's why I can endure half of me protesting and shouting, "Stop, you idiot! Get down off that stage!"

Did this come as a surprise to you? Why is it so difficult for you to understand that everything, *absolutely everything*, is subject to suspicion as long as there is life, and still a person can be one hundred percent serious, one hundred percent in love, one hundred percent faithful?

We can cancel our agreement, I can accept that. But give me one more moment. I want to say my goodbyes in peace.

I would say: I love you, Katie McKeen. If I could, that's what I'd say. My faithful assistant, my servant. I didn't receive warmth like that from anywhere else during the final years of my life.

I would also say: I love you, Moti and Malka. That will never change.

I would say: Mother, I love you too. Almost all mothers can be loved, and you weren't even close to the most difficult.

I say:

Farewell, Maimuna!

Farewell, Nina!

Wlibgis, you who left in anger, farewell!

Rosa, Rosa the forerunner, farewell!

Goodbye, Ulrike!

Farewell, Polina!

We were quite the madcap group, weren't we? We were fiercer than the legions of death! If I could feel anything, I'm sure I'd feel longing. Pure, numinous longing mingled with no shade of darkness or involuntary renunciation.

Now I'm ready. Thank you for your patience. Let's get going. Don't delay. If I can still hope for anything it's only that this won't take long . . .

Oh—was that it?

Just a thump in the pit of my stomach: I wouldn't even really call it pain . . .

I'm sitting on a wooden stool. On a red cushion. I look myself in the eyes. I can see that I'm already looking through everything; I see that I don't see anything any more. Viewed from a distance, for a few more seconds it still seems as if I'm ready to accept hugs and sign autographs.

I hear the rustling. People have organized themselves in a line. Katie McKeen notices something now and takes a step.

There's only one way . . .

My eyes snap wide. My mouth opens. I jerk, then slump. I don't have time to fall off the stool because Katie's hands catch me. Katie and a man with the look of a marathoner who has appeared next to her, lower me to the floor. The man begins CPR, and Katie talks into a radio, giving instructions.

The noise and commotion in the hall begin instantly. The whole goddamn circus we've practiced so many times, just in case, swings into motion. From the beginning this has been obvious to everyone, including me: my body won't necessarily hold out to the end.

Katie McKeen is golden and quick despite the panic.

All the people are fast, as if driven by the lash.

If I could, I'd say: Calm down. I'm dead.

Shlomith, farewell!

The New York Times

NEW YORK, AUGUST 22, 2007

Hunger Wins Out Over Art

Controversial performance artist Shlomith-Shkhina leaves behind a legacy of contradictions

SUZANNE LEBLANC

Performance artist SHEILA RUTH BERKOWITZ, better known by her stage name Shlomith-Shkhina, succumbed to anorexia on August 16 at the age of 61. Unique to the case is that she died before an audience in the Scheuer Auditorium at the Jewish Museum at the conclusion of her lecture performance on connections between anorexia and Judaism. At her death, Berkowitz weighed 62 pounds.

The technical cause of death appears to be heart failure. Although Berkowitz was quickly transported to a hospital, she could not be saved due to the poor health of her internal organs. Preliminary autopsy results reveal that Berkowitz's heart weighed half that which it should have weighed.

Sheila Berkowitz was born in New York in 1946 and spent her childhood and teenage years in Brooklyn. Prior to her main artistic career, she played drums in a Fluxus-inspired band named Entropy.

In 1967 Berkowitz married a Polish Jew, DOVID NIEWIAROWSKI. The couple soon moved to Israel to live on a kibbutz named Methuselah and had two children.

Seven years later, in 1974, Berkowitz divorced her husband. She returned to New York and began her career as a performance artist.

Berkowitz adopted the combination Shlomith-Shkhina as her stage name. "Shlomith" derives from the Hebrew word *shalom* (שלום), meaning peace, which also indicates perfection, welfare, and prosperity. "Shkhina" (שכינה), on the other hand, has reference in Judaism to the feminine aspect of God, the presence of God.

According to Jewish art specialist EVE KRONENBERG, this name evokes the idea that even God is not free from suffering. In the Talmud, the spirit of Shkhina is described as suffering along with her chosen people:

Whenever Israel went into exile, the Shkhina [God's presence] went along into exile. They went to exile to Egypt, the Shkhina went with them ... They went to Babylon in exile, and the Shkhina went with them . . . And when they will eventually be redeemed, the Shkhina will be redeemed along with them.

"The name Shlomith-Shkhina contains internal contradictions, and it also contradicts the content of Berkowitz's art," observes Kronenberg. "Of course this is intentional. Berkowitz's work drew its power from unresolved ambivalence."

———

Berkowitz intentionally exposed herself to malicious attention and criticism, which was often uncommonly aggressive. Religious circles considered Berkowitz's performances profane, while many in the art community saw her breaking of taboos as cheap attention-seeking.

"She's found the perfect recipe for getting publicity," said one anonymous New York art critic in 2004 while the founding members of the New York Feminist Art Institute, MIRIAM SCHAPIRO and CAROL STRONGHILOS, were curating a 30-year retrospective on Berkowitz's art at the Brooklyn Museum.

———

As early as 1976, in her work *Food Meditation*, the future trademarks of Berkowitz's art were visible: Jewish culture, in this case kosher rules, and a very personal, physical style.

In most of her performances, Berkowitz was naked or scantily clothed. She did not shy away from pain, whether emotional or physical.

All of these elements combined in her breakthrough 1979 work *I Shall Fear No Evil for Thou Art with Me*, in which the role of the audience was to demean the naked artist by reading anti-Semitic comments to her after choosing them blindly from a wicker basket.

"I still have the slip of paper I fished out of that basket," says the French performance artist ORLAN (b. 1947). "It was an excerpt from Hitler's Gemlich letter from 1919. I was also asked to pin a *Judensau* under Shlomith's left collarbone. I'm used to pain as an element of art, but I've never experienced the sort of unease that piece aroused in me then."

———

Prior to her fateful final performance, Berkowitz's most controversial work was the *The 614th Commandment* (1983). The basis for the piece was a thought experiment suggested by the Jewish Canadian philosopher EMIL FACKENHEIM (1916–2003).

The Torah contains 613 commandments and prohibitions, but Fackenheim developed a 614th commandment while attempting to find a theological explanation for the holocaust. According to the new commandment, "the authentic Jew of today is forbidden to hand Hitler yet another, posthumous victory."

For Fackenheim, fulfilling the

614th commandment meant protecting the Jewish identity, i.e. promoting marriage between Jews and separation from other cultures. In her performance, Berkowitz turned this arrangement on its head. She read aloud quotations from Jewish thinkers who explained the holocaust as the fulfillment of God's will.

"This if anything is a victory for the anti-Semitic mindset," Berkowitz said in a *Times* interview in October, 1983. "Any attempt at finding a theological explanation for genocide is a dead end. God was absent then, and God is absent now. There is no God. There is only a flood of increasingly complicated explanations that don't serve anyone."

In recent decades, feminist artists have mostly focused on mapping out and publicizing their own internal spaces. Female desire and sexuality, gender roles, body image, and corporeality have received ample study.

"A certain ironic double exposure and postmodern theoretical machinery have pervaded most performances," says performance art researcher NADIA KREIGHBAUM. As an example she cites ANNIE SPRINKLE'S classic performance *Post Porn Modernism* (1989), in which Sprinkle urinated on the stage and inserted a speculum in her vagina, among other things.

But, according to Kreighbaum, Berkowitz's works completely lack any ironic or erotic dimension. "Despite their strong physicality, they're very literary works, since they're based on the Book and interpretations of the Book. They deconstruct not only the word but also flesh. This was confirmed in tragic fashion in her final performance."

Shlomith-Shkhina's final performance, with its shocking ending, casts her entire career in a new light. Did her art refine her disease, or was it the other way round?

Performance artist MARINA ABRAMOVIČ (b. 1946) sees Berkowitz's final presentation exclusively as an apologia for anorexia. "You can use art to try to sanctify anything. We have to be honest. I think Berkowitz hadn't thought this performance all the way through."

Questions will continue, though. Did Berkowitz's death make her a martyr? If it did, is she a martyr for the Jewish religion, western culture, or art? Whatever the case, there's no doubt the performance that led to Berkowitz's death, which literally incarnated an artistic idea, will become one of the macabre classics of her field. Furthermore, what influence will it have on artists who draw their inspiration from suffering and destruction?

It may be too soon to answer these questions, but not for much longer. The Sean Kelly Gallery, which specializes in concept and performance art, is organizing a symposium on September 15 entitled "Destructive Art in a Destructive Society." The event is open to the public.

Contents

I

II

ACKNOWLEDGMENTS

The help I received from others during the writing of *Oneiron* was indispensable. Teemu Manninen wrote Polina's hypothetical ode (p. 173–174). Rami Saari translated Shlomith's letter into Hebrew (p. 223–224), and he and Riikka Tuori spared no effort helping me with questions related to Jewish culture and the Hebrew language. Joel and Ekaterina Geronik hosted me in Moscow and served not only as tour guides for the city but also the Russian mentality. For questions about the Russian language, I've frequently bothered Tintti Klapuri. Shlomith's New York took shape after two weeks I spent in the home of Monique Truog and Damijan Sacchio. In addition to Monique and Damijan, Alison Smith shared details about the Hasidic culture of Borough Park that fed my imagination. Monique checked and refined my English phrasing. Jouni Kaipia taught me everything I know about West African architecture. I spent two unforgettable months at Villa Karo in Grand-Popo, Benin, in 2009–2010. The Autio Funeral Home provided information about burials. Anna Ripatti corrected a ridiculous misconception. Lieven Ameel corrected my nonexistent Dutch. Kari-Pekka Pöykkö helped with the Wolof phrases. Satu Taskinen taught me that what happens on the mountain, stays on the mountain. At a critical moment Judith Schalansky gave this gentle but strict command: "Now forget everything else and write." Monica Vasku Machado gave Rosa Imaculada an authentic voice in *The Heart of Rosa Imaculada* (2013), a performance combining language, text, and heart sounds; thank you for the dancing, Auri Ahola, Valtteri Raekallio, and the rest of the Runovaara group! I consulted Timo

Suonsyrjä on a number of medical questions. Reijo Aulanko explained how fricatives work. Markku Eskelinen, Kristiina Sarasti, Sinikka Vuola, and my mother read the manuscript and all supported me in every way during this long process. Special thanks to Sinikka for her precise linguistic observations!

I owe the greatest debt of thanks to my life partner, Martti-Tapio Kuuskoski. He read and commented on the manuscript at every stage. We've had endless discussions about *Oneiron* and the laws of this otherworldly place. All of these journeys we made together.

Any possible mistakes and misunderstandings, intentional or unintentional, are my responsibility alone.

Financial support for the writing of this novel was provided by the Kone Foundation, the Uusimaa and Kainuu Regional Funds of the Finnish Cultural Foundation, Arts Promotion Centre Finland, the WSOY Literature Foundation, and the Otava Book Foundation.

REFERENCES

The epigraph for Part I of the novel comes from Tolstoy's *The Death of Ivan Ilyich*.

The epigraph for Part II is from Christoph Schlingensief's *Heaven Could Not Be As Beautiful As Here: A Cancer Diary* (*So schön wie hier kanns im Himmel gar nicht sein!*). Original translation based on the Finnish translation by Eeva Bergroth, *Kauniimpaa kuin taivaassa*, p. 90 (Kansallisteatterin kirja / Kirja kerrallaan and Finnish National Theatre, 2011).

The quotations on pages 38 and 39 are from *The Tibetan Book of the Dead: The Great Liberation Through Hearing in the Bardo*.

The quotations on page 78 are from David Nicholls's novel *One Day*, pp. 384–385 (Hodder & Stoughton, 2009).

On page 170–171 there are excerpts from *The Cherry Orchard* by Anton Chekhov. Original translations based on various English and Finnish translations.

The quotation on page 168 is from Emanuel Swedenborg's *Arcana Cœlestia Vol 1, Redesigned Standard Edition*, translated by John Clowes and revised by John Faulkner Potts, p. 8 (Pennsylvania: Swedenborg Foundation, 2009).

The quotations on pages 172 and 175 are from Emanuel Swedenborg's *A Hieroglyphic Key to Natural and Spiritual Mysteries, by Way of Representations and Correspondences*, translated from the Latin by James John Garth Wilkinson, pp. 13 and 14 (William Newberry, 1847).

The quotations on page 179 are from Emanuel Swedenborg's *New Jerusalem and Its Heavenly Doctrine* from the Redesigned Standard Edition of the Works of Emanuel Swedenborg, edited by William

Ross Woofenden, pp. 7 and 154 (Pennsylvania: Swedenborg Foundation, 2009).

As noted in the text, the quotations on page 195 come from *Faith after the Holocaust*, by Eliezer Berkovits, pp. 81–82, modified as described (Ktav, 1973).

The quotations on pages 195 and 196 are from Ignaz Maybaum's *The Face of God after Auschwitz*, pp. 61, 64, and 84 (Polak & Van Gennep, 1965).

The quotations that begin on page 219 are from Bruno Bettelheim's *The Children of the Dream*, in order of appearance from pp. 277, 278, 213, 288, & 320 (Macmillan, 1969). Some quotations have been altered slightly.

PERMISSIONS

OTHER IMPORTANT SOURCES

Esther Altmann: "Eating Disorders in the Jewish Community" (www. myjewishlearning.com/article/eating-disorders-in-the-jewish-community)

Dan Cohn-Sherbok: *Issues in Contemporary Judaism* (Macmillan, 1991)

Daniel Gavron: *The Kibbutz. Awakening from Utopia* (Rowman & Littlefield Publishers, Inc., 2000)

Stefanie Teri Greenberg: *An Investigation of Body Image Dissatisfaction Among Jewish American Females: An Application of The Tripartite Influence Model.* PhD dissertation (University of Iowa, 2009, ir.uiowa.edu/etd/368)

Benzion C. Kaganoff: *A Dictionary of Jewish Names and Their History* (Jason Aronson, 1996)

Edward Kessler: *What Do Jews Believe? The Customs and Culture of Modern Judaism* (Walker Books, 2007)

Jean-Luc Nancy: *Corpus* (Métailié, 1992) and *L'Intrus* (Galilée, 2000)

Michael Orbach: "Orthodox and Anorexic", *Tablet – A New Read on Jewish Life*, August 23, 2012 (tabletmag.com/jewish- life-and-religion/109958/orthodox-and-anorexic)

Roni Caryn Rabin: "Rabbis Sound an Alarm Over Eating Disorders", *The New York Times*, April 11, 2011 (www.nytimes.com/2011/04/12/health/12orthodox.html)

Jyrki Siukonen: Introduction to *Clavis Hieroglyphica. Hieroglyfinen avain ja muita filosofisia tekstejä*, selected translations of Emanuel Swedenborg's *Clavis Hieroglyphica*, Finnish translation by Jyrki

Siukonen, pp. 7–113. (Gaudeamus, 2000)

Rivkah Slonim: "The Mikvah", TheJewishWoman.org, from Rivkah Slonim's introduction to *Total Immersion: A Mikvah Anthology* (Jason Aronson, 1996), (www.chabad.org/theJewishWoman/article_cdo/ aid/1541/jewish/The-Mikvah.htm)

Oneworld, Many Voices

Bringing you exceptional writing from around the world

The Unit by Ninni Holmqvist (Swedish)
Translated by Marlaine Delargy

The Hen Who Dreamed She Could Fly by Sun-mi Hwang
(Korean) Translated by Chi-Young Kim

The Hilltop by Assaf Gavron (Hebrew)
Translated by Steven Cohen

A Perfect Crime by A Yi (Chinese)
Translated by Anna Holmwood

The Meursault Investigation by Kamel Daoud (French)
Translated by John Cullen

Laurus by Eugene Vodolazkin (Russian)
Translated by Lisa C. Hayden

Masha Regina by Vadim Levental (Russian)
Translated by Lisa C. Hayden

Umami by Laia Jufresa (Spanish)
Translated by Sophie Hughes

The Hermit by Thomas Rydahl (Danish)
Translated by K.E. Semmel

The Peculiar Life of a Lonely Postman by Denis Thériault
(French) Translated by Liedewy Hawke

Three Envelopes by Nir Hezroni (Hebrew)
Translated by Steven Cohen

Fever Dream by Samanta Schweblin (Spanish)
Translated by Megan McDowell

The Postman's Fiancée by Denis Thériault (French)
Translated by John Cullen
